**Praise for *New York Times* bestselling author
Joan Johnston**

"A guaranteed good read."
—*New York Times* bestselling author Heather Graham

"Joan Johnston does short contemporary
Westerns to perfection."
—*Publishers Weekly*

"Johnston warms your heart and tickles your fancy."
—*New York Daily News*

"Joan Johnston continually gives us everything we
want...fabulous details and atmosphere, memorable
characters, a story that you wish would never end,
and lots of tension and sensuality."
—*RT Book Reviews*

"Absolutely captivating...a delightful storyteller...
Joan Johnston [creates] unforgettable subplots and
characters who make every fine thread weave into a
touching tapestry."
—*Affaire de Coeur*

JOAN JOHNSTON

New York Times bestselling author Joan Johnston started reading romances to escape the stress of being an attorney with a major national law firm. She soon discovered that writing romances was a lot more fun than writing legal bond indentures. Since then she has published a number of historical and contemporary category romances. In addition to being an author, Joan is the mother of two children. In her spare time, she enjoys sailing, horseback riding and camping.

NEW YORK TIMES BESTSELLING AUTHOR

JOAN JOHNSTON

~ Hawk's Way ~
GROOMS

HARLEQUIN® FEATURE AUTHOR

Recycling programs for this product may not exist in your area.

ISBN-13: 978-0-373-60661-0

HAWK'S WAY GROOMS
Copyright © 2008 by Harlequin Books S.A.

The publisher acknowledges the copyright holder of the individual works as follows:

HAWK'S WAY: THE VIRGIN GROOM
Copyright © 1997 by Joan Mertens Johnston, Inc.
HAWK'S WAY: THE SUBSTITUTE GROOM
Copyright © 1998 by Joan Mertens Johnston, Inc.

Printed in U.S.A.

CONTENTS

HAWK'S WAY:
THE VIRGIN GROOM

CHAPTER ONE

SWEAT STREAMING FROM his temples, strong hands clenched tight on the parallel bars that supported him, Mac Macready put his full weight on his left leg. He felt a sharp pain, but the leg held. He gritted his teeth to keep from groaning. So far, so good.

Mac kept his eyes focused on the area between the bars in front of him, willing his leg to work. He took an easy step with his right leg, then called on the left again. The pain was less sharp the second time he put his weight on the restructured limb. He could handle the pain. More important, the leg had stayed under him. He glanced across the room at his friend and agent, Andy Dennison, and grinned.

Mac Macready could walk again.

"You did it, Mac," Andy said, crossing the room to slap him on the back. "It's great to see you back on your feet."

"About time," Mac said. "I've spent the better part of two years trying to get this damned leg of mine back into shape." A sharp pain seared up his leg, but he refused to sit down, not now, when he had just made it back onto his feet. He took more of his weight on his arms and kept walking. A bead of sweat trickled between his shoulder blades before it caught on his sleeveless T-shirt. He summoned another smile. "Give me a couple of months, and I'll be ready to start catching passes again for the Tornadoes."

Mac caught the skeptical look on Andy's face before his agent said, "Sure, Mac. Whatever you say."

He understood Andy's skepticism. Mac had said the same thing after every operation. Who would have suspected a broken leg—all right, so maybe it had been shattered—would be so difficult to mend? But his body had rejected the pins they had used to put things back together again at ankle and hip. They had finally had to invent something especially for him.

Then the long bones in his leg hadn't grown straight and had needed to be broken and set again. He had fought complications caused by infection. Finally, when he had pushed too hard to get well, he had ended up back in a cast.

The football injury had been devastating, coming as it had at the end of Mac's first phenomenal season with the Texas Tornadoes. His future couldn't have been brighter. He was a star receiver, with more touchdown catches than any other rookie in the league. His team was headed for the Super Bowl. With one crushing tackle, everything had fallen apart. The sportscasters had called it a career-ending injury. Mac wasn't willing to concede the issue.

"Good work, Mac," the physical therapist said, reaching out to help him into the wheelchair waiting for him at the end of the parallel bars. "Put your arm around me."

He flashed the young woman a killer grin, inwardly cursing the fact that after six measly steps he was on the verge of collapse. "Better watch out, Hartwell. Now that I'm back on my feet, I'm going to give your fiancé some serious competition."

Diane Hartwell blushed. Most women did when Mac turned on the charm. He had the kind of blond-haired, blue-eyed good looks that made female heads swivel to take a second look. Mac wondered what she would think if she knew the truth about him.

Diane answered wryly, "I'm sure George would gladly trade me to you for an autographed football."

"Done," Mac said brightly, biting back a grimace as Diane bent his injured leg and placed his foot on the wheelchair footrest.

"I was only kidding," Diane said.

"I wasn't," Mac said, smiling up at her. "Tell your fiancé I'll be glad to autograph that football for him anytime."

"Thanks, Mac," Diane said. "I appreciate it."

"Think nothing of it, Hartwell. And tell George to hang on to that ball. Someday it'll be worth something."

Once Mac resumed his career, he would break every record in the book. He had that kind of determination. And he had been that good. Of course, that was before the accident. Everybody—except himself—questioned whether he would ever be that good again.

It had been touch and go for a while whether he would even walk. But Mac had known he would walk again, and without the aid of a brace. He had done it today. It seemed he was the only one who wasn't surprised.

He had known he would succeed, because he had beaten the odds before. When he was eight, he had suffered from acute myelocytic leukemia. It should have killed him. He had recovered from the childhood disease and gone on to win the Heisman Trophy and be drafted in the first round by the Texas Tornadoes. Mac had no intention of giving up his dreams of a future in football.

Andy wheeled him down the hospital corridor to his room. "When do you get out of here?" his agent asked.

"The doctor said once I could stand on my leg, he would release me. I guess that means I can get out of here anytime now."

"The press will want a statement," Andy said as he

stopped the wheelchair beside Mac's hospital bed. "Do you want to talk to them? Or do you want me to do it?"

Mac thought of facing a dozen TV cameras from a wheelchair. Or standing with crutches. Or wavering on his own two feet. "Tell them I'll be back next season."

"Maybe that's not such a good—"

"Tell them I'll be back," Mac said, staring Andy in the eye.

Andy had once been a defensive lineman and wore a coveted Super Bowl ring on his right hand. He understood what it meant to play football. And what it meant to stop. He straightened the tie at his bull neck, shrugged his broad shoulders and smoothed the tie over his burgeoning belly, before he said, "You got it, Mac."

"Thanks, Andy. I am coming back, you know."

"Sure, Mac," Andy said.

Mac could see his agent didn't believe him any more than the doctors and nurses who had treated him over the past two years. Even Hartwell, though she encouraged him, didn't believe he would achieve the kind of mobility he needed to play in the pros. Mac needed to get away somewhere and heal himself. He knew he could do it. After all, he had done it once before.

"Where can I get in touch with you?" Andy asked.

"I'm headed to a ranch in northwest Texas owned by some friends of mine. I have an open invitation to visit, and I'm going to take them up on it. I'll call you when I get there and give you a number where I can be reached."

"Good enough. Take care, Mac. Don't—"

"Don't finish that sentence, Andy. Not if you're going to warn me not to get my hopes up."

Andy shook his head. "I was going to say don't be a fool and kill yourself trying to get well too fast."

"I'm going to get my job back from the kid who took

over for me," Mac said in a steely voice. "And I'm going to do it this year."

Andy didn't argue further, just shook Mac's hand and left him alone in the hospital room.

Mac looked around at the sterile walls, the white sheets, the chrome rails on the bed, listened to the muffled sounds that weren't quite silence and inhaled the overwhelming antiseptic smell that made him want to gag. He had spent too much of his life in hospital beds—more than any human being ought to have to. He wanted out of here, the sooner the better.

He could hardly wait to get to the wide open spaces of Zach and Rebecca Whitelaw's ranch, Hawk's Pride. More than Zach or Rebecca or the land, he had a yearning to see their daughter Jewel again. Jewel was the first of eight kids who had been adopted by the Whitelaws, and she had returned to Hawk's Pride after college to manage Camp LittleHawk, the camp for kids with cancer that Rebecca had started years ago.

Mac remembered his first impressions of Jewel—huge Mississippi-mud-brown eyes, shoulder-length dirt-brown hair and an even dirtier looking white T-shirt and jeans. She had been five years old to his eight, and she had been leaning against the corral at Camp LittleHawk watching him venture onto horseback for the first time.

"Don't be scared," Jewel had said.

"I'm not," he'd retorted, glancing around at the other five kids in the corral with him. The horses were stopped in a circle, and the wrangler was working with a little boy who was even more scared than he was.

"Buttercup wouldn't hurt a fly," Jewel reassured him.

He remembered feeling mortified at the thought of riding a horse named Buttercup. And terrified that Buttercup would throw him off her broad back and trample him underfoot. Even though he'd been dying of cancer, he'd been afraid of getting killed. Life, he had learned, was precious.

"I'm not scared," he lied. He wished he could reach up and tug his baseball cap down tighter over his bald head, but he was afraid to let go of his two-handed grip on the saddle horn.

Jewel scooted under the bottom rail of the corral on her hands and knees, which explained how she had gotten so dirty, and walked right up to the horse—all right, it was only a pony, but it was still big—without fear. He sat frozen as she patted Buttercup's graying jaw and crooned to her.

"What are you saying?" he demanded.

"I'm telling Buttercup to be good. I'm telling her you're sick and—"

"I'm dying," he blurted out. "I'll be dead by Christmas." It was June. He was currently in remission, but the last time he'd been sick, he'd heard the doctors figuring he had about six months to live. He knew it was only a matter of time before the disease came back. It always did.

"My momma died and my daddy and my brother," Jewel said. "I thought I was gonna die, too, but I didn't." She reached up and touched the crisscrossing pink scars on her face. "I had to stay in the hospital till I got well."

"Then you know it's a rotten place to be," he said.

She nodded. "Zach and 'Becca came and took me away. I never want to go back."

"Yeah, well I don't have much choice."

"Why not?" she asked.

"Because that's where you go when you're sick."

"But you're well now," she said, looking up at him with serious brown eyes. "Except you don't have any hair yet. But don't worry. 'Becca says it'll grow back."

He flushed and risked letting go of the horn to tug the cap down. It was one of the many humiliations he had endured—losing his hair...along with his privacy...and his childhood. He had always wanted to go to camp like his sister, Sadie, but he had been too sick. Then some lady had opened this place. He had jumped at the chance to get away from home. Away from the hospital.

"Your hair doesn't grow back till you stop getting sick," he pointed out to the fearless kid standing with her cheek next to the pony's.

"So, don't get sick again," she said.

He snickered. "Yeah. Right. It doesn't work like that."

"Just believe you can stay well, and you will," she said.

The circle of horses began to move again, and she headed back toward the fence. It was then he noticed her limp. "Hey!" he shouted after her. "What happened to your leg?"

"It got broken," she said matter-of-factly.

Mac hadn't thought much about it then, but now he knew the pain she must have endured to walk again. Jewel would know what he was feeling as he got out of the hospital for what he hoped would be the last time. Jewel would understand.

After that first meeting, he and Jewel had encountered each other often over the next several years. He had beaten the leukemia and returned as a teenager to become a counselor at Camp LittleHawk. That was when Jewel had become his best friend. Not his *girlfriend*. His *best friend*.

He already had a girlfriend back home in Dallas. Her name was Louise and he called her Lou and was violently in love with her. He had met Lou when she came to the junior-senior prom with another guy. She had only been in the eighth grade. By the time he was a senior and Lou was a freshman, they were going steady.

He told Jewel all about the agonies of being in love, and though she hadn't yet taken the plunge, she was all sympathetic ears. Jewel was the best buddy a guy could have, a confidante, a pal. A soul mate. He could tell her anything and, in fact, had told her some amazingly private things.

Like how he had cried the first time he had endured a procedure called a back-stick, where they stuck a needle in your back to figure out your blood count. How he had wet the bed once in the hospital rather than ask for a bedpan. And how humiliating it had been when the nurse treated him like a baby and put the thermometer into an orifice other than his mouth.

It was astonishing to think he could have been so frank with Jewel. But Jewel didn't only listen to his woes, she shared her own. So he knew how jealous and angry she had been when Zach and Rebecca adopted another little girl two years older than her named Rolleen. And how she had learned to accept each new child a little more willingly, until the youngest, Colt, had come along, and he had felt like her own flesh-and-blood baby brother.

Mac had also been there at the worst moment of her life. He had lost a good friend that fateful Fourth of July. And Jewel... Jewel had lost much more. After that hot, horrible summer day, she had refused to see him again. So far, he had respected her wish to be left alone. But there was an empty place inside him she had once helped to fill.

He had received an invitation to her wedding the previous spring. It was hard to say what his feelings had been. Joy for her, because he knew how hard it must have been for her to move past what had happened to her. And sadness, too, because he knew the closeness they had enjoyed in the past would be transferred to her husband.

Then had come the announcement, a few weeks before the wedding, that it had been canceled. He had wondered what had gone wrong, wondered which of them had called it off and worried about what she must be feeling.

He would never pry, but he was curious. After all, he and Jewel had once known everything there was to know about each other. He had picked up the phone to call her, but put it down. Too many years had passed.

Mac had never had another woman friend like Jewel. Sex always got in the way. Or rather, the woman's expectations. And his inability to fulfill them.

What kind of man is still a virgin at twenty-five? Mac mused.

An angry man. A onetime romantic fool who waited through college for his high school sweetheart to grow up, only to be left for another guy.

It hadn't seemed like such a terrible sacrifice remaining faithful to Louise all those years, turning down girls who showed up at his dorm room in T-shirts and not much else, girls who wanted to make it with a college football hero, girls who were attracted by his calendar-stud good looks. He had loved Lou and had his whole life with her ahead of him.

Until she had jilted him her senior year for Harry Warnecke, who had a bright future running his father's bowling alley.

Lou had been gentle but firm in her rejection of him. "I don't love you anymore, Mac. I love Harry. I'm pregnant, and we're going to be married."

Mac had been livid with fury. He had never touched her, had respected her wish to remain a virgin until she graduated from high school and they could marry, and she was pregnant with some guy named Harry's kid and wanted to marry him.

It had taken every ounce of self-control he had not to reach out and throttle her. "Have a nice life," he had managed to say.

His anger had prodded him to hunt up the first available woman and get laid. But his pain had sent him back to his dorm room to nurse his broken heart. How could he make love to another woman when he still loved Lou? If all he had wanted was to get screwed, he could have been doing that all along. His dad had always told him that sex felt good, but making love felt better. He had wanted it to be making love the first time.

His final year of college, after he broke up with Lou, he went through a lot of women. Dating them, that is. Kissing them and touching them and learning what made them respond to a man. But he never put himself inside one of them. He was looking for something more than sex in the relationship. What he found were women who admired his body, or his talent with a football, or his financial prospects. Not one of them wanted him.

It wasn't until he had been drafted by the pros and began traveling with the Tornadoes that he met Elizabeth Kale. She was a female TV sports commentator, a woman who felt comfortable with jocks and could banter with the best of them. She had taken his breath away. She had shiny brown hair and warm brown eyes and a smile that wouldn't quit. He had fallen faster than a wrestled steer in a rodeo.

She hadn't been impressed by his statistics—personal or football or financial. It had not been easy to get her to go out with him. She didn't want to get involved. She had her career, and marriage wasn't in the picture.

Mac didn't give up when he wanted something—and he'd wanted to marry Elizabeth. As the season progressed, they began to see each other when they were both in town. Elizabeth was a city girl, so they did city things—when they could both fit it into their busy schedules. Mac wooed her with every romantic gesture he could think of, and she responded. And when he proposed marriage, she accepted. Elizabeth made what time she could for him, and they exchanged a lot of passionate kisses at airports where their paths crossed.

He had carefully planned her seduction. He knew when and where it was going to happen. He was nervous and eager and restless. By a certain age—and Mac had already reached it—a woman expected a man to know all the right moves. Mac had been to the goal line plenty of times, but he had never scored a touchdown. He was ready and willing to take the plunge—figuratively speaking—but now that he had waited so long, the idea of making it with a woman for the first time was a little unnerving. Especially with Elizabeth, who meant so much to him.

What if he did it wrong? What if he couldn't please her? What if he left her unsatisfied? He read books. And planned. And postponed the moment.

Then he broke his leg. *Shattered his leg.*

Mac tasted bile in his throat, remembering what had happened next. Elizabeth had come to the hospital to see him, flashbulbs popping around her, as much in the news as his girlfriend as she was as a famous newscaster. She listened at his bedside to the prognosis.

His football career was over. He would be lucky if he ever walked again. He would always need a brace on his leg. Maybe he could manage with a cane.

He had seen it in her eyes before she spoke a word. The fear. And the determination. She said nothing until the doctors had left them alone.

"I can't—I won't—I can't do it, Mac."

"Do what, Elizabeth?" he asked in a bitter voice that revealed he knew exactly what she meant, though he pretended ignorance.

"I won't marry a man who can't walk." She slipped her widespread fingers slowly through the hair that fell forward on her face, carefully settling it back in place. He had always thought it a charming gesture, but now it only made her seem vain.

"I can't go through this with you," she said. "I mean, I…I hate hospitals and sick people and I can't…I can't be there for you, Mac."

He had known it was coming, but it hurt just the same. "Get out, Elizabeth."

She stood there waiting for…what?…for him to tell her it was all right? It wasn't, by God, all right! It was a hell of a thing to tell a man you couldn't stand by him in times of trouble. *For better or for worse.* It told him plenty about just how deep her feelings for him ran. Thin as sheet ice on a Texas pond.

"I said get out!" He was shouting by then, and she flinched and backed away. "Get out!"

She turned and ran.

His throat hurt from shouting and his leg throbbed and his eyes and nose burned with unshed tears. He shouted at the nurse when she tried to come in, but he couldn't even turn over and bury his head in a pillow because they had his leg so strapped up.

Mac forced his mind away from the painful memories. There had been no seductions during the past two years, though he had spent a great deal of time in bed. He had been too busy trying to get well. Now he was well. And he was going to have to face that zero on the scoreboard and do something about it.

He could find a woman who knew the ropes—there were certainly enough volunteers even now—and get it over with. But he found that a little cold and calculating. The first time ought to be with a special woman. Not that he would ever be stupid enough to fall in love again. After all, twice burned, thrice chary. But he wanted to like and respect and admire the woman he chose as his first sexual partner.

Lately his dreams had been unbelievably erotic. *Hot, sweat-slick bodies entwined in twisted sheets. Long female legs wrapped around his waist. A woman's hair draped across his chest. His mouth on her—* He shook off the vision. Now that he was finally healthy—meaning he could get out of bed as easily as he could fall into it—it was time he took care of unfinished business.

Jewel's face appeared in his mind's eye. He saw the faint, crisscrossing scars from the car accident that had left her an orphan which had never quite faded away. Her smile, winsome and mischievous. Heard the distressed sound of her voice when she admitted her breasts kept growing and growing like two balloons. And her laughter when he had offered to pop them for her.

With Jewel he wouldn't have to be afraid of making a fool of himself in bed. Jewel would understand his predicament. But she was the last person he could ever have sex with. Not after what had happened to her.

He was sure she would see the humor in the current situation. Jewel had a great sense of humor. At least, once upon a time she had. He could hardly believe six years had passed since they had last seen each other. They had both been through a great deal since then.

Mac hoped Jewel wouldn't mind him intruding on her this way. But he was coming, like it or not.

CHAPTER TWO

PETER "MAC" MACREADY was the last person Jewel Whitelaw wanted to see back at Hawk's Pride, because he was the one person besides her counselor who knew her deepest, darkest secret. She should have told someone else long ago—her parents, one of her three sisters or four brothers, her fiancé—but she had never been able to admit the truth to anyone. Only Mac knew. And now he was coming back.

If she could have left home while he was visiting, she would have done so. But Camp LittleHawk was scheduled to open in two weeks, and she had too much to do to get ready for the summer season to be able to pick up and leave. All she could do was avoid Mac as much as possible.

As she emerged from a steamy shower, draped herself in a floor-length white terry cloth robe and wrapped her long brown hair in a towel, she learned just how impossible that was going to be.

"Hi."

He was standing at the open bathroom door dressed in worn Levi's, a Tornadoes T-shirt and Nikes, leaning on a cane. He didn't even have the grace to look embarrassed. A grin split his face from ear to ear, creating two masculine dimples in his cheeks, while his vivid blue eyes gazed at her with the warmth of an August day in Texas.

"Hi," she said back. In spite of not wanting him here, she felt her lips curve in an answering smile. Her gaze skipped to the knotty-looking hickory cane he leaned on and back to his face. "I see you're standing on your own."

"Almost," he said. "Sorry about intruding. Your mom said to make myself comfortable." He gestured to the bedroom behind him, on the other side of the bathroom, where his suitcase sat on the double bed. "Looks like we'll be sharing a bath."

Jewel groaned inwardly. The new camp counselors' cottages had been built to match the single-story Spanish style of the main ranch house, with whitewashed adobe walls and a red barrel-tile roof. Each had two bedrooms, but shared a bath, living room and kitchen. As the camp manager, she should have had this cottage all to herself. "I thought you'd be staying at the house," she said.

"Your mom gave me a choice." He shrugged. "This seemed more private."

"I see." Her mother had asked her if she minded, since Jewel and Mac were such old friends, if she gave Mac a choice of staying at the cottage or in the house. Jewel hadn't objected, because she hadn't been able to think up a good reason to say no that wouldn't sound suspicious. As far as her parents knew, she and Mac still were good friends. And they were.

Only, Jewel had expected Mac to keep his distance, as he had for the past six years. And he had not.

Mac's brow furrowed in a way that was achingly familiar. "I can tell Rebecca I've changed my mind, if you don't want me here."

Jewel struggled between the desire to escape Mac's scrutiny and the yearning to have back the camaraderie they had once enjoyed. Maybe it would be all right. Maybe the subject wouldn't come up. *Yeah, and maybe horses come in green and pink.* "I..."

He started to turn away. "I'll get my bag."

"Wait."

He turned back. "I don't want to make you uncomfortable, Jewel. I won't talk about it. I won't even bring up the subject." His lips curled wryly. "Of course, I just brought up the subject to say I won't bring it up, but I promise it'll be off-limits. I need a place to rest and get better, and I thought you might not mind if I stayed here."

His eyes looked wounded, and her heart went out to him. She crossed to him, because that seemed easier than making him walk to her with the cane. His arms opened to her and she walked right into them and they hugged tightly.

"God, I've missed you," he said, his deep voice rumbling in her ear.

"This feels good," she admitted. "It's been too long, Mac."

There was nothing sexual in the embrace, just two old friends, two very good friends, reconnecting after a long separation. Except Jewel was aware of the strength in his arms, the way her breasts felt crushed against his muscular chest and the feel of his thighs pressed against her own. She stiffened, then forced herself to relax.

"You're taller than I remember," he said, tucking her towel-covered head under his chin.

"I've grown three inches since... I've grown," she said, realizing how difficult it was going to be avoiding the subject she wanted to avoid. "It's a good thing, or I'd get a crick in my neck looking up at you."

He had to be four inches over six feet. She remembered him being tall at nineteen, but he must have grown an inch or two since then, and of course his shoulders were broader, his angular features more mature. He was a man now, not a boy.

He was big. He was strong. He could physically overwhelm her. But she had known Mac forever. He would never hurt her. She reminded herself to relax.

The towel slipped off, and her hair cascaded to her waist.

"Good Lord," Mac said, his fingers tangling in the length of it. "Your hair was never this long, either."

"I like it long." She could drape it forward over her shoulders to help cover her Enormous Endowments.

"I think I'm going to like it, too," he said, smiling down at her with a teasing glint in his eyes.

She gave him an arch look. "Are you flirting with me, Mr. Macready?"

"Who, me? Naw. Wouldn't think of it, Ruby."

Jewel grinned. In the old days, he had often called her by the names of different precious gems—"Because you're a Jewel, get it?"—and the return to such familiarity made her feel even more comfortable with him. "Get out of here so I can get dressed," she said, stepping back from his embrace.

The robe gaped momentarily, and his glance slipped downward appreciatively. She self-consciously pulled the cloth over her breasts to cover them completely.

"Looks like they've grown, too," he quipped, leering at her comically.

She should have laughed. It was what she would have done six years ago, before disaster had struck. But she couldn't joke with him anymore about her overgenerous breasts. She blamed the size of them for what had happened to her. "Don't, Mac," she said quietly.

He sobered instantly. "I'm sorry, Jewel."

She managed a smile. "It's no big deal. Just get out of here and let me get dressed."

He backed up, and for the first time she saw how much

he needed the cane. His face turned white around the mouth with pain, and he swore under his breath.

"Are you all right?" she asked.

"No problem," he said. "Leg's almost as good as new. Figure I'll start jogging tomorrow."

"Jogging?"

He gave her a sheepish look. "So maybe I'll start out walking. Want to go with me?"

She daintily pointed the toe of her once-injured leg in his direction. "Walking isn't my forte. How about a horseback ride?"

He shook his head. "Gotta walk. Need the exercise to get back into shape. Come with me. My limp is worse than yours, so you won't have any trouble keeping up. Besides, it would give us a chance to catch up on what we've both been doing the past six years. Please come."

She wrinkled her nose.

"Pretty please with sugar on it?"

It was something she had taught him to say if he really wanted a woman to do something. She gave in to the smile and let her lips curve with the delight she felt. "All right, you hopeless romantic. I'll walk with you, but it'll have to be early because I've got a lot of work to do tomorrow."

"Figured I'd go early to beat the heat," he said. "Six-thirty?"

"Make it six, and you've got a deal." She reached out a hand, and Mac shook it.

The electric shock that raced up her arm was disturbing. It took an effort to keep the frown from her face. This wasn't supposed to happen. She wasn't supposed to be physically attracted to Mac Macready. They were just good friends. *Yeah, and horses come in purple and orange.*

She closed the bathroom door and sank onto the edge of the tub. She had always thought Mac was cute, but he had matured into a genuine hunk. No problem. She would handle the attraction the way she had from the beginning, by thinking of him as a brother.

But he wasn't her brother. He was a very attractive, very available man. Who once had been—still was?—her best friend.

She clung to that thought, which made it easier to keep their relationship in perspective. It was much more important to have a friend like Mac than a boyfriend.

JEWEL REPEATED THAT SENTENCE like a litany the next morning at 5:55 when Mac showed up in the kitchen dressed in Nikes and black running shorts and nothing else. The kitchen door was open and through the screen she was aware of flies buzzing and the lowing of cattle. A steady, squeaking sound meant that her youngest brother, Colt, hadn't gotten around to oiling the windmill beside the stock pond. But those distractions weren't enough to keep her from ogling Mac's body.

A wedge of golden hair on his chest became a line of soft down as it reached his navel and disappeared beneath his shorts. She consciously forced her gaze upward.

Mac's tousled, collar-length hair was a sun-kissed blond, and his eyes were as bright as the morning sky. He hadn't shaved, and the overnight beard made him look both dangerous and sexy.

Without the concealing T-shirt and jeans, she could see the sinewy muscles in his shoulders and arms, the washboard belly and the horrible mishmash of scars on his left leg. He leaned heavily on the cane.

She poured him a bowl of cornflakes and doused them with milk. "Eat. You're running late."

"Oh, that I were running," he said. "I'm afraid walking is the best I can do." He hobbled across the redbrick tile floor to the small wooden table, settled himself in the ladderback chair opposite her and began consuming cereal at an alarming rate.

"What's that you're wearing?" he asked.

She tugged at her bulky, short-sleeved sweatshirt, dusted off her cutoff jeans and readjusted her hair over her shoulders. "Some old things."

"Gonna be hot in that," he said between bites.

But the sweatshirt disguised her Bountiful Bosom, which was more important than comfort. "Hungry?" she inquired, her chin resting on her hand as she watched him eat ravenously.

"I missed supper last night."

She had checked his bedroom and found him asleep at suppertime and hadn't disturbed him. He had slept all through the afternoon and evening. "You must have been tired."

"I was. Completely exhausted. Not that I'd admit that to anyone but you." He poured himself another bowl of cereal, doused it with the milk she had left on the table and began eating again.

"Nothing wrong with your appetite," she observed.

He made a sound, but his mouth was too full to answer.

She watched him eat four bowls of cereal. That was about right—two for dinner and two for breakfast. "Ready to go walking now?" she asked.

"Sure." He took his dish to the sink and reached back for hers, which she handed to him.

Seeing the difficulty he was having trying to do everything one-handed, so he could hang on to his cane, she said, "I can do that for you."

"I'm not a cripple!" When he turned to snap at her, he lost his one-handed grip on the dishes. His cane fell as he lurched to catch the bowls with both hands. Without the cane, his left leg crumpled under him.

"Look out!" Jewel cried.

The dishes crashed into the sink as Mac grabbed hold of the counter to keep from falling backward.

"Damn it all to hell!" he raged.

Jewel reached out to comfort him, but he snarled, "Don't touch me. Leave me alone."

Jewel had whirled to leave, when he bit out, "Don't go."

She stopped where she was, but she wanted to run. She didn't want to see his pain. It reminded her too much of her own.

He stared out the window over the sink at the endless reaches of Hawk's Pride, with its vast, grassy plains and the jagged outcroppings of rock that marked the entrance to the canyons in the distance.

"It must be awful," she whispered, "to lose so much."

His eyes slid closed, and she watched his Adam's apple bob as he swallowed hard. He slowly opened his eyes and turned to look at her over his shoulder. "This…the way I am… It's just temporary. I'll be back as good as new next season."

"Will you?"

He met her gaze steadily. "Bet on it."

She knew him too well. Well enough to hear the sheer bravado in his answer and to see the unspoken fear in his eyes that his football career was over. They had always been deeply attuned to one another. He was vulnerable again, in a way he once had been as a youth—this time not to death itself, but to the death of his dreams.

"What can I do, Mac?"

He managed a smile. "Hand me my cane, will you?"

It was easier to do as he asked than to probe the painful issues that he was refusing to address. She crossed to pick up his cane and watched as he eased his weight off his hands and onto his leg with the cane's support.

"Are you sure it isn't too soon to be doing so much?" she asked as he hissed in a breath.

He headed determinedly for the screen door. "The only way my leg can get stronger is if I walk on it."

She followed after him, as she had for nearly a dozen years in their youth. "All right, cowboy. Head 'em up, and move 'em out."

He flashed her his killer grin, and she smiled back, letting the screen door slam behind her.

It was easier to pretend nothing was wrong. But she could already see that things were different between them. They had both been through a great deal in the years since they had last seen each other. She knew as well as he did what it felt like to live with fear, and with disappointment.

She had worked hard to put behind her what had happened the summer she was sixteen and Harvey Barnes had attacked her at the Fourth of July picnic. But even now the memory of that day haunted her.

She had been excited when Harvey, a senior who ran with the in crowd, asked her to the annual county-wide Fourth of July celebration. She'd had a crush on him for a long time, but he hadn't given her a second glance. During the previous year, her breasts had blossomed and given her a figure most movie stars would have paid good dollars to have. A lot of boys stared, including Harvey.

She had suspected why Harvey had asked her out, but she hadn't cared. She had just been so glad to be asked, she had accepted his invitation on the spot.

"Why would you want to go out with a guy who's so full of himself?" Mac asked after she introduced him to Harvey. "I'd be glad to take you." As he had previously, every year he'd been at Hawk's Pride.

"I might as well go with one of my brothers as go with you," she replied. "Harvey's cool. He's a hunk. He's—"

"Yeah, yeah, yeah. I get the message," he said, then teased in a singsong voice, "Pearl's got a boyfriend, Pearl's got a boyfriend."

She aimed a playful fist at his stomach to shut him up, but the truth was, she was hoping the picnic date with Harvey, their first, would lead to a steady relationship.

Mac caught her wrist to protect his belly and said, "All right, go with Harvey Barnes and have a good time. Forget all about me—"

Jewel laughed and said, "That mournful face isn't going to make any difference. I'm still going with Harvey. I'll see you at the picnic. We just won't spend as much time together."

Mac looked down at her, his brow furrowed. He opened his mouth to say something and shut it again.

"What is it?" she asked, seeing how troubled he looked.

"Just don't let him… If he does anything… If you think he's going to…"

"What?" she asked in exasperation.

He let go of her hands to shove both of his through his hair. "If you need help, just yell, and I'll be there."

He had already turned to walk away when she grabbed his arm and turned him back around. "What is it you think Harvey's going to do to me that's so terrible?"

"He's going to want to kiss you," Mac said.

"I want to kiss him back. So what's the problem?"

"Kissing's not the problem," Mac pointed out. "It's what comes after that. The touching and…and the rest. Sometimes it's not easy for a guy to stop. Not that I'm saying he'd try anything on a first date, but some guys… And with a body like yours…"

Her face felt heated from all the blood rushing to it.

Over the years they had managed not to talk seriously about such intimate subjects. Mac never brought them up except in fun, and until recently she hadn't been that interested in boys. She searched his face and found he looked as confused and awkward discussing the subject as she felt.

"How would you know?" she asked. "I mean, about it being hard to stop. Have you done it with Lou?"

His flush deepened. "You know I wouldn't tell you that, even if I had."

"Have you?" she persisted.

He tousled her hair like a brother and said, "Wouldn't you like to know!"

In the days before the picnic, Mac teased her mercilessly about her plan to wear a dress, since she only wore jeans and a T-shirt around the ranch.

Her eldest sister, Rolleen, had agreed to make a pink gingham dress for her, copying a spaghetti-strapped dress pattern that Jewel loved, but which she couldn't wear because her large breasts needed the support of a heavy-duty bra. Rolleen created essentially the same fitted-bodice, bare-shouldered, full-skirted dress, but made the shoulder straps an inch wide so they would hide her bra straps.

On the day of the picnic, Jewel donned the dress and tied up her shoulder-length hair in a ponytail with a pink gingham bow. Her newest Whitelaw sibling, fifteen-year-old Cherry, insisted that she needed pink lipstick on her lips, which Cherry applied for her with the expertise of one who had been wearing lipstick since she was twelve.

Then Jewel headed out the kitchen door to find Mac, who was driving her to the picnic grounds to meet Harvey.

"Wow!" Mac said when he saw her. "Wow!"

Jewel found it hard to believe the admiration she saw in Mac's eyes. She had long ago accepted the fact she wasn't pretty. She had sun-streaked brown hair and plain brown eyes and extraordinarily ordinary features. Her body was fit and healthy, but faint, crisscrossing scars laced her face, and she had a distinctive permanent limp.

The look in Mac's eyes made her feel radiantly beautiful.

She held out the gingham dress and twirled around for him. "Do you think Harvey will like it?"

"Harvey's gonna love it!" he assured her. "You look good enough to eat. I hope this Harvey character knows how lucky he is." The furrow reappeared on his brow. "He better not—"

She put a finger on the wrinkles in his forehead to smooth them out. "You worry too much, Mac. Nothing bad is going to happen."

Looking back now, Jewel wished she had listened to Mac. She wished she hadn't tried to look so pretty for Harvey Barnes. She wished...

Jewel had gotten counseling in college to help her deal with what had happened that day. The counselor had urged her to tell her parents, and when she had met Jerry Cain and fallen in love with him her junior year at Baylor, the counselor had urged her to tell Jerry, too.

She just couldn't.

Jerry had been a graduate student, years older than she was, and more mature than the other college boys she had met. He had figured out right away that she was self-conscious about the size of her breasts, and it was his consideration for her feelings that had first attracted her to him. It had been easy to fall in love with him. It had been more difficult—impossible—to trust him with her secret.

Jerry had been more patient with her than she had any right to expect. She had loved kissing him. Been more anxious—but finally accepting—of his caresses. They were engaged before he pressed her to sleep with him.

They had already sent out the wedding invitations by the time she did.

It had been a disaster.

They had called off the wedding.

That was a year ago. Jewel had decided that if she couldn't marry and have kids of her own, she could at least work with children who needed her.

So she had come back to Camp LittleHawk.

"Hey. You look like you're a million miles away."

Jewel glanced around and realized she could hardly see the white adobe ranch buildings, they had walked so far. "Oh. I was thinking."

"To tell you the truth, I enjoyed the quiet company." Sweat beaded Mac's forehead and his upper lip. He winced every time he took a step.

"Haven't we gone far enough?" she asked.

"The doctor said I can do as much as I can stand."

"You look like you're there already," she said.

"Just a little bit farther."

That attitude explained why Mac had become the best at what he did, but Jewel worried about him all the same. "Just don't expect me to carry you back," she joked.

Mac shot her one of his dimpled smiles and said, "Tell me what you've been doing with yourself lately."

"I've been figuring out the daily schedule for Camp LittleHawk."

"Need any help?"

She gave him a surprised look. "I'd love some. Do you have the time?"

He shrugged. "Don't have anything else planned. What kinds of things are you having the kids do these days?"

She told him, unable to keep the excitement from her voice. "Horseback riding, picnics and hayrides, of course. And handicrafts, naturally.

"But I've come up with something really exciting this year. We're going to have art sessions at the site of those primitive drawings on the canyon wall here at Hawk's Pride. Once the kids have copied down all the various symbols, we're going to send them off to an archaeologist at the state university for interpretation.

"When her findings are available, I'll forward a copy of them to the kids, wherever they are. It'll remind them what fun they had at camp even after they've gone."

"And maybe take their minds off their illness, if they're back in the hospital," Mac noted quietly.

Jewel sat silently watching Mac stare into the distance and knew he was remembering how it had been in the beginning, how they had provided solace to each other, a needed word of encouragement and a shoulder to lean on. She knew he had come back because she was here, a friend when he needed one.

"I can remember being fascinated by those drawings myself as a kid," Mac mused.

"Didn't you want to be an archaeologist once upon a time?"

"Paleontologist," he corrected.

"What's the difference?"

"An archaeologist studies the past by looking at what people have left behind. A paleontologist studies fossils to recreate a picture of life in the past."

"What happened to those plans?" she asked.

"It got harder and harder to focus on the past when I realized I was going to have a future."

"What college degree did you finally end up getting?"

He laughed self-consciously. "Business. I figured I'd need to know how to handle all the money I'd make playing football."

But his career had been cut short.

He turned abruptly and headed back toward the ranch without another word to her.

Jewel figured the distance they had come at about a mile. She looked at her watch. Six-thirty. Not very far or very fast for a man who depended on his speed for a living.

About a quarter of a mile from the house, Mac was using his hand to help move his left leg. Jewel stepped to his side and slipped her arm around his waist to help support his weight.

"Don't argue," she said, when he opened his mouth to protest. "If you want my company, you have to take the concern that comes along with it."

"Thanks, Opal," he said.

"Think nothing of it, Pete."

She hadn't called him Pete since he had started high school and acquired the nickname "Mac" from his football teammates. It brought back memories of better times for both of them. They were content to walk in silence the rest of the way back to the house.

Jewel had forgotten how good it felt to have a friend with whom you could communicate without saying a word. She knew what Mac was feeling right now as though he had spoken the words aloud. She understood his frustration. And his fear. She empathized with his drive to succeed, despite the obstacles he had to overcome. She understood his reluctance to accept her help and his willingness to do so.

It was as though the intervening years had never been.

Except, something else had been added to the mix between them. Something unexpected. Something as unwelcome as it was undeniable.

No *friend* should have felt the frisson of excitement Jewel had felt with her body snuggled up next to Mac's. No *friend* should have gotten the chill she got down her spine when Mac's warm breath feathered over her temple. No *friend's* heart would have started beating faster, as hers had, when Mac's arm circled her waist in return, his fingers closing on her flesh beneath the sweatshirt.

She would have to hide what she felt from him. Otherwise it would spoil everything. Friendship had always been enough in the past. Because of what had happened, because she was in no position to ask for—or accept—more, friendship was all they could ever have between them now.

As they reached the kitchen door, she smiled up at Mac, and he smiled back.

"Home again, home again, jiggety jog," she said.

"Same time tomorrow?"

She started to refuse. It would be easier if she kept her distance from him. But it was foolish to deny herself his friendship because she felt more than that for him.

She gave him a cheery smile and said, "Sure. Same time tomorrow." She breathed a sigh of relief that she wouldn't have to face him again for twenty-four hours.

"As soon as I shower, we can go to work planning all those activities for the kids," he said.

Jewel gave him a startled look.

"Changed your mind about wanting my help?"

She had forgotten all about it. "No. I…uh…"

He tousled her hair. "You can make up your mind while I shower. I'll be here if you need me."

A moment later he had disappeared into the house. It was only then she realized he was going to use up all the hot water.

"Hey!" she yelled, yanking the screen door open to follow after him. "I get the shower first!"

He leaned his head out of the bathroom door. She saw a length of naked flank and stopped in her tracks.

"You can have it first tomorrow," he said. His eyes twinkled as he added, "Unless you'd like to share?"

She put her hand flat on his bare chest, feeling the crisp, sweat-dampened curls under her palm, and shoved him back inside. "Go get cleaned up, stinky," she said, wrinkling her nose. "We've got work to do."

He saluted her and stepped back inside.

It was the right response. Just enough teasing and playful camaraderie to disguise her shiver of delight—and the sudden quiver of fear—at being invited to share Mac's shower.

CHAPTER THREE

"Wow! MAC MACREADY in the flesh!"

Mac felt embarrassed and humbled at the look of admiration—almost adulation—in Colt Whitelaw's eyes. Mac had just shoved open the kitchen screen door to admire the sunrise on his third day at Hawk's Pride when he encountered Jewel's fourteen-year-old brother on the back steps. He had known the boy since Colt came to the Whitelaw household as an infant, the only one of the eight Whitelaw kids who had known no other parents than Zach and Rebecca. "Hi there, kid."

Colt was wearing a white T-shirt cut off at the waist to expose his concave belly and ribs and with the arms ripped out to reveal sinewy biceps. Levi's covered his long, lanky legs. He was tossing a football from hand to hand as he shifted from foot to booted foot. With the soft black down of adolescence growing on his upper lip, he looked every bit the eager and excited teenager he was.

"Mom said you were coming, but I didn't really believe her. I mean, now that you're famous and all, I didn't think you'd ever come back here. I wanted to come over as soon as you got here, but Mom said you needed time to settle in without all of us bothering you, so I stayed away a whole extra day. I'm not bothering you, am I?"

Mac resisted the urge to ruffle Colt's shaggy, shoulder-length black hair. The kid wouldn't appreciate it. Mac knew from his own experience that a boy of fourteen considered himself pretty much grown up. Colt was six feet tall, but his shoulders were still almost as narrow as his hips. His blue eyes were filled with wonder and hope, without the cynicism and disappointment that appeared as you grew older and learned that life threw a lot of uncatchable balls your way.

"Sit down and tell me what you've been doing with yourself," Mac invited. He eased himself into one of the two slatted white wooden chairs situated on the flagstone patio at the back of the cottage. Colt perched on the wide arm of the other chair.

The patio was arbored, and purple bougainvillea woven within a white lattice framework provided shade to keep the early morning sun off their heads and a pleasant floral fragrance.

Mac was aware of Colt's scrutiny as he gently picked up his wounded leg and set the ankle on the opposite knee. When he was done, he laid his cane down on the flagstone and leaned back comfortably in the chair.

"I was watching the game on TV when your leg got busted," Colt said. "It looked pretty bad."

"It was," Mac agreed.

"I heard them say you'd never walk again," Colt blurted.

Mac managed a smile. "Looks like they were wrong."

"When you didn't come back after a whole year, they said you'd never play football again."

"It's taken me a while to get back on my feet, but I expect to be back on the football field in the fall as good as new and better than ever."

"Really?" Colt asked.

Mac was fresh out of the shower after his second morning of walking with Jewel, and wished now he had put on jeans and boots instead of shorts and Nikes. The kid was gawking at his scarred leg like he was a mutant from the latest horror movie.

Mac figured it was time to change the subject, or he'd end up crying his woes to the teenager. He gestured to the football in Colt's hands and said, "Are you on the football team at school?"

Colt made a disparaging face and mumbled, "Yeah. I'm the quarterback."

Most boys, especially in Texas, would have been ecstatic at the thought of being quarterback. "It sounds as if you don't care much for football."

"It's all right. It's just…" Colt slid off the arm backward into the slatted wooden chair, with his legs dangling over the arm, the football cradled in the notch of his elbow. "Did you always know what you wanted to do with your life?"

Mac nodded. He had always known he wanted to play football. He just hadn't been sure his body would give him the chance. "How about you?"

"I know exactly what I want to do," Colt said. "I just don't think I'm going to get the chance to do it."

"Why not?"

"Dad expects me to stay here and be a rancher."

"Is that so bad?"

"It is when I'd rather be doing something else."

Mac stared at Colt's troubled face. "Anything you'd like to talk about?"

Colt shrugged. "Naw. I guess not." He settled his feet on the ground and rose with an ease that Mac envied. "Guess I'd better get going. Now that school's out for the summer, I've got a lot of chores to do."

Mac turned his eyes in the direction of the squealing windmill.

Colt laughed. "I'll get to it right away. Hope it hasn't been keeping you awake."

"I've slept fine." Like the dead. He had slept straight through the afternoon and evening of his first day here, and yesterday he had been exhausted after a day spent mostly sitting down, working out a crafts program for the camp with Jewel. He knew his body needed rest to heal, but he was tired of being tired. He wanted to be well again.

Colt began loping away, then suddenly turned and threw the football in Mac's direction. Instinctively, Mac reached out to catch it. His fingertips settled on the well-thrown ball with remembered ease, and he drew it in.

Colt came loping back, a wide grin splitting his face. "Guess you haven't lost your touch." He held out his hand for the ball.

Mac looked up at the kid, an idea forming in his head. "How would you like to throw a few to me over the next couple of weeks, after I get a little more mobile?"

Colt's eyes went wide with wonder. "You mean it? Really? Hot damn, that would be great! I mean, golly, that would be great!" he quickly corrected himself, looking over his shoulder to see if any of his family had heard him. "Just say when and where."

"Let's say two weeks from today," Mac said. "I'll come and find you."

Colt eyed Mac's injured leg. "Are you sure—"

"Two weeks," Mac said certainly.

Colt grinned. "You got it." He took the ball and sauntered off toward the barn.

Mac let out a deep sigh. He had given himself two weeks to get back enough mobility to be able to run for a pass, when it was taking him thirty minutes to walk a mile.

He turned as he heard the screen door slam and saw Jewel. She was just out of the shower, having been second again this morning, since she had gotten a phone call the instant they came back in the door from their walk. She must have blown her hair dry, because it looked shiny and soft enough for him to want to put his hands in it.

The only time he had ever touched her hair in the past was to tousle it like an older brother or tug on her ponytail. He couldn't help wondering what it would feel like to have all that long, silky hair draped over his body.

Mac turned away. *This is Jewel. Your best friend. You'd better get laid soon, old buddy. You're starting to have really weird fantasies.*

She was wearing jeans and boots and a long-sleeved man's button-down, oxford-cloth shirt turned up at the cuffs with the tails hanging out. He wondered if the shirt had belonged to her fiancé and felt jealous of the man. Which was stupid, because Mac and Jewel had never been lovers.

Would you like to be?

He forced his mind away from that insidious thought. It would mess up everything if he made a move on his best friend. He needed Jewel's friendship too much to spoil things that way.

The shirt was big and blousy on her, and she wore her hair pulled over her shoulders in front to hide whatever there might have been left to see of her figure, which wasn't much.

He started to say "You look great!" and bit his tongue. It sounded too much like something a man might say to a woman he wanted to impress. "Hi," he said instead. "Hope you had enough hot water."

"Barely. I made it a quick shower. I'm definitely first tomorrow." She took the seat next to him, leaned back and inhaled a breath of flower-scented air that made her breasts rise under the shirt. The sight took his breath away.

Whenever he had thought about Jewel in the years they had been apart, it was her laughter he had remembered. The way her eyes crinkled at the corners and her lips curved, revealing even white teeth, and how the sound would kind of bubble up out of her, as effervescent as sparkling water.

He couldn't imagine why he hadn't remembered her breasts. He could see why a man might stare. Had they been that large six years ago? They must have been, or close to it, because he had joked with her about them a lot, he remembered. And she had laughed in response, that effervescent, sparkling laugh.

He realized he hadn't heard her laugh once since he had arrived. She had smiled, but her eyes had never joined her mouth. A sadness lingered, memories of more than uncatchable balls. More like forfeited games.

"Who was that on the phone?" he asked.

"Mrs. Templeton. Her eight-year-old son, Brad, is supposed to be a camper during the first two-week session, but he was having second thoughts about coming."

"Why?"

"She's not really sure. He was excited at first when his parents suggested the camp. She wanted me to talk to him."

"Were you able to change his mind?"

Her lips curved. "Brad's an avid football fan. I mentioned you were here—"

"You shouldn't have done that," Mac said brusquely.

She looked as if he'd kicked her in the stomach. "I'm sorry," she said. "I didn't think you'd mind. You always seemed to like spending time with the kids."

He made a face. "It isn't that I mind spending time with them. It's just—" He didn't want them to see him hobbling around with a cane. He didn't want them feeling sorry for him. He didn't want to be asked a lot of questions for which he had no answers.

He would know in the next few weeks whether his leg

was going to stand up to the rigors of running. He wanted time by himself to deal with his disappointment—if that was what it turned out to be. He wanted to be able to rage against fate without worrying about some sick kid's feelings.

"I'm sorry, Mac," Jewel said, reaching out to lay her hand on his forearm.

The hairs on his arms prickled at her touch, and his body responded in a way that both surprised and disturbed him. He resisted the urge to jerk his hand away. That would only hurt her again.

This is Jewel. My friend. There's nothing sexual intended by her touch.

Jewel might be his friend, but his body also recognized her as female. This sort of thing—unwanted arousal—had happened once or twice when they were teenagers, and she had touched him at an odd moment when he wasn't expecting it, but he had always attributed those incidents to randy teenage hormones. That excuse wouldn't work now.

All right, so she was an attractive woman.

That excuse wouldn't work either. Jewel wasn't pretty. Never had been. Her nose was straight and small, her chin was square, her mouth was a bit too big and her eyes were Mississippi-mud brown. Ordinary features all. She did have an extraordinary body. Her long legs, small waist and ample breasts were the stuff of male dreams. But Mac was offended on Jewel's behalf to think that any man could want her because of her body and not because of who she was inside.

So, it's her mind you find attractive?

As a teenager, he had liked her sense of humor, her enthusiasm for life and her willingness to reach out to others. He hadn't seen much of the first two traits this time around, and he wasn't sure whether it was a continued willingness to reach out to others that had made her return to Camp LittleHawk or, as he suspected, a desire to retreat from the world.

Mac had no explanation for his response to Jewel except that he had been celibate for too long. What had happened when Jewel touched him was merely the healthy response of a male animal to a female of the species. The problem would be solved when he found himself a woman and satisfied the simple physiological need that had been too long denied. Which meant he had better make a trip into town sometime soon and find a willing woman.

"Do you want me to call the Templetons back and tell them your plans have changed and you won't be here, after all?" Jewel asked.

He shook his head. "I guess it won't hurt me to be nice to one little boy."

"If you'd rather not—"

"I said I would." He slid his leg off his knee and reached for his cane. "It's not that big a deal, Jewel."

She rose and reached for his arm to help him up.

He jerked away. "I'm not an invalid. I wish you'd stop trying to help me."

He saw the hurt look on her face, but that was better than having her know the sharp sexual response her touch had provoked. That would ruin everything. Better to have her think he was in a lousy mood than find out that he wanted to suck on her breasts or put his hand between her legs and seek the damp heat there.

"I'm going in to town today," he said, realizing he'd better get away for a while and cool down.

"Perfect! I need some things from the hardware store. Could you give me a lift?"

Thank God she wasn't looking at him, or she would have known something was wrong. He opened his mouth to refuse and said, "Sure. Why not? Give me a chance to change into a shirt and jeans and some boots first."

She gave him a blazing smile that made his groin pull up tight. Hell. He'd better find himself a woman. And soon.

No DOUBT ABOUT IT, Jewel thought. Mac had been acting strange all day. Every errand he had run had taken him to the opposite end of town from her. Although they had made plans to meet for lunch at the Stanton Hotel Café, he hadn't arrived until she was nearly finished eating. She was sitting on one of the 1950's chrome seats at the lunch counter when he finally showed up, grabbed a cup of coffee, said he wasn't hungry, remembered something else he had to do in town and took off again.

If Jewel hadn't known better, she would have said he didn't want to be anywhere near her. But that was silly. They were best friends.

They had agreed to meet in the parking lot near the bank at four o'clock where Mac had parked his extended cab Chevy pickup and head back to Hawk's Pride. Jewel was sitting on the fender of the truck when Mac finally returned.

"You could have sat inside," he said. "It wasn't locked."

"It was too hot with the windows rolled up, and I needed a key to get them down," she said, lifting the hair at her nape to catch the late afternoon breeze. She heard him suck in a breath and had turned in his direction when a female voice distracted them both.

"Peter? Is that you?"

Jewel rose and turned at the same time as Mac to find a red-headed, green-eyed woman standing beside the bed of the pickup.

"Eve?" Mac replied in tones of astonishment that rivaled the woman's.

She ran toward him, and Jewel watched in awe as Mac dropped his cane to surround the woman with his arms. Jewel hurried to pick it up, certain Mac would lose his balance and need it at any moment.

Only he didn't.

Either he was stronger on his feet than he had been two days ago, or the petite redhead was stronger than she looked.

"Peter. Peter," the woman said, her gaze searching his face.

"Eve. I can't believe it's you!" he replied, his eyes searching her face with equal delight.

He suddenly looked around for Jewel and reached out a hand to draw her closer. "Jewel, this is Evelyn Latham. Eve and I dated for a while in college. She's the only person I ever let get away with calling me Peter."

Eve simpered. "It's because you have such a big—"

"Yeah," Mac cut her off. "Eve, this is my friend, Jewel Whitelaw. I'm spending some time at her parents' ranch."

Jewel saw Eve take one look at her plain face and her unshapely clothes and dismiss her as no competition.

Eve then gave Mac a quick, but thorough, once-over. "You look *purrr*fectly fit to me."

Jewel cringed at the way the woman drew out the word with her Texas accent. Eve obviously appreciated Mac's assets—one of which she had apparently seen up close and personal—and the sexual invitation she extended was clear, at least to Jewel.

Mac must have heard it, too. "What are you doing with yourself these days, Eve? I haven't seen you since…when was it?"

"Graduation day from UT, two years ago."

He looked for a ring on her left hand, but didn't find one. "I thought you were going to marry Joe Bob Struthers."

"I only told you that because I was mad at you for dumping me after only three dates…just when we were getting to know each other so well."

He's probably slept with her, Jewel thought. She couldn't fault Mac's taste. The woman was gorgeous. She wore a clingy green St. John knit dress, with a fashionable gold chain draped across her flat stomach.

Mac gave Eve a look that suggested he would be happy to pick up where they had left off. "So you're not a married woman?"

"I'm free as a bird," Eve confirmed.

"I thought you were a Dallas girl, born and bred. What are you doing out here in the far reaches of northwest Texas?" Mac asked.

"My dad bought the bank here in town. I've been the assistant manager for the past year."

"I never expected any less of you," Mac said, "graduating the way you did at the top of the class."

Pretty *and* smart. That was a lethal combination, Jewel thought. Not that Jewel was competing in any way with Evelyn Latham for Mac's affection. She and Mac were just friends. But she couldn't help thinking that if Mac got involved with Eve, she would see a whole lot less of him, and she did enjoy his company.

"What are you doing here?" Eve asked Mac in return. "Aren't you supposed to be off playing football, or something like that?"

Jewel couldn't believe the woman had dated Mac but had no idea when the football season began and ended.

"It's the off-season," Mac said with an indulgent smile. For the first time it must have occurred to him that he didn't have his cane. He looked around for it, and Jewel handed it to him. He took it and leaned on it. "I'm here visiting friends and recuperating from a football injury."

"You were hurt?" Eve asked.

Jewel rolled her eyes. Mac gave her a nudge with his hip, and she straightened up.

"You could say that," Mac said. "I guess you didn't hear about it."

Eve turned her mouth down in a delightful moue. "As you very well know I never cared much for football, only for the way you looked in those tight pants."

The sexual innuendo was even more blatant this time, and Jewel felt uncomfortable standing there listening to it. "Sorry we can't stay," she said. "Mac was just giving me a ride home."

The pout that appeared on Eve's face would have looked right at home on a three-year-old. "Oh, Mac. I was hoping you'd have dinner with me."

"I still can," Mac said. "I'll take Jewel home and come back. What time and where?"

"How about eight o'clock? My house." She gave Mac an address in the newest condominium complex in town.

Mac grinned. "I'll be there."

"Don't dress up," Eve purred. "I want you to be comfortable."

"You got it," Mac said.

With Jewel standing right there, Eve went up on tiptoe and gave Mac a kiss right on the mouth. Jewel noticed Mac's arm went around her waist quick enough to draw her close, so the kiss wasn't unwelcome. It went on a long time, and from the way their mouths shifted, their tongues were involved.

Jewel stood frozen, unable to move. At last the kiss broke, and Mac shot her a quick, embarrassed look. It was too little, too late. He should have thought of her feelings before he practically made love to another woman right in front of her.

Only it shouldn't have mattered if he kissed somebody else. They were only friends.

"See you at eight," Mac said as he backed away from Eve.

"I'll be waiting," Eve said in a sultry voice.

Mac went around to his side of the truck without stopping to open Jewel's door. Not that she needed her door opened for her. She got in and sat near the edge of the seat, opening the window as soon as Mac started the truck and sticking her elbow out.

"Sorry about that," he said after a few minutes. "I shouldn't have embarrassed you like that."

"I wasn't embarrassed," Jewel said. "Kiss all the girls you want. It doesn't make any difference to me."

"All right. If that's the way you feel. Just so you don't worry, I may not be back tonight."

"Thanks for telling me," Jewel said. "I won't wait up for you."

She really didn't care. He was just a friend. He'd had another girlfriend most of the time she had known him. This was no different. Except, the whole time she had watched Mac kissing Eve the most stunning thought had been running through her head.

I wish it were me.

CHAPTER FOUR

MAC WENT TO Evelyn Latham's house with one purpose in mind: to get laid. Eve opened the door wearing a clingy red velour jumpsuit that sent a wake-up call to his body. He was sure all it would take was one kiss to get the old machinery back into action. So he pulled her into his arms and kissed her and…nothing. Not a damned thing happened.

He worried about the situation all through supper and all through the glass of merlot they enjoyed by the fire he started for her in the stone fireplace. When they ended up entwined on the couch, he willed his body to react to the feel of her lips against his, to the feel of her body beneath his hands. He felt the sweat pop out on his forehead. But…nothing.

This wasn't supposed to happen. Just because he hadn't made love with a woman didn't mean that he didn't want to. He wanted to, all right. His damned body just wasn't cooperating! He made up some excuse for why he couldn't stay—his aching leg had come in handy for once—and bolted.

He drove around for two hours wondering if he was going to spend the rest of his life a virgin. What the hell had gone wrong? He hadn't been able to figure it out but had finally conceded that driving around all night wasn't going to give him any answers.

Then he remembered he had told Jewel he would probably be out all night. What was she going to think if he came back early?

That you don't take your time.

Yeah. Probably she'd just think he'd gotten his fill of Eve already. He couldn't imagine getting his fill of Jewel in bed. The thought of touching her skin, the feel of her hair against his body, the smell of her.

His body stirred in response.

It's too late, buddy. You already missed the party. You have to do that when there's a flesh-and-blood woman around.

And when it was some other woman besides Jewel. It wasn't going to do him any good getting aroused by thoughts of her, because she was the last person he could have sex with.

Hell, his leg *was* killing him. He had some exercises he was supposed to do at night that he hadn't done to relax the muscles. He needed to lay his leg flat in bed. He needed… he needed to know he could function as a man. The situation with Eve had been disturbing because it had never happened to him before. What if something was wrong with him? What if all those operations had done something to his libido?

You don't have any problem responding to Jewel.

He recalled his feelings for Jewel, the ones that had sent him off in search of another woman. They weren't as comforting as they should have been. He had felt the same sort of semi-arousal with Eve before he kissed her, but when it came time for action, his body had opted out.

Mac cut the pickup engine at the back door to the cottage. No lights. At least he'd be spared the ignominy of Jewel seeing him sneaking in at two in the morning. He didn't want to have to make some explanation about why he was home early. He wasn't about to tell her the truth, and he hated like hell to lie.

He eased the kitchen door open—Western doors were rarely locked, even in this day and age—and slipped inside.

"Hi."

Mac nearly lost his balance and fell. "What the hell are you doing sitting here in the dark?"

He reached for the light switch, but Jewel said, "Don't."

The rough, raw sound of her voice, as though she had been crying, stayed his hand. He remained where he was, waiting for his eyes to adjust to the dark. He finally located her in the shadows. She was sitting with her elbows perched on the kitchen table, her face buried in her hands.

He limped over, scraped a chair closer and sat beside her. He felt her stiffen as he laid an arm across her shoulder. "Are you all right?"

"I'm fine."

"You don't sound fine. You sound like you've been crying."

"I didn't think you'd be back tonight."

Which meant she had expected to have the privacy to cry without being disturbed. It didn't explain *why* she had been crying. She tried to rise, but he kept his arm around her and pressed her back down. "I'm here, Jewel."

"Why is that, Mac? I can't imagine any woman throwing you out. Which means you left on your own. What happened?"

This was exactly the scene Mac had been hoping to avoid. "She…uh…we…uh…"

"Don't tell me Eve didn't make a pass."

"She did," Mac conceded reluctantly.

"Then why aren't you spending the night with her?"

"I…uh…that sort of thing can give a woman ideas."

"I see."

"You do?"

"Sure. Spend the whole night in a woman's bed, and she tends to think you might be serious about her. Everyone knows you're a love'em and leave'em kind of guy."

"I am? I mean, I suppose I am. I haven't found a woman I'd want to settle down with who'd have me." That was certainly no lie.

Eve had wanted him, all right. It should have been the easiest thing in the world to take her in his arms and make love to her. The situation had been perfect: willing woman, intelligent, not a total stranger, attractive—hell, absolutely beautiful. And it had been absolutely impossible.

Mac bit back the sound of frustration that sought voice.

"You should go to bed if you're going to get up early and walk tomorrow," Jewel said.

"I'd rather sit here with you," Mac replied.

"I'd rather be alone."

"Are you sure?"

"I'll be fine."

Mac leaned over to kiss her softly on the temple. Her hair smelled of lilacs. It reminded him of warm, lazy summer days they had spent lying on the banks of the pond that bordered the Stonecreek Ranch. He resisted the urge to thread his fingers through her hair. It might comfort her, but it would drive him damn near crazy.

"Just know I'm here if you need me," he said. "You'd better get to bed, too, because I'm expecting you to walk with me tomorrow."

"I don't think that's a good idea. It would be better if you go alone."

He stared at her, wishing he could see the expression on her face. Moonlight filtered in through the kitchen window but left her mostly in shadow. "What's going on, Jewel? Why are you shutting me out?"

"I got along fine without you for six years, Mac. What makes you think I need you now?"

Mac was stunned as much by the virulence in her voice as by what she had said. "If you want me out of here, I'm gone."

She clutched his forearm as he rose, rubbing at her eyes with the knuckles of her other hand. "Don't leave. Don't leave."

He pulled her up and into his arms, and she grabbed him tight around his neck and sobbed against his shoulder. He rubbed her back with his open palms, aware suddenly that she was wearing a thin, sleeveless cotton nightgown and nothing else.

His body turned hard as a rock in two seconds flat.

His equipment worked all right. At the wrong time. With the wrong woman.

"Damn it all to hell," he muttered.

Jewel needed his comfort, not some male animal lusting after her. He kept their hips apart, not wanting his physical response to frighten or distress her. "Tell me what's wrong, Jewel. Let me help," he crooned in her ear.

"It's too embarrassing," she said, her face pressed tight against the curve of his shoulder.

"Nothing's too embarrassing for us to talk about, my little carbuncle."

She hiccuped a laugh. "Carbuncle? Isn't that an ugly inflammation—"

"It's a red precious stone. I swear."

She relaxed, chuckling, and it took all the willpower he had to keep from pulling her tight against him.

"You always could make me laugh," she said. "Oh, Mac, I wish you'd come back a long time ago. I missed you."

"And I missed you. Now tell me what's so embarrassing that you don't want to talk about it?"

She sighed, and her breasts swelled against his chest, soft and warm. His heartbeat picked up. Lord, she was dangerous. Why couldn't this have happened with Eve? Why did it have to be Jewel?

Her fingers began to play in the hair at his nape. He wondered if she knew what she was doing to him and decided she couldn't possibly. She wouldn't purposely turn him on. What she wanted was comfort from a friend. And he intended to give it to her.

But he wasn't any more able to stop his body from responding than he had been capable of making it respond. All he could do was try to ignore the part of him that was insisting he do something. He focused his attention on Jewel. She needed his help.

"Tell me what's wrong," he urged.

"I wish things were different, that's all."

"Don't we all?" he said, thinking of his own situation. "But frankly, that doesn't sound embarrassing enough to keep to yourself. What is it? Got bucked off your horse? Happens to the best of us. Broke a dish? Do it all the time. If you broke a heart I might worry, but you can always buy another dish."

She laughed. The bubbly, effervescent sound he hadn't heard for six years. He pulled her close and rocked her in his arms in the old, familiar, brotherly way.

She stiffened, and he realized what he had done. His hips, with the hard bulge in front, were pressed tight against hers. There was no way she could mistake his condition.

"Damn, Jewel," he said, backing away from her, putting her at arm's length and gripping her hands tightly in his.

He smiled, but she didn't smile back.

When she pulled free, he let her go. "We can still talk," he said, wanting her to stay, wanting to confess the truth to her. She was still his best friend. But somehow things had changed. He couldn't tell her everything, not the most private things. Not anymore.

Maybe he had been wrong to expect her to confide in him. Maybe she felt the same awkwardness he did, the distance that had never been there before. A distance he had put there, because he saw her not just as a friend, but as a woman he wanted to kiss and touch.

"I'm going to bed, Mac."

"Will you walk with me tomorrow?"

"I don't think—"

"Please, Jewel. You're my best friend. I'd really like the company."

She hesitated so long, he thought she was going to refuse. "All right, Mac. I suppose I owe you that much." She turned and left without another word.

He waited until her bedroom door closed before he moved, afraid that if he did, he would go after her.

He wondered what had been troubling her. He wondered what she would have done if he had lowered his head and sucked on her breasts through the thin cotton. Blood pulsed through his rock-hard body, and he swore under his breath.

Mac went to bed, but he didn't sleep. He tossed and turned, troubled by vivid erotic fantasies of himself and Jewel Whitelaw. *Their legs entangled, their bodies entwined, his tongue deep in her mouth, his shaft deep inside her. She was calling to him, calling his name.*

Mac awoke tangled in the sheets, his body hot, hard and ready, his heart racing. And all alone.

He heard Jewel calling from outside the door. "Mac. Are you awake?" She knocked twice quietly. "It's time to walk."

Mac groaned. "I'll be with you in a minute." As soon as he was decent.

From the look of Jewel at the breakfast table, she hadn't slept any better than he had. She was wearing something even less attractive than the sweatshirt and cutoffs she had worn previously. It didn't matter. He saw her naked.

Mac shook his head to clear it. The vision of her breasts, large and luscious as peaches, and her long, slim legs wrapped around his waist, remained as vivid as ever.

"Are you all right?" Jewel asked.

"Fine. Let's go."

She chattered the whole way to the canyon, but he would have been hard-pressed to remember a word of what she had said or his own responses.

Everything was different. Something was missing. And something had been added.

He wanted their old relationship back. He was determined to quench any desire he might feel for her, so things could get back to an even footing. He figured the best way to start was to bring the subject out into the open and deal with it. On the walk back to the house, he did.

"About what happened last night... It shouldn't have happened." His comment was vague, but he knew she understood exactly what he meant when pink roses blossomed on her cheekbones.

She shrugged. "I was just a woman in a skimpy nightgown."

"Jewel, I—"

She stopped and turned to him, looking into his eyes, her gaze earnest. "Please, Mac. Can we pretend it never happened?"

He gave a relieved sigh. "That's exactly what I'd like to do. It was an accident. I never intended for it to happen. I wish I could promise it won't happen again, but—" He shot her a chagrined look. "I'll be sure you're never embarrassed again. Am I forgiven?"

"There's no need—"

"Just say yes," he said.

"Yes."

She turned abruptly and started walking again, and he followed after her.

"I'm glad that's over with," he said. "I can't afford to lose a friend as good as you, Jewel."

"And I can't afford to lose a friend like you, Mac."

Jewel's eyes were as brown and sad as a motherless calf. Mac wished she had told him why she was crying last night. He wished she had let him comfort her. If she ever gave him another chance, he was going to do it right. He wasn't going to let his hormones get in the way of their friendship.

When they got back to the house, she hurried up the back steps ahead of him. "I get the shower first!"

"We could always share," he teased. He could have bitten his tongue out. That sort of sexual innuendo had to cease.

To his relief, Jewel gave him a wide smile and said, "In your dreams, Mac! I'll try to save you a little hot water."

Then she was gone.

Mac settled on the back stoop and rubbed the calf muscles of his injured leg. It was getting easier to walk. Practice was helping. And it would get easier to treat Jewel as merely a friend. All he had needed was a little more practice at that, too.

AFTER HE HAD SHOWERED, Mac made a point of seeking Jewel out, determined to work on reestablishing their friendship. He found her in the barn, cleaning stalls and shoveling in new hay for the dozen or so ponies Camp LittleHawk kept available for horseback rides. "Can I help?" he said.

"There's another pitchfork over by the door. Be my guest."

Mac noticed she didn't even look up from her work. Not a very promising sign. He grabbed the pitchfork and went to work in the stall next to the one she was working in. "I thought your mom usually hired someone to do this kind of heavy labor."

"I don't have anything better to do with my time," Jewel said.

"Why not?" Mac asked. "Pretty girl like you ought to be out enjoying herself."

Jewel stuck her pitchfork into the hay and turned to stare at him. "I enjoy my work."

"I'm sure you do," he said, throwing a pitchfork of manure into the nearby wheelbarrow. "But there's a time for work and a time for play. I don't see you doing enough playing."

"I'm a grown-up woman, Mac. Playing is for kids."

"You're never too old to play, Jewel." Mac filled his pitchfork with clean straw and threw it up over the stall so it landed on Jewel's head.

She came out of her stall sputtering and picking straw out of her mouth, mad as a peeled rattler. She confronted him, hands on hips and said, "That wasn't funny!"

He set his pitchfork against the stall and laughed. "I think you look darned cute with straw sticking out of your hair every whichaway." He headed toward her to help pull out some of the straw.

When he got close enough, she gave him a shove that sent him onto his behind. Only the straw Mac landed in wasn't clean. He gave a howl of outrage and struggled up out of the muck, glaring at the stain on the back of his jeans. "What'd you do that for?"

She grinned. "I think you look darned cute, all covered with muck."

"You know this means war."

"No, Mac. We're even now. Don't—"

He lunged toward her, caught her by the waist and threw her up over his shoulder in a fireman's carry.

"Watch out for your leg!" Jewel cried. "You're going to hurt yourself carrying me like this."

"My leg is fine," Mac growled. "Good enough to get you where I want you."

Mac headed for the short stack of hay at one end of the barn and when he got there, dropped Jewel into it. When she tried to jump free, he came down on top of her and pinned her hands on either side of her.

"Mac," she said breathlessly, laughing. "Get up."

"I want to play some more, Emerald, my dear," he said sprinkling her hair with hay.

"You're more green than I am," she taunted.

Mac took a look at the back of his jeans. "Yes, and I think you should pay a forfeit for that."

"You can have the shower first," she said with a bubbly laugh. "You need it!"

His laugh was cut off when he realized that what he really wanted was a kiss. He stared at her curving mouth, at the way her nose wrinkled when she laughed, at the teasing sparkle in her brown eyes. "I think I'll take something now."

He watched her face sober when she realized what he intended. He knew she must be able to feel his arousal, cradled as he was between her jean-clad thighs. He waited for her to tell him to let go, that the game was over. She stared up at him with luminous eyes and slicked her tongue quickly, nervously over her lips. But she didn't say get up or get off. And she didn't say no.

Friends, Mac. Not lovers. Friends.

Mac made himself kiss her eyelids closed before he kissed each cheek and then her nose and then…her forehead.

He rose abruptly and pulled her to her feet. She was dizzy, because her eyes had been closed, so he was forced to hold her in his arms until she was steady. She felt so good there, so very right. And so very wrong.

"I'm sorry, Jewel," he said. "That was totally out of line."

She took a deep breath and let it out. "Yes, I suppose it was. I think it's your turn to pay a forfeit, Mac."

He tensed. "What did you have in mind?"

She reached out, and for a moment he thought she was going to lay her hand on his chest and give him another shove. Instead, she grasped a nearby pitchfork and held it out to him. "You get to finish what I started. I'm going to get another shower and wash off all this itchy straw."

"Hey! That's not fair," he protested.

But she had already turned and stalked away.

"You and your bright ideas," Mac muttered to himself as he pitched manure into the wheelbarrow. "What were you thinking? Maybe you could throw straw around when you were kids and it was funny, but there was nothing funny about what almost happened in that haystack. What if you'd kissed her lips? How would you have felt when she got upset?

How do you know she'd have been upset?

Mac mused over that question for the next hour as he finished cleaning stalls. Actually, Jewel had seemed more upset that he hadn't kissed her lips. Could she have feelings for him that weren't merely friendly?

Don't even think about it, Macready. The woman's off-limits. She's your friend, and she needs your friendship.

Concentrate on somebody else's needs for a change and forget what you want.

Mac knew why he was having all these lurid thoughts about Jewel. He probably would be having such thoughts about any woman he came in close contact with at this stage in his life. It didn't help that Jewel turned him on so hard and fast.

Get over it, Mac.

"I intend to," Mac muttered as he set the pitchfork back where it belonged and headed for the house. "Jewel is my friend. And that's the way it's going to stay."

At the end of two weeks Mac was walking the mile to the canyon without the aid of a cane and doing it in seven minutes flat. Jewel had difficulty keeping up with him when he broke into a jog. His leg was getting better; hers never would. She could picture him moving away from her, going on with his life, leaving her behind. She was going to miss him. She was going to miss playing with him.

The scene in the barn hadn't been repeated. Nor had Mac teased her or taunted her or done any of the playful things he might have done when they were teenagers. He had become a serious grown-up over the past two weeks. She hadn't realized how much she had needed him to play with her. To her surprise, she hadn't been intimidated or frightened by him in the barn. Not even when she had thought he might kiss her.

She had wanted that kiss, she realized, and been sorely disappointed when he kissed her forehead instead. Then she'd realized he had been carried away by their physical closeness, and when he'd realized it was her—his old friend, Jewel—he had backed off. He liked her, but not that way. They were just friends.

It should have been enough. But lately, Jewel was realizing she wanted more. She was going to have to control those feelings, or she would ruin everything. Mac would be leaving soon enough. She didn't want to drive him away by asking for things from him he wasn't willing to give.

"Hey," she called ahead to him. "How about taking a break at the bottom of the canyon."

"You got it." He dropped onto the warm, sandy ground with his back against the stone wall that bore the primitive Native American drawings and sifted the soil through his fingers. She sank down across from him, leaning back on her palms, her legs in front of her.

"You'll be running full out by this time next week," she said.

"I expect so."

"I won't be coming with you then."

"Why not?"

She sat up and rubbed at the sore muscles in her thigh. "I can't keep up with you, Mac." In more ways than one. He would be going places, while she stayed behind.

Mac dusted off his hands on his shorts, scooted around to her side and, as though it were the most natural thing in the world, began to massage her thigh. She hadn't let a man touch her like that since she had broken her engagement. Chill bumps rose on her skin at the feel of Mac's callused fingers on her flesh. It felt amazingly good. It dawned on her that she didn't feel the least bit afraid. But then, this was Mac. He would never hurt her.

The past two weeks of waiting for Mac to repeat his behavior in the barn had been wonderful and horrible. She loved being with Mac. And she dreaded it. Since the night he had come home early from Evelyn Latham's house, he had remained an avuncular friend. He had been a tremendous help planning activities for the children. He had made her laugh often. But with the exception of that brief, unfulfilled promise in the barn, there was nothing the least bit sexual in his behavior toward her.

She was unsure of what her feelings were for Mac, but there was no doubting her profound physical reaction to his touch. It was difficult not to look at him as a virile, attractive man, rather than merely as a friend. Even now, she couldn't keep her eyes off of him.

The Texas sun had turned him a warm bronze, but a white strip of flesh showed around the waist of his running shorts, confirming the hidden skin was lighter. She caught herself wondering what he would look like without the shorts.

"How does that feel?" he asked as he massaged her thigh. "Better?"

She nodded because she couldn't speak. *It feels wonderful.* She wanted his hands to move higher, between her legs. As though she had willed it, his fingertips moved upward on her thigh. She let him keep up the massage, because it felt good. Then stopped him because it felt too good.

"Wait." She gripped his wrist with her hand, afraid that he would read her mind and realize that the last thing she wanted him to do was stop.

"If you exercised more, maybe your limp wouldn't be so bad," he said.

She brushed his hand away from where it lingered on her flesh. "One leg is slightly shorter than the other, Mac. That isn't going to change with exercise."

"It might with surgery. They can do remarkable things these days. Have you thought about—"

"What's going on here, Mac?" she interrupted. "You never said a word to me in the past about my limp. You always told me to ignore it, to pretend it didn't exist, that it didn't keep me from being who I am. What's changed?"

Mac backed up against the wall again. His gaze was

concentrated on the sand he began once more sifting through his fingers.

"Mac?" she persisted. "Answer me."

He looked up at her, his eyes searching her face. "How can you stand it—not being able to run?"

She shrugged. "I manage."

"I'd hate it if something like that happened to me."

"Something like that *has* happened to you."

He shook his head. "Uh-uh. I'm temporarily out of commission. I'm going to be as good as new."

Did he really believe that? Jewel wondered. Yes, he had made astonishing progress in two weeks, but even she could see the effort it had taken. One look at his leg—at the scar tissue on his leg—suggested there was never going to be as much muscle to work with as there had been in the past. "What if you can never run again like you used to, Mac? What if you can't get back to where you were?"

"I will."

"What if you can't?"

"I'll be playing again in the fall. Count on it."

"You're purposely avoiding my question. *What if you can't?*"

He rose, but it took obvious effort to do so without the cane. She said nothing while he accomplished the feat— a minor miracle considering the condition he'd been in two weeks ago.

"Let's go," he said gruffly, reaching down to help her to her feet.

She shoved his hand out of the way. "I'm not a cripple, either, Mac," she said. "I can manage on my own."

"Damn it, Jewel! What do you want from me?"

"Honesty," she said, rising and standing toe to toe with him, her eyes focused on his. "You never used to lie to me, Mac. Or to yourself."

"What is it you want to hear me say? I won't quit playing football! It's all I ever wanted to do."

"You wanted to be a paleontologist."

"That's what I said. But inside—" he thumped his bare
chest with his fist "—all I ever dreamed about, all I ever
wanted to do was run like the wind and catch footballs. It
was just so impossible for so long, I never let myself hope
for it too much. But I made it happen. And I'm not going
to give it up!"

Jewel felt her heart skip a beat. She hadn't known. She
hadn't realized. If what Mac said was true, then he was
facing a much greater crisis than she had imagined.

"Avoiding reality isn't going to make it go away, Mac,"
she said gently. "You have to face your demons."

"Like you have?" Mac retorted.

Jewel's face blanched. She turned her back on him and
headed up the trail toward the mouth of the canyon.

"Jewel, wait," Mac said as he hurried after her. He
grabbed her arm to stop her. "If you're going to insist on
honesty from me, how about a little from you?"

"What is it you want to know? You know everything,"
she said bitterly. "You're the only one who does!"

He gave her an incredulous look. "You never told anyone else? What about your fiancé?"

She shook her head violently.

"Why the hell not?"

"I couldn't tell Jerry. I just couldn't!"

In days gone by he would have put an arm around her
to offer her comfort. But things had changed somehow in
the two weeks since they had met again. His eyes offered
emotional support, instead. "God, Jewel. That's a heavy
burden to be carrying around all by yourself."

"I'm managing all right."

"What happened to Jerry What's-his-name? Why did you call off the wedding?"

"I couldn't... I wasn't able... I could never..."

She saw the dawning comprehension in his eyes. "I don't want or need your pity!" She tried to run from him in awkward, hobbling strides, but he quickly caught up to her and pulled her into his arms.

"Don't run away," he said, his arms closing tightly around her. "It doesn't matter, Jewel. It'll get better with time."

She made a keening sound in her throat. "It's been six years. I can't forget what happened, Mac. I can't get it out of my head. Jerry was so patient, but when he tried to make love to me, I couldn't let him do it. I couldn't!" Her throat ached. A hot tear spilled onto her cheek and a sob broke free.

She grasped Mac tight around the waist and pressed her face against his bare chest, sobbing as she never had on the day she had been attacked or at any time since then. She had been too numb with shock to cry six years ago. And she had been too full of guilt when she broke up with Jerry to allow herself the release of tears.

"Shh. Shh," Mac crooned as he rocked her in his arms. "It's all right. It doesn't matter. Everything will be all right."

She felt his lips against her hair, soothing, comforting, and then his hands on either side of her face as he raised it to kiss her tear-wet eyelids. He kissed her nose and her cheeks and finally her mouth. His lips were firm, yet gentle, against her own. She yielded to the insistent pressure of his mouth, her lips soft and damp beneath his. He kissed her again, his lips brushing across hers and sending a surprising frisson of desire skittering down her spine. *Oh, Mac...*

She pressed her lips back against his and heard a sharp intake of breath. She froze, then stepped back and stared up at him in confusion.

He opened his mouth to speak and shut it again, obviously upset and looking for a way to explain what had happened between them. She wondered if he had felt it, too, the wondrous stirring inside, the need to merge into one another. What if he did? Oh, God. It would ruin everything. She couldn't…and he would never… She took another step back from him.

"Wait, Jewel. Don't go," he said, reaching out a hand to her. "We have to talk about this."

"What is there to say?"

He took a step closer, and it took all her willpower not to run from him. She felt an equally driving need to press herself against him, which she resisted just as fiercely.

"I don't want what just happened to spoil things between us," he said, his voice anguished. "I could see you needed comfort, and I…I got a little carried away."

"All right, Mac. If that's the way you want it." She would ruin everything if she pressed for more. He obviously wanted things to stay the same between them. He wanted them to be friends. That was probably for the best. What if she tried loving him and failed, as she had with Jerry? She would lose everything. She couldn't bear that.

"What's wrong, Jewel?"

She mentally and physically squared her shoulders. "I shouldn't have fallen apart like that. I've spent a lot of time in counseling putting what happened six years ago behind me."

"Have you?"

"I'm as over it as I'm ever going to get," she conceded with a rueful twist of her mouth. "It doesn't matter, Mac, really. I have the kids at camp. I have friends. I have a full life."

"Without a man in it," he said flatly. "Or children."

She arched a brow. "Who says a woman needs a man in her life? And there are lots of children at Camp Little-Hawk who need me."

He held up his hands in surrender. "You win. I'm not going to argue the point."

Jewel released a breath that became a sigh, glad the subject was closed. "We'd better get back to the house."

He looked as though he wanted to continue the discussion, but she knew that wouldn't help the situation. She decided levity was what was needed. "I hope you saved some energy, because I know for a fact Colt will be waiting for you when you get back to the house."

Mac groaned. "I forgot. He's going to throw me some passes."

"I can always send him away."

"I suppose I can catch a few passes and keep him happy."

"And keep who happy?"

Mac grinned. "So I'm looking forward to it. Think what that'll mean to you."

She gave him a quizzical look. If Mac was up to catching passes, it meant he was getting well. If he was getting well, it meant he would be leaving soon. She wanted to hear him say it. Maybe then she could stop fantasizing about him. "What will it mean to me?" she asked.

Twin dimples appeared in his cheeks. "You get the shower first."

Jewel laughed. It beat the heck out of crying.

CHAPTER FIVE

IF THERE WAS one thing Colt Whitelaw wanted more than he wanted to fly jets someday, it was to have Jennifer Wright look at him the way she looked at his best friend, Huckleberry Duncan. Jenny didn't even care that Huck had a stupid name. When Huck was around, Jenny wouldn't have noticed if Colt dropped dead at her feet. She only had eyes for Huck.

Which meant Colt got to spend a lot of time watching her when she wasn't looking. Jenny wasn't what most guys would have called pretty. She was short and skinny, her nose was too long and her teeth were slightly crooked. But she had the prettiest eyes he'd ever seen. Jenny's eyes were about the bluest blue eyes could get.

It wasn't just the color of them that he found attractive. When he looked into Jenny's eyes he saw the pledge of warmth, the promise of humor and depths of wisdom far beyond what a fourteen-year-old girl ought to possess.

Jenny might be the same age as him and Huck, but it seemed she had grown up faster—in more ways than one. For a couple of years she'd been taller than Huck. This past year Huck had caught up and passed her. Colt had always been taller than Jenny. Not that she'd noticed.

This past year something else had happened to Jenny. She had started becoming a woman. Colt felt like walloping Huck when Huck kidded her about the bumps she was sprouting up front, but when she bent over laughing and her shirt fell away, he had sneaked a peek at them. They were pure white and pink-tipped. He had turned away pretty quick because the whole time he was looking, he couldn't seem to breathe.

His body did strange things these days whenever she was around. His stomach turned upside down and his heart started to race and his body embarrassed him by doing other things that were still pretty new and felt amazingly good and grown-up. He had it bad for Jenny Wright. Not that he'd ever let her or Huck know about it. Because Huck felt about Jenny the way Jenny felt about Huck. It was true love both ways. When they got old enough, Colt figured they'd marry for sure.

He kept his feelings to himself. He liked Huck too much to give him up as a friend. And it would have killed him to stop seeing Jenny. Even if she was always going to be Huck's girl.

"Hey, Colt. I thought you were going to throw me some passes," Huck said, giving him a friendly chuck on the shoulder.

Colt watched as Jenny climbed up onto the top rail of the corral near the new counselors' cottages and shoved her long blond ponytail back over her shoulder. "You gonna be all right up there?" he asked.

She laughed. "I'm not one of your mom's campers, Colt. I'm healthy as a horse. I'll be fine."

Colt couldn't help it if he worried about her. He didn't want her to fall and get hurt. Not that she appreciated his concern. He turned the football in his hands, finding the laces and placing his hands where he knew they needed to be.

"Go long!" he shouted to Huck, who had already started to run over the uneven terrain, which was dotted with clumps of buffalo grass and an occasional prickly pear cactus.

Colt threw the ball with ease and watched it fall perfectly, gently into Huck's outstretched hands. Huck did a victory dance and spiked the ball.

"We are the greatest!" Huck shouted, holding his pointed fingers upward on either side of him in the referee's signal for a touchdown.

They made a pretty good team, Colt conceded. About the best in the state. Both of them would likely be offered athletic scholarships to college. Huck was so rich—his father was a U.S. senator from Texas—he didn't need a scholarship to pay for college. Colt's family could easily afford to send him to college, too, but he kept playing football because he had heard it might help him get into the Air Force Academy.

If Huck had wanted to go to the Academy, his dad, the senator, could write a letter and get him appointed. Colt didn't have that advantage. He would never presume on his friendship with Huck to ask for that kind of favor from Senator Duncan. So he had to find another way to make sure he got in.

Huck retrieved the ball and started walking back toward Colt and Jenny. Colt took advantage of the opportunity to have Jenny's full attention. "He's pretty good," he said, knowing Huck was the one thing Jenny was always willing to discuss.

"He is, isn't he," she said, a worried frown forming between her brows.

"Something wrong with that?" Colt asked, leaning his elbow casually on the top rail next to Jenny's thigh where her cutoffs ended and her flesh began. Casual. Right. His mouth was bone-dry.

"I don't want him to go away," she said.

He watched her face as she watched Huck. "You think football will take him away?"

"No. Huck loves football, but I think he'd be willing to attend a college somewhere close just so we could be together. Only..." Her head swiveled suddenly, and she looked him right in the eye. "You're going to take him away."

He swallowed hard, his hormones going into overdrive as she continued staring at him. He managed to say, "I am?"

She nodded solemnly. "He's going to want to follow wherever you go, Colt, and I know your plans don't include staying here in Texas. I don't want to get left behind."

Jenny was dirt-poor, and even if she could have gotten a scholarship to a college somewhere else—which, with her brains, she probably could—she had to stay at the Double D Ranch to help take care of her sick mother and four younger brothers.

"Huck would never leave you behind," Colt said seriously.

"He might not have any choice. Not if he went off to fly jets somewhere with you."

Colt felt angry, vulnerable and exposed. "How did you know about that? About me wanting to fly jets?"

She shrugged and slipped down off the top rail of the corral. "Huck and I don't have any secrets."

"He shouldn't have told you," Colt said, feeling his heart begin to thud at the closeness of her. He wanted her to step back so he could breathe, so he could think straight. Didn't she see what she was doing to him? "That was private information," he snapped. "It doesn't concern you."

Her fisted hands found her hips. "It does when Huck is thinking about going with you."

"I never asked him to come along," he retorted.

"Hey, you two! What're my two favorite people arguing about?" Huck said, grinning as he stepped between them and slipped an arm around each of their shoulders. Colt stood rigid beneath his arm. Huck still had the football in one hand, and Colt knocked it to the ground.

"Ask your girlfriend," he said, bending to retrieve the ball and pulling free of Huck's arm. "I've got to go find Mac Macready. I'm supposed to throw some passes to him this morning."

Huck left Jenny standing where she was and headed after Colt. "Macready's really here? I mean, I heard rumors in town he was, but I wasn't sure. You're really going to throw some balls to him?"

"I said I was, didn't I?" Colt stopped where he was and looked back over Huck's shoulder to where Jenny stood abandoned. Her expression said it all.

See what I mean? You lead. Huck follows.

It wasn't his fault. It had always been that way. If Jenny didn't like it, she didn't have to hang around. Colt turned back to Huck.

Huck's sandy hair had fallen over his brow and into his eyes. His rarely combed hair, combined with his ski-slope nose and freckled cheeks and broad smile, gave him an affable appearance he deserved. Huck didn't make enemies. He wouldn't have hurt a fly. Colt was sure he hadn't meant to hurt Jenny's feelings. Huck just forgot to be thoughtful sometimes.

"What about Jenny?" Colt asked.

"Hey, Jenny," Huck called. "You want to hang around and meet Mac Macready?"

Jenny shook her head.

"See? She's not interested," Huck said. "But I am."

Colt sighed. "You want to stay?" he asked Huck.

"Does a cowboy wear spurs?" Huck replied with a lop-sided grin.

They headed for the counselor's cottage where Mac was staying, leaving Jenny behind at the corral. Colt glanced over his shoulder at her. It looked for a moment like she might follow them. Then she turned to where her horse was tied to the corral next to Huck's, mounted up and loped the gelding in the direction of her family's ranch.

"You shouldn't ignore Jenny like that," Colt said, turning back to Huck.

Huck seemed to notice suddenly that she had left. "What did I do?" He shook his head. "Women. They're mysterious creatures, old buddy. Don't ever try to understand them. It's a waste of time."

"Why did you tell her about me wanting to fly?" Colt asked.

Huck looked chagrined. "We were talking about the future and…it just came up."

"Make sure it doesn't come up again," Colt said. "That's my business, and I don't want the whole world knowing about it." Especially when he was afraid he wasn't going to be able to make his dream come true.

"Jenny isn't the whole world," Huck argued. "She's my girlfriend. I have to tell her things."

"Just don't tell her things about me," Colt insisted.

"That's hard to avoid when you're my best friend," Huck said. "Besides, if we're going to be jet pilots—"

"When did my plans become yours?" Colt asked.

Huck grinned and pulled an arm tight around Colt's neck in a wrestler's hold. "We're friends forever, pal. Where you go, I go. If you fly, I fly. Enough said?"

Colt wished it were that simple. He wished he could express his desire to be a jet fighter pilot and expect his parents to be happy about it. He had never said a word to them, because he knew they would hate the idea.

He might be one of eight adopted kids, but his mom and dad had made it pretty clear over the past couple of years that he was the one they expected to inherit Hawk's Pride. They already had his life planned for him. They expected him to come back home after college to manage the ranch.

He was grateful to have Zach and Rebecca Whitelaw for parents. He loved them enough to want to make them happy by fulfilling their expectations. It just wasn't what he wanted for himself. He wanted to fly.

So he made his plans surreptitiously, meanwhile letting his father teach him everything he would need to know to run the cattle and quarter horse end of the business. His father had told him his sister Jewel was taking over Camp LittleHawk, and that was fine with him. Although he kind of liked the ranching business, he wanted absolutely nothing to do with a camp for kids with cancer.

Not that he didn't have sympathy for the plight of all those sick kids. But he had learned his lesson early. He had befriended a couple of them when he was old enough to make friends. It was only later, when he asked why they hadn't returned the following summer, that he learned the awful truth. Sometimes sick people died.

It was a sobering lesson: *Illness could rob you of people you loved.* He had found a child's solution to the problem that had stood him in good stead. He stayed away from sick people. Which was why he hadn't been to Jenny's house much, even though Huck went there a lot. Her mom was dying slowly but surely of breast cancer.

Colt might have argued further with Huck, except he caught sight of Mac Macready coming around the corner of the house with his sister, Jewel.

"Hey!" Colt called. "Ready to catch a few passes?"

"You bet," Mac called back.

Colt looked for signs of reluctance or resignation on Mac's face. After all, Colt was just a kid. He didn't see anything but delight.

"Just give me a minute," Mac said with a smile and a wave. "Be right with you." He turned and said something in Jewel's ear, then headed in Colt's direction.

JEWEL HEARD THE kitchen screen door open and called, "Is that you, Mac?"

"Jewel?"

"Colt?" At the sound of her brother's frightened voice, Jewel hurried from her bedroom wearing an oversized plaid Western shirt, jeans and boots, her hair still wet from her shower. She met Colt halfway to the kitchen. "What's wrong?"

Her brother stood white-faced before her. "It's Mac. He fell."

Oh, dear God. "Should I call an ambulance?"

"I don't know," Colt said, his hands visibly trembling. "I thought maybe you ought to come and see for yourself first. It was awful, Jewel. One minute Mac was fine, and then Huck tackled him and…he didn't get up."

"Huck *tackled* him? What on earth were you boys thinking, Colt? You know Mac's recovering from surgery!"

"We thought it would be more fun—"

"Did he hit his head when he fell?"

"I don't think so. I think—"

Before Jewel could make the decision whether to call 911, Mac appeared at the kitchen door, one arm around Huck's shoulder, the other pressed against the thigh of his scarred leg.

Colt had been pale, but Mac's face was completely drained of blood. His teeth were gritted against the pain, and he was leaning heavily on Huck Duncan's shoulder and favoring his leg. It took her a second to realize it wasn't his poor, wounded and scarred left leg he was favoring, it was the other one. Now both legs were injured!

"What happened?" she asked as she crossed quickly to hold the screen door open for him. As soon as she moved, Colt seemed to wake from his shocked trance and took a place on Mac's other side. The two boys helped him keep his weight off both legs as they eased him through the kitchen and onto the sofa in the living room.

While the boys stood awkwardly at her side, Jewel dropped to her knees and eased Mac's foot up onto a rawhide stool that Grandpa Garth had given her one Christmas, a relic of bygone days at his ranch, Hawk's Way. Then she started untying the laces of Mac's athletic shoe.

"I can do that," he said, trying to brush her hands away.

"Sure you can, but let me," she insisted. She eased off the shoe and the sock beneath it and immediately saw the problem. His ankle was swelling. "Can you move it?" she asked.

Slowly, hissing in a breath, he rotated the ankle. "Doesn't feel broken," he said. "I've had enough sprains to recognize one when I see it. Damn. This is all I needed."

"I'm sorry, Mr. Macready," Huck said in an anguished voice. "I didn't mean to hurt you."

Mac looked up at the boy and said, "Call me Mac. And it wasn't your fault, Huck. Your tackle wasn't what caused the problem. I just didn't see that gopher hole soon enough."

Jewel watched him smile at the boy, pretending it was no big deal, when she knew very well it was. This was a setback, no doubt about it.

"But your leg—" Huck protested, his eyes skipping

from the awful scars on Mac's left leg to the swelling on
his right ankle. "How're you gonna walk now?"

"One step at a time," Mac quipped with an easy grin.
"Fortunately, I brought a cane with me. That should help
matters some."

Jewel turned to Colt and said, "Wrap some ice in a towel
and bring it here. You go help him, Huck."

When they were both gone, she gently moved the ankle.
"Are you sure it isn't broken?"

He sighed. It was a sound of disgust. "It's a sprain,
Jewel. Not even a bad one."

"I should have warned you about gopher holes," she
said.

"I didn't step in a gopher hole," he said quietly, looking
at the hands he held fisted against his thighs.

"Then what—" She saw the truth in the wary look he
gave her. His leg—his *right* leg—must not have supported
him. She reached out a hand, and he clutched it with one
of his.

She didn't offer him words of comfort. She could see
from the grim look on his face that words wouldn't change
what had happened. She didn't point out the obvious—that
his football career was over. He had to see that for himself.

But if she had thought this accident would make Mac
quit, he quickly disabused her of the notion.

"This'll slow down my rehabilitation some," he said.
"Will you mind if I hang around a little longer? I know
camp's starting in a day or so—"

She rose to her feet, her hand coming free of his. "Of
course you can stay!" she said, her voice unnaturally sharp.
She didn't want him to go away. She liked having him here.
But she couldn't believe he was ignoring the implications
of this injury. How long was he going to go on batting his

head against the wall? Couldn't he see the truth? Didn't he understand what this accident meant?

"Mac—"

He cut her off with a shake of his head. "Don't say it. Don't even suggest it."

"Suggest what?"

"This doesn't change my plans."

"But—"

His face turned hard, jaw jutting, shoulders braced in determination. She had seen that look before, but she had been too young and naive to recognize it for what it was.

"Be my friend, Jewel," he said. "Don't tell me why I can't do what I want to do. Just help me to do it."

She stared at him as though she had never seen him before. She knew now why Peter Macready had survived a form of cancer that killed most kids. Why he had become the best rookie receiver in the NFL, despite the fact he had never been the fastest athlete on the field. Mac didn't give up. Mac didn't see obstacles. He saw his goal and headed for it without worrying about whether it could be reached. And so he invariably reached it.

Jewel wished she had half his confidence. She might be a married woman now with a baby in her arms.

Maybe it wasn't too late for her. Maybe she could learn from him how it was done. Maybe she could take advantage of Mac's presence to give her the impetus to change her life. If Mac could recover from a shattered leg, why couldn't she recover from a shattered life?

The boys returned with two dish towels loaded with ice and fell all over each other arranging the cold compresses around Mac's ankle. Jewel saw Mac wince when their overenthusiasm rocked his ankle, but instead of snapping at them, he launched into a story about how he had played a whole football game with a taped-up sprained ankle, thanks to an injection of painkiller.

The teenage boys dropped to his feet in awe and admiration. Jewel started to leave, but Mac reached up and caught her hand. "Join us," he said.

"I have work—"

"Just for a few minutes."

She figured maybe he didn't want to be stuck alone with the boys. She would stay with him long enough to let them hear a story or two before shooing them away. She settled beside Mac on the worn leather couch—another donation from her grandfather's house at Hawk's Way. Mac's arm slid around her as naturally as if he did it every day.

She resisted the urge to lay her head on his shoulder. Putting his arm around her had been a friendly gesture, nothing more. But she was aware of the way his hand cupped her shoulder, massaging it as he regaled the three of them with stories of life in the pro football arena.

As she sat listening to him, an insidious idea took root. *What if she came to Mac tonight and explained her problem and asked him to help her out?*

She trusted Mac not to hurt her. She trusted him to go slow, to be patient. He didn't love her, and she didn't love him, so there wouldn't be that particular pitfall complicating matters. It would be just one friend helping out another.

She could even explain to him how she had gotten the idea. That she had seen his determination to play football again and been inspired to try to solve a problem that she had thought would never be resolved.

All she wanted him to do was teach her how to arouse a man and satisfy him...and be satisfied by him.

She tried to imagine how Mac might react to such a suggestion. He was obviously an experienced man of the world. Only... What if he wasn't attracted to her that way?

Her mind flashed back to the scene in the canyon earlier that afternoon, when she had felt Mac's arousal. But he had apologized for that. Maybe when push came to shove, he wouldn't want to get involved with her.

Jewel didn't hear much of what Mac said to Colt and Huck. She wasn't even aware when he sent them away. She was lost deep in her own thoughts. And fears.

She wished the idea hadn't come to her so early in the day. Now she would be stuck thinking about it until dark, worrying it like a dog worried a bone.

All she had to do was cross the hall tonight and knock on Mac's door and... She didn't let her imagination take her any farther than that. Oh, how she wished night were here already! It was so much easier to act on impulse than to do something like this with cold calculation.

Of course, she was far from cold when she thought about Mac. Her whole body felt warm at the thought of having him touch her, having him kiss and caress her. She just wanted to get through the entire sexual act once without cringing or falling apart. That's all she wanted Mac to do for her. Just get her through the moments of panic before he did it. Get in and get out, like a quick lube job on the truck.

The absurdity of that comparison made her chuckle.

"Are you going to let me in on the joke?" Mac said.

"Maybe." If she didn't lose her nerve before nightfall.

CHAPTER SIX

MAC WAS LYING in bed wondering what Jewel would do if he crossed the hall, knocked on her door and told her he wanted to make love to her. She would probably think he had lost his mind. He had to resist the urge to pursue her. Jewel didn't need a fumbling, first-time lover. He, of all people, knew how much she needed a kind, considerate, *knowledgeable* bed partner. Which, of course, he wasn't.

She needed a slow hand, an easy touch—wasn't that what the song said? He had a lot of pent-up passion, a lot of celibate years to make up for. He was afraid the first time for him was going to be fast and hard. Which might be fine for him. But not for her.

Mac wished he didn't have such vivid memories of what had happened to Jewel that day in July six years ago. Any man who had seen her after Harvey Barnes had attacked her... He made himself think the word. After Harvey Barnes had *raped* her...

He had never wanted to kill a man before or since. He had been there to come to her rescue because he had seen Harvey drinking too much and worried about her, like a brother might worry about his sister. Jewel would have pounded him flat if she'd known he had followed her and Harvey when they slipped off into the trees down by the river.

He had kept his distance, even considered turning around and heading back to the noise of the carnival rides at the picnic, which seemed a world away from the sooth-ing rustle of leaves down by the river. He had heard her laugh and then…silence.

He figured Harvey must be kissing her. He was stand-ing at the edge of the river skipping stones, thinking he'd been an idiot to follow her, when he heard her cry out. Even then, he hadn't been sure at first whether it was a cry of passion.

The second cry had chilled his blood and started him running toward the sound. He could remember the feeling of terror as he searched frantically for her amid the thick laurel bushes and the tangle of wild ivy at the river's edge, calling her name and getting no answer.

There were no more cries. He saw why when he finally found them. Harvey had his hand pressed tight over Jew-el's mouth, and she was struggling vainly beneath him. He saw something white on the ground nearby and realized it was her underpants.

He might have killed Harvey, if Jewel hadn't stopped him. He hadn't even been aware of his hands clenched in the flesh at Harvey's throat. It was only Jewel's anguished voice in his ear, pleading with him, that made him stop before he strangled the life out of the boy.

Harvey was nearly unconscious by the time Mac finally let go and turned to Jewel. Seeing her torn, grass-stained dress and the trickle of blood coming from her lip enraged him all over again. Jewel whimpered with fear—of him, he realized suddenly—and the fight went out of him.

He started toward her to hold her, to comfort her, but she clutched her arms tight around herself, turned her back to him and cried, "Don't touch me! Don't look at me!"

His heart was thudding loudly in his chest. "Jewel," he said. "You need to go to the hospital. Let me find your parents—"

She whirled on him and rasped, "No! Please don't tell anybody."

"But you're hurt!"

"My father will kill him," she whispered.

He could understand that. He had almost killed Harvey Barnes himself. Then she gave the reason that persuaded him to keep his silence.

"Everyone will know," she said, her brown eyes stark. "I couldn't bear it, Mac. Please. Help me."

"We'll have to say something to explain that cut on your lip," he said tersely. "And the grass stains on your dress."

"My beautiful dress." The tears welled in her eyes as she pulled the skirt around to look at the grass stains on the back of it.

He realized it wasn't the dress she was crying for, but the other beautiful thing she had lost. Her innocence.

"We'll tell your father Harvey attacked you—"

"No. Please!"

He reached out to take her shoulders, and she shrank from him. His hands dropped to his sides. He realized they were trembling and curled them into tight fists. "We'll tell them Harvey attacked you, but you fought him off," he said in an urgent voice. "Unless you tell that much of the tale, they're liable to believe the worst."

He had never seen—never hoped to see again—a look as desolate as the one she gave him.

"All right," she said. "But tell them you came in time. Tell them...nothing happened."

"What if...what if you're pregnant?" he asked.

"I don't think...I don't think..."

He realized she was in too much shock to even contemplate the possibility.

She shook her head, looking dazed and confused. "I don't think..."

He thought concealing the truth was a bad idea. She needed medical attention. She needed the comfort her mother and father could give her. "Jewel, let me tell your parents," he pleaded quietly.

She shook her head and began to shiver.

"Give me your hand, Jewel," he said, afraid to put his arms around her, afraid she might scream or faint or something equally terrifying.

She kept her arms wrapped around herself and started walking in the opposite direction from the revelers at the picnic. "Take me home, Mac," she said. "Please, just take me home."

He snatched up her underpants, stuffed them in his Levi's pocket and followed her to his truck. But it was too much to hope they would escape unnoticed. Not with Jewel's seven brothers and sisters at the picnic.

It was Rolleen who caught them before they could escape. She insisted Mac find her parents, and he'd had no choice except to go hunting for Zach and Rebecca. He had found Zach first.

The older man's eyes had turned flinty as he listened to Mac's abbreviated—and edited—version of what had happened.

The dangerous, animal sound that erupted from Zach's throat when he saw Jewel's torn dress and her bruised face and swollen lip made Mac's neck hairs stand upright. He realized suddenly that Jewel had known her father better than he had. Zach became a lethal predator. Only the lack of a quarry contained his killing rage.

Jewel's family surrounded her protectively, unconsciously shutting him out. He was forced to stand aside as they led her away. It wasn't until he got back to his private room in the cottage he shared with a half-dozen boys aged eight to twelve and stripped off his jeans, that he realized he still had Jewel's underwear in his pocket.

The garment was white cotton, with a delicate lace trim. It was stained with blood.

A painful lump rose in his throat, and his eyes burned with tears he was too grown up to shed. He fought the sobs that bunched like a fist in his chest, afraid one of the campers would return and hear him through the wall that separated his room from theirs. He pressed his mouth against a pillow in the bedroom and held it there until the ache eased, and he thought the danger was over.

In the shower later, where no one could see or hear, he shed tears of frustration and rage and despair. He had known, even then, that Harvey Barnes had stolen something precious from him that day, as well.

Mac learned later that Zach had found Harvey Barnes and horsewhipped him within an inch of his life. And Zach hadn't even known the full extent of Harvey's crime against his daughter. It seemed Jewel had been right not to tell her father the truth. Zach would have killed the boy for sure. Harvey's parents had sent him away, and he hadn't been seen since.

Things weren't the same between him and Jewel after that. She smiled and pretended everything was all right in front of him and her family. But the smile on her lips never reached her eyes.

The end of the summer came too soon, before they had reconciled their friendship. He went to her the night before he left, seeking somehow to mend the breach between them, to say goodbye for the summer and to ask if she was all right.

"Harvey Barnes is gone," she said. "And tomorrow you will be, too. Then I can forget about what happened."

"I'll be back next year," he reminded her.

She had been looking at her knotted hands when she said, "I hope you won't come, Mac."

Something bunched up tight inside of him. "Not come? I come every summer, Jewel."

"Don't come back. As a favor to me, Mac. Please don't come back."

"But why? You're my best friend, Jewel. I—"

"You know," she said in a brittle voice. She raised her eyes and looked at him and let him see her pain. "You know the truth. It's in your eyes every time you look at me."

He felt like crying again and forced himself to swallow back the tickle in his throat. "Jewel—"

"I want to forget, Mac," she said. "I need to forget. Please, please don't come back."

A lump of grief caught in his throat and made it impossible to say more. When he left that summer, a part of himself—the lighthearted, teasing friend—had stayed behind.

Mac had honored Jewel's wishes and stayed away for six long years. The really sad thing was, it had all been for nothing. She wasn't over what had happened. The past had not been forgotten.

He had often wondered if he'd done the wrong thing. Should he have told her parents the truth, anyway? Should he have come back the following summer? Should he have tried harder to get in touch with her over the years, to talk to her about what had happened?

A soft knock on the door forced Mac from his reverie. Before he could reply, the door opened, and Jewel stood silhouetted in the light from the hall. She was wearing a sleeveless white nightgown with a square-cut neck. The gown only covered her to mid-thigh. He could see the shape of her through the thin garment, the slender legs and slim waist and bountiful bosom.

He sat up, dragging the sheets around him to cover his nakedness and to conceal the sudden arousal caused by the enticing sight of her in his bedroom doorway. "Jewel? Is something wrong?"

She slipped inside and closed the door, so that momentarily he lost sight of her as his eyes adjusted to the dark. He heard the rustle of sheets and suddenly felt her body next to his beneath the covers.

"Jewel? What's going on?" He hoped his voice didn't sound as shocked as he felt. He didn't know what she thought she was doing, but he intended to find out before things went much farther.

He had expected an answer. He hadn't counted on her laying her palm on his bare chest. She followed that with a scattering of kisses across his chest that led her to the sensitive flesh beneath his ear. His body was trembling with desire when she finally paused to speak.

"Nothing's wrong, Mac," she murmured in his ear. "I came because..." She nibbled on his earlobe, and he groaned at the exquisite pleasure of it. "I need your help," she finished.

He put an arm around her shoulder, realized suddenly he was naked and clutched at the sheet again. "Anything, Jewel. You know I'd do anything for you. But—"

"I was hoping you'd say that. Because what I need you to do... It won't be easy."

He waited, his breath caught in his chest, for what she had to say. "Anything, Jewel," he repeated, his heart thundering so loud he figured she could probably hear it.

She pressed her breasts against his chest and said, "I want you to make love to me."

His heart pounded, and his shaft pulsed. In another moment, things would be out of hand. His eyes had adapted to the dark, and with the moonlight from the window he at last could see the feelings etched on her face. Not desire, but fear and vulnerability.

"I want to feel like a woman," she said in a halting voice. "I want to stop being afraid."

He couldn't keep the dismay from his voice. "Aw, Jewel."

A cry of despair issued from her throat, and she made a frantic lurch toward the edge of the bed and escape.

He grabbed for her, knowing she had misinterpreted his words. It wasn't that he didn't want her. He wanted her something fierce. He just wasn't the experienced bed partner she thought he was. He caught her by the wrist and pulled her back into his arms and held her tight, biting back a groan at the exquisite feel of her breasts crushed against his chest with only the sheer cloth between them.

"It's all right, Mac," she said in a brittle voice. "I made a mistake. Let me go, and we'll forget this ever happened."

She held herself stiff and unyielding in his arms. "Jewel—"

"Don't try to make me feel better. I deserve to feel like an idiot, throwing myself at you like this. I just thought… with all your experience…"

This time he did groan.

She tried to pull away, and he said, "You don't understand."

"I understand you don't find me attractive. I'm sorry for forcing myself on you like this."

"No!" *Tell her the truth, Macready. She's your friend. She'll understand.*

But the words stuck in his throat. If he hadn't cared for her, if he didn't want her so badly, if things hadn't changed between them like they had, maybe he could have confessed the truth.

"It's not that I'm not attracted to you," he said.

He saw the look on her face and realized she didn't believe him. How could she not see the truth when it was throbbing like mad beneath the thin sheet that separated them?

"Then why won't you make love to me?" she challenged.

"Because…"

He couldn't tell her the truth, and he saw she believed the worst—that she had imposed herself where she wasn't wanted, and he was rejecting her as kindly as he could.

"Aw, Jewel," he said again. His voice was tender, as gentle as he wished he could be with her.

She made a keening sound in her throat, a mournful sound that made him ache somewhere deep inside.

He realized he had no choice. He had to try to make love to her. He couldn't botch things much worse than he already had. He leaned over and pressed his mouth against hers, restraining the rush of passion he felt at the touch of her soft, damp lips.

She moaned and arched her body against his. Her mouth clung to his, and he felt her need and her desire.

Maybe it's going to be all right. Maybe I can get us both through this.

He tried to hold back, so he wouldn't scare her. Yet when his tongue slipped into her mouth it found an eager welcome. He thrust deep, mimicking the sex act, and she riposted with her tongue in his mouth.

He thought the top of his head was going to come off. He had never felt so out of control. His hands slid down her arms, feeling the goose bumps and her shiver of anticipation. She was as excited as he was. She wanted him, too.

His lips started down her slender throat, across the silky flesh that led to her breastbone and downward, giving her plenty of warning where he was headed. She could have stopped him anytime she wanted. He wasn't an animal. He had his desire on a firm leash.

She cried out when his mouth latched onto her nipple, and he sucked hard through the cotton. Mac knew it wasn't a cry of fear, because her hands grasped his hair and held him there.

Her moan of pleasure urged him on. He released her breast momentarily and kissed her mouth again, an accolade for her trust in him. "I won't hurt you, Jewel. I would never hurt you," he murmured against her lips.

"I know, Mac. I know," she replied in gasping breaths.

Their tongues dueled dangerously, inciting them both to greater passion. He clasped her shoulders, making himself go slow, telling himself *Go Slow.* He slid his hand across the damp cotton that covered her breasts all the way down to her belly, wishing the damned nightgown wasn't between his palm and her flesh, but feeling the heat of her even through the thin shift.

He grabbed the bottom edge of it, anxious to get it out of his way, and brushed her thigh with his fingertips. Just her thigh. She tensed slightly but didn't pull away. He managed not to heave a sigh of relief.

It's going to be all right. I'll be able to do this for her.

But he was overeager and excited, worried about whether he would be able to satisfy her, and a moment later his hand accidentally brushed against the soft mound between her legs.

She jerked away from him with a cry of alarm. But he still had hold of the nightgown, and the fragile material tore. He let go, but it was too late. She was already rolled up in a tight, fetal ball with her back to him.

"Jewel—"

"I can't!" she cried. "I can't."

He laid a hand on her shoulder, and she cringed away.

"Please don't touch me," she whispered.

He lay staring at her in shock. He should have known better than to try this. He should have known he didn't have the experience to do it right. "What can I do?"

She turned to him, her eyes awash in despair. "I'm sorry, Mac."

"Aw, Jewel."

"I thought it would be all right. Because it was you," she sobbed. "Because you're my friend."

He would have to confess the truth. He owed her that much. "It isn't you, Jewel, it's me," he said flatly.

"You're just saying that to make me feel better," she said.

"No. I'm not." He forced himself to continue as she stared up at him. "You mustn't be discouraged by what happened here tonight. I'm sure another man, a more experienced man, could have managed things better. I lost control and frightened you."

"But I trust you," she protested.

"All the more reason I should have kept my hands off of you." He huffed out a breath of air and shoved a hand through his hair in agitation.

"When you find a man you love," he said earnestly, "a man who loves you enough to take his time and do things right, I'm sure you'll be able to get past what happened to you."

She sat up slowly, her chin sunk to her chest, her hands knotted in front of her knees, which were clutched to her chest. She swallowed hard. "What you're saying is that you're not that man."

"No. I'm not."

"I see."

Evidently not. Evidently he hadn't hinted broadly enough at his inexperience for her to realize the truth.

Now it was too late. In the heat of the moment he might have confessed his virginity. But as his passion cooled, he felt appalled at how close he had come to exposing himself to her laughter.

And she would laugh. It would be gentle laughter, kind laughter, an effervescent bubble of disbelief. But he couldn't bear to hear it.

"If you won't do this for me, I don't know where to turn," she said at last.

"There are lots of men out there who'd be attracted to you, if you'd let them see your charms."

She shot him a twisted smile. "You mean my Enormous Endowments?"

"I wouldn't call them that," he protested with a startled laugh.

"What would you call them?" She thrust her chest out, and his mouth went dry.

He hesitated a heartbeat and said, "Astonishing Assets?"

She laughed, the bubbly, effervescent sound he remembered from long ago. "Oh, God, now I've got you doing it!" She grabbed a pillow and hugged it tight against her ribs, effectively hiding the Generous Giants.

"Look, Jewel, for a start, you're going to have to stop doing that."

"Doing what?"

"Hiding behind clothes, behind your hair, behind pillows." He tugged on the pillow, and she reluctantly gave it up. He was immediately sorry, because it was hard to keep his eyes off her. He could see her brownish-pink nipples beneath the damp cloth.

"It was my breasts that got me into trouble in the first place," she said. "Can you blame me for wanting to hide them?"

"Maybe not," he conceded. "But hiding your light behind a bushel is not the way to find your Prince Charming. You're going to have to want to attract a man to find the right one."

"I'm afraid, Mac."

He saw that in her shadowed eyes. In her drawn features. From the instinctive way she circled her arms protectively around herself. But if he couldn't help her out by making love to her, the least he could do was help her find another man to do it.

"You can start small—no pun intended—and do this in baby steps. You've got to crawl before you can walk."

"Meaning?"

"Go back to basics, to flirting, to wanting to attract a man's attention."

"I can't do that."

"Can't? Or won't?"

"Won't."

"You can start with me," he coaxed. "I'll be your lab rat."

She grinned wryly. "Hold that thought. Man as rat. I like it."

He gave her a crooked smile. "The idea is for you to start seeing men as *men*—get it?"

"All right," she conceded with a sigh. "I'll give it a try. Where do I start?"

"Wear some clothes that fit better. Something that shows off—"

"My Plentiful Peaches?"

He laughed. "Actually, yeah, that would do it."

She slid her legs over the edge of the bed and looked back over her shoulder at him. "I'm not so sure about this, Mac."

"Believe me, it'll work," he said, wrapping the sheet around his waist as he rose to follow her to the door.

"You'll have the guys around here on their knees begging to take you out."

She arched a skeptical brow. "You really think so?"

"I guarantee it."

She paused at the door and put a hand on his naked chest. His heart thudded. His loins throbbed. She searched his face, and he hoped his lurid thoughts weren't apparent.

"What if I attract the wrong kind of attention?" she asked. "What if someone…some man…"

"Start here on the ranch. I'll keep an eye out for you. If any of the cowhands or counselors makes a wrong move, I'll be there. You can use me as your guinea pig."

"Hmm. Man as pig. I like that even better."

He laughed and tousled her hair. "Cut it out."

"You'll help me through this, won't you?" she asked, her heart in her eyes.

"If you want to try out your seductive wiles on someone safe, I'm your man," he volunteered. He would keep his libido in check if it killed him.

"You don't know how much that means to me, Mac. You really think this will work?"

"It's sure as hell worth a try."

"Thanks, Mac. Still friends?"

He wrapped his hand around her nape—to keep her at arm's distance—and said, "You bet. And don't worry. Anybody makes the wrong kind of move, I'll cut him off at the pass."

"My hero," she said, an impish grin forming on her lips.

"You bet." He knew he should shove her out the door and put temptation from his path, but he couldn't resist one last kiss.

He leaned down to her, keeping their bodies separated and pressed his mouth against hers with all the gentleness he could muster.

Her lips were pliant under his, soft and supple and incredibly sweet.

"Good night, Jewel. Go to bed and get some sleep."

"Good night, Mac. You, too."

He must have nodded, or grunted an assent, because she left the room and closed the door behind her. But he knew damned well he wasn't going to sleep.

Mac replayed the events of the evening in his head. If only he'd had more experience. If only his hand hadn't brushed against her and scared her. If only he'd known what to do to reassure her.

What was done was done. He'd had his chance and he'd blown it. The least he could do was help her find another guy to help her out, while keeping his own hormones in check. The last thing he wanted to do was scare her again. Which meant he'd better make sure she never found out her Beautiful Breasts turned him hard as a rock.

If she was going to start wearing clothes that fit, he'd better go shopping for some baggy jeans.

CHAPTER SEVEN

JEWEL DECIDED THE best way to avoid hiding behind her hair was to remove that option. She drove to the Stonecreek Ranch at the crack of dawn to have her sister Cherry whack it off. She had known Cherry would understand what she wanted to do and help her because, of all her adopted brothers and sisters, Cherry understood best what it meant to feel different.

Cherry was the last Whitelaw Brat to be adopted and had come to the family when she was fourteen, an extremely tall, redheaded, blue-eyed Irish girl—and an incorrigible juvenile delinquent. Jewel had been closest to her in age, only a year older. After a rocky start, during which Cherry did her best to break every rule—and offend every member—in the Whitelaw household, they had ended up becoming best friends.

The night Cherry was accused of spiking the punch bowl at the senior prom and expelled from high school, she had eloped with Billy Stonecreek to avoid facing Zach and Rebecca. Cherry had become an instant mom to Billy's twin six-year-old daughters Raejean and Annie. Three years later, Cherry was six months pregnant, and as far as Jewel could tell, happy as a cat in a dairy.

Cherry had made the Stonecreek Ranch a comfortable place to live, substituting leather and wood furniture for the silks and satins bought by Billy's first wife, Laura, who had died in a car accident. Jewel was surprised, when she showed up at Cherry's back screen door unannounced, to catch her sister and brother-in-law kissing in the kitchen.

It wasn't the kiss that shocked her. It was the passion behind it. Billy's hands avidly cupped Cherry's breasts, and her hands clutched his buttocks. They were pressed together like flies on flypaper.

She cleared her throat noisily. "Excuse me."

Jewel imagined a ripping sound as they sprang apart.

"Jewel!" Cherry exclaimed, her voice revealing both relief and irritation. "What are you doing here?"

"Obviously interrupting something important," Jewel said with a teasing grin.

Her sister flushed a delightful pink, and Billy stuck his hands in his front pockets, a move that didn't do as much as he probably hoped to hide his state of arousal.

Jewel felt a little guilty for intruding, and if it hadn't been an emergency she might have turned and left. But she was afraid she would lose her nerve if she waited. She stepped into the kitchen, careful not to let the screen door slam behind her and wake the twins. "I need my hair cut. Could you do it for me?"

"Now?" Cherry asked, her brows rising practically to her hairline.

"Yes, now."

Jewel was wearing a sleeveless white knit shell and tight-fitting jeans that had been shut away in a drawer for six years. She watched as Cherry perused her attire and exchanged a look with Billy, whose eyes had opened wide with astonishment once she stepped inside. Jewel resisted the urge to cross her arms over her chest. She was going to have to get used to men looking at her.

"Hi, Billy," she said.

"Hi, Jewel." It came out as a croak. He cleared his throat

and tried again. "You look…" He searched for a word and came up with, "Nice. What's the occasion?"

He was clearly curious, as she suspected her family would be, about why she was suddenly exposing assets she had kept hidden for the past six years. "No occasion," she said. "I just want to get my hair cut. Can you help me out?" she asked Cherry.

"Sure," Cherry said. She turned to Billy. "You don't mind if we postpone breakfast for half an hour, do you?"

"I've got some chores I can do in the barn. Give a holler when you want me." Billy grabbed his Stetson from the antler rack on the wall and headed out the screen door. Cherry caught it before it could slam.

"All right," Cherry said once she had scissors in hand and Jewel was settled in a kitchen chair with a towel around her shoulders. "Spill the jelly beans. What's going on?"

"Nothing much."

"For the first time in six years I can see you have breasts," Cherry retorted tartly. "Believe me, anyone seeing your breasts for the first time wouldn't say they're 'nothing much.'"

Jewel laughed. That was why she liked Cherry so much. She didn't pull her punches. Cherry said exactly what she was thinking, even if it wasn't necessarily what you wanted to hear.

"I had a talk with Mac Macready last night," Jewel said. "He convinced me it's time to come out of my shell."

"I see," Cherry said.

Jewel realized Cherry was *seeing* a great deal more than she wished or intended. "It isn't like that."

"Like what?"

"It's not Mac I'm trying to attract."

"It isn't?"

"No. Not that I don't love him dearly. I do. As a friend."

"A *friend*," Cherry repeated.

Jewel winced as nine-inch-long hanks of brown hair began falling to the kitchen floor. There was no turning back now. "A friend," she confirmed.

"And this *friend* suggested you'd look better in skin-tight jeans and short hair?"

Jewel laughed. "Not exactly. He simply said I should dress to attract a man."

"What you're wearing ought to do it," Cherry confirmed.

"You think so? It's not too…enticing?"

"You're dressed fine, Jewel. Half the young women in this country are probably wearing similar outfits this morning. You can't help it if you have big breasts."

Jewel noticed Cherry said it without the capital B's. Jewel automatically thought Big Breasts, something she was going to have to get over if she was going to have any hope of surviving this metamorphosis.

"There," Cherry said, surveying her handiwork. "A few turns with my curling iron, and I think you'll be pleased with the result."

When Cherry was done, she held a mirror in front of Jewel's face. "Take a look."

Her hair swept along her chin in a shiny bob, with soft bangs across her brow. Jewel sighed. "Oh, Cherry, you're a marvel. I look—"

"Cute," Cherry said with an irreverent laugh. "No getting around it. You're darned cute."

"I'm twenty-two. That's too old for cute. Besides, my features are too ordinary to be—"

"Cute," Cherry persisted with a grin. "Let me call Billy, and he can confirm it." She called out the door for Billy, who bounded up the back steps and into the kitchen.

He paused in the acting of pulling off his leather work

gloves as he looked Jewel up and down. "Who would've believed a haircut could make such a difference?"

"Isn't she cute?" Cherry asked.

"Sexy," Billy countered. When his wife nudged him in the ribs, he amended, "Sexy and cute."

Jewel's brow furrowed. She had never been pretty, and "cute" sounded like something you said about a one-year-old with a lollipop. One glance down explained the "sexy." Jewel felt the heat start in her throat and work its way up her neck to sit like red flags on her cheeks. "Good God," she said. "Have you got an extra shirt I can borrow?" she asked Billy.

"What for?" Billy said.

"She wants to go back into hiding," Cherry said scornfully. "Well, we're not going to help you do it. You turn right around and head out that door with your head held high. You've got nothing to be ashamed of. What happened to you six years ago wasn't your fault. It's about time you shoved Harvey Barnes out of your life and started enjoying it again."

"That's pretty much what Mac said."

"Good for Mac," Cherry said. "Am I going to have to go with you to make sure you don't cover yourself up like a nun?"

"No," Jewel conceded with a chagrined look. "I'll be all right."

"Stand up straight and enjoy the looks you get. Because you darn sure deserve them!"

"Thanks, Cherry," Jewel said, giving her sister a quick hug. "Thanks for everything."

Her brother-in-law gave her a quick hug and teased, "Definitely sexy. Go get 'em, Jewel."

Cherry and Billy stood arm in arm on the back porch

waving as she drove away. They were already kissing again as the dust rose behind her pickup.

It wasn't easy resisting the urge to slip a long-sleeved shirt over the figure-exposing knit shell the instant she returned home. It would have been easier if Mac had been there waiting, and she could have gotten that first meeting over with.

But he wasn't there.

She had left a note hanging on Mac's door when she snuck out to get her hair cut. The note she found stuck on her door when she got back said that he had taped up his ankle and gone walking despite the sprain. She left a third note for Mac saying that she was eating breakfast with her family and inviting him to join them, then left the cottage before she lost her courage.

Jewel figured it couldn't hurt to have a buffer between her and Mac when he saw her for the first time in her new guise. Not that she thought he wouldn't approve. After all, it had been his idea for her to feature her assets more prominently. But after last night...

In the bright light of day, Jewel found it hard to believe she had crossed the hall to Mac's bedroom last night. Or that she had actually asked him to make love to her. Or that he had refused.

She wished he had done it before kissing her. Good Lord. Who would have thought a kiss from Mac Macready could turn her to mush like that? His lips had been soft and slightly damp, and he had tasted...like Mac. Familiar and good.

If that was all she had felt, she would never have gotten frightened the way she had. But there had also been something dark and dangerous about his kisses. A threat of leashed passion that once freed might... When Mac had accidentally touched her, that awful sense of powerlessness had returned, and the bad memories had all come crashing down on her.

She couldn't blame Mac for backing away like he had. What man wouldn't cut his losses? Mac had gently but firmly told her to find somebody else to make love to her. He wasn't available for the job.

She didn't want somebody else, she had realized. She wanted Mac. Which was why she was dressed like this. Cherry had seen right through her feeble protests. The only man she wanted to attract was Mac Macready. She would never have found the courage to shed her protective skin of clothing if she hadn't conceded this was one sure way of getting Mac's attention.

He had certainly seemed interested last night. That is, before she had gotten scared and scared him off. Before he had accidentally touched her below the waist, everything had been wonderful. Her knee-jerk reaction had come before her rational mind could tell her it was Mac.

That had been followed by the disturbing thought that maybe even Mac couldn't make it all right. That maybe she would forever fear a man's touch in bed. She had kept herself curled up in a ball to avoid testing the truth. Because that possibility was too devastating to contemplate.

Jewel was determined to get over her fear. She was determined to give Mac another chance. And she wanted Mac to want another chance. She was understandably nervous about her next meeting with him. It made a lot of sense to diffuse the situation by including her family in the equation. Hence the unusual visit to her family's breakfast table. This morning she needed the support they had always given her. She wanted their reassurance that she looked all right, that she would not "stick out" in a crowd.

Jewel could smell biscuits and bacon through the screen door. She smiled and stepped inside, knowing she would find the warmth of hearth and home. She stopped just inside the door, enjoying the cacophony of seven voices—Rolleen was away at medical school—raised in excited chatter.

"Wow! You look different!"

Jewel smiled self-consciously at Colt as she settled into an empty chair at the breakfast table. She was tempted to slump down, but forced herself to sit up straight. This was the new and improved Jewel Whitelaw.

Her mom gave her a bright smile and said, "You look lovely today, sweetheart."

"Why'd you cut off all your—"

Nineteen-year-old Jake elbowed fifteen-year-old Rabbit to shut him up. "You look real nice, Jewel," Jake said. He exchanged a knowing look with their father at the head of the table.

Jewel felt her cheeks heating. They had noticed the difference, all right, but so far had avoided commenting directly on it. She decided to keep their attention focused on her hair. "It's been so hot lately, I decided to get a trim," she said to appease the curious looks she was getting from sixteen-year-old Frannie and twenty-year-old Avery.

"Good idea," her father said, buttering a fluffy biscuit.

"I've got some time this morning if you need any last-minute help getting ready for the first drove of campers," her mother offered, as she set a bowl of scrambled eggs and a second platter of bacon in the center of the table.

"Everything's under control, Mom," Jewel said.

"When do you go to the airport?" her father asked.

"The flight from Dallas arrives at 9:30 this morning with about a half-dozen kids," she replied. "There's another half dozen and the two counselors arriving from Houston shortly afterward. Mac has volunteered to go with me in the van to pick them up. I invited him to join us for breakfast," she said. "I hope that's all right."

"Of course it's all right," her mother replied. "It'll be nice to visit with him. We've barely seen hide or hair of either of you. What have you been doing?"

"Mac's been walking in the mornings—"

"Is his ankle better?" Colt asked.

"What's wrong with his ankle?" her father asked.

Colt got busy scooping another spoonful of eggs on his plate and sent a pleading look toward Jewel not to betray him.

"He tripped and twisted it yesterday," Jewel said. "It seems to be all right this morning."

"It's fine," Mac said as he opened the screen door and stepped into the kitchen. "How's everyone this morning?"

He was greeted with a chorus of smiles and "hellos" and "hi's."

Jewel feasted her eyes on him. His blond hair was still damp from the shower, and the rugged planes of his face were shadowed by a day's growth of beard, so he hadn't even stopped to shave. He must have been afraid of missing breakfast. He was wearing a Western shirt tucked into beltless, butter-soft jeans and cowboy boots.

She looked up at him defiantly, daring him not to like what he saw. He was the one who had wanted change. She had provided it. He had better not complain.

Jewel saw nothing in his blue eyes but admiration. That flustered her as much, and perhaps more than the opposite reaction. She hadn't been ready for the blatant male appreciation of her figure that she found on his face.

"I hope I'm not too late for breakfast," he said as he slipped into the last empty chair, which happened to be across from Jewel.

"Just in time," Zach said.

Jewel could feel Mac's eyes on her but kept her gaze lowered as she ate her scrambled eggs. It was going to take some time for her to adjust to having men look at her with sexual interest. It was all right when Mac did it, because she did not feel frightened by him. But he was right. If she wanted to get over the past, this was a start in the right direction.

She heard Mac exchange comments with her father about the cattle and cutting horse businesses that supported Hawk's Pride, listened to him discuss football with Colt, smiled along with him as he teased Rabbit about his nickname, which dated from his childhood when he had loved carrots. Mac obviously knew her family well, and they apparently liked him as much as he liked them.

Jewel felt a rush of guilt at having deprived Mac of their company all these years. Having been Mac's friend, she knew how hard it was for his own family to treat him normally. His parents and older sister, Sadie, had hovered over him long after he was well, afraid to let him try things for fear he would get hurt and end up back in the hospital.

Zach and Rebecca loved Mac like a son, but they hadn't spent years with him in a hospital setting where he was fighting for his life against a disease that killed kids. They were willing to let him do a man's work. Jewel knew Mac had needed his summers as a counselor at Camp Little-Hawk as much as Zach and Rebecca had needed his help with the kids.

"Right, Jewel?"

Jewel looked up at Mac, startled to realize he was speaking to her. "Excuse me. I wasn't listening. What was the question?"

Her family laughed.

"What's so funny?" she demanded, looking at them suspiciously.

"I said the reason the kids keep coming back year after year is that you're constantly making changes to keep things interesting," Mac said with a grin.

Jewel realized that this year she had made a huge change that was bound to be noticed—by the other counselors, if not the kids. One of the reasons she loved working with kids was that they never seemed to notice her ample bosom. "Change is good," she said, both chin and chest outthrust defiantly.

"Of course it is, darling," her mother said in a soothing voice.

"I wasn't complaining, Jewel," Mac said, his gaze staying level with hers.

She kept waiting for it to drop to her breasts. But it never did. There was nothing sexual in his gaze now. What she saw was approval and appreciation of her as a person. A thickness in her throat made it hard to speak. "We'd better get going," she said. "We don't want to be late to the airport."

"I'm ready when you are," Mac said, pushing back from the table. "Thanks for the breakfast, Rebecca. I don't know when I've enjoyed a meal so much. It's great to be back."

"It's great to have you back," Zach said, rising and putting a hand on Mac's shoulder as he walked him to the door. "You're welcome anytime."

"Thanks, Zach," Mac said, shaking hands with the older man.

Jewel felt exposed once she and Mac emerged from the throng of hugging and backslapping brothers and sisters and parents and headed across the backyard toward the van.

She felt Mac's gaze trained on her again, intense, disturbing, because this time he was obviously looking at more than her face. She paused as soon as they were hidden by a large bougainvillea and turned to confront him.

She propped her balled hands on her hips, thrust her shoulders back and held her chin high. "All right, Mac. You were the one who asked for this. Look your fill and get it over with."

His lips curved. His eyes surveyed her intently. His voice turned whiskey rough as he said, "You could stand there till doomsday, and I wouldn't get my fill of looking at you."

Jewel would have scoffed, but the sound got caught in her throat. "Mac…"

He stepped close enough to put them toe to toe.

She struggled not to give ground. "Say what you think. Spit it out. I can take it."

His thumb caressed the faint scars on her bared cheek, then edged into her hair. "Your hair's so soft. So shiny. So sleek." His hand slid through her hair to capture her nape and hold her still as he lowered his head. "I find you irresistible, Jewel."

Jewel felt her heart thudding, had trouble catching her breath, then stopped breathing altogether as his mouth closed over hers.

He kept their bodies separated, touching her only with his mouth. The searing kiss was enough to curl her toes inside her boots.

He lifted his head and said, "Welcome back, Jewel. I missed the old you."

"Oh, Mac—" She was on the verge of blurting out her strong feelings for him—the same feelings his kiss had suggested he had for her—when he interrupted.

"I don't think you're going to have any trouble at all attracting the man of your dreams." He smiled ruefully. "You're going to have to remind me to keep my distance.

I don't want any good prospects to think I have any kind of claim on you except as a friend."

Jewel stared at him with stunned eyes, but quickly recovered her composure. "No sweat, Mac," she said, turning and heading for the van. "I'll make sure any men I meet know exactly where you stand."

She owed Mac too much to make him feel uncomfortable by revealing her new feelings for him before he was ready to hear them. But if kissing her like this only reinforced the bonds of *friendship*, she had her work cut out for her. The changes in her hair and wardrobe had been useful in helping Mac to see her as a desirable female. All she had to do now was figure out how to make him fall in love with her.

CHAPTER EIGHT

MAC STARED OUT the window of the van at the flat grassland that lined the road between Hawk's Pride and the airport, rather than at the woman behind the wheel. But he very much wanted to feast his eyes on Jewel.

He liked the bouncy new haircut that showed off the line of her chin and made her cheekbones more prominent. He liked the formfitting clothes that outlined a lush figure he yearned to hold close to his own. He was intrigued by the sparkle of wonder and delight—and unfulfilled promise—in her dark brown eyes.

Mac wished he had a Stetson to set on his lap.

He hadn't realized he would be so physically susceptible to the striking change in Jewel's appearance. A friend would have settled for giving her an approving pat on the back. His kiss had been a purely male impulse, an effort to stake his claim on an intensely desirable female.

Mac recognized his problem. He simply had no idea how to solve it. How did a man stop desiring a woman? Especially one he not only lusted after but also liked very much?

Jewel sat across from him behind the wheel not saying a word. But speaking volumes.

Tension radiated between them. Sexual tension.

He had told her to find another man, but now he wasn't so sure. She had certainly seemed to enjoy his kiss. Maybe if he seduced her in stages... If they took it slow and easy...

Who was he kidding? When it came down to the nitty-gritty, it was still going to be the first time for him. He was still going to be guessing at what he was doing. Besides, it wasn't fair to change his mind at this late date.

Who said life was fair?

"I appreciate you coming along to help today," Jewel said, interrupting his thoughts.

"My pleasure. How many people are we picking up?"

"Twelve kids, two counselors."

"Are you still hiring college kids?"

"Patty Freeburg is still in college. Gavin Talbot is in graduate school. I should warn you, this group of kids includes Brad Templeton."

"The kid who wanted to meet me?"

Jewel nodded. "His leukemia is in its second remission. You know how that works. You're afraid to get your hopes up that this remission will last, because you've already slipped out of remission once."

"You have to keep believing you can beat the disease," Mac said.

"Most kids aren't as lucky as you were."

"You think it was luck that I beat myelocytic leukemia?" he asked.

"Statistics say the chances of a kid surviving that kind of leukemia aren't good. What else could it have been?"

"Sheer determination. Willpower. It can move mountains. Recently it put me back on my own two feet when the doctors said I would never walk again without a brace."

"Granted, willpower is important. Determination counts for a lot. But are they enough to get your leg back into shape for pro football?" Jewel asked.

Mac felt a spurt of panic. "Sure. Why not?"

"Willpower can't replace the missing muscle in your leg, Mac. Determination can't make the scars disappear."

"I can compensate."

She nodded. "For your sake, I hope so."

"Why are you being so negative about this?" Mac demanded, using anger to force back the fear that had surfaced with her doubts.

"I'm not being negative, just realistic. You learn to accept—"

"Don't accept anything that isn't exactly what you want. Don't expect anything less than the best for yourself or those sick kids, Jewel. You deserve it. And so do they."

Jewel smiled ruefully. "To tell the truth, this is an argument I don't want to win. I want to believe in happily ever after for these kids and for you. And I'm hoping desperately for it myself. I've taken the first steps toward a new me. I have to admit it feels good, even though it is a little scary."

He met her glance briefly and saw the fear, before she returned her gaze to the road in front of her. "Why scary?"

"Because I'm not sure how well I'll handle all the male attention once I have it."

"Encourage the men you're interested in, and discourage the ones you don't want."

She grunted her disgust. "You make it sound so easy. Encourage how? Discourage how?"

"Smiles. And frowns."

Jewel looked at him incredulously, then gave a bubbly laugh. "If it were only that simple!"

"It is," Mac assured her.

She eyed him doubtfully. "That's all there is to it?"

"Why not try an experiment? When this Gavin What's-his-name—"

"Talbot," Jewel provided.

"When Talbot gets off the plane, give him a 'You're the one!' smile, and see what kind of response you get."

They had arrived at the local airport just as the commuter plane from Dallas was landing. Jewel stopped the van close to the terminal and stepped out to wait for the plane door to open and the kids to come down the portable stairs to the tarmac.

The three girls and four boys on the Dallas flight all wore hats of some kind, a means of hiding the ravages of chemotherapy on their hair. Baseball caps, berets, slouch hats, straw hats, bandannas, Jewel had seen them all. Beneath the hats their eyes looked haunted, their mouths grim. Jewel looked forward to easing their worries for two weeks, to helping them forget for a short time that their lives were threatened with extinction.

A scuffle broke out between two of the boys the instant they reached the tarmac. The other kids spread out in a circle to watch.

"Hey!" Jewel cried, running to reach them.

Mac was there before her and picked up the boy who had done the shoving, leaving the other boy with no one to fight. "What's the problem?" Mac asked in a calm voice.

The boy on the tarmac was in tears. He pointed to the boy in Mac's arms. "He said I'm going to die."

"We're all going to die," Mac replied. "Could get hit by a bus tomorrow."

The other kids smiled. It was an old joke for them, but it still worked every time.

The crying boy was not amused. He pointed to the kid in Mac's arms. "He said I can't beat it. He said no one can. He said—"

Mac perused the thin, gangly boy held snug against his side. "Doesn't look like a doctor to me," he said. "Where do you suppose he got the information to make his diagnosis? You a doctor?" Mac asked the kid.

The boy clenched his teeth and said nothing.

"Guess that settles that," Mac said. "Any other questions?" he asked the crying boy.

The kid wiped his nose on the shoulder of his T-shirt and pulled his Harwell Grain and Feed cap snugly over his eyes. "Guess not."

Mac exchanged a look with Jewel, who began herding the children toward the terminal.

"Why don't you all come inside with me," she said. "We'll get a soda while we wait for the kids from Houston to arrive, along with your counselors."

As soon as they were gone, Mac set the boy down on his feet in front of him. Knowing the kid would likely run the instant he let go, Mac settled onto one knee, his hands trapping the kid's frail shoulders, and tried to see the boy's eyes under his baseball cap. The kid's chin was tucked so close to his chest, it was impossible.

"What's your name?" Mac asked.

"I want to go home."

"You sound pretty mad."

"I never wanted to come here in the first place. My mom made me!"

"Why'd you tell that boy he was going to die?"

"'Cause he is!"

"Who says?"

"He's got acute myelocytic leukemia, same as me. It kills you for sure!"

"I'm not dead."

The boy's chin jerked up, and his pale blue eyes focused on Mac's. "You're not sick."

"I was. Same as you."

The boy shook his head. "But you're—"

"I'm Mac Macready."

The blue eyes widened. "*You're* him? You look different from the picture on your trading card."

"I was younger then," Mac replied. *And twenty pounds heavier with muscle.*

"My mom said you'd be here, but I didn't believe her."

"You must be Brad Templeton." Mac let go of the kid's shoulders, rose and stuck out his hand. "Nice to meet you, Brad."

The boy stared at Mac's hand suspiciously before he laid his own tiny palm against it. Mac figured the kid for eleven or twelve, but he didn't look much more than eight or nine. The slight body, the gaunt cheeks, the hopeless look in his eyes, told how the disease had decimated him—body and soul.

"You ready to join the others?" Mac asked.

He watched as the boy looked toward the kids bunched in the front window of the terminal and made a face. "This is a waste of time."

"Why is that?"

"I mean, why bother pretending everything is all right, when it's not?"

Mac put a hand on the boy's back, and they began walking toward the terminal. "Why not pretend? Why not enjoy every moment you've got?"

The boy met his gaze, and Mac knew the answer without having to hear it. He had been through it all himself.

This was a child going through the stages that prepared him for death. The anger. The grieving. And finally, the acceptance. Brad Templeton had done it all before, when the first remission ended. Then death had given him a brief reprieve—a second remission. But having once accepted the fact he was going to die, it was awfully hard to start living all over again.

"Death doesn't always win," Mac said quietly.

Brad looked up at him. "How did you beat it?"

"Determination. Willpower."

Brad shook his head. "That isn't enough. If it was, I'd already be well."

"Don't give up."

"I have to," Brad said. "It hurts too bad to hope when you know it isn't going to make any difference."

They had reached the door to the terminal, but before going inside, Mac stooped down and turned the boy to face him. "Sometimes you have to forget about what the doctors say and believe in yourself."

Brad looked skeptical.

Mac didn't know who he was trying to convince, himself or the kid. Sometimes the doctors were right. Kids died. And football players got career-ending injuries.

He rose and said, "Come on, Brad. We can keep each other company this week and have some fun."

Brad snorted. "Fun. Yeah. Right."

Mac smiled. "If you're not smiling ear to ear when you get back on that plane in two weeks, I'll—"

"How are you two doing?" Jewel interrupted. A whoosh of cold air escaped the terminal as she joined them in the Texas heat that was already rising from the tarmac.

"I was making a bet with Brad that he would be smiling by the end of next week."

Brad grimaced.

Jewel eyed Brad, then murmured to Mac, "Looks like you have your work cut out for you."

"Come on, Brad," Mac said, giving the boy a nudge toward the door. "Let's go inside and meet the other kids."

"I've already met them," Brad said sullenly. "They all hate me."

"We'll have to work on that, too," Mac said, sending Jewel a look that said "Help!" over his shoulder.

"I'd appreciate it if you'd keep an eye on everybody while I greet the folks on the plane from Houston," she said.

Mac realized the second commuter plane had arrived, Jewel was headed back out onto the tarmac. "Don't forget," he said. "Smile."

Jewel shot him a radiant smile. "How's this?"

Mac put an exaggerated hand to his heart. "Lord have mercy, girl, that's potent stuff!"

Jewel laughed and turned away, her hips swaying seductively in the tight jeans.

Mac was glad she'd turned away when she had. His hand was still on his heart, but it was keeping the damned thing from flying out of his chest. If she kept walking like that, he wasn't going to be able to go inside anytime soon.

He felt a tug on his shirtsleeve and looked down to see Brad staring up at him.

"You got the hots for her?"

Mac stared, agog. "The *hots?*"

"You know. Sexy chick like that—"

Mac put a hand over Brad's mouth. "Where did a kid your age learn—? Don't answer that. She's Miss Whitelaw to you."

The kid reached up to uncover his mouth. "I'm twelve. I was here when I was nine and Jewel said we can call her Jewel and she's a lot prettier now."

"And you're old enough to notice, is that it?"

Brad gave Mac a man-to-man shrug. "I haven't thought too much about girls 'cause...you know."

Mac put a hand on Brad's shoulder. "Yeah, I know how that is, too."

He ushered Brad inside thinking it was going to be a very long two weeks.

JEWEL'S HEART WAS beating rapidly. Even kidding the way he was, Mac's admiring look had been enough to take her breath away. It was easy to keep the smile on her face long enough to greet the other five campers, Patty Free-burg and Gavin Talbot.

Patty was petite and pretty, with long blond hair she wore in a youthful ponytail, blue eyes and a wonderfully open smile. "Hello," she said. "I'm glad to be back."

"Good to have you back, Patty," Jewel said. "You know the drill. Would you mind helping the kids locate their luggage inside?"

"Sure," Patty said. "Come on, you guys, hup, two, three, four!"

The two boys marched, and the three girls giggled as they followed Patty toward the terminal.

Jewel turned to greet Gavin Talbot, who was hefting a duffel bag over his shoulder. She knew Gavin's credentials backward and forward. He was twenty-six and working on a Ph.D. in child psychology. Eventually he planned to become a clinical psychologist, and work with dying kids. He was spending time at Camp LittleHawk because it catered to children with cancer.

She knew Gavin would have to be an empathetic and caring man to choose such a career. She had not imagined he would also be stunningly handsome.

He was over six feet tall, with the sort of rangy body Jewel was used to seeing on cowhands, who led physically active lives. His sun-streaked, tobacco-brown hair suggested a lot of time out-of-doors, and the spray of tan lines around his dark brown eyes confirmed it. He was dressed in a white, oxford-cloth shirt, unbuttoned at the throat and turned up to his forearms, well-worn—though not ragged—jeans and cowboy boots.

"Hello, Miss Whitelaw," he said, reaching out to shake her hand as they followed Patty and the kids back to the terminal.

His large, callused hand engulfed hers, offering comfort, reassurance and something else…a spark of sexual interest.

Jewel didn't think she was imagining it. She felt a small frisson of pleasure merely from his firm handclasp. It was probably the way he looked into her eyes, as though seeking a connection, that made her insides jump a little.

"Call me Jewel, please, Gavin," she replied.

"Jewel," he repeated, the smile broadening, becoming more relaxed. "The name fits."

Jewel only had an instant to decide whether to frown or smile, as Mac had instructed. Jewel smiled.

She had only taken two steps when Gavin put a hand under her elbow and said, "You're hurt."

"It's an old injury that causes me to limp," she said, wondering if the interest she had previously seen would diminish, now that he knew she was considerably less than perfect.

Her opinion of him went up a notch when he said, "It doesn't seem to slow you down much." She felt a spurt of anxiety when Gavin made eye contact with her again, because the sexual spark was still there. Well, she had wanted to attract him and she had. So now what did she do with him? She turned to find Mac staring at her through the terminal's front picture window.

Mac was safe. Mac was nonthreatening.

Mac also was not volunteering to help her get over the lingering fear that had kept her celibate all these years. Maybe seeing that someone else was interested in her would spur him to action.

She turned back to Gavin and forced another smile onto her face. "You look like you spend a lot of time outdoors."

"I own a cattle ranch south of Houston," he said. "I spend my weekends there when I can."

"You should be right at home here," she said. "We do

a lot of trail rides in the early morning and late afternoon for the children."

"What about moonlight rides for the grown-ups?" he asked. "Ending with a romantic campfire and toasted marshmallows?"

Jewel was a little shocked at how fast Gavin had made his move. She swallowed back the knot of fear and shot him a calculated come-hither glance. "I suppose that could be arranged."

"How about tonight?"

"How about what tonight?" Mac asked.

Jewel had been so busy staring back into Gavin's brown eyes, she hadn't realized they had reached the terminal. Mac's question caught her unawares. "What?"

"Jewel and I were just setting up a moonlight ride for tonight," Gavin said.

Jewel heard the warning in Gavin's voice. *Stay clear. This one's mine. We don't want company.*

Mac ignored it. "Sounds like a fine idea," he said. "Hey, Patty, you want to go for a moonlight ride tonight?"

Patty smiled. "Sure. Who all's going?"

"Everybody," Gavin said wryly, his gaze never leaving Mac's.

At least Gavin was a good sport, Jewel thought. She was grateful that Mac had realized how uncomfortable she would have been all alone with Gavin and had invited himself and Patty. With Mac along she would feel safer flirting with Gavin. And perhaps Mac would be moved to do a little flirting himself.

Jewel was amused to see how Gavin maneuvered to be in the front seat with her on the trip back, forcing Mac into the back with Patty and the kids. Gavin wasn't the least impressed by Mac's football hero status, because he wasn't a big football fan.

"I know that sounds like blasphemy in Texas," he said. "But I'd rather spend my Saturday and Sunday afternoons at the ranch, since I'm stuck indoors reading and writing the rest of the week."

"What's the name of your ranch?" Jewel asked as she started the van and headed back toward the ranch.

"Let's not talk about me," Gavin said, avoiding an answer. "Tell me about yourself."

Jewel watched Gavin stiffen as Mac suddenly leaned forward, bracing his arms on the back of the front seat, effectively interposing himself between Jewel and the counselor. "Mind if I listen?" Mac said. "Jewel and I haven't had much time to catch up on things since the last time we were together."

Jewel heard the insinuation in Mac's voice that suggested "together" meant more than sitting on a garden swing next to each other.

"You two are old friends?" Gavin asked, eyeing the two of them speculatively.

"We're rooming together," Mac said. "Didn't Jewel tell you?"

Jewel turned a fiery red at the knowing look Gavin gave her, even though the situation with Mac was perfectly innocent. She was a little perturbed at Mac. He seemed to be saying everything he could to keep Gavin at a distance. She appreciated his concern, but until he volunteered to take Gavin's place, she was determined to be brave enough to pursue the relationship.

She forced a laugh and said, "Mac has been like a big brother to me for years. He gets a little protective at times."

Gavin's brows rose, and the smile returned. "I see. Don't worry, Mac," he said, patting Mac's arm. "I'll take good care of her."

Mac grunted and shifted back into the backseat, his arms crossed over his chest.

Jewel shivered as she made brief eye contact with Gavin. It looked like she was going to get a chance to try out her feminine wiles tonight. Mac would be there, so she wouldn't have to worry about things getting out of hand. Toasting marshmallows over a campfire would be a marvelously romantic setting, perfect for establishing a friendly rapport with Gavin.

She wondered if Gavin would try to kiss her. She wondered if she should let him. She caught Mac's narrowed gaze in the rearview mirror and wondered, with a smile, if *Mac* would let him. She had better have a talk with Mac before the trail ride and let him know she welcomed Gavin's attentions for the practice they would provide.

Jewel shivered in anticipation. She only hoped that when the time came, and Gavin made advances, she would have the nerve to follow through.

CHAPTER NINE

MAC STARED THROUGH his horse's ears at Jewel, riding side by side with Gavin on the moonlit trail ahead of him. Patty had decided to stay at the ranch, so he had no riding partner. Mac watched Jewel lean close to hear what Gavin was saying. A trilling burble of laughter floated back to him on the wind. His neck hairs rose, and he gritted his teeth in frustration.

That could have been him riding beside Jewel. That could have been him making her laugh. Instead, he was reduced to the role of chaperon. And not enjoying it one bit.

Mac turned to see who was coming as another horse cantered up beside him bearing one of the three late additions to their trail ride. "Hey, Colt. What's new?"

"You know anything about that Gavin guy?" Colt asked, aiming his chin toward the couple ahead of them.

Mac stared at Gavin. "He's as comfortable on a horse as any cowboy I've ever seen, he's educated, friendly, courteous and he appears to be interested in Jewel."

"You think he'll try to hurt her?"

Mac saw the worry on Colt's young face. Six years ago the kid had been only eight, but obviously Jewel's trauma had left a lasting impression on her family. "There's not much Gavin can do with me along," Mac reassured the teenager.

Colt heaved a sigh of relief. "Thanks, Mac. Jewel is... well, she's pretty special."

"I know."

Colt glanced over his shoulder, frowned, then looked straight ahead again. "I thought I might get to see a little more of Jenny if we came along tonight. I should have known she'd stick like glue to Huck."

Mac arched a brow. "You have feelings for her yourself?"

Colt readjusted his Western straw hat, setting it lower over his eyes to hide his expression. "She's Huck's girl."

"You didn't answer my question."

"So what if I like her?" Colt retorted. "Nothing's gonna come of it. They'll probably get married as soon as Huck finishes college."

"College is a long way off. Maybe Huck will change his mind. Or Jenny will."

Colt snorted. "What difference would that make? She doesn't know I'm alive."

Mac wasn't sure what to say. He hadn't been too fortunate in the romance department himself. But he knew what he would do if he loved a woman. "Mind if I offer you some advice?"

Colt shrugged.

"If you get a chance to make Jenny your girl, grab it with both hands." He grinned at Colt. "It's awful hard for a woman to resist a man who loves her, heart and soul."

Colt eyed him sideways. "If you say so."

They had reached the ring of stones Camp LittleHawk used as a campfire site for barbecues. Mac watched as Gavin lifted Jewel from her horse, sliding her down the front of him as he settled her feet on the ground. He saw the stunned look on Jewel's face as she gazed up at Gavin. Was it fear or wonder she had felt at the intimate contact?

He kneed his horse into a lope to catch up to them. He was out of the saddle and at her side seconds later. "Hey,

Jewel," he said, putting a hand on her shoulder. "Let's get the fire going for those marshmallows."

When she looked at him, he saw dazed pleasure in her eyes. Damn. She was definitely aroused. A quick glance at the front of her—at the pebbled nipples that showed through the knit top—confirmed his diagnosis.

So what was he supposed to do now? Disappear, so Gavin could get on with his seduction?

The hell he would.

He grabbed Jewel's hand. "Come on, Jewel. Let's get some firewood."

Jewel glanced at him in surprise, smiled and followed him to the box of firewood that was kept nearby. He loaded her arms with kindling and picked up a few logs to carry back himself. By the time they returned to the fire, Colt had unpacked the wire clothes hangers they had brought along and was unbending them to make marshmallow roasting sticks.

Mac and Jewel knelt together before the ring of stones that Jenny and Huck were straightening and began arranging the kindling and logs. Gavin arrived moments later with the bag of marshmallows, a thermos of hot chocolate and some paper cups from his saddlebag and a couple of blankets that had been tied behind Jewel's saddle.

"Up, you two," he said to Mac and Jewel. "Let me get this down under you."

Mac and Jewel scooted to the side, and Gavin spread the gray wool blanket where they had been, settling himself on the opposite side of Jewel from Mac and leaning close to whisper, "I think you've already started my fire."

Mac couldn't help overhearing. Or seeing Jewel stiffen slightly before she managed a smile and replied, "Give me a match, and I'll show you a real blaze."

Gavin, damn him, laughed and handed her a box of

matches. Instead of letting her light the match by herself, Gavin held her hand as she drew the match along the edge of the box and lit the kindling. When the fire from the match had almost reached her fingers, Gavin lifted her hand to his mouth and blew it out.

Jewel made a mewling sound that had Mac's insides clenching. His hands fisted unconsciously, and his body tensed to fight.

Until that moment, Mac had not realized the extent of his feelings for Jewel. He had always liked her and considered himself her friend. He had missed talking to her in the years they had been apart. He was more than a little attracted to her. But the instinctual need to claim her, to make her his and only his, rose unbidden from somewhere deep inside him.

He resisted the strong urge to hit Gavin Talbot in the nose and began straightening out a clothes hanger to use as a roasting stick. Fighting the metal was a better release for his tension than starting an uncivilized brawl.

It was abundantly clear to him now, as it had not been before, that he wanted to be the man Jewel gave herself to for the first time. He wanted to see her eyes when their bodies were joined, hear her sighs as she learned the pleasure to be found in loving each other.

But Gavin moved fast, and Mac wasn't sure he was going to get a second chance with Jewel if something didn't happen pretty quick to separate the two. It didn't take much of a fire to toast marshmallows, and it wasn't long before Colt opened the bag and began tossing marshmallows around. Gavin was making Jewel laugh again, putting a marshmallow on the end of her roasting stick and whispering in her ear as it toasted on the fire.

"Jewel," Mac said quietly.

To his surprise, she looked immediately at him. "Yes, Mac?"

"Your marshmallow is on fire."

Because she was looking at him, she swung the burning marshmallow in his direction. Mac caught the coat hanger far enough back not to burn himself and blew out the fire. "Hope you like it charred," he said with a smile.

He blew on it to cool it, then pulled the gooey marshmallow off the end of the wire and held it out to her between thumb and forefinger. She leaned forward, her mouth open, and grabbed Mac's wrist as she bit into it. She held on to his wrist while she chewed, waving her hand at her mouth and making noises because the gooey marshmallow was both hot and deliciously sweet.

Then, as though it were the most natural thing in the world, she leaned over and sucked the rest of the marshmallow off of his thumb, licking it clean with her tongue.

Mac stared at her with avid eyes. She could have no idea what she was doing. By the time she was done with his thumb and had started on his forefinger, his body was strung as tight as a bowstring.

Jewel looked up at him, his forefinger still in her mouth, and caught his gaze with hers. She might not have realized beforehand what effect she was having on him, but he saw she recognized immediately what she had done.

Ever so slowly, she withdrew his forefinger from her mouth, then let go of his wrist. She had to clear her throat to speak. "I forgot to bring along wet wipes," she said. "I figured that was the best way to get rid of the marshmallow."

Mac took the fingers that had been in her mouth and slowly licked off imaginary specks of sugar. "It seems to be all gone."

He watched Jewel swallow hard before Gavin distracted her attention.

"How about sharing this one with me?" Gavin said, putting a hand on her forearm to stake his claim and holding out a perfectly toasted marshmallow.

Mac saw the goose bumps rise on her flesh where Gavin's hand lay. Saw her tentative smile as she turned back to the other man.

"Sure, Gavin," she said. "I'd like that."

She pulled the gooey marshmallow from the wire and ate half of it before Gavin caught her wrist and, with a grin, turned the marshmallow toward himself. Mac watched in helpless fury as Gavin ate the rest of the marshmallow from her hand and licked her fingers clean.

When Gavin started kissing her fingertips, something inside Mac snapped. "That's it!"

"What?" Jewel said, turning bewildered eyes on him.

"Let's go, Jewel." Mac stood and grabbed Jewel's wrist to drag her to her feet. He was surprised when she resisted.

"What's wrong with you, Mac?" she said.

"I think this has gone far enough." He said the words to the counselor, who understood exactly what his problem was.

Gavin rose to his feet, his legs widespread. "I didn't hear the lady complaining about my attentions."

Gavin had a point. But Mac wasn't in a rational mood. "The lady is too polite to say anything."

Gavin raised a questioning brow and faced Jewel. "Is that true, Jewel?"

"I don't see… I mean, I think I may have encouraged… I just wanted to see…"

Gavin's lip curved wryly on one side. "Your point is taken," he said to Mac.

By then, Colt was on his feet on the other side of the fire. "You need any help, Mac?"

Jenny grabbed Colt's T-shirt where it hung out of his jeans and yanked on it. "Sit down, Colt. This doesn't concern you."

"She's my sister."

"Sit down, Colt," Jenny repeated.

Mac watched as Colt met Jenny's gaze and settled back onto the ground beside her.

By then, Jewel was up and standing nose to nose with Mac. "What's gotten into you?" she demanded in a harsh whisper. "You're the one who told me to flirt with him in the first place!"

"I didn't think it would go this far," Mac said stubbornly.

"Thanks to you," she hissed, "it's not likely to go much further!"

"That's fine by me," Mac retorted.

"I think I'll excuse myself and let you two settle this alone," Gavin said. "I can find my own way back."

"We'd better get going, too," Jenny said, rising and pulling Huck and Colt to their feet. "I don't want to be late getting home."

Within moments, everything had been picked up and repacked, and the four of them were on their way back to the ranch house, leaving Mac and Jewel to put out the fire.

"All right, Mac," Jewel said. "I want to hear from your own lips what possessed you to cause such a scene."

JEWEL WAS CONFUSED by Mac's strange behavior. "You're the one who told me to try out my feminine wiles," she said. "The first time I do, you act like a jealous lover."

She thought Mac flushed, but it was hard to tell in the firelight.

"I thought you wanted me along to protect you," he said.

"If I needed protection. Which I did not."

Mac kicked sand over the fire, creating a cloud of smoke. "You *liked* the way he was pawing you?"

"*Pawing* me?" she said. "Gavin's attentions weren't at all unwelcome."

When Gavin had smiled at her, she had allowed herself to feel the pleasure of being attractive to—and attracted to—a handsome man. When he had blown out the match, and his warm, moist breath touched her hand, she had not cut off the frisson of awareness that skittered down her spine. When he had kissed her fingertips, she had felt her heart beat more rapidly in response.

But none of those feelings in any way compared to the shock of awareness she felt when she had met Mac's gaze and discovered he had been aroused by the way she had sucked and licked his fingers clean.

It was the difference between a pinprick and being stabbed with a knife. While she was completely aware of both, one was slight and fleeting, while the other burned deep inside. One would disappear quickly; the other would not soon be forgotten.

She wasn't about to admit her vulnerability to Mac when he was behaving like a jealous idiot. Especially when he wasn't volunteering to take Gavin's place. "I liked what Gavin did," she said.

"I didn't," Mac said flatly.

"Why not?" Jewel demanded.

"He was moving too fast. You hardly know the guy."

"He didn't do anything I didn't allow."

"That's another thing," Mac said. "Just how far were you intending to go? Would you have let him kiss you?"

"Why not?" she said tartly.

Mac made a threatening, rumbly sound in his throat.

"I can kiss you as well as some stranger can. If it's kisses you want, come to me."

"Last night you said—"

"Forget about last night. It never happened. We start new, here and now. You want to practice being a woman, practice with me."

Jewel eyed Mac in astonishment. She had exactly what she had thought she wanted. All she had to do was find the courage to follow through and take Mac up on his offer. She took a deep breath, let it out and said, "All right. I'll practice with you."

Mac heaved a sigh and knelt down to stir the ashes with a stick to make certain the fire was out. "Thank God that's settled."

"I want to be kissed, Mac."

She watched his shoulders tense, saw him drop the stick, then rise to face her.

"You want to be kissed now?"

"If you hadn't scared Gavin away, he'd be kissing me now," she pointed out.

It was hard to tell what Mac was feeling. His eyes were narrowed in—anger? His lips were twisted in a moue of—frustration? And his brow was furrowed deep with—apprehension? Which showed how good she was at reading men. What did Mac Macready have to be anxious about? He must have kissed a hundred women. She was the one who needed lessons.

"Come here, Jewel," Mac said in a voice that grated like an unoiled hinge.

It only took a couple of steps for her to reach him. His arms opened wide, and as she stepped between them, they folded around her. One hand caught at her nape, the other low on her spine, just above her buttocks. She was aware of goose bumps rising along her nape as his hand slid up and grasped a handful of her hair.

He did not pull her any closer, simply angled her head and lowered his mouth. His lips felt warm and full as he rubbed them against hers. "Are you sure about this, Jewel?" he breathed against her half-open mouth.

She made a sound in her throat which he must have taken as assent, because he kissed the left side of her mouth, then the right, before returning to the center. He slipped his tongue beneath her upper lip, then nipped at her lips with his teeth.

Jewel shivered. It was strange, standing upright, being held—but not held—in a man's arms. She leaned into the kiss, returning the gentle pressure of his mouth. She slid her tongue along the seam of his lips, and he opened for her. Jewel had never been the aggressor with a man. It felt wonderful to be able to taste and tease to her heart's content without being afraid.

Her arms roamed up Mac's back, feeling the corded sinew. One hand slid into the hair at his nape and played with it as she indulged herself kissing him, feeling the damp softness of his lips, tasting the inside of his mouth with soft, tentative thrusts that he returned. She felt him begin to tremble.

"Jewel," he murmured.

"Hmm." Her lips followed the line of his chin to a spot below his ear, and she heard him hiss in a breath.

"I think we'd better stop."

She leaned back and looked up into his hooded eyes, at lips rigid with passion. She smiled. "If I look anything like you do, perhaps you're right."

"You look beautiful," he said fervently.

"You don't have to say that," Jewel protested. "I know what I—"

He put his mouth on hers to silence her, pouring his feelings into a kiss that had her straining to be closer to him, closing the distance between them, until they were pressed close from breast to thigh. Jewel was so entranced by what Mac was doing with his mouth that it took her a moment to realize he had widened his stance enough to fit her between his legs.

He was aroused.

She squeezed her eyes shut and tried to concentrate on the kiss. It was so lovely. It felt so good. But her body below the waist had turned to stone.

Mac broke the kiss and looked down at her, his eyes worried. "Jewel?"

"Let me go, Mac."

"I won't hurt you, Jewel." He put one hand on her buttocks to keep her where she was. He smiled tenderly. "I'd very much like to put myself inside you."

Jewel felt the heat climbing up her throat at such plain speaking. "Mac—"

"But I'm not going to do anything until you're ready," he said, leaning down to give her a gentle kiss on the lips. "We have plenty of time."

"Your recuperation is almost complete," Jewel countered. "Look how far you've come in—"

He stopped her with another kiss. "We have plenty of time for you to get used to me touching you, wanting you."

"It doesn't seem fair, Mac. I mean, for me to use you like this."

He smiled. "Believe me, I don't mind."

His eyes seemed to be promising things she knew he could not mean. She looked down and said, "In a couple of weeks you'll be leaving here, and I won't be seeing you again."

He lifted her chin until she was looking into his eyes.

"You'll always be special to me, Jewel. You have no idea how special." He opened his mouth as though to say something else and closed it again. "Look, let's just take this one day at a time. You can start with simple stuff like kisses and touches. Anytime you want to practice, just let me know. How does that sound?"

"Are you sure I won't be imposing?" Jewel asked.

"It'll be my pleasure," Mac said with a grin, rocking his body against hers.

"Oh!"

His brow wrinkled in concern. "What's wrong?"

"You're still…and I'm not… It's working!" she said with delight. "I'm hardly affected at all." Except that her pulse was throbbing, and she felt the strangest urge to push back against the hardness that rested between her legs.

Mac's smile looked a little forced. "See. You're already getting used to me."

He released her, and Jewel took a step back.

"I suppose we'd better get back," she said. "Camp starts tomorrow, and I'll be getting up early."

"I can help you after my workout."

Jewel smiled. "I'd like that."

"Don't forget. Anytime you feel like you want to practice, just let me know. There's no need to flirt with that Gavin character."

"I thought I might try my wings—"

"Try your wings on me!" He swung her back into his arms, kissed her hard on the lips, then stomped off toward his horse, leaving her standing there.

It took a minute for Jewel to catch her breath and steady her racing pulse. "I was just teasing!" she called after him, as she hurried to catch up.

Mac made a growling sound in his throat. "Let's go. It's late."

She stomped right over and stood in front of him. "For heaven's sake! Where's your sense of humor?"

He grabbed her hand and placed it on the bulge in his jeans. "Right there. I'm not feeling too damn funny at the moment."

Even though he had immediately let go of her hand, Jewel was too shocked to jerk away. She left her hand where Mac had put it, feeling the length and hardness of him. This part of him didn't seem nearly so threatening through a layer of denim and cotton, warm and pulsing beneath her hand.

"Jewel," he said through gritted teeth. "What are you doing?"

"Learning."

He gave a choked laugh. "I think my sense of humor is—"

"In very fine shape," she said with a gamine grin. "Want to test it again?"

He caught her wrist and removed her hand. "I think I've had enough testing for one evening. Let's save this for another time."

"Anything you say, Mac," she answered cheerfully. "You're the teacher."

And Jewel was determined to be a very good pupil.

CHAPTER TEN

MAC REALIZED THE DILEMMA he had put himself in. He was going to be kissing and touching Jewel over the next several weeks—and encouraging her to kiss and touch him—even though he had serious reservations about making love to her. Not because he didn't desire her, but because he was afraid if he did something wrong, he would mess things up for her even more. He decided he owed it to both of them to get some professional advice.

"Something's come up that I need to discuss with my agent," Mac said to Jewel at breakfast the next morning. "I've made reservations to fly to Dallas this afternoon."

"Couldn't you do it over the phone?" Jewel asked.

Mac shook his head and raised another spoonful of cornflakes. "Too sensitive. Requires face-to-face consultation."

"Why didn't you say something about this last night?" she asked suspiciously.

He grinned. "I was distracted last night."

Jewel blushed. Mac thought she had never looked lovelier. She was wearing a plaid Western shirt, tucked in at the waist of her jeans, that hinted at the fullness of her figure. Her brown hair looked sun kissed, and her brown eyes gleamed. As she turned toward him, the faded crisscross scars on her face took him back to a time when they were both much younger and someone had teased her about them.

Mac realized he must have cared a great deal for her even then. He could remember wiping away her tears with his thumbs, kissing her scarred cheek and saying, "These scars are as precious as any other part of you, Jewel, more facets to add texture to the diamond you are."

He had meant it then, and he could see it now.

Jewel laid her spoon in her cereal bowl and said, "I'll miss you, Mac. When will you be back?"

Mac met her troubled gaze and said, "I don't know." He had no idea how long it would take to get an appointment with the one sex therapist he knew. Dr. Timothy Douglas might be too busy to fit him in for several days.

"You're not coming back, are you?" Jewel said flatly. "You've changed your mind about wanting to teach me, and you're leaving." The glow had left her face and the sparkle had faded from her eyes.

"What do I have to do to convince you I'm not going away?"

"Kiss me," she said. "That was the deal. I could ask anytime, and I'm asking now." She crossed her arms over her chest as though she thought he might refuse.

Silly woman. He wasn't about to refuse.

Mac crossed to Jewel in two steps, tipped her chin up and slanted his mouth over hers, kissing her with all the passion he felt, hoping to convince her he meant what he said. They were both breathing hard when he lifted his head. "I'm coming back," he said. "I just have some business to do in Dallas."

Tears filled her eyes as she looked up at him. "That was goodbye. I know it."

Mac shook his head in disbelief. He stood and put his hands on his hips. "Look, Jewel. Why would I make an offer like the one I made last night and leave the next day for good?"

"Because you had second thoughts," she said.

"No, I did not."

"Because you realized I might fall in love with you or something stupid like that, if you started kissing me all the time."

"That never crossed my mind!" The thought hadn't occurred to him, but he liked the idea now that she mentioned it.

"Probably you never thought of me falling in love, because kisses don't mean much to a man like you," she said, lips pouting.

How wrong she was! Mac thought. Her kisses, at least, made him feel a great deal, though he wasn't willing to go so far as to think in terms of love. A great deal of *like*. That was what he felt for Jewel Whitelaw.

But he couldn't resist kissing her again. He slipped his tongue inside her mouth and tasted her thoroughly. When he stood again, the revealing bulge was back in his jeans. He noticed that she noticed and felt his body tighten in expectation.

"I'll be back, Jewel. Trust me."

It was a lot to ask a woman who hadn't found much about men to trust.

She blinked back the tears and said, "All right, Mac."

He kissed her again, to thank her for trusting him, but when he felt the urge to pull her up and into his arms, he stepped back. "You've got campers to see to, and I've got a few things to do before I join you."

"You're still going to help me with the campers this morning?"

"Of course. Why wouldn't I?"

"I thought you might have to pack..."

"I'm only taking a few things."

She walked back to him and put her arms around him

and hugged him tight. "I'm so glad you're coming back," she said. "I'll be waiting for you. I won't even flirt with Gavin while you're gone."

She was already halfway to the door by the time he realized what she had said. She turned back, winked and laughed, then headed out the door.

Mac watched her till she was gone, realizing he had more problems to solve than just hers, if they were to have any hope of a future together. He had gotten a big signing bonus when he joined the Tornadoes, but his five-year contract had provided for a smaller salary in the first few years. He had most of the signing bonus left, but he had pretty much spent his first year's salary.

What if he didn't make it back onto the team?

Don't even think *that!*

Mac didn't believe in quitting or giving up or giving in. But it was time for a reality check. He had accomplished more than most men would have. He was walking—hell, he was running again—when the doctors said he'd be in a leg brace the rest of his life. He should quit while he was ahead. If he went back to playing football, chances were good he'd reinjure his leg. Maybe next time his prognosis would be even worse.

Mac called his agent's office and got Andy's secretary. "Tell Andy I'll be in his office about four o'clock this afternoon. I'll fill him in on everything when I see him."

He headed out the door dressed in a starched white oxford-cloth shirt belted into crisp new jeans and almost new ostrich cowboy boots, so he'd be ready if the media caught sight of him in Dallas. Mac wanted to look confident and ready to go back to work for the Tornadoes on the outside, even if he didn't feel quite that way inside.

He stopped at the boys' bunkhouse to check on Brad Templeton, but apparently the kids had already headed over to the cookhouse for breakfast. He was about to leave when he heard something hit the tile floor in the communal bathroom. He stepped inside. "Who's there?"

Nobody answered, but Mac knocked on the frame of the open bathroom doorway and said, "Anybody here?"

Brad Templeton stepped out of one of the four shower-curtained stalls. "How'd you know I was here?"

"I heard something drop."

He made a face. "My plastic cup."

"Why aren't you at breakfast with the other kids?" Mac asked, leaning casually against the bathroom doorway to put the kid at ease.

"I told Gavin I didn't feel well."

Mac's easy pose evaporated. He took the few steps to bring him to Brad's side, whipped off the kid's New York Mets baseball cap and pressed his hand on Brad's forehead. It all happened so fast, Brad didn't have a chance to complain until Mac had already found out what he wanted to know. He replaced the cap. "No fever," he said.

Brad tugged the ball cap back down over his nearly bald head. "Naw. I'm okay."

Fever was one of the first—and worst—signs that a remission was over, that the leukemia was back. It wasn't something to be ignored. "Why'd you tell Gavin you were sick?" Mac asked.

Brad shrugged, the kind of kid gesture that could have meant anything, but really meant, *I couldn't tell him the truth.*

"What's on the agenda this morning?" Mac asked.

"Horseback riding," Brad mumbled.

"That sounds like fun. What's the problem?"

"I've never been on a horse before. I'd probably get bucked off and stomped to death. I don't want to die any sooner than I have to."

Mac grinned.

"That's not funny!" Brad said.

"You sound exactly like I did when I went riding the first time. Funny how being sick makes you want to live all the more, isn't it?"

Brad's brows rose almost to the brim of his ball cap. It was one thing for Mac to say he'd been sick, another for him to express a feeling that could only be had by someone who had personally faced death.

"Come on," Mac said, putting a hand on Brad's shoulder and ushering him toward the door. "Let's get you fed. I know just the pony for you. Gentle as a lamb."

"What's his name?" Brad asked.

Mac grinned. "Buttercup."

MAC PACED THE confines of Andy Dennison's office, from the bat signed by Ken Griffey, Jr., in one corner, to the football signed by Joe Montana in the other and back again. His agent had become his friend, and now he needed some friendly advice. But Andy was late.

He had too much time to think.

Andy must have leaked what time Mac was landing at Dallas/Fort Worth International Airport, because a bunch of photographers and reporters had been waiting for him when he exited the jetway. He had smiled for the cameras as he walked quickly toward the chauffeur-driven limousine waiting for him outside.

"It's great to see you walking so well, Mac," one reporter commented. "Will you be back with the Tornadoes this fall?"

"That's my plan," Mac said.

"You can walk. But can you run?" another reporter asked.

Mac smiled more broadly. "Does a Texas dog have fleas?"

Everybody laughed, but the reporter persisted. "What's your time for the förty?"

Mac's time for the forty-yard dash wasn't anywhere near the four-point-something-second range of most wide receivers, and nothing close to his own previous time. His hesitation in answering hinted at the problems he was having, and the reporters, smelling blood, attacked in earnest.

"Have you come to Dallas to announce your retirement?" one speculated.

"No," Mac said flatly.

"Are you here to see a doctor about your leg?"

"No."

"Are you negotiating with the Tornadoes to get your spot on the team back?"

"No comment."

That gave them more meat to chew on and distracted them from other lines of questioning. They asked a dozen more questions aimed at determining his exact status with the Tornadoes, before he reached the limousine and safety.

"Remind me to kill Andy when I see him," he muttered to Andy's driver.

The old man laughed. "He thought you could use the publicity."

"Why wasn't he here to keep the wolves off of me?"

"He's working on a big deal. Said he'd see you at the office at four, like you asked. You're all set up to stay at the Wyndham Hotel. I can take you there to freshen up, if you'd like."

"I need to make another stop first." Mac gave Andy's chauffeur the address of the sex therapist, who had agreed to see him today during a time someone else had canceled an appointment.

Dr. Timothy Douglas had first talked to Mac in the hospital after one of his operations, when Mac was scared to death that he would be impotent for life because nothing seemed to be working. The doctor had reassured Mac that the medication he was taking—and his state of agitation over the problem—had caused his lack of sex drive.

Douglas was not much older than Mac, but he was balding and wore spectacles, both of which made him look more distinguished. The good doctor had returned several times over the years to talk to Mac in the hospital, and it was during one of those discussions that Mac had admitted he was a virgin.

Douglas hadn't been able to control a smile. "Good for you," he'd said. "Too many men are indiscriminate these days."

"Sorry to burst your bubble, Doc, but I doubt I'd be able to say that if I'd been out of this bed more than a day at a time over the past couple of years."

Douglas patted his shoulder and said, "Wait for the right woman, Mac. You won't be sorry."

Douglas was the only person in the world who knew Mac's secret. And the only one he felt comfortable telling about Jewel's secret. Surely the good doctor could come up with some suggestions for how Mac could help Jewel without hurting her.

"This is a doctor's office," the chauffeur said when he stopped in front of the address Mac had given him.

"Sure is," Mac said. "Meet me back here in an hour."

Mac let himself out of the sleek black car and headed inside the office building.

The hour Mac spent with Timothy Douglas had been well worth the time and trouble to get there. As he paced his agent's office, Mac worked through the various suggestions Douglas had made for how he could help Jewel.

"Patience is essential," Douglas said. "Thoughtfulness. Consideration. All the things you would normally expect in a loving relationship. Only, each step of the way, you need to check with Jewel to make sure she's still with you. Understand?"

Mac understood all right. The man was supposed to control himself while he attended to the woman first. "What if I can't wait?" he blurted, his face crimson with embarrassment.

"Do you care for this woman?" Douglas asked.

"Why the hell do you think I'm so worried?" Mac shot back. "What if I lose control and make things worse?"

"Be sure you're thinking of her at the crucial moment, instead of yourself, and everything will turn out fine."

"That's all there is to it?" Mac asked skeptically.

"Sex is a natural bodily function," Douglas said. "We're supposed to procreate. Your body will know what to do, even if you don't."

Mac took comfort in that last word of advice. But as he was very well aware, knowing technically what to do, and actually doing it, sometimes turned out to be two entirely different things.

On Mac's next lap across his agent's office, the door opened and Andy Dennison stepped inside.

"Hi there, Mac. What's new?"

"I can walk. And I can run."

Andy smiled and crossed to shake Mac's hand. "Congratulations. I should have known you would do what you promised. How about a cigar to celebrate?"

"No thanks," Mac said with a smile. "I'm in training."

"You don't mind if I have one." Andy crossed to his desk, took a cigar from a box on top of it, clipped the end with a sterling silver device, sniffed it and rolled the tobacco lovingly between his fingers. That was as far as he could go. No smoking was allowed in the building.

"When can I set up an appointment with the Tornadoes?" Andy asked.

"Not so fast," Mac said, seating himself in one of the two modern chrome and black leather chairs facing the desk. "What's the last date I could show up in training camp and still have a chance to make the team?"

"Depends on how fast you can run when you show up," Andy said bluntly.

"How fast is the new kid?"

Andy gave Mac a figure for the forty that made sweat bead on Mac's forehead. It was two seconds better than Mac's best time before he was injured.

"What about his hands?"

"Misses a few. Fumbles now and again."

Mac smiled. "Then I have a chance. Being fastest isn't everything. I proved that when I played."

"Yeah. But being slow will get you cut from the team," Andy pointed out.

"How slow is too slow?" Mac asked, leaning forward, his elbows on his knees.

Andy shrugged. "Hard to say. But if you aren't within a second or two of your best time…" Andy shrugged again.

Mac sighed and sat back, crossing his good ankle over his scarred knee. "I was afraid of that."

"Look, there's been some interest in using you as a sports commentator. Why not let me follow up and—"

"That isn't what I want to do with my life."

"What are you planning to do? I mean, if you don't make the team?"

Mac drew a complete blank. "I don't know. I haven't thought about it much."

"Maybe you should," Andy said. "Think about that sportscasting job. It's national television, lots of exposure, possibility of advertising bucks. Lot of dough in a job like that."

"Lots of travel, too," Mac said.

"Yeah, there's that."

"I want to settle down somewhere and have a family."

Andy cleared his throat. "Uh. I heard about that stop you made this afternoon. Anything I can do to help?"

Mac laughed. "It's taken care of, but thanks for the offer."

"Sure, Mac, just know I'm there if you need me. By the way, who's the girl?"

"Knowing your penchant for publicity I figure I'll keep that to myself for a while."

"Hey. Whatever you want," Andy said. "By the way, how long are you going to be in town?"

"Just overnight."

"Anxious to get back to your girl?" Andy said with a sly smile.

Mac thought about it, smiled and answered, "Yeah. I am."

"Look, I know some folks who'd like to have dinner with you. How about it?"

"Will it help you out?"

Andy grinned. "You're a great guy, Mac. I knew you'd come through. I'll have a tux delivered to your hotel room, and I'll have my limo pick you up at eight."

"A tux! What kind of shindig is this?"

"Charity ball in Fort Worth, complete with politicians and socialites. Won't hurt you to be seen there, Mac. You can use all the good press you can get. You'll be sitting at the mayor's table."

Mac shook his head. "How do I let you talk me into these things?"

Andy stuck the cigar between his teeth and grinned. "You like me?"

Instead of laughing, Mac looked Andy in the eye and said, "You stuck with me when a lot of other folks didn't. I'm not likely to forget that anytime soon." He left before Andy could form a response.

CHAPTER ELEVEN

COLT SAT ON THE sagging back porch of Jenny's house waiting for Huck to come back out. He tugged at the frayed knee of his jeans, making the tear worse, then glanced up at the hot, noonday sun. He couldn't get what Mac had said about Huck and Jenny out of his mind.

College is a long way off. Maybe they'll change their minds about each other.

Colt would never do anything to separate the two of them—not that he believed anything could alter Jenny's devotion to Huck—but Mac had offered him a sort of hope he hadn't allowed himself to feel in a very long time.

Lately, Colt let his eyes linger on her more. He let his heart fall more completely under her spell. Even though his head said it was a stupid thing to do.

"Hey, Colt. You ready to go?"

Colt leapt up guiltily as the kitchen screen door slammed and stuck his hands deep into his back pockets. "Yeah. Sure." *Good thing Huck couldn't read his mind.*

"You're acting awful jumpy lately. What's your problem?" Huck asked as he crossed past Colt and down the creaking steps. "Some girl finally caught your eye?" he teased.

Maybe Huck could read minds, Colt thought uncomfortably.

"Who is it? Sarah Logan? Freda Barnett? I know— Betty Lou Tucker!"

Betty Lou Tucker was the prettiest—and most curvaceous—girl in school. Huck was way off the mark. The only girl Colt ever thought about was Jenny. And Jenny wasn't beautiful, she was just...Jenny. Colt thought of Jenny looking up at him with her bluer-than-blue eyes and felt the heat rising up his throat to make visible spots on his cheeks.

"Thought so," Huck said with a laugh. "Betty Lou's been looking at a lot of guys since she broke up with Bobby Ray." Huck unlooped the reins from the tie rail in front of the Double D ranch house and mounted his horse. "You coming with me, or you gonna sit on Jenny's back porch all day?"

"I...uh...think I'll wait to talk to Jenny before I leave... about some stuff."

Huck shook his head in disgust. "Jenny's gotta feed the little ones before she can do anything. You might be waiting a while. She was asking me if I could help her out, but I've got better things to do with my time than housework. You're welcome to take my place."

"Maybe I'll do that," Colt said, his heart thumping a little harder.

"See you tonight at the movies?" Huck asked.

"Naw. My dad asked me to do some bookkeeping with him."

"When are you gonna tell him you're not gonna stay on the ranch?" Huck asked.

"Sometime," Colt said.

"Better be soon, or he'll be depending on you so much you'll never get out," Huck warned.

"I hear you," Colt said irritably.

Huck kicked his horse into a lope, raising a choking cloud of dust from the dry, sunbaked dirt around the house.

Colt stepped back and waved away the worst of it so he

could breathe, then turned and stared at the screen door. All he had to do was knock and offer his help. It was bound to seem a little odd to Jenny for him to volunteer, since he'd never been in her house before.

There was a reason for that. He stayed away from sick people, and her mother had been sick nearly the whole time he'd known her. Her mother's breast cancer had gone into remission for a long time, but after the youngest child was born, it had come back.

Now Mrs. Wright was dying of cancer. Colt knew what that meant. Hair falling out from chemotherapy. Frail limbs. Eyes dead long before the body was. He had seen too much of it at Camp LittleHawk. Enough to know that it hurt desperately to like—let alone love—someone who was ill and who might or might not survive another week, another month, another year.

The only thing that could make him go inside Jenny's house right now was the knowledge that he would get to spend time alone with her. They would probably talk and maybe laugh together. That possibility was worth having to share Jenny's pain as she tended to her dying mother.

But Huck had said Jenny was feeding the little ones. Colt was the baby in his family, but he figured he could probably manage whatever Jenny asked of him.

Colt knocked on the door, said, "Jenny, I'm coming in," and let himself inside. He immediately took off his Western straw hat and stood still inside the screen door until his eyes adjusted to the darker room. When he could see, he found Jenny staring at him, her jaw hanging open.

"Colt. What are you doing in here?"

"Huck thought you might need some help." He clutched the hat against his chest feeling foolish, but said, "Here I am."

She smiled, and he knew it was going to be all right. He looked for a place to hang his hat, but didn't see anything.

"Put it on top of the refrigerator," she said. "That way Tyler and James can't get to it."

He looked at the baby sitting in the high chair before her and the older child sitting in a youth chair next to him. "They seem pretty well lassoed," he said, but he put the hat where she told him, anyway.

She gestured him toward her. "This is Randy," she said, sticking another spoonful of something gross looking in the baby's mouth, "and next to him is Sam. Tyler and James are playing in their room.

"Here. You can take my place." She rose and handed Colt the baby spoon and the open jar of baby food. "Randy loves peas."

Colt took one look at the contents of the jar and nearly gagged. "This doesn't look edible."

Jenny laughed, and he felt his whole body go still at the sound. "Don't tell Randy. He eats it like it was green ice cream."

Colt sat in the chair she had vacated and aimed a spoon of peas in Randy's direction. When his mouth opened, Colt shoved it in, and Randy cleaned it off. "He's a human vacuum cleaner!"

"He'll probably end up as big and tall as my dad," Jenny said as she set a plate of more recognizable food in front of Sam. The music had gone out of her voice by the time she got to the end of her sentence.

"Where is your dad?"

"He left," she said, her eyes focused on Sam. "Took off when Mom got sick the second time."

"I'm sorry, Jenny. I didn't know."

She tried to make light of it. "Can't really blame him.

It isn't pretty to watch someone die. He loved her very much, you know."

Colt couldn't believe how matter-of-factly she was speaking about such a tragic situation. "It must be hard for you and your mom to get along on your own."

Her chin came up, and she looked at him with her incredible blue eyes. "We manage."

He heard her message loud and clear: *Don't feel sorry for me.* He admired her gumption. But what choice did she have? She wasn't old enough to leave home and get a job. Where would she go? He realized now why she had been so worried about being left behind by Huck.

"Good thing you have so much help around the house," he said. "All those brothers, I mean."

"I'm the eldest," she said. "Tyler is ten, James is nine, Sam is five and Randy will be one in a couple of months."

"Who takes care of them when you're in school?"

"Mom has a sister who takes care of her during the days and keeps an eye on the little ones. I pick up the slack at night and give Aunt Lenore a rest."

Colt caught her glance for a moment and saw a sort of desperation he had often felt himself. A yearning to be free to follow your own path, to see the world, to explore to your heart's content. And the knowledge that destiny—or your parents or family—had other plans for you.

He had thought Huck was the only impediment to having Jenny. He saw now what the future held for her as well as she probably saw it herself. Unless she ran away, and he did not see Jenny as the kind of person who ran away from anything, she would be tied to her family until the boys were grown.

Huck would leave her behind when she couldn't go with him, because Huck would never understand why she couldn't go. Colt understood, though. It was the same rea-

son he might never fly jets. Because she couldn't bear to
hurt her family to please herself. As he could never bear
to hurt his.

Colt wanted to tell her that he understood. That he knew
what she faced. That he would be there for her, even if
Huck wasn't.

What if you get a chance to fly jets? an inner voice
asked. *Would you stay and work at Hawk's Pride just to
be near Jenny?*

Colt was glad he didn't have to make that kind of decision for four years. He would be here for her now. Even
though she was Huck's girl. And might always be.

JEWEL, PATTY AND GAVIN were sitting in the sand at the bottom of a canyon with eleven campers, pencils and notepads
in hand, sketching the primitive art etched on the stone
canyon wall that rose up on one side of them.

Some of the kids were sitting cross-legged, some lay on
their stomachs. Only one child had not relaxed and made
himself comfortable. The twelfth camper, Brad Templeton,
stood directly in front of the wall, staring up at it intently.

"How are you doing?" Jewel asked the campers as she
rose and began to walk among them to see what they had
produced in the half hour they had been drawing.

"Okay."

"Pretty good."

"What's that thing there?" A girl's finger pointed to a
stick horse etched on the stone wall.

"What does it look like?" Jewel asked.

"It's a horse, dummy," the boy sitting next to the girl
said scornfully.

"Yes, it is, Louis," Jewel said. "But you can see why
Nolie might not recognize it. It could be some other animal."

"It has a long tail and pointy ears like a horse," Louis said.

"True. But some dogs have long tails and pointy ears."

"Oh," Louis said thoughtfully. "It looked like a horse to me."

"That's why we're making these drawings," Jewel explained. "And writing down what we think they mean." She put a supportive hand on Patty's shoulder as she encouraged one of the campers and exchanged a thankful look with Gavin, who had one of the youngest—and most homesick—campers sitting in his lap.

"We'll send your drawings to an archaeologist at the university who studies primitive art. She can tell us what she thinks the drawing means. When I send you her findings later this summer, you can compare your conclusions with hers."

"Does the drawing really mean something?" another little girl asked, staring at the primitive figures.

Jewel shrugged and smiled. "I don't know. Maybe someone a long time ago was just having fun drawing."

The kids laughed.

Jewel had reached Brad's side and noticed his drawing pad was blank. "Is something wrong, Brad?" she asked quietly.

He kept his eyes on the stone wall and spoke in a voice that only she could hear. "I know what it means," he said.

"You do?" Jewel turned to stare at the wall of stick figures and arrows pointing in different directions with a sun above it all. "Tell me. I've always been curious."

"What does it matter? What does anything matter?"

Jewel's brow furrowed. "You can't give up, Brad," she said.

"Why not?" he shot back. "People give up on stuff all the time. They quit hobbies and they quit school and they quit jobs."

"They don't quit living," she said.

"Some do," he said stubbornly. "They just stop doing things. You know what I mean."

Jewel felt a chill run down her spine. *People like her. As afraid of living as Brad was of dying.* "Tell me about the drawings, Brad."

He turned to look up at the wall. "The man wants to go somewhere far away, to have an adventure. But he isn't sure which is the best way to go. So he doesn't go anywhere at all. He stays right where he is. Where it's safe."

Jewel stared at the wall. The sun shone brightly above a stick-figure man and his stick-figure horse. They were surrounded by arrows pointing in all different directions—some of them back at the man himself.

He doesn't go anywhere at all. He stays right where he is. Where it's safe.

Jewel's throat squeezed closed. Brad might have been describing her own life for the past six years. Recently she had begun to make changes, but even so, she had been relying on Mac to get her over the worst hurdles. That had to stop. She had to start thinking about moving forward on her own. Or she might end up stuck forever right where she was.

She had to stop letting the past control her present. She had to open herself to new relationships. She couldn't count on Mac to solve her problems. He wanted to be her friend, nothing more. That had become apparent when she discovered from reading the newspapers the real reason he had gone to Dallas three days ago.

She had died a little inside when she opened the Dallas newspaper the day after Mac had left and found a picture of Mac and Eve Latham smiling at each other at a Fort Worth charity function. If Eve was the woman Mac wanted, Jewel had to accept that and move on. She had to find the courage to start living again—without Mac's help.

The same way Brad had to keep on living, despite the fact he might be dying. "Do you think he ever took the trip?" Jewel asked softly.

Brad shook his head, and a tear spilled on his cheek. He knuckled it away with his fist. "He waited too late," Brad whispered.

Jewel took a step closer and enfolded Brad in her arms. Her chin quivered, and she gritted her teeth to keep from making any sound. How could she have been working here all these years and not have seen what Brad could see so clearly? How could she have let so many years go by not living life when it was so precious? How could she have given fear such a stranglehold on her future?

"It's never too late, Brad," she said fiercely. "All you have to do is take that first step, and then another, and another." She rubbed his shoulders soothingly, then pushed him back and tipped up his chin so she could see his eyes beneath the baseball cap. "Just one step, Brad. And the adventure begins."

"Everything all right here?" Gavin had brought the homesick child with him in his arms.

Jewel swallowed back the knot in her throat and turned to Gavin with a smile. "Sure. I think Brad is ready to do some drawing. Right, Brad?"

"Yeah," he mumbled.

"This one is about ready to go back," Gavin said, gesturing to the little girl with his chin. She looked happy and comfortable in Gavin's arms. He really was a great guy, Jewel thought, just not the guy for her.

"Tell you what," Jewel said. "Why don't you and Patty gather up everyone else and get them started back. I'll stay here a little while longer with Brad."

"You sure?" Gavin asked doubtfully. "It's pretty isolated out here."

Jewel laughed. "Hawk's Pride is safer than most big cities. Brad and I will be fine."

"Okay," Gavin said with a smile. "See you later."

"Thanks, Gavin."

"You're welcome, Boss," he said over his shoulder. "Come on, guys. Let's get you all mounted up," he called to the campers. "Day's wastin'."

Jewel helped Gavin and Patty make sure all the campers were comfortable for the horseback ride up out of the canyon. Then she crossed back to where Brad was industriously working on his drawing.

"That's looking pretty good," Jewel said, admiring his sketch.

"I've had a lot of time to practice," Brad said, his lips curling wryly.

"What do you want to be when you grow up?" Jewel asked.

"I wanted to be a football player," Brad said, changing it to the past tense. "Like Mac Macready."

"Let's get some practice, then," Mac said.

Jewel and Brad both jerked their heads toward the sound of Mac's voice. He dismounted from his horse, a football tucked into his elbow.

Jewel was surprised Mac had returned, especially after seeing the photo of him with his arm around Eve Latham. Her first impulse was to rail at him, but she had no claims on Mac Macready. What "business" he did in his free time was up to him. She just wished he hadn't lied to her about why he had gone to Dallas. That wasn't something friends did to friends.

"What are you doing here?" Jewel said, her voice sharp despite her wish to keep it level.

"I brought a football, figuring I'd throw a few passes to the kids, but I passed them on the way down, headed back for lunch. Gavin told me you'd stayed behind with Brad, so I thought I'd join you."

"Hi, Mac," Brad said shyly.

"Hi, Brad," Mac said, tossing him the football. "I need to talk with Jewel for a minute. Why don't you go find us a place where you can throw me a few?"

"You want me to throw to you?"

"You want to be a football player someday, don't you? No time like the present to start practicing."

Brad shot Jewel a questioning look. *Should I let myself hope? Should I take him up on his offer?*

"One step, Brad," she said softly. "And the adventure begins."

The boy smiled broadly and turned back to Mac. "Okay, Mac. I'll go find us a good spot." He turned and headed on the run toward a sandy stretch that extended around a curve in the canyon wall.

Jewel compared the Mac in the newspaper photo to the Mac standing before her. He had looked impressively handsome in a tuxedo. But he was just as impressive dressed in a cutoff T-shirt that showed off a washboard midriff and rippling biceps. Cutoff jeans revealed his scarred leg, but emphasized his height. Tennis shoes and a Texas Rangers baseball cap with his blond hair sticking out every which-away made him look like one of the kids.

She was quite aware he was not.

Jewel forced herself to stand still as Mac eyed her up and down in return. She was wearing a T-shirt with the neck cut out that was also cut off at midriff, exposing her narrow waist, and very short, fringed cutoffs that showed off her long legs. She might as well have been naked. The look in his eyes made her skin feel prickly all over.

Now that he was back, his gaze seemed to say, they could pick up where they had left off, kissing and touching.

But she could not forget the possessive look in Eve's eyes, or the way Mac's arm reached snugly around her. She was very well aware of how long he had been gone and who he had been with, but she couldn't very well confront him with Brad nearby.

"I missed you," he said softly.

"From the picture in the newspaper I wouldn't have said you were too lonely."

He frowned. "What picture?"

"The one of you with your arm around Eve Latham at a charity ball."

Mac groaned. "I can explain—"

"Later," she said, turning to walk away from him. "Brad is waiting for you."

He caught her arm. "I want this cleared up now. It was nothing, Jewel. Publicity my agent set up."

"With Eve Latham?" she said, raising a doubtful brow.

"With her father, actually. He's a big fan of the Tornadoes."

"I suppose Eve just happened to be there?"

"Believe me, I didn't set that up. In fact, I'd planned to come right back the next morning, but Eve's father arranged a golf game the next morning with the manager of the Tornadoes that I couldn't very well get out of, and my agent snuck a few more appearances into the mix. Believe me, I only wanted to get back here as quickly as I could."

"Why?" she said, staring him in the eye. "So you could throw footballs to adoring campers?"

For the first time he looked angry. "You know better," he said through clenched teeth.

"Do I? I have no claim on you, Mac. If you'd rather not

follow through on what you promised, all you have to do is say so. It isn't necessary to make excuses."

An instant later, he was kissing her hard on the mouth. It was as much a kiss of anger as of passion. Jewel felt both angry and passionate in return. Mac let her go abruptly, his breathing erratic, and said, "I have no intention of backing out on my promise to you. It's up to you whether you choose to take advantage of my offer."

Jewel stared at Mac, appalled at how easily he had aroused her, how easily he had made her want him. She was afraid to let Mac back in. "I thought you'd lied to me about why you went to Dallas," she admitted.

"I would never lie to you, Jewel. That's not something friends do."

She wanted to believe him. She wanted to go back to trusting him. Fear made her cautious. Fear made her reluctant to let him back into her life. Fear could keep her stuck in the same rut forever.

Jewel glanced at the etching on the stone wall. She took a deep breath and let it out. "All right, Mac. You've got yourself a deal."

She held out her hand for him to shake, and Mac raised it to his mouth, kissing it like a courtier of old. His grin reappeared, and she felt her insides flip-flop.

"Very well, my little hyacinth," he said.

"That's a flower."

"And a precious stone," he assured her. "See you in a little while." He let go of her and loped across the sand, calling out to Brad to throw him the ball.

Jewel stared at her hand where Mac had kissed it, then raised her fingertips to her recently kissed lips. Mac had plainly thrown down the gauntlet. She had a chance to grab for life with both hands. She had a chance to practice kissing and touching with him. And she had a chance to explore a relationship with him beyond the friendship they had shared for so many years. She could take it, or reject it. The choice was hers.

What she must not do was make no choice at all.

If she hadn't spent the past half hour in Brad Templeton's company, she might have chickened out. But Jewel couldn't very well demand Brad reach out for life, if she wasn't going to do it herself.

Brad threw Mac the ball and came racing back to her holding out his notepad and pencil.

Jewel exchanged a glance with Mac that was the closest she had ever come to flirting with him. It promised everything…later. She was rewarded with a look that made her body curl inside and her breasts feel achy and swollen.

Jewel felt a tug on her T-shirt and looked down at Brad, who stood beside her again, his eyes gleaming with delight. Oh, yes. Football. And hope.

"I'll take those things," she said, reaching out for Brad's notepad and pencil.

Brad turned and trotted right back to Mac. She saw the boy swallow hard as he reached out for the football Mac was handing him. Jewel thanked Mac with her eyes and got a wink that flustered her in return.

She knew better than to tell either male not to overdo it. But Jewel was concerned as the sun rose higher and Brad continued to throw the ball and Mac continued to run for it. They were both drenched with sweat. Brad looked flushed. And Mac was starting to limp.

"Hey, you two. How about a break?"

She caught Mac's eye and gave him a warning look. He glanced at Brad and said, "I'm whipped, partner. How about a tall, cold glass? Of water, that is," he said, slapping Brad on the shoulder as they started back toward where Jewel sat in the shade of the canyon wall.

Jewel stood up with the canteens ready and handed one to each of them. She lifted Brad's hat as though to rearrange it on his head and surreptitiously checked for a fever. He seemed warm, but the sun was hot. "How are you feeling?" she asked, unable to keep the concern from her voice.

"Fantastic," Brad said, grinning for the first time since he had arrived at camp. "That was fun, Mac. Thanks."

"Tell you what I'm going to do, partner. I'm going to autograph this football to you with thanks for a strong throwing arm, so you can take it home with you."

"Wow! That would be neat," Brad said, sounding more like a kid his age every minute. He flopped down onto the sand, looking exhausted but happy.

Jewel was aware of Mac's wince as he settled onto the ground beside Brad.

"I've got some snacks that'll keep us until we can get some lunch," she said, dropping to her knees and opening what was left of the graham crackers and peanut butter and celery she had brought for the campers. "That'll also give you two a chance to cool off before we make the ride home."

As they munched, Mac and Brad talked. Jewel watched them closely. Brad had a smile on his face and talked a mile a minute, as though someone had turned up the rpms on a record. Mac listened. He didn't look at her often, but often enough to remind her that he was ready and willing whenever she wanted to take that final leap of faith. "Are you ready to head back now?" Jewel asked, when Brad had wound down a little.

"I guess," Brad said. "Can we do this again?" he asked Mac as he shoved himself to his feet.

"As often as you want before you leave," Mac said.

Jewel noticed Mac wincing again as he straightened his scarred leg.

He caught her watching him and grinned, as though he hadn't just been in pain. "Don't worry. Everything important is working just fine." He leered at her, making it clear exactly what he meant.

Jewel felt flustered and excited. And anxious. Mac looked exhausted. He was using humor—and sexual tension—to distract her and doing a pretty good job. She was also concerned about Brad. He seemed awfully red-faced even after his rest. "Are you sure you're both feeling all right?" she asked.

"I'm doing great!" Brad said.

"I'm just fine," Mac said.

Jewel pursed her lips. Typical males. Everything was fine until they keeled over. She decided to keep a close eye on both of them.

Mac was still grinning as he ushered Brad past her and headed for the horses, whispering for her ears only, "You look beautiful, Amethyst. And very, very desirable. I can't wait for…later."

Jewel's heart started to pound as she stared at Mac's back, wondering if she would have the courage to do this evening what she had been waiting six years to do. His calling her "Amethyst" reminded her that they had been friends for a very long time. That he would never hurt her. That she could trust him.

Surely Brad's admonition about postponing life had made a difference. Surely she would be able to let go of the fear and move forward with her life. All she had to do was take one step. And the adventure would begin.

CHAPTER TWELVE

BRAD WAS A different child when he entered the cookhouse for lunch—happy, talkative, showing off his football to the other kids and stuffing down a plateful of lasagna as though it was the best meal he had ever eaten. Jewel was proud of Brad for reaching out with both hands toward the future and grateful to Mac for putting an ear-to-ear smile on the boy's face.

However, Mac had not joined them for lunch, pleading the need for a shower. The entire time Jewel ate, she could not get the image of him naked in the shower out of her mind. She had the craziest urge to join him there which, of course, she did not indulge.

After lunch, when the campers took a rest break in their cottages, Jewel had no excuse to linger in the cookhouse. She drew herself up from the bench where she had been sitting and headed toward her cottage, not sure whether she wanted Mac to be out of the shower or not.

When she entered the cottage she felt disappointed not to hear the shower running. There was her answer. She had wanted an excuse to see all of Mac and had been thwarted. She headed for the bathroom anyway, thinking it would be nice to take a quick, cool shower herself while the campers were napping. The bathroom door was open on her side, so she assumed the room was empty.

It was not.

Mac sat in the tub covered with white bubbles—which

she presumed had come from the glass-stoppered container of bubble bath she kept on the edge of the tub. He was leaning forward, his teeth gritted, his hands apparently gripping his scarred leg.

"Mac?"

He whipped his head around, swore, then groaned. She saw his biceps ripple as he applied tremendous pressure to his leg.

"What is it?" she asked. "What's wrong?"

"Cramp," he gritted through his teeth.

She dropped to her knees on the fluffy bath mat beside the tub, her eyes focused on his straining face. "What can I do? How can I help?"

"I can't move...can't get out of the damned tub!"

"Do you want me to help you stand up?"

He shook his head violently and groaned again.

"How long has the muscle been cramped?" she asked.

"Too long," he snapped back.

His face was blanched with pain. The sweat on his brow and above his lip, which she at first thought had to be from the heat of the water, was apparently the result of fighting the cramp. For how long? Fifteen minutes? Twenty? "I'll call 911," she said, pushing off from the tub to stand up.

"Don't! I don't want news of this getting out."

"You need help, Mac," she said, angry because she was frightened.

"Then help me, damn it!"

"How?"

"Maybe two sets of hands working on the muscle will get it to uncramp more quickly."

She hesitated only a moment before dropping back down onto the bath mat. Before she could change her mind, she stuck her hands beneath the thin layer of bubbles into the water—which was merely lukewarm—and reached for his leg. Her hands tangled with his before she moved them upward, closer to his knee.

As she worked her fingers into the tightly clenched calf muscle she asked, "Has this happened before?"

He nodded. "Never this bad." His head rolled back and she watched his jaw muscles work as he struggled to endure the pain without making a sound.

"Please let me call someone, Mac."

"No," he grated out.

"Then let me run some more hot water. Wouldn't that help?"

He met her gaze, struggled with the decision, then nodded.

She tipped the lever to empty the tub, realizing after she did so, that the bubbles were going to run out with the water, leaving Mac exposed. But she couldn't worry about his modesty—or hers—right now. She was too worried about his pain and the ramifications of Mac having such severe cramps in his leg after what would have been a very light workout if he had really been playing football.

The water drained quickly, and a slurping sound announced the tub was empty. Jewel shot the lever closed and turned on the water, making it as hot as she thought he could stand.

"Too hot?" she asked, turning to look at him for the first time since the tub had begun draining.

"No. It feels good."

Her breath caught at the sight of him covered here and there with bubbles. She quickly turned her head away, but the image of him, wet curls caught on his nape, water pearled on his shoulders, bubbles caught in the curls on his chest—and on other curls—stayed with her.

But not for long. For the first time, she took a good look

at the leg she was massaging. "Mac, there's not much muscle left here. It's all scar tissue."

"I know," he said with a discouraged sigh. "That's the problem. What muscle there is left isn't enough to—" His hands gripped his ankle as an agonized cry tore from his throat. She moved her hands near his at the back of his ankle and felt the muscle spasming. The steaming hot water covered their hands as she held on tight with him for the sixty-five long seconds it took the spasm to pass. Suddenly, she felt the entire muscle ease.

Mac hissed out a breath and, after waiting to see if the tension would return, cautiously let go of his leg.

Jewel turned to look at him and saw his face was turned toward the tile wall. And that tears streamed from his eyes. "Oh, Mac."

"Go away, Jewel," he grated out.

She couldn't do that. Not with what she knew now.

Mac's football career was over. He knew it. And was grieving for it.

She didn't think about what she was doing, she just did it. Two seconds later she had her tennis shoes and socks off and had eased herself sideways into the tub on Mac's lap, her legs hanging over the side of the tub, her arms around his neck, her nose plastered against his throat. "I'm so sorry, Mac," she said, her nose burning, her eyes stinging with tears. "I'm so sorry."

At first she thought he was going to push her away, but his arms closed tight around her and he pulled her close, pressing his cheek tight against hers. She could feel him trembling, feel him struggling to hold back the sobs, until at last they broke free.

She held him close, crooning words that made no sense, offering the comfort of her arms and her love. *Oh, my God. I love him.* It was a stunning realization. A frightening one when she knew his life, now that his future was so uncertain, might very well move in a different direction than hers. But that would not stop what she felt for him. He was another part of her, a part she needed to feel whole inside.

Jewel had no idea how much time had passed when Mac's heaving body finally quieted. He seemed completely relaxed, as though he had accepted the inevitable and was now ready to move beyond it.

"You'd better turn off the water," he said in a voice that was amazingly calm.

Jewel lifted her head and realized the water had reached the rim of the tub and was threatening to spill over. She reached around and shut it off, then turned shyly back to Mac. "I should get off of you and let you finish your bath."

"I wish you wouldn't."

She laughed uncertainly. "What did you have in mind?"

In answer, he lifted her at the waist and rearranged her so she was facing him, her knees on either side of his hips. The extra weight of her legs caused the water to lap over the side of the tub, but Jewel had more important things to think about than a little water on the bathroom floor.

"Mac, do you think we should be doing this now? I mean, what if your leg—"

"Let me worry about my leg," he said.

When she opened her mouth to protest again, he covered it with his hand and said, "I'm fine. Really. Please, Jewel, don't leave me."

She kept her eyes focused on Mac's as he reached for the bottom of her soaked T-shirt and began to lift it up over her head. She raised her arms and let him remove it.

I love him. And I trust him, she realized.

Mac dropped the T-shirt onto the already soaked bath mat and reached behind her for the clasp of her bra. She gripped his shoulders and said nervously, "This is a first for me."

It was a warning and an offering and a prayer. *Please be careful. Please let my body please you. Please let me not be afraid.* She did not ask for what she wanted most. She did not say, *Please love me.* That was something Mac would have to offer on his own.

His eyes were intent on her face as he pulled her lacy, heavy-duty bra off and her Beautiful Breasts—with wonderful big B's, because Mac looked at them that way—fell free. The bra went the way of her T-shirt, and Mac reached out gently, reverently, to cup her breasts in his hands.

"Exquisite," he said, his thumbs flicking the nipples.

Jewel had to remind herself to breathe as sensation streaked from her nipples to a drawstring somewhere deep inside her womb and pulled it up tight. Her hands threaded into the damp hair at Mac's nape as he lowered his head to kiss each breast. His mouth latched onto a nipple and he sucked, gently at first, then more strongly.

Jewel's hips arched instinctively toward him.

"Easy," he said, his hands gripping her hips atop her cutoff jeans. "Slow and easy, Jewel. We have all the time in the world."

"I don't know what to do with my hands," she said anxiously. "Tell me what to do to please you."

He smiled. "You're doing fine."

"I'm not doing anything!" she replied pertly.

He lifted his hips, and she could feel his arousal.

"Oh. Well. I see."

Mac laughed, a rumbly sound, and kissed her quickly on the lips. "I love your innocence," he said, his eyes staring intently into hers. "I want to be the first, Jewel. I am so honored to be the first."

"But—"

He put his fingertips to her lips. "The first," he repeated.

In truth, this situation was so incredibly different from what had happened to her all those years ago, that the past didn't seem real anymore. Mac made her feel innocent, made her feel the joy and excitement—and normal fear— of an untouched woman.

He teased her and touched her and tasted her until they were both wrinkled from the water. And she did the same, enjoying the pleasure of rubbing her breasts against the crisp curls on his chest and returning the favor of kissing and caressing and sucking his nipples—which turned out to be surprisingly sensitive.

"We'd better get out of here," Mac said, "or we're going to turn into prunes."

Jewel felt a little shy standing up and stepping out of the tub. As much as she was tempted to look, she turned her back on Mac as he stood and stepped out of the tub behind her. She had already reached for a towel to cover her breasts, when he took it away from her.

He aligned his body with hers from behind, put his arms around her to cup her breasts and played with her nipples until they were aching and pointy. His mouth teased her throat beneath her ear with kisses, before he latched onto a particular spot and sucked hard enough to make her moan with pleasure.

"I'm only going to touch you," he said, explaining as his hands slid down the front of her, unsnapped her jeans, spread them wide and slid his hand beneath her panties. "To let you feel my hands on you."

She held her breath, expecting the fear to return. But it didn't. She felt only the warmth of his hand against her cooling flesh and the feel of his fingertips probing gently between her thighs. Slowly, carefully, he insinuated one finger inside her.

"Are you all right?" he asked.

"Uh-huh."

She felt his mouth curve into a smile against her cheek. "I think maybe you'd better breathe," he said.

She exhaled and then gasped a breath of air as his finger slid deeper inside her. "Oh."

He paused. "Did I hurt you?"

"No. I feel…" She searched for the word. *Strange. Full. Achy.* Yes, but more than that. "I feel good," she said. "This feels so right."

"I'm glad." He used his other hand to encourage her to spread her legs, so he would have easier access to her. And slipped another finger inside her.

Her breath was coming in erratic spurts, and she reminded herself to keep breathing.

"Still okay?" he asked.

She nodded, then made a sound when his thumb found the tiny bud at the apex of her thighs and began to caress it. Her knees started to buckle, nature's way of getting her prone, and Mac compensated by putting a strong arm around her midriff and pulling her back tight against him. She could feel his arousal against her buttocks, hard and pulsing.

Instead of being afraid, she was aroused. She was sure she could make love to him this time without running away. She was ready to move forward. She wanted to feel him inside her. "Mac," she said. "I'm not afraid anymore."

"Good," he replied, his voice husky. "Just relax and let me make love to you."

Let me make love to you. It was what she had wanted for a very long time. Jewel let herself fully enjoy what Mac was doing to her—making love to her—without worrying about whether he was *in love* with her. He was as considerate a lover as she could ever have hoped for. He cared for her. That would have to be enough for now.

Mac had one hand inside her jeans, the other tantalizing her nipple, while his mouth teased the flesh at her throat. She writhed against him as her body experienced all the joy and pleasure she had not allowed herself to feel in the past.

As the tension built inside her, she reached out to the pleasure, indulged in it, delighted in it, until she felt herself losing control. "Mac," she said, the fright back in her voice. "What's happening to me?"

"Something wonderful. Let it happen, Jewel. Let me do this for you."

She trusted Mac. As he had trusted her to comfort him. More than that. She loved him.

Jewel gave her body into his hands and was rewarded moments later with a shattering climax, her body shuddering with wave after wave of intense pleasure. "Mac," she gasped. "Mac."

"I know," he said, his voice gentle, his breathing as erratic as hers. "I know."

Jewel felt totally enervated and was barely aware when Mac picked her up in his arms and carried her to her bedroom. He pulled the sheets down on her bed, stood her up long enough to strip the wet cutoffs and panties off her, then tucked her under the covers before she had time to feel embarrassed at being naked.

She expected him to join her. But the last thing she saw before her eyes slid closed was Mac's taut, untanned buttocks as he walked out of the room.

MAC KNEW THAT JEWEL had expected him to join her in bed, and that he would have been welcome there. He could have eased the ache in his loins and gotten them both over hurdles that had stood in their way for years. He had learned from their recent lovemaking that he had not only the self-control—but the desire—to put Jewel's feelings and needs before his own.

Several things had stopped him from staying.

Mac had realized, as he was making love to Jewel, that he loved her. And not just as a friend, but as an inseparable part of himself. He wanted to spend his life with her. He wanted to plant his seed inside her and help her raise the children they would make together. He wanted to grow old with her.

Which raised a second problem. Mac Macready was another football has-been, who had no idea what he wanted to do with the rest of his life. After the horrific episode with his scarred leg in the tub, there was no denying the truth any longer. He would never play pro football again. Mac had not beaten the odds this time. He had lost.

It was a devastating realization.

If he had not had Jewel to hang on to, he didn't know what he would have done. She had understood his pain and his loss. She had offered comfort without platitudes. She obviously cared for him—even after seeing him at his most vulnerable.

None of the reasons he had for fearing commitment with a woman existed where Jewel was concerned. With her, Mac felt safe making that leap into the unknown, certain he could trust her to be there when he landed.

Which brought him to a third problem. Mac had no idea whether Jewel loved him merely as a friend or the way he wanted to be loved. As a man. As her lover. As her future husband.

Mac had collected Jewel's clothes before he left the bedroom, wrung out all her wet things and hung them in the bathroom to dry. He had dressed himself in Levi's and a

Western shirt, then laid himself down on his bed, his hands behind his head, to think.

On the way up out of the canyon at lunchtime, Jewel had encouraged Brad to tell Mac his interpretation of the primitive drawings on the canyon wall. Mac had listened attentively and heard in Brad's explanation an analogy of what life was like when it was lived in fear of reaching out for dreams. After all, dreams might never come true. You might end up disappointed, or in worse shape than if you had been satisfied with what you already had.

Mac had always believed in pursuing his dreams. He had never been indecisive. But clearly there were moments when old dreams had to be abandoned—and new dreams dreamed. Mac could no longer be a professional football player. So what else did he want to do with his life?

That wasn't an easy question to answer, because Mac had been so determined to regain the use of his scarred leg that he had refused to think about alternatives. Now he must. And he had to factor Jewel, and her commitment to Camp LittleHawk, into the equation.

The idea that rose immediately in his mind was such a simple solution—and yet so revolutionary in terms of how he had intended to spend his life—that Mac felt both excited and cautious about pursuing it. Maybe the best thing to do was to approach Jewel and see what she thought.

He was on his way back to her room when someone knocked hard and fast on the door to the cottage. He hurried to the door and opened it to find Gavin Talbot standing there.

"I think you better get Jewel and come to the boys' bunkhouse," he said. "Brad Templeton has a fever."

CHAPTER THIRTEEN

JEWEL BLAMED HERSELF for not recognizing that Brad's flushed face at lunch was caused not only by excitement but also by the fever that signaled the return of his leukemia—and the end of his second remission.

She could barely manage to keep a smile on her face as she belted Brad into the seat of the chartered plane for the short flight back to Dallas Children's Hospital, which was waiting to readmit him. Brad was gripping Mac's football tightly in the crook of one arm. His eyes were feverishly bright, and he had a smile plastered on his face as phony as the one on hers.

Jewel felt Mac's presence at her side. She saw the muscles in his scarred leg as he knelt facing Brad. Mac knew what the end of Brad's remission meant as well as she did. The boy's chances of survival were considerably less now than they had been at the beginning of the week. Mac might very well be bidding Brad Templeton goodbye for the last time.

"Hey, tiger," Mac said, tugging the brim of Brad's cap down playfully. "How's it going?"

Brad readjusted the cap and said, "It's back."

"I know," Mac said. "Remember what I said."

"Yeah. Doctors don't know everything."

Mac nodded soberly. "You keep fighting," he said, his voice low and fierce. He spoke so softly Jewel could barely hear him. "Don't give up. I expect to see you back here next summer. In fact, I expect you to be a counselor someday at a sports camp I'm thinking about starting, where lots of football players like Troy Aikman and Dan Marino and Reggie White and Jerry Rice will come and spend a little time with kids like you."

Jewel wondered where Mac had come up with the idea of a sports camp to encourage Brad. The way Brad's face had lit up, it had certainly been a good idea. She was surprised by the other message Brad had heard in Mac's speech.

"Does that mean you're not gonna play football anymore?" Brad asked.

Mac shook his head. "My leg can't tolerate it."

"So sometimes the doctors *are* right," Brad said.

Jewel watched as Mac gripped Brad's free hand in his and said, "Believe in yourself, and you'll come through fine."

"Time for takeoff, folks," the pilot announced. The nurse who was traveling with Brad was already buckled into her seat.

Mac stood, but Brad held on to his hand and pulled him back down onto his knee. "Good-bye, Mac," he said, a farewell in case he never came back. His chin wobbled and tears welled in his eyes.

"See you soon, Brad," Mac replied. He hugged the boy, who dropped the football and reached up to grab Mac tight around the neck with both hands.

"I don't want to go back to the hospital," Brad said. "Please don't make me leave."

"You have to go. You need help to get well."

"I'm not going to get well. I'm going to die!" Brad cried.

"You'd better not," Mac said severely. "I'm counting on you to come through for me."

Jewel watched as Mac pulled Brad's hands free and

reached down to retrieve the football from the floor of the plane and put it back in Brad's arms. "Remember, if I made it, you can make it, too," Mac said.

A tear spilled over as Brad glanced at Jewel for confirmation of Mac's promise.

Her throat was too swollen to speak. She whispered, "Come back soon, Brad," then backed away, keeping the smile on her face as long as she could. It was gone before she reached the door.

Once off the plane, Jewel ran all the way to the van. She had freely chosen to work with kids like Brad, knowing they didn't all make it. With some of them, it was especially hard to let go. Brad's life had seemed so full of possibilities, as Mac's had been all those years ago. Now Mac had lost his dream. And Brad might lose his life.

Jewel felt Mac's arms close around her from behind. He turned her to face the runway, which she saw through a haze of tears, and lifted her arm so she was waving at Brad as the chartered plane took off. Then Mac turned her to face him and closed his arms tightly around her, offering her a comforting shoulder to lay her head on.

"I can't bear it," she said. "First to see you so unhappy, and now Brad…" She couldn't say the word *dying*.

"Brad will make it," Mac said fervently.

"How can you be so sure?" she sobbed.

"I know these things," he said. "Besides, I'm going to need him when I start my sports camp for kids with cancer."

It took a moment for what he said to sink in. When it did, Jewel backed out of his arms and stared at him in shocked disbelief. "I thought you made that up for Brad's sake."

"Nope. It's for real." He opened the door of the van

and hustled her inside, then got into the driver's seat and started up the vehicle.

"Why haven't I heard about this sports camp before?" Jewel asked, wiping the tears from her eyes.

He grinned at her. "Because I just thought it up this afternoon."

"Oh."

"I wanted to talk to you about it before I went much further with the idea. What do you think about it?"

Jewel's first thought was that it would take Mac away from Hawk's Pride. That was selfish. What Mac planned to do would help a great many children. "I think what you're planning is one of the noblest, most considerate—"

The van veered to the berm and skidded to a halt. Before Jewel could say another word, Mac's arms were around her and his mouth had covered hers.

She had no time to think, only to feel. What she felt was overflowing love for this man who had so much strength, yet had let her see him when he was at his most vulnerable. She reached out to touch Mac's face tenderly, to thank him for being who he was.

He broke off the kiss abruptly, and she was caught by his gaze, which promised so much—hope, happiness and something else she was afraid to name, because she wanted it so much she feared she had merely wished it there.

"Look at me like that too long, love, and you're liable to get what you want right here and now, instead of when we get back to the cottage."

Jewel stared into Mac's blue eyes, her heart pounding. Had he really called her *love*? Had he said they were going to be making love in a few minutes? He didn't repeat himself, merely started up the van and pulled back onto the road.

Jewel suddenly realized why Mac had reached out to her

physically. Making love was an act to reaffirm life in the presence of death. *We can reach out for joy. We still have our lives ahead of us, whatever those lives may bring. This offer of lovemaking has nothing to do with Mac actually loving me. It's a reaction to Brad's illness.* She couldn't disagree with Mac's motive. Or with wanting to be held close, no matter what the reason. She wasn't going to deny him, or herself, the lovemaking he had promised.

"Tell me more about the camp," she said to break the strained silence.

"There isn't any more to tell," he replied. "It's just an idea right now. Do you have any suggestions?"

"Where do you plan to locate it?"

He frowned. "That's a problem. I probably have enough money left from my signing bonus with the Tornadoes to advertise the place and hire help for the first year. But I doubt whether I have enough to buy a piece of land and build buildings. Any suggestions?"

Jewel would have offered her facilities immediately, if she had thought he would accept. His explanation seemed to suggest he would be perfectly happy to open his camp right here.

The way he was looking at her, his heart in his eyes, gave her the courage to speak. "Camp LittleHawk belongs to my mother, but she's said it can be mine whenever I want it. I think having a sports program here—with famous football players participating on occasion—would be a welcome addition."

Mac smiled at her, and she felt her throat swell with emotion. "Thanks, Jewel. Incorporating my idea with what you've already established at Camp LittleHawk would please me very much."

They had arrived back at the cottage, and Mac quickly left the van and came around to help Jewel out. He took her hand and practically dragged her into the cottage. She realized why he was in such a hurry when, the instant they were inside with the door closed behind them, he pulled her into his arms and pressed her to him from breast to thigh. The evidence of his desire was hard to miss.

"I love you, Jewel."

The way he blurted it out seemed to surprise him as much as it surprised her. His eyes looked wary, as though he wished he hadn't spoken.

She shoved back the hurt and said, "It's all right, Mac. You don't have to say things like that."

The wary look disappeared, and his jaw firmed. "I don't *have* to say it. I *want* to say it. I love you, Jewel. I think I have for a very long time. I was afraid to do anything about it, afraid even to admit it, I think, because of all the bad things that happened when I loved someone in the past.

"What's happened to Brad made me realize I don't want to wait any longer. Life is too precious to waste a single day of it. I love you," he repeated. "And I want to make love with you."

Jewel took a deep breath and let it out. If he could find the courage to speak, so could she. "I love you, too, Mac. I've been afraid to tell you, afraid you wouldn't feel the same way. Afraid—"

She never got a chance to finish. His mouth captured hers at the same time he reached down to lift her up and carry her toward his bedroom.

MAC LAID JEWEL down on his bed as gently as he could and sat down beside her. He hadn't expected his courage to desert him, but it seemed for a moment that he wouldn't be able to go through with what he had planned.

It was late in the day, and the growing dusk gave everything in the room a soft, rosy glow. Jewel had never looked more beautiful to him. Or more trusting.

He had never been more nervous. Or frightened.

Think of her feelings, not your own.

"Are you all right?" he asked.

"More than all right," she said, a tender smile on her lips. "Kiss me please, Mac."

He had never been more gentle, more tender, more considerate of a woman. He brushed his mouth against hers, teased her lips, nipped at her and eased his tongue into her mouth to taste her. He felt her growing desire, her growing urgency to touch and taste in return.

He put his arms around her and pulled her close, feeling the tips of her breasts turn as pointy as pebbles when they made contact with his chest. "Would you like me to undress you?" he asked.

"I'd rather undress you," she said with a mischievous smile.

Mac was surprised, but when he thought about it, it seemed like a good idea. If he was undressed while she was still clothed, she would have the opportunity of escaping anytime she didn't feel comfortable. "Okay," he said. "Where would you like to start?"

She got off the bed and said, "Sit back on the bed, so I can take off your boots." She turned her back to him and tugged at each of his boot heels, while he gave her a shove with the opposite foot to help get the cowboy boots off. Then she pulled off his socks and said, "Stand up."

He stood barefoot on the wooden floor and watched as she slowly pulled his Western shirt out of his jeans and unsnapped the snaps, one at a time from the top downward. He wasn't wearing an undershirt, and she kissed her way down his chest. He was quivering by the time she reached the soft line of down that disappeared into his jeans.

When she ran her tongue around his navel, he nearly jumped out of his skin. "Good God," he muttered.

"You didn't like it?" she asked, looking up into his face.

He shoved both hands through his hair in agitation. "I'm about to explode because of it," he admitted.

Jewel smiled. "That's good, don't you think?"

Patience. Patience. Patience. He said it like a mantra, hoping he could endure her innocent exploration. He bit the inside of his cheek when she undid his belt, pulled it through the loops of his jeans and let it drop to the floor.

She unbuttoned the top button of his Levi's and began to lower the zipper. Her hand brushed against his tumescence, and he grabbed her wrist to avoid disaster. He wanted desperately to tell her it was the first time for him, but the words wouldn't come out. Instead he said, "It's been a while for me, Jewel. I don't want to disappoint you."

"What about Eve?" she asked.

He had forgotten all about Eve. "Nothing happened with her," he said.

"But you were gone so long that first night. And when you met her in Dallas, I thought—"

"She never turned me on," Mac blurted. "I couldn't... I didn't... Damn it, Jewel! You know what I'm trying to say." He could feel the heat rising on his throat. He couldn't believe what he had just confessed.

He waited for the laughter, and it came—a warm, happy sound that made his heart soar.

"Oh, Mac," Jewel said, her dark brown eyes bright with joy. "If you only knew how much I've wanted to hear you say those exact words—or something very like them."

"You have?"

"I've been terribly jealous," she admitted. Jewel rubbed her cheek against the curls on his chest, then kissed him, sending goose bumps skittering across his flesh. "I'm so glad," she said. "I've wanted you all to myself." The smile returned as she said, "And now I've got you."

She pushed his shirt off his shoulders until it caught at his wrists, effectively making him a prisoner. Instead of releasing the snaps, she shot him a grin and said, "You're my captive now. I can do whatever I want with you."

He leaned down to kiss her, and she stepped back and wagged her finger at him.

"Oh, no, you don't. I'm going to be doing the kissing and touching." She reached down and cupped him with her hand.

"You're going to kill me," Mac said through gritted teeth.

"You don't like it?" she teased.

"You know I like it," he retorted. "I like it so much I'm about to burst."

"Good," she said. "Now you stand right there while I undress."

Mac's eyes went wide when Jewel began a striptease in front of him. No woman had ever removed a T-shirt, bra, jeans and panties quite so seductively.

Don't think of yourself. Think of her.

Mac's pulse was pounding in his temples—and elsewhere. His whole body quivered with excitement.

"You're so beautiful," he said when she was naked at last.

She touched the crisscrossing scars on her face and the more visible scar on her thigh, where the operations to mend her leg had been performed. "You don't mind?"

He solved the problem of the imprisoning shirt by pulling his arms up over his head and using the shirt between his hands as a chain to encircle her and pull her close. "All I see is a beautiful, desirable woman."

She made a sound of pleasure when her breasts were finally pillowed against his naked chest. He spread his legs and urged her between them. Her hands curved around his waist and ventured up his back all the way to his nape. His blood raced as her hands caressed him.

He shuddered out a breath. *Think of her. Give her pleasure. Make it good for her. Don't think about yourself.*

He lowered his mouth to hers, sealing them together, mimicking the sex act with his tongue. The sounds she made in her throat caused his groin to tighten even more—if that was possible. He pushed against her and felt the heat of her through the denim as she rubbed her mound against him.

"I never knew it could feel so good," she whispered. "I never imagined how wonderful it would be."

He kissed her eyes and cheeks and nose before he reached her mouth again. She kissed him back eagerly, her tongue thrusting into his mouth, tasting him, dueling with him as he sought to return the favor.

Mac had forgotten about his jeans. She obviously had not. He felt her hands on the zipper again, and this time he let her lower it and reach inside.

"Okay?" she asked.

Think of her. Think of her. "Okay," he rasped.

But if she thought she was going to have it all her way, she was wrong. When Jewel reached for him, Mac got rid of his shirt and reached for her. He slipped two fingers inside her quickly, before she could protest, and settled his thumb on the tiny nub that was the source of so much delight.

"I can't…concentrate on you…when you're doing that…to me…" she panted.

His body was hard, pulsing in an agony of delight. It was a good thing she was not more experienced, although her innocence was likely to be his undoing.

He concentrated on bringing Jewel to a climax, focusing his attention on kissing her, touching her, pleasing her. Soon her hand was lax against him, her eyes closed, her jaw clenched as the pleasure overtook her. She leaned into him with her hips and arched her body toward him, making it easy for him to kiss her breasts, to suckle them and to tease them with his teeth and tongue.

Sweat beaded on his forehead, as he watched the play of expressions on her face. The rapture. The delight. The confusion as her body tightened more and more, as he pushed her higher and higher. The ecstasy as her body rippled with pleasure. And the love, as she looked up at him from hooded eyes and rose on tiptoe to find his mouth with hers and thank him with a kiss.

He picked her up, pulled down his bedcovers and laid her on the sheet. Her eyes had already slid closed before he pulled off his jeans and briefs and slid into bed beside her. He wrapped his arms around her and pulled her back into the hollow of his belly. He lay there bone hard and unsatisfied—but very pleased with himself.

He had brought Jewel to climax twice now and managed to control his own urgent need. Surely it would not be so difficult to put himself inside her and do it so she would not recognize his inexperience. She seemed to have put completely out of her mind what had happened six years ago.

He wished she were awake now. He wished he did not have to wait. If he could just make love to her this instant, he knew everything would be fine. But she seemed perfectly satisfied to lie beside him. She did not seem the least bit interested in any more touching or kissing.

Mac got the first hint of his error when he felt Jewel's hand sliding up his thigh, headed for the barely relaxed, unsatisfied part of him.

"Jewel? What's going on?"

She turned in his arms to face him. Her eyes were two shiny spots in the darkness. "I want to make love to you, Mac."

"We just—"

"I want you to put yourself inside me as deep as you can. I want to make you feel as wonderful as you've made me feel."

Mac swallowed hard. He felt like crying. "God, Jewel. Now?"

"Now." She touched him, and his body stood at rigid attention. She lay back and urged him over her.

She didn't have to urge him very hard.

For a moment she hesitated, and Mac realized she was remembering the past. This was the way he had found her with Harvey Barnes. Harvey was on top, and she was helpless beneath him. Like Harvey, Mac was stronger. He could do to her whatever he wanted.

Mac saw her rising fear and said, "It's me, Jewel."

Her whole body relaxed, and she smiled up at him sweetly. "I know, Mac. Love me, please. And let me love you."

Patience. Patience.

Patience went out the window the instant his body reached the entrance to hers. Mac tried to go slow, but she was wet and hot, and he wanted to be inside her so bad, that it took only three brief thrusts before he was buried deep inside her.

Mac paused, his weight on his elbows, his hips cradled in hers, and looked down, ashamed of his haste and afraid of what he would see on her face. "Jewel?"

"I'm fine," she said, her eyes glowing, her fingertips caressing his cheeks. "I'm wonderful."

It was all right. She couldn't tell it was his first time... because it was also the first time for her, he realized.

It was easy then, to think of her and not himself. "I don't want to hurt you," he said.

In response, she lifted her knees on either side of him, then wrapped her legs around his buttocks, seating him even more deeply inside her.

"My God," he muttered. "Jewel, I..." He withdrew and thrust as slowly and gently as he could, but the inevitable urge to mate, to put his seed inside her, drove him to move faster. When she lifted her hips and pushed back, the friction created unbelievably exquisite sensations.

Go slow. Slow down. Wait for her.

He saw Jewel's face through a haze of desire, heard her guttural sounds of pleasure and finally felt her body, slick and wet beneath him, begin to convulse.

Her body squeezed him, wringing pleasure beyond anything he could have imagined. He arched his head backward in an agony of joy as he spilled his seed inside her. His body pulsed, emptying itself in powerful thrusts before he lowered himself to lie beside her and wrapped her in his arms.

His breathing was ragged, his blood still pumping so hard it throbbed in his veins. He could not find breath for words, and would not have known what to say if he could have spoken.

"Thank you, Mac," Jewel whispered, snuggling close. "No man could have made me feel more lovely...or more loved."

Mac kissed her on the temple, a wordless thanks for saying what he had not been able to find words to express. The pleasure of this first time for him was all the sweeter, knowing she was happy.

Mac thought of all the women he could have made love to and had not. All the sex he had turned down in those early years, which had put him in the position of making love for the first time to the very woman he hoped to marry. As far as Mac was concerned, that meant Jewel was the only woman he would ever make love with.

Maybe he should have felt deprived. He did not.

Intuitively Mac knew that sex with a stranger—or even an acquaintance, would not have been as earth-shattering, or as bone-melting, as his experience with Jewel. Without the love he felt for her—and the love she felt for him in return—the sex act would not have brought him nearly so much joy.

"What are you thinking?" Jewel murmured.

"How much I enjoyed making love to you," he replied with a smile.

She kept her eyes lowered, and she was obviously struggling to speak as she said, "Considering the experience of the other women you must have slept with, I can't imagine my first efforts were much to shout about."

"Will you marry me?"

Mac had meant to distract her from a discussion of his sexual experience, and the proposal worked. But not in the way he had hoped.

"Does that mean you were satisfied?" she said, arching a brow. "I don't want to spend my life wondering how I stack up against the competition," she said wryly.

"I'm never going to be comparing you to anyone else," he muttered.

"Why don't I believe you?"

"Believe me."

"How can I believe you?" she said, rising to her elbow and staring down at him. "Are you telling me you never found a single other woman who was more appealing to you in bed than me?"

"That's exactly what I'm saying," he retorted, sitting up abruptly. "Because there were no other women."

She sat up just as quickly to face him, and the sheet dropped to her waist, exposing her breasts. "You're kidding, right?"

The sight of her nipples, full and rosy, set his pulse to galloping. "No man would kid about something like that. Until a few minutes ago I was a virgin. Now damn it, will you or won't you marry me?"

He had known she would laugh if she ever found out the truth. But he had never expected such gentle laughter. Such joyful laughter. Such loving laughter.

Jewel pushed him onto his back and straddled him with only the sheet between them. She leaned down, her lips close to his and said, "Oh, yes, my darling. I will most definitely marry you."

"It doesn't bother you that I don't have more experience in bed?" he demanded.

She chuckled. "Why should it? This way we can both learn exactly what pleases us. For instance, do you like it when I bite your earlobe like this?"

He shivered at the searing sensation of pleasure.

"Or would you rather I kissed this spot below your ear?"

Mac groaned. He had switched their positions and had her beneath him in two seconds flat. "I like it all," he said, nipping her earlobe and then kissing her below the ear, feeling the frisson of pleasure that rippled through her. "Just so long as I'm doing it with you."

"Well, then," she said, smiling up at him, "why don't we practice making a baby?"

Mac laughed, then cheerfully indulged the future mother of his children.

EPILOGUE

JEWEL SAT IN a rocker on the covered porch of the two-story Victorian house Mac had built for them. It stood on Hawk's Pride land her father had given them as a wedding present four years ago. Jewel had wanted a white house with lots of gingerbread trim with morning glories entwined in it, and that was exactly what she had.

She sighed with pleasure every time she looked around her. This was her favorite place to be these days. She was nursing her second son, while the first, blond-haired, blue-eyed, three-year-old Evan, played with a football at her feet.

"Daddy!" Evan cried, leaping up as Mac appeared around the corner of the house.

Mac opened his arms when he reached the foot of the steps that led up to the front door, and Evan launched himself into his father's arms. The two looked very much alike, down to the twin dimples in their cheeks.

"Welcome home," Jewel said with a smile.

"It's good to be home," Mac replied, settling into the rocker beside her with Evan on his lap. "How's Dustin?"

"Hungry, as always."

"I can see why he enjoys dinner so much," Mac said with a teasing smile, as he eyed the breast that provided his son's nourishment.

Jewel blushed. Even after four years of marriage, Mac

talked about her breasts as though they were the best gift he had ever been given. "How did your trip go?" she asked.

"I got two Pro-Bowl quarterbacks, a former Heisman Trophy winner and a record-setting kicker to commit to a week each at Camp LittleHawk."

"Fabulous!" Jewel said. "I knew you could do it! What about the fund-raiser?"

Jewel had been as surprised as Mac when Andy Dennison suggested they raise money for Mac's sports camp from the public. The Camp LittleHawk fund-raiser had become a highlight on the sports calendar and football players from around the league were delighted to be invited to participate.

"Everything is in place," Mac said. "Andy says he thinks we can double what we made last year."

"That'll mean we can build another couple of bunkhouses," Jewel said. "And hire the help we'll need to staff them."

Mac nodded and set his rocker to moving. "How were things around here while I was gone?"

"The high school-age summer counselors arrived yesterday for their week of training."

"Did he come?"

Jewel smiled. "He came."

Mac leaned his head back and turned his face away, but Jewel had already seen the tears that leaped to his eyes.

"He's been in remission for three years, Mac. Don't you think it's safe now to admit how much you like the kid?"

Mac turned back to her and reached out to take her hand in his. "I suppose it is."

"I thought so. That's why I asked him over for dinner tonight."

"What?"

"You can come out now, Brad," Jewel said.

The screen door opened, and Brad Templeton stepped onto the front porch. "Hi, Mac."

Mac rose and set Evan down.

It was questionable which of the two men moved first, but the instant they met, they wrapped their arms around each other and hugged tight.

Neither of them said anything, but if they were as moved as Jewel was, they were both too emotional to speak.

Mac recovered first, pushed Brad an arm's length away and said, "Let me look at you. How old are you now?"

"Sixteen," Brad said.

"You've gotten taller."

"You look the same."

Mac pulled off the New York Mets baseball cap and tousled Brad's dark hair. "Looks like you need a trim."

Brad grabbed the ball cap and tugged it down. "Now that I've got a little hair, I'm not about to cut it off. Besides, the chicks like it like this."

Mac laughed as he put an arm around Brad's shoulder and headed back toward Jewel. "Just remember," he said, pointing his thumb at Jewel, "this one's taken."

"I thought you had the hots for her," Brad said, winking at Jewel. "Guess I was right."

Mac laughed, then sobered. "I'm so glad you made it back here," he said, his voice breaking with emotion.

"I owe it all to you. I kept on fighting, like you said. And here I am."

The screen door slammed again and Jewel's brother Colt appeared on the front porch, tossing a football from hand to hand. At eighteen, his shoulders had broadened, and he had grown a few more inches. His hair was too long, and his face held a perpetual look of defiance. "If the reunion is over, I promised to throw Brad a few passes."

"Sure," Mac said, giving Brad a nudge in Colt's direction. "Let's see what kind of speed you have, Brad."

Mac returned to the rocker and settled down, picking up Evan again and holding him in his lap.

"Football," Evan said, pointing to Colt and Brad.

"Yep. Someday you're going to be playing, sport. But right now we're going to watch your uncle Colt and my friend Brad."

As the two of them watched Brad run in a zigzagging pattern, Jewel said, "Colt finally told Dad he's been accepted to the Air Force Academy."

Mac missed seeing Colt throw the football, because his attention had switched to Jewel. "What did Zach say?"

"He was angry that Colt hadn't said anything to him before now about wanting to go into the Air Force."

"And?"

"They're not speaking at the moment."

"What did Rebecca say?" Mac asked, his eyes back on Colt.

"Mom was hurt by all the secrecy. And she's afraid for Colt, because what he wants to do will put him in the path of danger."

Mac's mouth turned up wryly. "That shouldn't surprise her. Colt has led a pretty reckless life the past four years. It's a wonder he got through high school alive."

"I can't help thinking how unhappy Colt must have been all these years, knowing he was going to disappoint Dad and hurt Mom when he finally told them the truth about what he wanted to do with his life."

"Who'd have thought it," Mac said, watching the perfect spiraling pass Colt had thrown land gently in Brad's outstretched arms. "He would have made one hell of a pro quarterback."

"Apparently he'll play football for the Air Force Academy," Jewel said. "When he's done, he plans to fly jets."

Mac brushed his thumb across Jewel's knuckles, sending a frisson of pleasure streaking up her arm. "Do you think Colt would talk to me?"

"I'm sure he could use an ear to listen," Jewel said. "I've invited him for dinner, too."

Mac smiled. "Have I told you lately how much I love you?"

"It's been twenty-four hours, at least."

"I love you, Jewel." Mac raised her hand and kissed her palm.

Jewel found herself breathless as she met his avid gaze. "It's time for another lesson in the bedroom," she said.

"Oh? What are we learning this time?"

"How to make a baby *girl*," Jewel said.

"Sounds interesting," Mac said. "When does class start?"

"Right after the dinner dishes are done," Jewel said, "and you talk to Colt and he drives Brad back to Camp LittleHawk and we get these two into bed."

"I'll be there," Mac promised with a grin. "This is a lesson I don't want to miss."

Jewel laughed. "Just get it right this time, or you're liable to find yourself with a whole football team before we're through."

"I wouldn't mind," Mac said softly. "As long as we get at least one girl who looks just like you."

Before Jewel could answer, a football came flying onto the porch, and Mac and Evan abandoned her to play football with the two teenagers.

Jewel fingered the soft curls at Dustin's nape and brushed her hand across his baby-soft cheek. She was looking forward to Mac's inventive lovemaking tonight.

Knowing his determination to do everything to the best of his ability, it was bound to be a delightful adventure, full of fun and laughter.

Only this time, she would have the last laugh. Jewel's smile grew as she imagined the look on Mac's face when she told him—after the lesson, of course—that his daughter was already on the way.

* * * * *

HAWK'S WAY: THE SUBSTITUTE GROOM

CHAPTER ONE

*"WATCH YOUR WINGTIP! You're too close. We're going to—
Bail out, Huck! God, no, Huck!"*

Colt Whitelaw sat bolt upright in bed, his eyes wild
with remembered terror. His heart was racing, his hands
were clenched, and his sheet-draped body was drenched
in sweat. It took him a moment to realize where he was.
Home, at Hawk's Pride, his parents' ranch in northwest
Texas. He'd been jet-lagged when he'd arrived late last
night. That was the excuse he'd used, anyway, to go right
to bed. To avoid doing what had to be done.

*I have to see Jenny. I have to tell her there won't be any
wedding next month, that Huck was killed six days ago in
a midair collision over the Egyptian desert.*

Colt felt the sting in his nose, the tickle at the back of
his throat. He wasn't going to cry anymore. His best friend
was gone, and nothing could bring him back.

"Colt, I heard some noise. Are you all right?"

"I'm fine, Mom," Colt said, blinking against the afternoon sun. He had locked the bedroom door, or he knew
his mother would already have been inside. He was thirty-
two, but he was her baby, the youngest of eight adopted
kids and the only one who'd been an infant when Zach and
Rebecca Whitelaw had made him a part of their family.

"Are you ready to get up?" his mother asked through
the door. "Can I make you something to eat? Or do you
need more sleep?"

He couldn't eat. He couldn't sleep anymore. He couldn't do anything until he'd spoken to Jenny. "I'm fine, Mom," he said. "I think I'll take a shower."

"Everything you need is in the bathroom. Make yourself at home."

Make yourself at home. He supposed he deserved that. Three of his sisters were married and lived nearby, while the rest of his siblings worked on the family ranch. He hadn't been back to Hawk's Pride except for a brief visit at Labor Day or Christmas for ten years. It wasn't his home anymore, although at one time his father had expected him to manage the ranch. Colt had wanted to fly jets.

His brother Jake had become ramrod instead. His brother Louis—who was calling himself Rabb these days, short for Rabbit, a nickname he'd acquired as a result of eating a lot of carrots as a kid—worked the cattle, while his sister Frannie trained cutting horses. His brother Avery did the bookkeeping and legal work.

There was no place for him at Hawk's Pride now.

Colt made himself get out of bed. He groaned as his bruised right knee protested, along with his left shoulder. He'd survived the crash between his and Huck's training jets with minor injuries. The Air Force had exonerated him of blame in the incident, but he was on leave until he was fully recuperated.

He walked gingerly across the hall to the bathroom wearing only a pair of Jockey shorts and caught his mother peeking around the corner at the end of the hall. She jumped back out of sight, and he felt himself grinning as he closed the bathroom door behind him. Even if he didn't plan to stay, it was good to be home.

A half hour later Colt looked himself over in the mirror above the dresser in his former bedroom. The doctor had said the six stitches across his chin wouldn't leave much of a scar, but he'd decided not to try to shave around them. The day's growth of beard made him look disreputable but was countered by a military haircut that had left his black hair just long enough to part.

He rubbed his hands over the thighs of a pair of butter-soft jeans he'd found in a drawer and curled his toes in the scuffed leather cowboy boots he'd found in the closet. He wore a tucked-in white T-shirt but didn't have a Western belt, so the jeans rode low on his hips. He settled a battered Stetson on his head, completing his transformation into the Texas cowboy he once had been.

"Colt?"

Colt turned and found his mother standing in his open bedroom doorway, her heart in her eyes. There had always been a chance he'd be killed flying jets. This time he'd come damned close. He reached out and pulled her into his arms.

His birth mother had been a teenager, alone and in trouble, when she'd given him up to the Whitelaws for adoption. He often wondered about her, but he didn't miss her. In Rebecca Whitelaw he had the best mother any kid could want.

"Are you all right?" she asked, leaning back to look into his eyes. "How about some breakfast? Is there anything I can do for you?"

"I'm fine, Mom. Really. I don't think I could eat anything. I need to see Jenny, to tell her about Huck."

His mother leaned back, her eyes wide with disbelief. "You mean the Air Force hasn't contacted her?"

Colt shook his head. "Huck named his father as next of kin for notification purposes. The way things are between her and the senator, you can bet Huck's dad hasn't said a word to her, and I didn't want to tell her over the phone."

"I can't believe what's happened. Jenny's been waiting years for her brothers to grow up, so she'd be free to marry. And now, with the youngest graduating in June and her wedding day set, Huck is killed. It's just not fair!"

Colt rocked his mother in his arms. "I know, Mom." Colt felt his throat swelling closed. *Oh, God, Jenny. I'm so sorry. For your sake, I wish it had been me.*

He let go of his mother and took a step back. "I may be gone awhile. If Jenny needs anything, I want to be there for her."

"I understand," his mother said. She brushed her fingertips across his chin, coming as near as she dared without touching his stitches. "I know how close the three of you were."

Inseparable, Colt thought. *We were inseparable.*

"I'm sure Jenny will appreciate having you there," his mother continued. "Tell her to call if there's anything we can do."

"I will, Mom."

Colt decided to ride horseback to Jenny's ranch, mostly because it postponed the moment when he would have to tell her about Huck's death. It also gave him a chance to see the changes that had been wrought in the eight months since he'd last been home. Hawk's Pride looked more successful than ever. Which, by contrast, made the poverty on Jenny's ranch, the Double D, even more evident.

Fields that should have been planted in hay lay barren, a windmill wobbled and squeaked, fence posts needed to be repaired or replaced, the stock needed fattening, and a sun-scorched barn needed paint. Nevertheless, with its deep canyons and myriad arroyos, the land possessed a certain rugged charm.

His first sight of the ranch house, which looked as though it belonged in a Depression-era movie, confirmed his growing suspicion. If Jenny wasn't flat broke, he'd eat his hat.

Colt was surprised when he rode around the side of the barn to find himself staring at another rider on horseback. "Jenny. Hi."

The instantaneous smile made her bluer-than-blue eyes crinkle at the corners. His gut clenched.

I thought with Huck dead I'd feel different. But, heaven help me, I'm still in love with my best friend's girl.

"Colt! What a wonderful surprise!" Jenny cried. "Where's Huck? Did he come home on leave with you?"

"I'm alone," he managed to say.

She wore frayed jeans and a faded Western plaid shirt and sat on a rawboned nag that looked like it was a week from the glue factory. She nudged the animal, and it took the few steps that put them knee to knee. He could see the spattering of freckles on her nose and the corn silk blond wisps at her temples that had escaped her ponytail.

"I'm so glad to see you!" she said, reaching out to lay a hand on his thigh. "How long has it been?"

His flesh felt seared where she touched him. He reined his horse sideways to break the contact between them. "Since Labor Day."

"It seems like yesterday."

It seemed like forever. "How are you?" he asked.

Her smile broadened, creating an enchanting dimple in her left cheek. "Great! Counting down. After ten long years, just forty-two more days till I'm Mrs. Huckleberry Duncan."

Huck should have married her ten years ago, Colt thought. But Huck had followed where Colt led, and Colt had taken him off to fly jets. Jenny had stayed behind to raise her four younger brothers.

She was thirty-two now, Colt knew, because they were

the same age. The freckles and the ponytail gave her a youthful appearance, but she wasn't a girl any longer. He loved the laugh crinkles that age had put at the corners of her eyes, but he hated the worry lines in her forehead, because he was at least partly responsible for putting them there.

Colt knew life hadn't been easy for Jenny. She'd been a nurse for her mother, who'd died of breast cancer when Jenny turned fifteen, and then mother to her four brothers. It was finally time for her chance at happily-ever-after. Only Huck was dead. "Jenny—"

"Come inside," she said, turning her horse toward the house. He kneed his horse and followed her.

There was no lush green lawn, no purple morning glories trailing up the porch rail, nothing to lessen the starkness of the faded, single-story, wood-frame ranch house that sat in the middle of the northwest Texas prairie. Jenny rode around back to the kitchen door, dismounted and tied the reins to a hitching post.

As she stepped up onto the sagging covered porch she said, "Let me get you something to drink. You must be thirsty after such a long, hot ride."

"A glass of iced tea would be nice," he said as he dismounted. "Are any of your brothers around?"

"I don't see much of Tyler or James or Sam, now that they're out on their own. Randy won't be home from school for another hour."

"Good," Colt said as he followed her into the kitchen. "That'll give us some time alone to talk. How are things going?"

She shot him a mischievous grin as the screen door slammed behind him, then crossed to an old, round-cornered Coldspot refrigerator and pulled out a jar of iced tea. "It's a good thing Huck and I are finally getting hitched. If it weren't for the money he'll get from his trust fund when he marries, I'd have to turn the Double D over to the bank."

He hadn't expected her to be so honest. Maybe if she'd known about Huck, she wouldn't have been. "You're about to lose the Double D?"

"Not that I'd miss all the hard work, you understand, but this ranch has been in my family for so many generations, it'd be a shame to let it go."

"I didn't realize things had gotten so bad," he said.

"In forty-two days, all my troubles will be over. But enough about me. How'd you cut your chin? Fooling around with Huck, I'll bet. His last letter was full of—"

"Jenny, Huck is…" *Dead. Gone forever. Never coming back.* He swallowed hard.

"Huck is what?" she asked, her back to him as she reached for a glass from the cupboard above the sink.

"Huck died six days ago."

As she turned, her eyes wide, her mouth open in shocked surprise, the glass slipped from her hand and crashed to the floor. "No!" She pressed a clenched fist against her heart."How?"

"I killed him."

ALL THE BLOOD left Jenny's head in a *whoosh,* and she swayed. She heard broken glass crunch under Colt's boots as he stepped close enough to catch her before her knees gave way and lifted her into his arms. She clung to his neck in a daze as he carried her into the bedroom and sat her on her four-poster bed.

He tried to stand up, to move away, but she clutched at him and wouldn't let go. "Stay here," she rasped past a throat that had swollen closed. "Explain."

She felt the tension in his shoulders. Felt the shudder that racked his frame as he settled down beside her. It took a long time for him to speak. She noticed the dust motes in the sunlight streaming through her bedroom window, the country tune about "friends in low places" on the radio that always played in the kitchen, the screech of a windmill that needed repair.

Everything was just as it had been a moment before. And nothing was the same.

Colt cleared his throat. "I knew Huck had been sick with some kind of flu bug the night before we were scheduled for a training flight. He said he was fine, but I should have known better and grounded him. Whatever illness he had affected his equilibrium."

She felt the slight shrug in Colt's shoulders before he said, "His wingtip brushed mine and..." He swallowed hard. "I bailed out. Huck didn't."

This isn't real. I'm dreaming. Colt isn't really sitting here beside me. He's with Huck, training jet pilots in Egypt.

She brushed a hand across the short dark hair at Colt's nape. *So soft.* She laid her cheek against his and felt the night's growth of beard. *So prickly.*

I can feel. So this must be real, she thought. As real as the tight band of pain that bound her chest and made it so hard to breathe.

Colt leaned back and looked into her face. She had never seen such agony in a human being's eyes. "I'm so sorry, Jenny. So very sorry. I should have done something. I should have—"

"I doubt you could've kept him on the ground," she said in a shaky voice. "Huck was as crazy about flying as you are."

"I outranked him. I could've made it an order."

"You loved him too much to deny him anything he wanted," Jenny said simply. *Even me.*

Jenny didn't know where that last thought had come

from, but she pushed it back into whatever dark hole it lived in. When they were kids, she'd known Colt Whitelaw had a crush on her. She'd even thought she might like to go out with him, if he asked. But Huck had liked her, too, and once Colt found out his best friend wanted her, he'd kept his distance. She had become—would always be— Huck's girl.

Only, now Huck was dead.

"Oh, God, Colt. I don't think I can bear it!" Jenny cried. "I don't think I can live without him!"

Many times over the past ten years she'd wondered what she would do if something happened to Huck, and he didn't come back to her. But he always did. Lately, like a combat veteran who counts the days until he can leave the battlefield, she'd counted the days until Huck would come home at last, and they'd be married and live happily ever after.

"It's not fair, Colt. It's not fair!" she wailed.

"I know," he said, rubbing her back soothingly. "I know."

The tears came then, spilling over in hot tracks down her face. And excruciating grief. She let out a howl of rage and pain. Throughout it all she clung to Colt, held tight to him, as though the mere presence of another human could keep her from hurting so much.

Jenny cried until her throat was raw, until she was too weak to lift a hand to wipe away the tears. It didn't take long for exhaustion to claim her. She was already wornout from overwork and from too many sleepless nights spent worrying about how she was going to keep the ranch afloat on a sea of debt.

Jenny had pinned all her hopes for saving the ranch on the trust funds Huck would receive when they married. Now there would be no wedding. She hadn't merely lost the man she loved. She had also lost her home.

"What am I going to do, Colt?" she whispered. "How can I go on now?"

"I'm here, Jenny. I'll always be here for you," Colt murmured in her ear. "I love you, Jenny."

Jenny knew Colt hadn't meant it the way it sounded. Colt loved her the same way he loved Huck. He'd been a good friend to her, always willing to pitch in to help with her brothers, something Huck never seemed to have the time to do. It had been easy to lean on Colt, to lay her troubles on his strong shoulders whenever Huck was too busy to lend a hand.

Jenny was suddenly aware of how tightly her arms were wrapped around Colt's neck. And in turn, how his hands were tangled in her hair.

"Colt, let go. Let me go!" She struggled to free herself from his embrace, from the illusion of safety, the awful, welcome comfort he offered.

He stared at her in confusion. "What's wrong, Jenny? Tell me what I can do to help."

"Nothing!" She took a deep, shuddering breath. "Get out, Colt. Go away. I don't want you here."

"Because I killed him?"

She should have let him believe that was why she wanted him gone. One look at his face, and she couldn't do it. "Oh, Colt, don't you see? It would be so easy to turn to you, to depend on you. That wouldn't be fair to you. No one can take Huck's place."

The color faded from his face, until there were only two blotches of red on his cheeks. "I feel responsible for what happened. The least I can do is make sure you don't lose the Double D. I've got money. Let me help you, Jenny."

"You've always been there for me, and I love you for it. But money can't give me what I need most. Money can't bring Huck back."

She saw him wince before he said, "I miss him, too. He's going to leave a big hole in both our lives. But that doesn't change the fact this place needs a lot of work."

The words stung. "I've done the best I can."

"I know that! But admit it, Jenny. You're going to need help holding on to this place."

"I'm not admitting anything," she said stubbornly.

"You know Huck would want me to help you. Let me do this for him."

She shook her head. "I couldn't take your money, Colt. And I know how committed you are to flying jets. You'll be long gone before—"

"I've got up to sixty days' leave for recuperation. That's enough time to get some work done around here. I want to be here for you. Let me help you, Jenny. Please."

She lifted her chin. "I won't take charity, Colt. Even from you."

"Don't be ridiculous. We're friends."

"Friends. Not relations," Jenny said. "You have no obligation to help me, Colt."

His expression made it plain she'd offended him, but the only thing she had left was her pride. It was humiliating enough to be left at the altar—even if unwillingly—by Huck, without having to go begging for help to bail the Double D out of debt.

"You would have taken Huck's money," he said.

"He would have been my husband."

"Then marry me, Jenny, if that's what it takes. But damn it, let me help!"

The silence that followed his statement hung between them like temptation in the Garden of Eden. Jenny threaded her hands together to hide the fact they were trembling. "I know you must be hurting as badly as I am right now. But I won't take advantage of your grief—"

"Marry me, Jenny," he said, reaching out to separate her hands and hold them tightly in his. "On the day you would've married Huck. You should have a June wedding. You've waited long enough for it. You should walk down the aisle looking beautiful and knowing there's someone waiting who's willing to shoulder half the burden the rest of your life. We both know it's been your dream for a very long time. Let me make it come true. I owe you that much."

She stared at Colt, unable to look away. He understood about lost dreams. He almost hadn't made good on his dream of becoming a jet pilot. She was the one who'd urged him to confront his parents and tell them he didn't want to be a rancher, that he wanted to fly jets. She'd also been the one who shared his joy when he realized his parents were happy for him, not disappointed as he'd expected them to be.

Colt knew better than anyone what it had meant to her to sacrifice her own dreams for the sake of her brothers. She looked down at Colt's hands—large and strong and capable—then up into his blue eyes, as red-rimmed as her own, and focused on her with such earnest entreaty that she found it hard to look away.

"Suppose we did marry, Colt. Then what? I can't follow you around the world the way Huck did. My home is here on the Double D. Are you willing to give up flying?"

She watched his Adam's apple bob as he swallowed. "I can't."

"Then I can't marry you."

"Why not?"

"I won't trade one absentee partner for another," she said flatly. "I deserve better."

"Then take the damned money!"

"I don't need your charity."

"You sure as hell do!"

She yanked her hands free and said, "Get out, Colt. Leave. Go."

Colt stood his ground. "I owe Huck for not protecting him better. *I* stole your dream of happily ever after. Let me do this for you. For Huck. Marry me, Jenny."

Her chin quivered. She wanted so much to accept. It was the easy way out. But it was all wrong. "It wouldn't work, Colt."

"Why not?"

"For one thing, I don't love you."

"That doesn't matter."

She shook her head. "I can't believe you'd want to marry someone who—"

"Say yes, Jenny."

"What would people think—"

"To hell with what people think! At least you'd keep the Double D."

She stared at him, wanting to accept, but knowing such a marriage would be disastrous for both of them. "What happens when you fall in love with some other woman?"

"That isn't going to happen."

"How do you know?" she insisted.

He looked away, then turned back. "I gave my heart to someone a long time ago. There won't be anyone else."

"Oh." She was surprised by the jolt of jealousy she felt at his admission. Colt had often dated, but all the relationships had been brief. She'd never imagined him in love with some other woman. It had always been—only been—the three of them.

He reached for her hands again and held them tight. "If we don't get married, you're going to lose the only home you've ever known."

"Don't threaten me, Colt."

"It's the situation that's threatening."

"What about sex?" She lifted her eyes to his and saw the glint of humor there, despite everything. They'd always spoken freely to each other. She wasn't going to pull her punches now. "Or were you planning on a celibate marriage?"

"I wouldn't expect you to come to bed with me right away," he said, answering with as much care as the subject deserved. "But I'd expect our marriage to include physical relations eventually."

"I see." There had been a time—one time—about six years ago when his hand had accidentally brushed against her breast, and she'd felt her insides draw up tight. They'd both been horribly embarrassed, and it had never happened again. But she'd been aware of him ever since in a way she hadn't been before that day.

Still, it was unsettling to think of Colt having the right to touch her as a man touched a woman. It had always been forbidden, because she was Huck's girl.

Huck is dead. Huck is never coming back.

"Say yes, Jenny."

She looked into Colt's eyes, searching for the right answer. He looked so sure of himself. So certain he was doing the right thing. She shuddered to think what people would say if she showed up at church on the day she'd planned to marry Huck with a substitute groom.

Then she imagined what it would be like if she lost the ranch and had to go to work in town. Or had to live as a maiden aunt in the home of one of her brothers. And there were other considerations, things Colt didn't know about and which she could never tell him, that made her want to cling to the only home she had ever known.

She needed time, but there wasn't much. Her wedding date, June 20, was forty-two days away. Ten days after that, another mortgage payment would come due. And she had no money to pay.

It was selfish to marry Colt under the circumstances. She was crazy even to consider the possibility. But it was the only solution she could see—at the moment—for her desperate situation.

"All right," she said at last. "I'll consider your proposal."

"When will I know your answer?"

Jenny managed a crooked smile. "As soon as I do."

CHAPTER TWO

"HEY, JENNY, WAKE UP!"

Jenny rolled over in bed and stared, bleary-eyed, at her eighteen-year-old brother, Randy. She'd spent most of the night crying and had only gotten to sleep as the sun was coming up. She groaned, rolled back over and mumbled, "Let me sleep."

"Colt's in the kitchen. He wants to know where he should start to work."

"Tell him..." She snuggled deeper into the covers, already drifting back to sleep.

"I've got to get moving, or I'm going to miss the bus," Randy said. He gave her shoulder a shove and asked, "What do you want me to tell Colt?"

"Tell him to go away," she said, covering her head with a pillow.

"Are you sure?"

"I'm sure."

A persistent knock on her bedroom door drew her back to consciousness. She decided to ignore it. With any luck, Colt would take the hint and go away. She didn't want to see him. She didn't want to see anyone, looking and feeling like she did.

The door opened a crack and Colt said, "Jenny? Are you awake?"

"How can I sleep with all these interruptions?" she muttered irritably.

He took that as an invitation to come in, and a moment later she felt his presence by the bed. Which was when she realized she was wearing one of Randy's old football jerseys, and from what she could feel of the breeze from the open window on her bare thighs, it wasn't covering much.

She rolled onto her back, reaching for the sheet and blanket she must have kicked off and dragging them up to cover her. "What do you want, Colt?"

"I brought you a cup of coffee."

She squinted one eye open. "You expect me to drink that?"

"Why not?"

"It's likely to wake me up."

She saw the smile tilt his lips and the appearance of devastating twin dimples in his cheeks. "That's the general idea," he said. He seated himself beside her on the mattress and tousled her hair. "Come on, sleepyhead. Rise and shine."

She brushed his hand away. "I don't want to get up."

"Too bad," he said, sliding an arm under her shoulders to lift her up and sticking the coffee cup against her lips. "I need some marching orders, and you're the only one here to give them to me."

Against her better judgment, she took a sip of the scalding liquid. "Oh, Lord. That's strong enough that it might even work."

"I hope so," he said. "Because I'm planning to spend the day with you. I'll be glad to join you in bed, if that's what you'd prefer—"

She pushed the coffee away and scooted across the bed and out of it, tugging on the hem of the football jersey as she stood. "Give me a minute to get showered and dressed." She headed for her chest of drawers to retrieve clean underwear and socks.

"I'll leave the coffee here, in case you need another jolt," he said, setting the heavy ceramic mug on the end table beside her bed. "Oh, and Jenny..."

She turned to look at him over her shoulder.

"If you're wearing Saturday on Wednesday, what happens when you get to the weekend?"

Jenny stared at him uncomprehendingly until she realized she was wearing panties her brother Randy had given her for Christmas that were labeled with the days of the week. "So you'll only have to do laundry once every seven days," Randy had quipped.

She flushed with embarrassment at the thought of Colt glimpsing her underwear and snapped, "Well, you could always barge into my bedroom again on Saturday to find out."

"Touché," he said with a mock salute. "I'll be waiting for you in the kitchen."

The shower didn't help. Jenny's eyelids felt like they weighed a pound each, and they scratched her eyeballs every time she blinked. Her mouth was dry, her throat was sore, and her whole body ached. She was angry at being forced out of bed, but she didn't have the energy to fight.

"Your breakfast is on the table," Colt said when she arrived in the kitchen doorway.

She stared at the trestle table, where he'd put out a wrinkled cloth place mat and napkin—who had time to iron?—with a set of mix-matched silverware. He'd made scrambled eggs and toast and provided a cup of orange juice beside another cup of steaming coffee. She felt both grateful and resentful. "I could have made something for myself."

He pulled out the ladder-back chair at the head of the table and shoved her into it. "Sure you could. If you weren't dead on your feet. Eat."

"Are you going to join me?"

"I ate before I came over."

"Are you going to hover like that, watching every bite that goes into my mouth?"

He sat down in the chair to her right, then bounced up again. "Ouch!"

"Oh. Watch out for the nail in that chair."

"You've got nails sticking out of the kitchen chairs?"

She nodded, since her mouth was full of toast, then swallowed and answered, "My brothers' football buddies did a lot of leaning back in those chairs. Afraid they couldn't take the strain. Had to nail them back together."

"Why don't you fix them right?"

She shrugged. "No time. No money. No need." She gave him a beatific smile. "We know where the nails are."

"Any other sharp points I need to avoid—besides your barbed tongue?" he said. "If Huck were here—" Colt caught himself too late. The words were out, invoking Huck's presence.

Jenny felt the beginning of tears and blinked to fight them back. The fork fell from her hand and clattered onto her plate. She covered her face with her hands as an awful wave of grief rolled over her. "Why did this have to happen?"

She felt herself being lifted into Colt's arms, then felt him settling into the ladder-back chair in her stead. Her arms slid around his neck, and she hid her face against his throat. "I can't pretend this is just another day, Colt. Please, let me go back to bed. I want to sleep."

"When you wake up, he'll still be gone," Colt said soberly. "I know. I've had a week longer than you to deal with Huck's death. The only thing that helps is work."

"I'm so tired. I didn't sleep last night."

"If I let you sleep now, you'll be awake all night tonight," Colt said. "Then you'll be tired again tomorrow. Work now. Sleep later. Can you eat any more?"

She shook her head.

He forced her off his lap and onto her feet. "Where do you suggest we start?" he asked as he led her toward the back door.

"The cattle and horses need to be fed. I've got a few chickens that have probably laid eggs. The barn needs to be scraped and painted, the windmill in the west pasture isn't working, the back porch needs some new posts before it falls down, there's a leak in the roof that should be patched, I've got supplies to pick up in town—"

"Whoa!" Colt said. "We'll start with feeding the stock, then go pick up the supplies in town. Everything else can wait till we've both had a good night's sleep."

Jenny looked at Colt—really looked at him. Judging by the dark circles under his eyes, he hadn't slept much, either. Perhaps he was right. Perhaps work was the best way to keep the demons at bay. But they both needed to rest, as well, and she'd just come up with a solution for the problem.

"The stock tank in the south pasture needs to be checked before the day is over," she said. There happened to be a sprawling live oak near that tank. Once they got there, she'd tell Colt she needed to lie down for a little while in the shade and take a nap, and that she needed him to keep her company.

EVEN THOUGH JENNY was clearly exhausted, Colt had trouble keeping up with her throughout the day. The worst moments came when friends in town offered their condolences, along with memories of Huck that were so poignant they were painful.

At the feed store Mr. Brubaker said to Jenny, "Remem-

ber the time you and Huck and Colt climbed up and painted
J.W. + H.D. — True Love on the town's water tower? If I
ain't mistaken, it's still there."

Tom Tuttle at Tuttle's Hardware said to Colt, "Always
knew one of you boys would get hisself killed flying them
jets. Glad it weren't you, Colt. Sorry about Huck, Miss
Jenny."

At the Stanton Hotel Café, Ida Mae Cooper said, "I recall the first time the three of you came in here together
for a cherry soda. You were skinny as a beanpole in those
days, Colt, and couldn't take your eyes off Huck's girl."

Colt shot a look at Jenny to see if she'd made anything
of Ida Mae's announcement, but she merely looked forlorn.
She settled onto the red plastic seat of one of several stools
along the 1950s-era soda fountain and said, "No cherry
soda for me, Ida Mae. Just strong black coffee."

Colt slid onto the stool next to her. "I'd like that cherry
soda, Ida Mae."

Jenny glared at him as though he'd betrayed some trust,
as though they couldn't have cherry sodas anymore because Huck wasn't there to have one with them.

He met her stare with sympathetic eyes. "Huck won't
mind if we have a cherry soda, Jenny."

"Why does everybody keep talking about him?" she
muttered. "Don't they understand it hurts?"

"They miss him, too," Colt said simply.

"Here's that soda, Colt," Ida Mae said. She eyed him
speculatively and asked, "You planning to take care of
Huck's girl, now that he's gone?"

The question was loud enough—and volatile enough—
to bring conversation in the café to a halt. Colt felt everyone's eyes focus on him except Jenny's. She stared
determinedly into her coffee cup. Ida Mae waited expectantly for an answer.

He took a deep breath and let it out. "Jenny and I haven't made any plans beyond a memorial service a week from Friday. We'd like to invite everyone to come, if you'd be kind enough to pass along the word."

"Sure, Colt," Ida Mae said, patting his hand. "I can understand it wouldn't be a good idea to announce any more than that right now."

Colt opened his mouth to tell her she was way off the mark and closed it again. A denial that anything was going on between him and Jenny would likely stir up more gossip than saying nothing.

It was late afternoon by the time they got back to the ranch. Jenny suggested they ride horseback to the stock tank. Apparently the spigot in the stock tank in her south pasture needed to be fixed. She was running on fumes by the time they got there. She dismounted and led her horse over to the aluminium tank for a drink, and Colt followed suit.

"Where's that faulty spigot?" he asked, checking the spigot on the tank, which wasn't leaking as far as he could tell.

"I guess Randy must have fixed it. As long as we're here, we might as well take advantage of the shade."

He eyed her suspiciously. "There never was anything wrong with that spigot, was there?"

"Nope."

There wasn't much grass growing in the shade of the sprawling live oak growing near the tank, but he watched Jenny find a patch of it and sit down. She patted the ground beside her and said, "Join me. It's time for a nap."

Colt sighed. "If we sleep now—"

"Sit down," she ordered, "and shut up."

That brought a snappy salute and a "Yes, ma'am." He

dropped onto the ground beside her, suddenly feeling the results of too many haunted nights. He lay stretched out on his side, supporting his head with his palm. "Now what?"

She stretched out, facing him, and laid her cheek on her arm. "Lie down. I can't talk to you when your head's so far above mine."

Reluctantly, he came down off his elbow and laid his head on his arm, facing her. For a long time they stared at one another without speaking. He reached out to touch her cheek, to brush away a tear. "Don't cry, Jenny. I can't bear it when you cry."

"I can't help it. So many memories are shuffling around in my head."

"Mine, too," he admitted.

"Do you remember the last time we were here?"

He chuckled. "That isn't a day I'm likely to forget."

"I asked you if you'd teach me how to kiss," she said. "Do you remember what you said?"

"'No.' Or more precisely, 'Hell no!'"

Her eyes lit with laughter, and her lips curled up at the corners. "I begged until you relented, because I didn't want my first kiss with Huck to go awry."

"Craziest thing I've ever done in my life," he said. "Teaching my best friend's girl how to kiss."

"I wanted to know where my hands should go and where he'd put his hands."

"All over you," Colt muttered, "if he could get away with it."

He heard Jenny's laugh, a sound like a burbling brook, and realized it had been a very long time since he'd heard anything so pleasing. He smiled at her and let the memory of that long-ago day wash over him.

They'd ridden horseback to the stock tank, because

she'd said she had something important to discuss with him in private. While their horses had taken a drink, she'd popped the question. After his refusal, she'd gone to work convincing him.

"You have to help me, Colt," she pleaded. "My first kiss with Huck has to be perfect, because I'll be remembering it the rest of my life. I don't want anything to go wrong."

"That's what makes the first kiss memorable," he argued. "Things go wrong."

She shook her head, her long blond hair shimmering like corn silk in the sunlight. "Please. Do this for me."

He'd been aware of his attraction to Jenny from the first moment he'd looked into her bluer-than-blue eyes, but Huck had been the first one to speak of her. Colt had felt honor-bound to wait and see if things developed between Jenny and Huck before he made his move. To his dismay, Jenny had said yes to Huck's overtures.

More than once Colt had thought of trying to steal Jenny away from Huck. But he knew in his heart that he couldn't live with himself if he betrayed his friend like that. It would taint what he felt for Jenny. So he went along and remained a good friend to both of them.

See how virtue had been rewarded? Jenny wanted him to kiss her first!

More than anything in the world he wanted to hold Jenny Wright in his arms. But he had panicked when she came up with the harebrained notion that he should teach her to kiss. Would she be able to tell from his kiss how much he liked her? What if he got carried away and did something that scared her?

"I'll do this on one condition," he conceded at last.

"Anything," she promptly agreed.

"You never *ever* tell Huck."

"Why not?"

"Believe me, he wouldn't understand."

"Why not?"

"It's a guy thing," he said. "Promise," he insisted.

She crossed her heart with her forefinger. "Cross my heart and hope to die, stick a needle in my eye."

"I guess that'll do," he said.

"Okay, I'm ready," she said.

He rubbed his sweaty palms on the thighs of his jeans. "I'm not. I have no idea where to start."

"Why not put your arms around me?" she suggested.

He reached forward at the same time she reached up, and their arms knocked into each other.

"Oops."

"Sorry."

"See what I mean?" she said, wrinkling her nose. "I guess I'll need to stand still while Huck puts his arms around me. You want to try again?"

"Sure." He slid his left arm around her waist and tugged her toward him. But she didn't move.

She looked up at him in confusion. "What?"

"You need to take a step to get closer," he instructed. He applied pressure to her back again, and this time she responded by closing the distance between them until her breasts were a hairsbreadth from his chest.

"Is this close enough?"

There was no spit left in his mouth, and he croaked, "Yeah. That's probably close enough."

She looked up expectantly. "Now what?"

"Huck will probably put his hand on your head to angle it in the right direction."

"Okay. I'm ready. Go ahead."

He'd only intended to palm her head with his hand, but

somehow his fingers got tangled in her hair. "You've got really soft hair," he murmured.

He saw her cheeks pinken. "Thank you. Do you think Huck will do what you're doing? I mean, slide his fingers through my hair like that?"

"Why do you ask?"

She gave a negligent shrug. "It feels good."

Colt reminded himself he was holding Huck's girl. "He might run his hands through your hair. But don't worry if he doesn't. Every guy is different."

"Okay. Now what?"

"I'm a little taller than Huck, so some of what I'm saying might need to be adjusted for height," he said, trying to remain objective. He reminded himself to keep his hips apart from hers, so she wouldn't discover that his body was reacting as though this game of hers was the real thing. "I can bend down to you, or you can come up on tiptoe to reach me," he explained.

"Or Huck and I could move toward each other—me up, him down." She frowned thoughtfully. "It would be easier if I had my hands on Huck's shoulders. When should I do that?"

"Can you get your arms up between mine?" he asked.

She slowly slid her hands up his chest and around his neck. "How's that?"

His heart felt like a caged bird, racketing around inside his ribs. "That's fine," he managed to rasp. "Now, you slide up on tiptoe, and I'll lower my head."

As she came up on tiptoe she lost her balance. She grabbed him around the neck, and his arm tightened around her, pressing her soft, warm breasts against his chest. He met her startled gaze and said, "Are you all right?"

"I think so. Whew! See why I need the practice? Who knew there were so many pitfalls to a simple kiss?"

He started to push her away, but she clung to his neck and said, "Let's keep going. What is Huck likely to do next?"

Kiss you till he can't see straight, Colt thought. But he said, "Let's see how good you are at hitting a target."

She grinned. "You mean, can I find his lips with mine?"

"Give it a shot."

Her fingertips at his nape urged his head down toward hers. He kept his eyes locked with hers until he couldn't bear the excitement anymore, then closed his eyes and waited for her lips to touch his. When they didn't, he opened his eyes to find her staring at him, her brow furrowed. "What's wrong?" he asked.

"I shouldn't be the one doing the kissing," she said. "Huck will want to be the aggressor."

"The *aggressor?*" Colt said.

"You know, the wolf stalking his prey, the Neanderthal dragging his woman back to his cave."

"Where do women get these ideas?" he said, shaking his head.

"From men," she said with a grin. "Admit it. Men like to make the first move. What would Huck think if *I* kissed *him* first?"

"That you liked him," Colt said flatly.

She looked thoughtful, then shook her head. "I'm an old-fashioned girl. Huck has to be the one to kiss first."

Which meant *he* had to kiss *her* first, Colt realized. "Let's get this over with." He leaned down, but before he could kiss her, she put her fingertips to his lips. "What's wrong now?" he asked in exasperation.

"Huck wouldn't do it like that."

"Like what?"

"In a big hurry."

"He might."

"He'll take his time. He'll make it count. He'll know how important this first kiss is. Do it right," she said.

"Do it right?" he muttered. "I'll do it right. Watch me *do it right*."

He threaded his fingers through her hair again, then used his hold to angle her head back so her lips were aimed up at his. He lowered his head slowly, keeping his eyes on hers, *making it count*. This was the first time he was going to kiss the girl he loved. And he wanted her to know how important this moment was.

He felt a shock as their lips touched, and backed off to stare at her. She looked dazed. He lowered his mouth over hers a second time, feeling the firmness of her lips and then the supple give as she responded to him. He pressed a little harder and felt her hands slide into his hair.

He wanted to taste her, so he teased his tongue along the edge of her lips, waiting for her to open to him.

She broke the kiss abruptly and leaned back to stare at him, her pupils dilated, her lips wet, her body trembling. "What were you doing with your tongue?"

"I was tasting you."

"Will Huck want to do that?"

"I would if I were him," he said simply.

"Why?"

"Because it feels good."

"It makes me feel funny inside." She laughed nervously and said, "Look at me. I'm shaking."

"You want to quit?"

She hesitated, then shook her head. "I'd better practice

if I'm going to get it right with Huck. I'm ready now, if you want to try again."

He leaned down and touched her mouth lightly with his once, and then again, teasing kisses that urged her to accept what was coming. He felt her lips become less rigid, felt them ease apart as his tongue slid along the crease, heard her moan as his tongue slid inside her mouth. Her hands clutched his hair as her hips arched instinctively into his.

Then she was jerking herself away and backing up, her hand rubbing at her mouth, her eyes wide, her body trembling. "Ohmigod. What am I doing? What are we doing?"

He stood without moving. He saw her eyes drop to the thick ridge along the zipper of his jeans and knew what had frightened her. But that was going to happen to Huck, too. She might as well know it now, as later.

"It's all right," he said in a matter-of-fact voice. "What happened to you—to us—is normal. It's what happens between a man and a woman when they kiss. I'm sorry if I scared you."

"Will Huck—? Of course he will," she said, thrusting an agitated hand through her hair. "I had no idea it would be like that. So…powerful. You stop thinking, you stop being a rational person, your body just sort of…explodes."

"Yeah," he said, huffing out a breath of air. "That pretty well describes it."

She looked up at him earnestly and said, "Thanks, Colt. I'm going to be forever in your debt. There aren't many friends who'd be willing to help out like this."

"Anytime," he said.

Colt became aware of a horse ripping up grass with his teeth near his head and opened his eyes, reluctantly letting go of the memory. He leaned up on his elbow and looked down at Jenny. She was sound asleep, her breathing quiet and even. He wondered if her first kiss with Huck had been everything she'd hoped. He'd never asked, and she'd never spoken about it.

"This is for you from Huck," he murmured as he leaned over and gently touched her lips with his. "A kiss goodbye."

CHAPTER THREE

TOO LATE, JENNY REALIZED the trip TO the stock tank in the south pasture had been a big mistake. It reminded her of something she'd chosen to forget: Her "first kiss" with Huck had come nowhere close to arousing in her the emotions of her "practice kiss" with Colt.

She had blamed the disturbing difference on the fact a girl could only get her "first kiss" once, and due to her own stupidity, she'd had her first kiss with the wrong man. It was only natural that her "second kiss" wasn't quite so exciting. Of course she'd loved Huck's kisses, because she'd loved Huck. But the spark she'd felt with Colt, that delicious electricity—that total loss of shame and scruples—had never occurred with Huck.

Since lying beside Colt yesterday in the shade of the live oak, those bewitching memories had made their insidious way back into her consciousness. Jenny's mind had begun replaying the moment when Colt's lips first touched hers, when his tongue first traced the seam of her mouth, when she first tasted him.

It was simple curiosity, she told herself, that made her wonder if that electricity had merely been the result of a "first kiss," or whether it would happen if they kissed again. She was ashamed of herself for what she was thinking, but she couldn't get the idea out of her head.

What if Colt could make her feel more than Huck ever

had? What if she hadn't been kissed first by the wrong man? What if she'd been engaged to him?

That thought was too painful to face, since it would've meant she'd wasted ten years of her life—and Huck's. If she was going to have second thoughts, she should've had them a long time ago.

When? a voice asked. *After Huck was graduated from the Air Force Academy, he was never around for more than a few days at a time. You were busy with your brothers. You barely had time to make school lunches, let alone worry about your love life. It was convenient for both of you to be "in love." There was no time to stop and think. Until now.*

Jenny supposed everyone went through this sort of soul-searching at the time of such a significant loss. But she wasn't getting the answers she'd expected. She found her thoughts—and her eyes—focused more and more on Colt.

Sunday she went to church and surrounded herself protectively with her brothers. If anyone could keep Colt at a distance, it was Sam and Tyler and James and Randy. The idiot man simply shook each brother's hand as he moved past them into the pew and settled himself right beside her. It was a tight squeeze, because the pews weren't that large, and Sam wouldn't move over at first.

Colt finally speared Sam with a look that sent him scooting. "Hi, Jenny," he said. "I thought you might want company this first Sunday without Huck."

What were her brothers? Sliced baloney? With four brothers at her side, why did Colt think she needed him?

He shared a hymnal with her and sang the familiar refrains in a strong baritone voice that sent shivers down her spine. She found herself wondering how he would sound whispering love words in her ear.

It wasn't until after church, when everyone crowded

around, that she conceded she was grateful for Colt's presence. Her brothers hovered, but they were clearly uncomfortable responding to the offers of condolence.

Colt slid an arm around her waist to hold her close enough that their hips occasionally bumped. He shook hands with the men and pulled several blue-haired old ladies close enough to kiss their cheeks. As though he coped with such emergencies every day, he enfolded Randy in a one-armed embrace when her brother unexpectedly broke into tears.

Colt didn't even let go when Sam and Tyler and James came one at a time to bid her good-bye. They were all big, tall men, like their father had been. Sam and Tyler were dark-haired and brown-eyed, while James had green eyes and chestnut hair. They were dressed in suits, but that didn't make them look particularly civilized. They might have been wolves from a free-roaming pack.

They would have intimidated a lesser man. Colt met them without backing off, staring down Sam when he eyed the way Colt's arm was wrapped around her.

"You look like hell," Sam said to her. "Get some sleep."

"Thanks a lot, Sam," she replied, making a face at him. "I'm trying."

"Try harder," Sam said, chucking her gently under the chin. It wasn't a large gesture of affection, but it was the equivalent of a bear hug from Sam. She met his gaze and saw the worry there and smiled to reassure him. "I'll be fine, Sam."

He turned to Colt and said, "I guess we won't be seeing as much of you, now that Huck's gone."

Jenny held her breath, waiting for Colt to tell Sam that he'd offered to marry her.

Colt shot her a quick look, but all he said was, "I'll be around for a while."

Sam was followed by Tyler, who brushed his knuckles against her cheek and said, "Take care of yourself, sis." He gave Colt a hard look and said, "You be careful now."

Jenny wasn't sure whether it was an admonition to be careful flying jets, or whether Tyler was warning Colt to watch his step around her.

Colt replied, "I'm always careful."

James kissed her brow and whispered, "God works in mysterious ways. We can't know what he has planned for us."

She felt a moment of panic, wondering if James had somehow surmised her unsettling daydreams about Colt. But when she met his gaze, he only looked sad and sympathetic.

"Where's Randy?" Colt asked when her other brothers had all taken their leave.

Jenny looked around the church hall and saw Randy standing in a crowd of teenagers. "He's over there by the Butler twins, Faith and Hope."

"Let's go get him. My mom has invited the two of you to Sunday dinner at Hawk's Pride."

She freed herself at last from Colt's embrace and turned to face him, her hands knotted to keep him from reaching for them. "I can't go, Colt."

"Why not?"

"I couldn't face your parents. Not when I haven't made up my mind yet whether I'm going to marry you."

"They don't know about my proposal," Colt said.

"*I* know about it. I wouldn't feel comfortable. Please, Colt. Give them my regrets."

"I'll tell them now and follow you home. We can pick up something to have for dinner on the way."

Jenny stared after him as he stalked off, wondering how the situation had gotten so completely out of her control.

Her attraction for Colt seemed to be growing stronger by the minute—along with her guilt over the rapidity with which she seemed to be transferring her affections from one man to another.

All I have to do is spend a little more time with Colt, and his faults will begin to show, Jenny thought as she waited for Colt to return.

She and Colt and Randy spent the afternoon sitting on the floor around the coffee table in the living room playing a game of Scrabble. She found herself fascinated by Colt's hands. Blue veins were prominent in the backs of his hands, and his knuckles bore tiny tufts of black hair. His nails were clean and cut bluntly, and his fingers were long and thick, with callused pads. She imagined what it might feel like if he slid one inside her. And blushed hotly.

"You look kinda warm, Jenny," Randy said. "You want me to open another window?"

She kept her eyes on the table. "That's a good idea. What's the score?" she asked,

"Colt's beating the pants off you," Randy said.

Jenny closed her eyes and bit her lip to stop the moan from escaping her throat. She'd had a flashing mental image of Colt tearing off her white cotton underwear—she was wearing Tuesday on Sunday. His hand lay on the table right beside hers, large and strong.

"You have such a big, strong...vocabulary," Jenny said, catching herself at the last moment.

"Thanks," Colt said. "I think it's my turn."

"'Xenophile'?" Randy questioned suspiciously as Colt laid down the *x* and *e* before Randy's two-letter word and then the *p-h-i-l-e*. "What's it mean?"

"Someone who's attracted to foreign things."

"Like eels and caviar?" Randy asked.

"Like veiled women," Colt quipped, leering at Jenny.

Jenny picked up a doilie that was covering a hole in the arm of the couch upholstery, held it across her nose and mouth and batted her eyelashes. "Take me away, O Sheikh of Araby!" she said melodramatically.

Randy laughed. "I give up. You win, Colt. Game's over."

"Not quite yet," Colt said. He rose and did a swami's bow toward Jenny. "Your wish is my command, O Maiden of the East."

"Is that East *Texas,* suh?" Jenny said with a deep Southern accent, once again batting her lashes.

Colt grabbed a patterned cotton blanket that was draped across the couch—hiding another worn bit of upholstery—and threw it over Jenny's head as though he were really a sheikh come to kidnap her. While she was laughing uncontrollably, he whisked her up over his shoulder, hauled her into her bedroom and threw her onto the four-poster.

Jenny was still giggling when Colt pulled the blanket off her face. "I don't know when I've had such a good time. Thanks, Colt. I—"

She stopped talking and stared at him. When had he gotten so handsome? Had his cheekbones always been so sharp? His lips so full and wide? She wasn't aware of licking her lips until she heard Colt's sharp intake of air.

She met his gaze and caught a glimpse of something—what?—before his eyes were shuttered.

"Get some rest," he said as he backed his way out of the room. "I'll see you tomorrow."

No faults, she thought with a groan. *Not one damn fault.*

She dreamed of a woman in flowing, see-through silks being carried across the desert by a turbanned sheikh riding a magnificent Arabian stallion. They were running from something, but they couldn't escape because the horse kept getting bogged down in the sand. She looked up and realized a jet was falling out of the sky, about to crash right on top of their heads.

Jenny woke up before the jet hit the ground. She sat up in bed breathing hard and staring at the rising sun, wondering how she could have been laughing and playing such games last night when Huck was never coming back.

On Monday, Colt put new shingles on the leaky roof. Shirtless. His broad chest was covered in thick, dark curls. She couldn't help making the comparison to sandy-haired Huck, who'd had very little chest hair and not nearly so much muscle. Colt's shoulders bunched and relaxed as the hammer rose and fell.

She stood mesmerized as a single drop of sweat slid down the center of his back until it met his denim jeans. She found herself fascinated by the way the worn blue cloth molded his buttocks.

No faults there, either, she conceded.

Tuesday, Colt dug postholes to repair the rotten gate on the corral. "They used to punish cowboys with this job in the old days," he said, his eyes twinkling.

She found herself entranced by his gaze, unable to look away. His eyes reminded her of sapphires, except they weren't cold, like stone, but warm and welcoming. She noticed the spray of lines at the corners of his eyes where the sun had weathered his skin and realized he wasn't a boy anymore. He was a grown man. A very attractive grown man.

On Wednesday, she sat with Colt on the back porch after supper to drink a chocolate milkshake. She watched his Adam's apple bob as he leaned his head back and swallowed down the thick ice cream. Her body drew up tight as his tongue slipped out to lick the last of the milky chocolate off his upper lip.

"Are you going to drink the rest of that?" he asked, pointing to her half-finished shake.

She held out her frosty glass and said, "Help yourself."

He put his lips on the edge of the glass where hers had been and watched her as he took a sip. Tasting chocolate. Tasting her.

Her mouth went dry with desire.

She leaped up without excusing herself and ran inside, letting the screen door slam behind her, not stopping until she'd reached her bedroom. She closed the door and leaned back against it, aware of her pounding heart and the ache deep inside her.

She wanted him. It was sinful how much she wanted him. And they hadn't even had the memorial service for Huck.

What's wrong with me? How can I be having such thoughts about Colt when it's Huck I love…loved?

Several loud knocks on the door made her skitter away toward the center of the room. "Who's there?"

"It's me, Colt. Are you all right?"

"No, I'm not all right!" she said. *There's something terribly wrong with me. I can't help thinking of you. Wanting you.*

"Open the door, Jenny, and talk to me. I know something's been troubling you these past few days. I'd like to help."

"Go away, Colt." *Don't you understand? You're the problem!*

"Are you upset about that marriage proposal?"

Jenny grabbed at the excuse he'd offered. "It's been on my mind."

"Look, there's no need for you to decide about marriage right away. If you need money for the mortgage payment, I'll provide it, no matter what."

She yanked the door open. "I thought we agreed I can't take your money, Colt."

"It's no big deal, Jenny."

"It is to me."

He reached out and clasped her free hand in his. She felt the calluses on his fingertips, remembered what she'd been imagining his hands doing and jerked her hand out of his. "This isn't going to work!" she said desperately. "You can't keep coming here every day, Colt."

"Why not?"

"It's indecent!"

"Indecent? What the hell are you talking about?"

"I'm practically a widow—"

"You and Huck were never married. And in case you've forgotten, he was my friend, too."

Jenny stared at him, stricken. It wasn't Colt's fault she was attracted to him. *There's nothing wrong with him. I'm the one who's flawed.*

"I'm sorry," she said.

"If you really don't want me here, I'll stay away," he offered.

"No. Come tomorrow."

On Thursday, Jenny sent Colt out to repair a stall door in the barn while she stripped the beds, did the laundry and mopped the floors. She figured the distance would be good for both of them. If she wasn't forced to look at Colt all day, she was sure she wouldn't find herself thinking about him so much.

By noon she conceded that "absence makes the heart grow fonder." She went hunting for Colt to tell him lunch was ready, because that was the best excuse she'd been able to come up with to go after him.

"Colt? Are you out here?"

"Up here," Colt called down from the loft.

"Lunch is ready," Jenny said.

"Come on up here a minute. There's something I want to show you."

Jenny hesitated, then started up the ladder. When she reached the top, Colt grabbed her under the arms and lifted her the rest of the way up. She felt his touch all the way to her core. She was still standing where he'd left her when he turned and walked toward the corner of the loft.

"Over here," he said, going down on one knee.

Jenny told her feet to move, and they obediently headed in Colt's direction. She knelt beside him to look at what had been hidden in a bed of straw in the corner, then turned to share a smile with him. "They're adorable."

"Their eyes are still closed. They can't be more than a few days old."

"Six of them," Jenny said, counting the nursing kittens. "Jezebel, I didn't even know you'd been courting," she chided the mother cat.

Jezebel purred under Jenny's stroking.

Jenny looked at Colt and realized he was staring at her hand. His eyes locked with hers, his gaze heavy-lidded, his lips full and rigid. She stopped stroking the cat and rose abruptly.

"That stew is going to burn—"

Colt rose and grabbed her arm to keep her from fleeing. "You feel it, too."

She turned to him, her eyes wide with fright. "What are you talking about?"

"Don't bother pretending, Jenny. I've felt your eyes on me all week. I haven't been able to zip my damn jeans in the morning, thinking about you watching me."

She didn't know what to say, so she didn't say anything. A trickle of sweat tickled its way down her back. A fly buzzed, and one of the kittens mewed.

Colt let go of her and shoved his hand through his hair. "I'm afraid I don't know the proper etiquette for this situation. I suppose I should have kept on pretending right along with you, Jenny. But that wouldn't be fair to either of us."

"I can't help it," Jenny said quietly. She searched his face, saw the flare of heat in his eyes and responded to it.

"Neither can I," he replied in a hoarse voice.

"What are we going to do?"

"I could stay away."

"That wouldn't change how I feel," Jenny said. "I wonder if an experiment would help."

"What kind of experiment?" Colt said warily.

"I think maybe you should kiss me."

Colt stared at her. "What will that accomplish?"

She gave a shuddering sigh. "I'm not sure. Maybe nothing."

Colt shook his head and grinned wryly. "I feel like a fifteen-year-old kid again. How do you want to do this?"

She cocked a brow. "You're the expert, as I recall."

"All right. Come here."

As he slipped his arm around her waist, her hands slid up his chest and around his neck. He pulled the rubber band out of her ponytail and threaded his hand into her hair, angling her head for his kiss. She rose a little on tiptoe as his head lowered toward hers. She closed her eyes as his mouth covered hers.

Jenny waited with bated breath as Colt's lips pressed against hers, soft and a little damp. A frisson chased up her spine as his tongue teased the seam of her lips. She opened her mouth eagerly, and his tongue slipped inside. Without any warning, without any urging, her hips rocked into the cradle of his thighs, and she rode the hard ridge that promised so much pleasure.

So much feeling. So much heat. So much more than she had ever felt with Huck.

Jenny sobbed against Colt's mouth.

He put his hands on her shoulders and shoved her away. "Jenny?"

She sobbed again, unable to admit the horrible discovery she'd made. Her eyes blurred with tears until she could no longer see the stark look in his eyes.

He pulled her close, pressing her face against his chest and rubbing her scalp. "I guess your experiment didn't work," he said. "I'm sorry. What happens now?"

There were so many things Colt didn't know. So many things she couldn't tell him. A clock was ticking. She didn't have the luxury of waiting until the guilt was gone. They'd already lost so much time. She didn't want to lose any more. This physical thing between them wasn't love, but she was smart enough to know it was something very special. It didn't happen all the time. It hadn't happened between her and Huck.

Jenny didn't know how long they'd been standing in the loft before she became aware of Colt's heart thudding beneath her ear, of his hand stroking her hair, of his strength wrapped around her frailty. "I have—" She cleared the frog from her throat. "I have a favor to ask."

"Name it," Colt said.

She leaned back and laid her hand on his cheek. "Will you marry me?"

"Are you sure that's what you want?"

"It's the practical thing to do. Considering…everything."

Colt pulled her back into his arms. "It's been awful damned tough on you, hasn't it? All right, we'll do the practical thing and get married."

"In June," she said. "When I would have married Huck."

"Right. I'll just step up to the altar in place of my best friend and say 'I do.' Do you suppose anyone will notice?"

"I will," she said quietly.

CHAPTER FOUR

"I'M MOVING IN WITH Jenny Wright tomorrow," Colt announced to his family at supper that evening.

The astonished faces of his brothers and sisters, the gasp from his mother and the frown on his father's face all demanded an explanation. "We're getting married in June," he said baldly, "on the day Jenny would have married Huck. I'm moving in so I'll be able to finish the repairs that need to be made at the Double D before my leave is over."

"I knew you wanted her for yourself," Jake said in disgust. "But Huck isn't even cold in his grave!"

Colt was out of his seat and reaching for his brother before the last words were out of his mouth. Their father intervened, catching Colt around the chest and holding him back, while Rabb and Avery did the same with Jake.

Colt's hands were fisted at his sides, and his face was flushed with rage. "Take it back, Jake."

"It's the truth," Jake said.

"Did Jenny agree to this?" his mother asked.

Colt tried to answer, but when he couldn't get words past the knot in his throat, just nodded.

"You can't marry Jenny!" Frannie exclaimed. "She's Huck's girl."

Colt felt his stomach roll. They were only saying what everyone else in town would say when they heard what he and Jenny had decided. He'd hoped for more understanding from his family, but he didn't give a damn whether he got it or not. He was going to marry Jenny. "My mind is made up," he said.

"What's the rush?" Avery asked.

"Jenny's going to lose the Double D unless she gets some quick financial help. Marriage is the best security I can offer her."

"I knew she was having trouble making ends meet," his father said. "Are you sure marriage is the best solution to the problem?"

Colt shook himself free. "Huck was my best friend. I owe Jenny whatever help I can give her."

"Everybody sit down, please," his mother said. "Let's discuss this calmly and rationally."

Rabb and Avery let Jake go, and he sat down. Colt was too agitated to rejoin his family at the table. "Look," he said. "There's really nothing to discuss. Jenny and I are getting married, and nothing anybody says is going to stop us."

"We're not trying—"

Colt interrupted his father. "I'm sorry, Dad. I think it'll be more comfortable for everybody if I just move in with Jenny tonight." He turned and headed for his bedroom to pack.

He heard a knock at the door a moment later. He should have known they wouldn't let him go without another lecture. When he opened the door, he found Jenny standing there.

"What are you doing here?"

"I needed to talk to you."

He looked out into the hall, which was surprisingly empty of his parents and siblings, then dragged her inside and closed the door behind her. "What's going on?"

"You tell me," she said. "I sneaked in through the patio door and heard a lot of yelling in the dining room."

His lips flattened. "My family isn't exactly thrilled at my upcoming nuptials."

"Neither is mine," she said. "I called my brothers and told them what we'd decided, and they all came over to try to talk me out of it. Sam was furious. He accused me of carrying on with you all these years. I couldn't believe the things he said. I…" She took a shuddering breath. "It was horrible."

He saw the anguish in her eyes and pulled her into his arms. "I know," he said. "Jake accused me of jumping the gun, too."

"We can't go through with this, Colt."

His heart lurched. He couldn't give her up now. Wouldn't give her up. Even if he was only going to have her for a matter of weeks before he left to return to Egypt.

"Do these second thoughts have anything to do with what happened in the loft? Because—"

She covered his mouth with her hand to silence him. "It's not that. It's the opposition from both our families. I don't want to be at war with my brothers, and I know you love your family as much as I love mine. How can we do this to them?"

"What other choice do we have?"

"I can give up the ranch and move into town."

"You don't want to do that."

She sighed. "No, I don't."

"Our families have been told, and we're both still walking and talking. I'd say the worst is over."

"Is it?" she asked, looking up at him.

"In fifty years, I guarantee you nobody will remember how we ended up married."

She managed a wobbly smile, and Colt felt his heart

begin to thump a little harder. He was grateful he no longer had to hide his physical attraction to her, but a larger problem remained. Colt was *in love* with Jenny. It complicated everything; it didn't change anything. The only way to help her was to marry her. Unless she'd take money from him without the connection.

"If you really think marriage is a bad idea, let me make you a loan," he said. "I can work for you at the Double D until my leave is up."

She shook her head. "I couldn't borrow as much money from you as it would take to put the ranch back on sound footing. I'd never be able to pay it all back. And I'm going to need help on the Double D for a very long time. A lifetime."

"Then marry me, Jenny. Huck wouldn't want you to lose the ranch. Huck would kill me if I let you lose the ranch."

The attempt at humor brought a fleeting smile to her lips. She brushed her fingertips across the front of his shirt, pressing away a wrinkle and causing his body to tense beneath her hand. He held himself perfectly still, loving the touch, wanting it, yet aware of how precarious their relationship was precisely because of their fierce attraction to each other.

Her hand paused near his heart, and he wondered if she could feel it jumping in response to her touch. She looked deep into his eyes, searching, he supposed, for whatever reservations she might find there. There were none. At least none he was willing to let her see.

Finally she said, "All right, Colt. If you're willing to go through with this marriage despite the opposition from our families, I'll go along."

"There is one thing," he said.

"What?" she asked.

"I told my family I was moving in with you tonight."

She shook her head in disbelief. "Colt—"

"I guess I can stay at a hotel in town."

"You can sleep in one of my brothers' rooms."

"Is Randy going to give you any trouble about this?"

"If he does, he can do his own cooking and laundry until he goes off to college." She laid her head on his chest. "I hope we're doing the right thing."

"As long as we're both convinced it's the right thing, then it is," he said with a certainty he wasn't feeling inside. He had plenty of fears.

What if she never learns to love me? What if I can't make her happy?

There were bound to be problems, especially since he would be away in the Air Force. And there was going to be talk. But together they could weather the storm. And Jenny would be his at last.

He'd imagined making love to her a thousand times over the years he'd known her. But that was all he'd ever done. Imagine. He'd never thought his dreams would come true. Soon he'd have the right to hold her naked in his arms. To put himself inside her. He wanted to make love to her. More important, he wanted her love.

There isn't enough time, a voice warned. *You've got less than sixty days before you have to report back for duty in Egypt. Sixty days isn't much time to woo a grieving woman.*

He had to find a way. He had to find the time.

Colt smoothed his hand over Jenny's hair with a sense of wonder. He was going to be sleeping in a room nearby her tonight. In a little more than a month he'd have the right to lie beside her.

I'm sorry, Huck, but she needs me. I know you wouldn't want her to be alone. And I love her.

"How did you get here tonight?" he asked.

"I drove Old Nellie."

Old Nellie was a rusted-out '56 Chevy pickup. "If you'll give me a minute to finish packing, I'll ride back with you," Colt said.

The door opened without anyone knocking, and Colt found himself staring at his brother Jake over Jenny's head. His arms were around her—in comfort—just as her arms held tight to him.

Jake took one look, and his eyes narrowed. "I came here to apologize. Looks like I was right all along."

Colt stared his brother down. He'd done nothing wrong. He'd loved Jenny for years, but he'd never by word or deed done anything to suggest to her how he felt. If Huck had come home and married her, he would have lived his life without her ever knowing he cared. He'd done nothing that required an apology. "Get out, Jake, and leave us alone."

"If alone is what you want, little brother, alone is what you'll get!" Jake backed out, slamming the door behind him.

Colt heaved a gusty sigh. "Damn it all to hell."

"Colt, if this marriage is going to cause problems—"

Colt laid his fingertips against Jenny's lips to silence her and felt himself quiver at that small touch. "Jake only sees things in black and white. He'll get over it—in fifty years or so."

He saw her try to smile…and fail.

"Cheer up," he said, tipping her chin up so he could look into her eyes. "The cavalry is riding to the rescue."

She stepped back, away from his touch. "Thanks, Colt. The least I can do is help you pack. Where do you want to start?"

It didn't take long to pack his things. He hadn't brought much with him from Egypt. He grabbed the small bag and headed down the hall.

His mother was waiting for him there.

"Hello, Jenny," she said, reaching out for Jenny's hand. "I'm very happy for you both."

"Thank you, Mrs. Whitelaw," Jenny replied.

The two women held hands for a moment before his mother turned to him. She didn't say anything, just stared, her heart back in her eyes.

"I'm sorry, Mom," he said at last. "I can't stay here."

She smiled bravely. "I know. I just wish..." She turned quickly back to Jenny and gave her a hug. "I wish you both the best." Then she reached up to touch his cheek. "Take care of yourself, Colt. Don't be a stranger."

She'd made no comment about whether they all planned to attend the wedding next month. He opened his mouth to ask and shut it again. It was better to let sleeping dogs lie.

Jenny slipped behind the wheel of the pickup as he threw his bag into the rusted-out truck bed. He settled onto the torn passenger seat, and she released the clutch and stepped on the gas.

The short drive from his home to hers had never seemed so long. He listened to the noisy rattle in the dash. The *clunk* as the carriage of the truck hit the frame when the worn-out shock absorbers failed. The sound of sand and gravel crunching under the bald tires. And, of course, every breath she took.

Colt searched for some safe subject to discuss. Everything seemed fraught with memories of Huck. Maybe that wasn't so bad. The three of them had been best friends. It was fitting that Huck should be here on this journey with them.

"I miss him already," Colt said into the silence.

"I keep asking myself what he would think about what we're doing," she said.

"He'd understand," Colt said.

"Would he?" she asked, turning to look at him.

"He loved us both. He wouldn't want you to lose the ranch."

Jenny shot him an agonized glance. "I can't believe we're even thinking about—"

"Huck is dead, Jenny. We have to go on living."

"To marry you so soon… It seems… I feel like I'm betraying Huck. His memory, anyway. I'm attracted to you, Colt, but I don't love you. I loved Huck."

"We both loved him, Jenny. That's why getting married is the right thing to do."

"There's something wrong with the logic in that statement, but I'm too tired to figure it out right now." She pulled up to the kitchen door and shut off the engine. It ran for another couple of seconds before it died. "It looks like Randy's still up."

"Do you want me to talk to him?" Colt asked. "To explain?"

"Randy hasn't said a word against this marriage. I think he understands how bad things are."

And maybe how alone you'd be with Huck never coming back, Colt thought.

Jenny sighed, then pushed the truck door open and stepped down. "Come on in, and I'll show you where to sleep."

Colt grabbed his bag from the truck bed, then followed her up the back steps and into the kitchen. Randy was leaning back against the sink, a can of Pepsi in his hand.

"Hello, Randy. Long time no see," he said, extending his hand to the lanky teenager. Randy's hair was the same blond as Jenny's, but his eyes were hazel instead of blue and looked like they'd seen a great deal more of life than a boy his age should.

Randy hesitated, then took Colt's hand and shook it.

"Hi, Colt. What's up?" He flushed as he realized the can of worms such a question might open up. "I mean…I thought you were moving in tomorrow."

"Change of plans," Colt replied. He turned to Jenny, whose face looked drawn. "Where do you want me?"

"Follow me," she said, hurrying from the kitchen.

"You gonna stay in Sam's room?" Randy asked, tagging along behind them.

"I'll stay wherever Jenny puts me."

"Sam's room is next to mine," Randy said. "Down the hall from Jenny's."

"Sounds like a good place to be," Colt said, meeting Jenny's glance over her shoulder. It seemed *down the hall* was as close to his sister as Randy wanted Colt.

Colt didn't know if Sam's old room was where she'd initially wanted to put him, but she took her cue from Randy's suggestion, and he found himself in the doorway to a small, feminine room a moment later.

"This is my sewing room now," she said. "I'll get my things out of here tomorrow."

The small room held a single, brass-railed bed and a bedside table with a delicate porcelain lamp. Her sewing machine sat on a table heaped with clothes that she was either making or mending. In the corner stood a clothing dummy wearing what looked like the beginning of a wedding gown.

The gingham curtains were trimmed in eyelet lace, and the bed was heaped with a bunch of frilly pillows and a pair of rag dolls. It might have been Sam's room once upon a time, but Jenny had made it hers.

This was a side of Jenny he'd rarely seen: the soft, feminine side. She'd done a man's work on the Double D for as long as he could remember, and he'd rarely seen her wearing anything but jeans. Everything in this room was soft, decorated in pastel pink and pale green. The dolls were a surprise. It smelled flowery, like maybe the drawers were filled with some kind of potpourri.

She flushed as he met her gaze. "I'll just take these with me," she said, scooping up the lacy pillows and the dolls, as though she were embarrassed for him to see them. "Randy can get you anything you need," she said as she backed out of the room.

"What bee got into her bonnet?" Randy asked, staring after her.

"I guess she wasn't expecting company tonight," Colt said.

"Why did you come tonight?" Randy asked.

Colt met Randy's troubled gaze and decided to tell the truth. "My family doesn't approve of this marriage any more than your brothers do. I thought it would make everybody more comfortable if I got this move over with."

"If you hurt her, I'll take you out myself."

Colt met the teenager's warning look with a steady gaze. "There isn't a man alive who cares more for your sister than I do, Randy. I only want to help her."

The boy stared at him a moment longer before his shoulders sagged. "Jeez, Colt. We sure can use the help. Things have been pretty tight around here. Jenny hasn't let on to the others how bad things are, but it's a little hard to hide the truth from me, when all we ever have for supper is macaroni and cheese."

Trust a youth to judge the state of things by what he put in his stomach, Colt thought wryly. "Things are going to get better, Randy. I'm here to make sure of it."

"Thanks, Colt. Guess I'll get some sleep. The school bus comes early in the morning."

"Good night, Randy. I'll see you at breakfast."

Colt stripped to his shorts, which was what he'd worn

to sleep in for the past ten years, when he might find himself jumping into a flight suit in the middle of the night, and slipped between the covers.

The sheets were printed with roses. The pillow smelled like…Jenny. The springs squeaked and squealed as he turned over, trying to get comfortable. The mattress sagged in the middle, a reminder that everything in the house was old and worn-out and needed to be replaced. He turned out the delicate porcelain lamp and stared into the darkness. He could hear the crickets outside his window and the rustle of the wind through the grass.

It must have been hard to be the one female in a house full of men. With most of them gone, she'd created this feminine haven for herself. When he thought about it a little more, Colt realized it wasn't a woman's room, it was a girl's room. A place, perhaps, to recapture a lost childhood?

Colt remembered a time when he'd come to visit and had helped Jenny feed Randy. The kid loved squashed-up peas. Huck had decided he would rather go play than stay and help, so he'd had Jenny to himself for the whole afternoon—along with her four younger brothers. Her mother had been confined to her bed, watched over by Jenny's aunt.

Colt had enjoyed himself tremendously that day because it was all new to him—feeding Randy, changing Sam's diaper, then making sure Tyler and James took a bath. He'd been able to go home at the end of the day. Jenny had not.

The door opened almost before he heard the knock and was shut again after Jenny slipped inside.

"Colt?" she said.

He sat up and turned on the light. She was wearing an old chenille bathrobe and a pair of fluffy slippers. Her hair was down on her shoulders, and her face looked scrubbed.

He felt his body tighten. "What are you doing in here, Jenny?"

"I can't do it, Colt."

He slid his legs over the side of the bed, but kept the sheet over his hips. "Do what?"

"I can't marry you."

He forgot about the sheet as he stood and crossed to take her by the arms. "What's going on, Jenny? I thought this was all settled."

Tears welled in her eyes and one plopped onto her cheek. He brushed it away with his thumb.

"Huck will always be there between us. Don't you see? Someday you're going to want a wife who can love you back, and I—"

"Let me worry about what I need," Colt said, pulling her into his arms. Her body was stiff and unyielding. He leaned back and separated her hands and put them around his waist, then pulled her close.

He was sorry as soon as he did. He could feel the soft warmth of her breasts against his naked chest. Feel her thighs through the wafer-thin robe. He angled his hips away, so she wouldn't become aware of his arousal. *I'm sorry, Huck. I can't help wanting her.*

He took Jenny's head between his hands and tilted her face up to his. "Listen to me, Jenny. I don't expect you to stop loving Huck. His memory will always be with us. I loved him, too, you know." He kissed a tear from her cheek and tasted the salt…and the sweetness of her. "Let me do this for him, for you, for both of you."

"I feel so guilty," she whispered.

"Why?"

"Because I'm glad you're here. Because I'm glad I don't have to face life alone anymore. And you're not even the man who was supposed to come home to me. What's wrong with me, Colt?"

He hugged her tight against him. "Nothing's wrong with you, Jenny. You're just human."

"I'm so tired of trying to hold everything together by myself. You can't imagine what it's been like, Colt. I've been counting the days until Huck got here to take some of the burden off my shoulders. I know it's not fair to lay so much on you. I just can't do it by myself anymore. I can't."

She was weeping in earnest, and Colt lifted her into his arms and sat down on the sagging bed and let her cry. She kept her mouth against his neck to mute the sound, as aware as he was that her brother was in the next room. When the sobs became hiccups, he felt her fingertips move tentatively across his chest. Gooseflesh rose where she touched.

"You're cold," she said.

"It's the breeze from the window," he lied. "I'll close it later."

"I should go to bed. It's late." But she made no move to leave his lap. Her hand stole around his neck, and he quivered as she played with the short hair at his nape. "I'm sorry I fell apart like that."

"You're entitled. I don't know how you've managed to do so much with so little help. Why haven't you said something to Sam and Tyler and James?"

"They've got their own lives. The ranch is my problem."

"And mine now."

"Until your leave is up."

"Yeah," he said, realizing for the first time how little help he was going to be if he left her behind and returned to Egypt.

At last she lifted her head. Her eyes were red-rimmed, and her lower lip was swollen where she'd chewed on it.

"I'm so used to carrying all the responsibility on my shoulders, I'm not sure how I'll adjust to having someone around to help."

"I'm sure you'll manage. You always have."

She looked at him strangely. "Yes. I have."

It took Colt a moment to identify what he was feeling, what she'd heard in his voice. He was angry. Furious, really. At his friend. How could Huck have left her alone all these years and gone off to fly jets? Why hadn't Huck stayed home and married Jenny and run the ranch with her? Why hadn't Huck given her babies of her own, instead of leaving her alone to raise her brothers?

He was no better. He'd known for a long time how little time Huck spent with her, how little help Huck had provided, but he hadn't encouraged his friend to marry her. *Because as long as Huck never married Jenny there was always the chance she might be yours someday.*

Colt felt sick inside. It was hard to face such truths. He had a chance now to redress the wrongs of the past. He could be there for Jenny. Love her. Take care of her.

For Huck's sake? Or for your own? a voice asked.

For Jenny's sake, he answered. She deserved a better life, and he was going to make sure she got it.

"You'll feel better after a night's sleep," Colt said as he stood and set Jenny's feet on the floor. He had to unwrap her arms from around his neck. He held her hands for a moment, his thumbs moving across her work-worn knuckles. "I promise I'll always take care of you, Jenny. It's the least I can do for Huck." *And for the woman I love.*

CHAPTER FIVE

JENNY ROSE THE NEXT morning feeling—for the first time in a very long time—like anything was possible. She dressed in the same worn jeans, another faded Western shirt, and the same boots with the holes in the soles that were layered with newspaper. But she didn't feel the least forlorn. *Why do I feel so different?* she wondered. Hope. It was as simple as that.

"Good morning."

Jenny was surprised to find Colt in the kitchen ahead of her. His short black hair was still shiny wet from the shower. She must have been more exhausted than she'd thought, to sleep through the groaning water pipes.

He rubbed at the beard darkening his cheeks and chin and said, "Hope you don't mind. Figured I'd wait to shave again till these stitches come out."

Growing up in a houseful of men, she'd seen many an unshaven face at the breakfast table, but never one she found so appealing. "I'll make us some coffee," she said, suddenly aware that she'd been standing there admiring the way his chest filled out his white T-shirt and the way his jeans molded…everything.

He pointed to the percolator. "Coffee's made." He had a pan on the stove and was laying strips of bacon in it.

"I should be making your breakfast," she said.

He grinned. "Tell you what. You clean up the mess, and we'll call it even."

"Deal," she said, crossing to stand beside him and pour herself a cup of coffee.

The heat of his body reminded her that she was no longer alone. And revived the unwanted attraction that lay between them. She hadn't stopped loving Huck; she'd merely acknowledged this physical *thing* that existed between her and Huck's best friend. She refused to feel guilty for taking the only road open to her.

Jenny took a sip of hot, black coffee, savoring the bitter taste of it, before she swallowed. According to Colt, there had been some delay in returning Huck's body to the States, but the senator had promised to contact Colt regarding the funeral arrangements. "Do you know yet when and where Huck's funeral is being held?" she asked. "I'll need to make arrangements to be there."

"Huck's being buried on the family farm in Virginia, where the senator makes his home when he's in Washington. Family and close friends only. I'm sorry, Jenny. I told the senator you should be there."

"Oh." Huck's father had never accepted her, but it hurt to be excluded from the funeral more than she'd thought it would. Her hands began to tremble, and she carefully set down the coffee cup. Huck wouldn't know she wasn't there. But it was hard to let him go when she'd never gotten the chance to say good-bye. She blinked furiously to fight back the tears. She was done with crying for what couldn't be changed.

Colt's arms closed tightly around her. "Huck will know you wanted to be there. And why you weren't."

"It hurts. Oh, God, I hurt inside."

"Me, too," he admitted hoarsely.

They stood wrapped in a comforting embrace until the smell of burning bacon forced them apart. Colt let go of her, grabbed a fork and turned the blackened bacon. "I hope you like your bacon crisp," he said.

"I like bacon any way I can get it." Jenny flushed as she realized Colt must have made an early morning trip to the convenience store. She and Randy hadn't eaten bacon at breakfast for quite a while, because it didn't fit into their meager budget.

She met Colt's eyes, which urged her not to make a big deal of it. It rankled to accept even this much charity. "Colt, I don't think you should be buying food—"

Randy arrived in the kitchen with his hair askew, teenage whiskers mottling his face, wearing a pair of pajama bottoms and scratching his bare stomach. "I smell bacon."

"Go get dressed," Jenny told him, wanting Randy out of the kitchen so she could finish making her point to Colt. "Breakfast will be ready by the time you are."

"Will you make me a lunch?" Randy asked.

"Sure," Jenny said. "Get moving." Randy was supposed to make his own lunch, but she knew why he hadn't. He hated the monotonous menu of peanut butter and jelly sandwiches, but that was all they could afford. She opened the refrigerator to get out the jelly and gasped. "What did you do? Buy out the store?"

She shot a look at Colt, whose face had taken on a mulish cast. "If I'm going to be eating your food, I figured I ought to provide my share of it," he said.

"Oh, Colt, you shouldn't have done this."

"Don't push me," he said, throwing down the fork he was using to turn the bacon and putting his fisted hands on his hips. "I'm mad as hell about what I've found here. It wouldn't take much to send me over the edge."

"Mad? About what?"

"That you never told me—or Huck, who would've told me—just how bad things are around here. Damn it all,

Jenny! Macaroni and cheese? Peanut butter and jelly? Huck was rich, and I've got a trust fund of my own. Why didn't you ask us for help?"

"I didn't want your help."

"Why the hell not?"

Jenny felt her stomach twist into a knot. *Because if I'd asked for help, you'd have found out the secret I've been keeping from both of you.* "Pride," she said, her own fisted hands landing on her hips. "I didn't want to admit how badly I'd failed. There. Are you satisfied?"

Colt huffed out a gust of air, then hooked his thumbs in his back pockets. "I'm sorry. I guess it's easy to criticize when you're not around to see how difficult it is to shoulder the load. But please let me help, now that I'm here."

"All right, Colt." She reached up to get plates from the cupboard and noticed her hands were shaking. Another bullet dodged. She didn't dare tell Colt the truth. No one knew the truth. Not even Randy, who lived with her.

"Where's breakfast?" Randy asked, setting his book bag on the floor beside the empty table. "The bus'll be here in a couple of minutes!"

Jenny set plates and silverware on the table, then made Randy's lunch while Colt fried a couple of eggs for her brother "over easy," as he'd requested. They were just sitting down with their own eggs, toast and bacon, when Randy stuffed down his third slice of toast and bolted for the door. "See you after school!" he said as the screen door slammed behind him.

"Whew!" Colt said with a grin. "I'd forgotten how hectic school mornings can be."

Jenny managed a smile. "It's hard to believe there's less than a month left before he's done."

Jenny thought of all the years she'd made sure her brothers got off to school. She'd been looking forward to the day when Randy graduated, because it meant she could begin her life with Huck. That wasn't going to happen now. She looked across the table and met Colt's concerned gaze.

"I'm here, Jenny. It's going to be all right."

The comforting words did nothing to ease the tension in her shoulders. "I'm afraid you'll regret this later, Colt." *When you find out the truth about me.*

"Let's take it one day at a time, shall we?"

Jenny released a shuddering breath. "All right. Where do you want to start today?"

"Suppose you tell me."

"If I don't get some fence repaired, what few cattle I have are going to be long gone."

"Fence it is," Colt said as he rose to take his plate to the sink.

The fence was barbed wire stretched between mesquite posts. Some of the posts had rotted, and some of them had been pushed down by cattle rubbing against them. It was hard work digging new postholes and restretching the barbed wire. Jenny told herself the lack of supplies had discouraged her from tackling the job. The truth was, it was grueling work that required more brute strength than she had.

As she watched the corded sinews flex in Colt's arms, Jenny conceded there were simply some things a man could do better than a woman. "Thanks, Colt," she said as she stapled the barbed wire into place. "I couldn't have done this without you."

He grabbed the kerchief from his back pocket, lifted his hat and wiped the sweat from his face and neck. He retrieved his T-shirt from the post where he'd left it, hung his Stetson there while he slipped his shirt back on, then resettled the Stetson low enough to shade his eyes. "Digging postholes is a lot harder work than flying jets," he said with a crooked smile.

She pointed at the white contrail left by a jet flying overhead. "So you'd rather be up there than down here?"

He tipped up his Stetson and squinted at the plane overhead. "Flying is all I ever wanted to do." He looked back at her. "But right now, there's no place I'd rather be than here with you."

"Digging postholes?" she said with a teasing grin.

"Better me than you," he said, his voice turning serious.

She turned and headed for the truck, tools in hand. "I don't mind a little hard work."

He caught her by the elbow and swung her around. He held on to her arm while he took the posthole digger and the staple gun out of her hands one at a time and threw them into the rusted-out bed of the pickup. Then he grasped both arms and turned her to face him.

"A little hard work is one thing, Jenny. Running yourself into the ground trying to do too much by yourself is another thing entirely. I've been watching you this past week, and it's plain to me that you're worn-out."

"I can't sleep," she retorted.

"This is more than lost sleep," he said. "You're wrung out. And so skinny a hard wind could blow you over."

She pulled herself free and took a step back. Colt was so much more perceptive than Huck. Huck hadn't noticed how thin she was—and how tired she was—four months ago, when he'd come for the Christmas holidays. Colt was so close to discovering the truth. She wanted to blurt it out to him. But that would send him running for sure.

"I'll admit I'm overworked," she said, feeling her way carefully. "It's been tough doing everything myself. I guarantee you I'll sleep better—and eat better, especially with the way you're shopping—now that you're here."

"I wish you'd said something sooner."

"Would you have stopped flying jets and come home to help me?" she asked in a quiet voice.

He looked stunned at the suggestion. "I... You know I would have..." He shrugged. "I don't honestly know. I like to think I'd have come if you'd said you needed me."

She shook her head. "You're only fooling yourself, Colt. You're just like Huck. All you have to do is sniff jet fuel, and you're off into the wild blue yonder."

He laughed. "I'm not that bad."

"You've asked me to marry you knowing full well you intend to return to Egypt to finish your tour there. What if I said I needed you here? That I wanted you to stay here with me? Would you resign from the Air Force?"

A shuddery breath escaped before Colt said, "Are you asking me to resign?"

Jenny made a face. "I don't know. It hardly seems fair to ask you to stay here when we aren't going to have a real marriage."

"Whoa, there, woman. Who said it wasn't going to be a real marriage?"

She flushed. "I suppose I meant a normal marriage. You know, where the two parties love each other and plan to spend their lives together."

Colt's brow furrowed, and his hands caressed her arms where he'd been tightly gripping her. "I wish I could give you that. I really do, but—"

"We don't love each other, and you plan to spend your life flying jets," she finished for him. She reached up to gently smooth the furrows from his brow with her thumb. "Don't worry, Colt. I'll be fine. I don't blame you for what happened to Huck. Truly I don't."

"I just wish—"

She put her fingertips over his lips. "No regrets. I'm

grateful for whatever help you're able to give me during the next few weeks. I'm not going to ask for more."

He pulled her hand down, grasping it in his own. "That's the problem," he said. "You never ask for anything. What is it you want out of life, Jenny? I mean, besides scraping a meager living out of this place?"

"I want—wanted—to wake with my husband beside me and lie in bed listening to the morning sounds. I wanted us to work side by side, making the Double D as wonderful a place to live as it once was. And I wanted children of my own." She sighed wistfully. "It's too late for a family now."

"Why?" Colt asked.

She realized what she'd almost revealed and smiled to distract him. "I'm too old, for one thing. And the man I'm about to marry would rather fly jets." She stepped back and pulled her hand free, breaking all contact between them.

Colt cleared his throat and stuck his thumbs in his back pockets to keep from reaching for her again. "So you're going to spend your life on this godforsaken ranch all alone?"

"I'm sure my brothers will come around on holidays."

"Don't any of them want to live here with you? What's Randy going to do when he finishes college?" Colt asked.

"He wants to go into business for himself and earn lots of money."

"Fine. What about Sam and Tyler and James?"

"Sam's foreman for a nearby ranch," Jenny said. "Tyler's headed to medical school in Houston. And James…"

"What about James?"

She gave him a wondering look. "James is studying to become a minister. So you see, I'm on my own."

Colt saw a great deal. She'd given up her own hopes and dreams to make sure her brothers realized theirs. Every extra penny must have gone for tuition or books or clothes.

That was why the ranch had suffered. She was obviously very proud of them, and their opposition to this marriage was proof of how much they cared for her.

He couldn't just marry her and leave her here to manage on her own. On the other hand, he didn't think he could give up flying, either.

"Have you ever thought about selling the Double D?" he asked.

"I've thought about it," she admitted.

"And?"

Her eyes searched the horizon. He looked along with her and didn't see much, just a few scrub mesquite, some cactus and buffalo grass and bluebonnets, and in the distance, a few craggy bluffs that marked deep canyons similar to those that graced Hawk's Pride.

"I know it doesn't seem like much," she said. "But I love it. I feel connected to everyone who came before me." She turned to look at him. "I want—wanted—my children to grow up here and to love their heritage as much as I do."

Colt imagined Jenny playing with a bunch of kids, tickling them and laughing with them and having fun...without him. Because he'd be off flying jets.

It wouldn't be fair to leave her alone and pregnant.

Is it any more fair to deprive her of the one thing she wants that you can give her?

Colt took two steps toward Jenny and brushed a stray wisp of hair from her brow. His hand lingered on her cheek. "It's not too late for children, if you really want them."

"I can't raise them alone, Colt. Or rather, I won't do that to them. My dad left us and...I just wouldn't do that to any child of mine. Not if I could help it."

"I see." Colt looked deep into Jenny's eyes, wondering how it had come to this—a choice between the woman he had always loved, and the thing he loved doing most.

It didn't make it any easier to know that she didn't love him. That her heart belonged—would always belong—to his best friend.

CHAPTER SIX

COLT STUDIED JENNY in the sleeveless black sheath she'd worn to the memorial service for Huck. She was surrounded by friends who'd come to the Double D to bring mountains of food and offer their condolences. Her hair was gathered in a shiny golden knot at her crown, leaving her neck and shoulders bare, so he could see her body curved in all the right places. But she left a frail shadow on the ground, and her face looked wan. It dawned on him suddenly that she might be sick.

Sick people sometimes die.

Colt forced back the feeling of panic. *Jenny isn't sick. She's just tired.* The fear that she might be ill was like a living thing inside him, clawing at him, tearing at his insides. He knew his feelings were irrational, but his dread was born of firsthand experience.

When he was too young to know better, he'd made friends of the kids who attended Camp LittleHawk, the camp for kids with cancer started by his mother at Hawk's Pride. He was eight when he met Tom Hartwell. Like many of the kids at camp, Tom had leukemia, but it was in remission. He and Tom had become blood brothers. Tom wanted to fly jets someday. Colt said he'd never thought much about it, but it sounded like fun.

Colt felt his insides squeeze at the memory of the freckle-faced, blue-eyed boy. Tom had worn a baseball cap to cover his head, left bald by chemotherapy. "My hair's really, really red," Tom had said with a grin. "Wait till it grows back in. You won't believe it!"

But the leukemia had come back, and neither Colt's raging nor his prayers—nor the best doctors money could buy—had been able to save his blood brother. Tom had died before Colt ever got a chance to see his red hair.

Jenny's not sick. She's just tired, he repeated to himself.

Nevertheless, he moved hurriedly through the crowd of mourners, briefly greeting neighbors he hadn't seen in years, catching brief snatches of conversation.

"...Remember when Huck and Jenny and Colt..."

"Then Huck and Jenny and Colt went galloping across..."

"—going to take Huck's place at the altar. Can you believe..."

He stood at Jenny's shoulder and knew she was aware of him when she leaned back against him and reached for his hand. He interrupted old Mrs. Carmichael to say, "Jenny and I are going out onto the porch for some air. Please excuse us," and led her away without looking back.

It wasn't easy getting through the kitchen, which was also full of people, including most of his own siblings. He didn't allow anyone to stop them. "Jenny needs some air," he said as he headed inexorably for the back porch.

Even there they found no respite. His mother and father stood on the porch, along with two of Jenny's brothers.

"There they are now," Sam said when he spied them. "I want to talk to you, Colt. I don't think—"

"Not now," Colt said without stopping. "Jenny and I are going for a walk." He put himself between her and everyone else and headed off down the rutted dirt road that led away from the ranch.

Jenny stumbled once in her black pumps, and he put his arm around her waist and kept on walking.

"Where's the fire?" Jenny asked.

Colt stopped abruptly and stared at her. "What?"

"Where are we going in such a hurry?"

Colt realized he'd been blindly running from his fear, which stabbed him anew when he looked down and saw the gauntness beneath her cheekbones and the shadows beneath her eyes. He had to work to keep his voice steady as he asked, "Are you all right?"

She gave him a quizzical look. "My fiancé is dead, and I've agreed to marry another man in a matter of weeks, but otherwise I suppose—"

He shook his head impatiently. "I mean, are you feeling all right? You look so thin, so exhausted. I thought you might be...sick."

She stiffened and looked away. "If I were, I wouldn't expect you to take care of me."

The air soughed slowly from Colt's lungs. Jenny knew better than anyone how assiduously he avoided sick people. When they were kids, he hadn't come near her house for a long time because her mother was dying of cancer, and he couldn't face seeing the ravages of the disease. He put a hand on her shoulder, and she jerked free and turned to face him.

"To answer your question, I'm fine, just very tired and very unhappy," she snapped. "We should go back now."

She'd already started back toward the house when he caught her elbow and turned her around again. "This way," he said, leading her along the twin dirt tracks that had been created by wagon wheels more than a century before.

She went along but asked, "Where are we going?"

"You need to rest."

She laughed. "Rest? You've practically got me jogging in high heels. I'm going to sprain an ankle—"

He scooped her up into his arms, making her cry out

in surprise and grab his shoulders. He left the road, heading across country toward a single live oak that created a circle of shade.

She laughed at him uneasily. "Colt, where are you taking me?"

"Somewhere you can take a nap in peace and quiet."

"I've got company at the house."

"All of whom are perfectly capable of entertaining themselves with stories of 'Huck and Jenny and Colt,'" he said.

He set her down on the patchy grass, then sat with his back against the trunk of the live oak, his legs stretched out in front of him, and pulled her down beside him. "Lay your head on my lap and relax," he said.

"Colt—"

He tugged on her hand. "Humor me, Jenny."

When she was settled with her head on his thigh, she closed her eyes and heaved a great sigh. The wind rustled the leaves of the live oak, and cattle lowed in the distance. A jay complained on a branch above them. They might have been a thousand miles from another human being.

"Thank you, Colt," Jenny murmured. "I didn't realize how much I needed a little peace and quiet."

He reached down and pulled the pins from her hair, then ran his fingers through the silky mass, massaging her scalp where the knot had been.

"That feels wonderful," she said.

Colt wanted to do a lot more, to hold her in his arms, to lie next to her, body to body. Instead he settled his hand on her nape, where he gently massaged the tense muscles.

"I'm not sure I could have heard one more story about Huck and me and you without breaking into tears," Jenny confessed in a quiet voice. "Thanks for rescuing me."

"That's too bad. I've got one I'd like to tell," Colt said.

Jenny's eyes opened, and she started to sit up. "Oh?"

He pressed her back down and said, "Relax. It's a good story, I promise."

"All right. Go ahead."

He could feel the rigidity in her body, the physical wariness. She'd taken so many blows lately, and he wanted to spare her any more pain. But avoiding the subject wasn't the answer. Neither of them was likely to forget the part Huck had played in their lives. They both had to accept his loss and move on.

Colt brushed a stray curl from Jenny's brow and said, "Huck and I were riding camels—"

Jenny's head popped up. "Camels? Really?"

"Lie down and listen," Colt said with a chuckle. When Jenny was settled again with her cheek on his thigh, he continued. "Huck and I were riding camels in Cairo, tourists traveling from one pyramid to the next, when he turned to me and said, 'I wish Jenny were here, because she'd have the nerve to see just how fast this beast can go. We'd be galloping across the desert instead of walking sedately behind some guide.'"

"Did Huck really say that?"

"He did," Colt confirmed. "And he was right. You're an amazing woman, Jenny."

She lifted her head and looked at him. "If I'm so amazing, why didn't he come back sooner? Why did he leave me alone so long?"

Colt hesitated. There was no excuse for Huck's behavior. There was an explanation. "He loved flying."

"More than he loved me," she said bitterly. She sat up abruptly, her back to Colt, her head bowed.

He saw her shoulders heave and knew she was crying again, though she made no sound. He sought words to comfort her. "He missed you terribly, Jenny. He ached

for you. He admired you for taking care of your brothers."
He had never heard Huck say any of those things out loud,
but he had felt them himself, and he couldn't believe Huck
hadn't felt them, as well.

"I hate those damned jets!" Jenny said vehemently. "I
hate—" A sob cut her off.

Colt could resist no longer. He wrapped his arms tightly
around her from behind, pressing his cheek against hers.
"Huck's father had a great deal to do with keeping him
away, Jenny. The senator didn't think his son should be
saddled with the responsibility of raising someone else's
family. It didn't help that Huck was rich, and you were
poor."

"He thought Huck could do better," Jenny said. "He told
me so to my face the one time I met him."

Colt bit back a gasp of disbelief. He'd known how
Huck's father felt; he hadn't known Senator Duncan had
been so blunt with Jenny. "Huck never let the senator sway
him, Jenny. He always loved you."

"Just not enough," Jenny said.

RANDY HAD BEEN watching Faith Butler for almost an hour
without going anywhere near her. Faith stuck pretty close
to her twin sister, Hope, who'd gathered a crowd of admiring boys around her. Faith stood behind Hope like a
shadow of her sister. It had been that way for as long as
Randy could remember.

Hope Butler's behavior was *outrageous*. At least, that
was the word Jenny used to describe her. Her face was
usually slathered with makeup, and she wore her dresses
cut low enough to cause problems with the fit of a guy's
jeans. She smoked and drank and drove her car like a bat
out of hell.

Randy figured she worked so hard to attract attention

to herself so nobody would notice Faith. That is, so people would spend more time talking about the difference in their personalities rather than the other, more obvious difference between them.

They were both beautiful, with long, straight black hair they wore parted in the middle, and dark chocolate eyes and smooth, creamy skin. But something had gone wrong when they were in the womb, and Faith's left hand had stopped growing. Her arm ended shortly beyond the wrist, and she wore a plastic prosthetic device with a metal hook that substituted for her missing hand.

Like most of the guys, Randy had been attracted to Hope at first. Some guys said she "put out," and he'd been hoping he'd get lucky and score with her. Somewhere along the line, he'd gotten distracted by Faith.

He watched her now, standing serenely behind her sister, her left hand unobtrusively tucked behind her back. Faith smiled at Hope's anecdotes and seemed not to mind that her sister was the center of attention. Faith never made a big deal about the fact she didn't have a left hand.

Randy wondered if Faith ever minded all the guys paying attention to her sister instead of her, or if she ever felt angry or bitter about being the "imperfect" twin. He wondered what it would be like to date a girl like that. And shuddered involuntarily when he thought of that hook at the end of her arm anywhere near him.

He flushed with shame. It wasn't Faith's fault she was born like that. Remorse moved him in her direction. He walked right up to her and said, "Hi. I noticed your glass is almost empty. Can I get you something else to drink?"

She looked startled and frightened, like a deer he'd come upon suddenly in the brush when he was hunting. He was no more able to hurt her than he'd been able to kill that deer. "I noticed you from across the room," he said.

That only seemed to make her more self-conscious, so he quickly added, "I mean, I was noticing how pretty you look."

Her lashes lowered over her eyes, and two red spots appeared on her cheeks. "Thank you," she said in a barely audible voice.

The more shy she was, the more protective he felt. "I wondered if you might want to go to the movies with me sometime."

Her lashes lifted and she looked up at him and he felt his heart skip a beat. "Are you asking me out?" she asked.

With the full force of her gaze directed at him, he couldn't catch his breath to speak. His mind had turned to mush.

She smiled at his confusion and for the first time her left hand came out from behind her back. "You must have mistaken me for my sister."

He made himself look at the hooked hand she'd brought out to make sure he knew she was the imperfect twin. He shook his head, but was still unable to speak.

She smiled sweetly. "I'll tell Hope—"

"I meant you," he blurted. "I want to take you out on a date."

She looked surprised again. "Why?"

He was startled into a laugh. "That's a stupid question."

She lowered her lashes again. "I meant it seriously. And I'd like an answer."

He wished she would look up, but she didn't, and he didn't have the nerve to reach over and tip her chin up. He noticed they were starting to get attention from some friends of his, and he figured he'd better get this over with before they came over and started giving him a hard time. "I just thought it might be interesting to get to know you," he said.

When she looked up, she caught him glancing at two buddies of his who were whispering behind their hands. "Did someone dare you to go out with me?"

"Are you kidding?" He saw from her face that she wasn't.

"It's happened to me before," she said defensively.

He felt his insides clench and struggled to keep the pity—and anger—from his voice. "All I want to do is take you out on a date."

"So you say."

Frustrated, he'd already turned to leave when she reached out, touching him with the hook. He barely managed to keep himself from jerking away.

"Wait," she said. "If you want to see me, you can come over to my house tomorrow morning."

He raised a brow in question. "What's going on at your house?"

She smiled and his loins tightened. "I'm in charge of making favors for your sister's wedding. You can help. I'll provide lunch."

"All right. I'll see you then."

"Everything all right here?"

Randy was surprised by Hope's interruption. He wouldn't have thought she paid much attention to what her sister did. He caught the militant look in Hope's eyes and realized she was there to protect Faith. "We're done," he said. He opened his mouth to say "See you tomorrow" to Faith, but shut it again when he realized everybody's attention was now turned in their direction.

He walked away without looking back, because he didn't want to see what Faith thought of his hasty retreat. It wasn't that he was embarrassed about their date or anything, but he didn't want to put up with his friends teasing him about it. He knew he wouldn't be able to keep from getting upset, and the more upset he got, the more brutal their teasing would be. Better to keep the whole business to himself.

"Are you all right?" Hope whispered to her sister.

"I'm fine," Faith said.

"He didn't—"

"I'm fine," Faith said with a smile that Hope recognized. Faith used smiles the way a knight used a shield to ward off harmful blows.

Hope would have urged Faith to leave right then, except she hadn't yet found an opportunity to talk with Jake Whitelaw. Not that he wanted to talk to her. Or even knew she was alive. When she'd said hello to him earlier, he'd scowled and replied, "That's the wrong dress for a funeral."

She'd bitten back a sharp retort. Since she'd only worn the dress to get his attention, it had served its purpose. Hope sighed as she looked down at the long legs revealed by the short skirt. Why couldn't Jake have admired her legs instead of criticizing the dress?

Everything she did—smoking, driving fast, even wearing makeup so she'd look older—was calculated to make him notice her. But she might as well be eight years old instead of eighteen. All he saw was a kid. Someday she was going to figure out a way to convince Jake Whitelaw that Hope Butler was the woman of his dreams.

COLT KEPT JENNY away from the house as long as he dared, but brought her back in time to say good-bye to everyone. Her family and his were the last to leave, and they stood on the back porch together bidding them farewell.

"We're so glad you're going to be part of the family," his mother said as she hugged Jenny good-bye.

"Colt's a lucky man," his father said as he gave Jenny a kiss on the forehead.

"You'd better take damned good care of her," Jenny's brother Sam warned quietly as he shook Colt's hand.

Colt knew Sam was only worried about his sister, so he simply said, "I will." He wished he could tell Sam that he loved Jenny, but it was too soon after Huck's death to admit to such feelings. Besides, loving her wasn't enough. Huck had loved Jenny, yet he'd left her alone to raise her brothers.

Jake was last in line to say good-bye, and Colt met his elder brother's hard-eyed look without flinching.

"I hope you know what you're doing," Jake said. "I think you're asking for heartache."

"It's my heart," Colt said. "Let me worry about it."

Jake gave a grudging nod. "All right, little brother. Don't say I didn't warn you."

When Colt and Jenny were finally alone, they were completely alone, since Randy had escaped to the movies with some friends. Colt was surprised when he ushered Jenny inside to find the kitchen as clean as a whistle.

"I expected to spend the evening washing casserole dishes," he said. "What are we going to do with all this free time?"

"I've got books that need to be balanced," Jenny said.

Colt shook his head. "Not tonight. You're too tired."

"I'll decide whether I'm too tired," Jenny retorted irritably.

"There. See? You're so tired you're snapping at me."

"I'm not—" Jenny cut herself off and hissed out a breath of air. She gave him a plaintive look. "I don't know how to do nothing, Colt."

"Then we'll do something," he promised as he slid his arm around her waist and headed her into the living room.

"Like what?" she demanded as she plopped down onto the couch.

"Well, there's always necking," he teased as he dropped down beside her. "Let's see if I remember how it's done. I sneak my arm along the back of the couch, like so."

Jenny giggled as she watched his arm move snakelike along the couch behind her.

"Then I take your hand in mine, to kind of distract you from what my other hand is doing." He suited word to deed and threaded the fingers of her left hand with the fingers of his. He waggled his right hand, which now completely encircled her. "Then this hand comes to rest ever so lightly on your shoulder. *Voilà! I yam readee for zee zeduction,*" he said in a terrible French accent.

Jenny laughed. "Being the very good girl that I am, I will, of course, pretend not to notice your hand on my shoulder," she said, joining his game.

"Of course," he agreed, returning her grin with one of his own.

"But secretly," she said, shooting him an impish look, "I'll be enticing you to do more."

His brows waggled. "You will?"

She nodded, grinning broadly.

"How?" he asked, intrigued.

"Oh, in little ways, like making sure that our hands rest on *your* thigh, instead of mine."

Colt looked down and discovered that their joined hands were indeed lying on his thigh instead of hers. He could suddenly feel the heat of her hand through his black suit trousers. A more intense physical response was not long in coming. He hoped to hell she didn't notice. "Then what?" he asked in a raspy voice.

"I'd lean a little closer and bat my eyelashes at you and look demure." She did so in a way that should have been funny, but which merely left him wondering what secrets she was hiding beneath her lowered lids.

He leaned close to her ear and whispered, "Then what?" and felt her body quiver.

"I'd wait to see if you took the bait," she murmured.

"Look at me, Jenny."

She lifted her lids, and their gazes caught and held. He lowered his head toward hers, drawn by her parted lips. He kept his eyes on her mouth, waiting for even the slightest indication that she didn't want this to happen. Sure enough, she backed away.

"I'd resist at first," she said, her eyes lambent but still full of mischief. "But when you least expected it, I'd turn to you and make all your adolescent male dreams come true." She reached out with her free hand, caught his nape and drew his head down to hers, their mouths meshing before she slipped her tongue between his lips to taste him.

An instant later she was on her feet, wiping her mouth and backing away from him. "Ohmigod. I shouldn't have done that."

He was on his feet and headed toward her, his hands outstretched in supplication. "It was just a game, Jenny."

"You're right. I'm tired. I need to rest. Good night, Colt."

An instant later she was gone.

Colt took a step after her and stopped himself. His body was rock hard with no hope of satisfaction, but he only had himself to blame. "What did you expect, Whitelaw?" he muttered. "When you play with fire, you'd better damn well expect to get burned."

CHAPTER SEVEN

JENNY WOKE TO THE sound of a hammer against wood. The sun was high and a warm breeze billowed the lace curtains at the open window. She hadn't set her alarm because it was Saturday, and she didn't have to make sure Randy got off to school on time. But it was rare that she slept so late.

Then she remembered. *I kissed Colt last night. And not by accident. I wanted it to happen. I helped it to happen. And I could have done a lot more. He wouldn't have stopped me.*

She had fled, afraid of the powerful feelings evoked by that brief meeting of lips. It wasn't like her to run away, but nothing about the past ten days had been the least bit normal. It was time to face facts. Time to stop pretending her life had even the remotest chance of turning out happily ever after.

She couldn't marry Colt. It wouldn't be fair. Not unless she told him the truth about herself. And she knew what would happen if she did that. She had to call the whole thing off. Now. Before it was too late.

Jenny yanked on a pair of jeans and slipped into a chambray shirt. She ran a brush through her hair but didn't even take time to put it up in a ponytail. The noise was coming from the back of the house, and as she hurried through the kitchen she saw the remnants of two blueberry pancake breakfasts in the sink. She stopped at the screen door and stared.

Colt and Randy were working side by side, both stripped to the waist. Colt's shoulder muscles flexed as he supported a portion of the back porch roof while Randy slipped a new post in place under it. Colt's bronzed skin glistened with sweat and beads of perspiration pearled in the dark hair on his chest. His jeans had slid down so she could see his navel and the line of black down leading into his jeans.

Her body tightened viscerally.

Jenny was shocked at how quickly she'd responded to the sight of Colt's half-naked body and clutched at the doorjamb to keep herself from bolting again. She would surely get over this aberrant attraction once Colt was gone. She started to push the screen door open but hesitated when he spoke.

"That's it, boy. Easy does it." Colt let go of the rotting post he'd been holding, and the weight of the roof settled onto the new post.

"Holy cow! We did it!" Randy exclaimed.

"We make a good team," Colt said, laying a hand across Randy's youthful shoulders. Her brother beamed with pride.

Jenny felt her throat swell closed. This was what her brothers had missed. A father to teach them to be men. She'd done her best, but there were some things a mother couldn't provide.

She swallowed down the ache in her throat that arose whenever she acknowledged what had been stolen from her...from all of them...when their father had run away rather than face their mother's illness. She'd been the eldest, the one who remembered him best, so his abandonment had hit her the hardest. She wasn't about to set herself up for that kind of heartache again.

"How long are you going to hang around?" Randy asked.

Jenny saw the startled look on Colt's face. She didn't usually eavesdrop, but she was curious to hear his answer.

Colt picked up a hammer to knock the post farther into place and said, "Long enough to help your sister put this place back together."

"How long is that?" Randy persisted.

"What does it matter to you?" Colt asked. "If I understood your sister right, you're headed off to college in the fall. Bring me one of those rails, will you?"

Randy brought him a porch rail and squatted beside him as he measured and began to saw. "I'm asking because I am going off to college. I hate the thought of leaving Jenny here all alone."

"Yeah," Colt agreed. "That's tough. You want to try nailing this in place?"

"Sure," Randy said.

Jenny watched as Colt showed Randy how to run a plumb line so the porch rail would be straight. She wondered for a moment how he could know so much about carpentry, until she remembered Colt had been trained his whole life to take over Hawk's Pride. There wasn't much he didn't know about running a ranch, and that included the kind of repairs he'd been doing for the past ten days.

Jenny had discovered it was easier to do the repairs herself than take the time to train her brothers. She realized now that she had cheated them of the pride in a job well-done and herself of the pleasure of teaching them that she saw on Colt's face.

"I'm real worried about Jenny living here all alone," Randy admitted as he began nailing the rail in place. "I mean, when you go back to flying jets."

"Maybe I can talk Jenny into selling this place and coming with me."

Randy turned to gape at Colt, and the hammer came

down on his thumb. "Yow!" He leaped up and flung his hand around, trying to ease the pain. Eventually the thumb ended up in his mouth.

By then Jenny was out the door and standing on the porch beside her brother, reaching for his hand. "Are you all right?"

Randy yanked his hand away and said angrily, "Why are we bothering to fix this place up, if you're just going to sell it?"

"I never agreed—"

"This is our home," Randy interrupted. "You can't sell it!"

Jenny was furious with Colt for putting such an idea in Randy's head, but equally annoyed with her brother. "You know I'd never sell the Double D if I had a choice." She shot a quick glance at Colt, who looked chagrined. "It appears I may not have a choice."

Randy turned to Colt. "Is that true, Colt? Are you going to force Jenny to sell the Double D?"

Colt's lips pursed, and he shook his head. "I was only suggesting it might be better if she did."

"How would you feel if your parents sold Hawk's Pride?" Randy demanded. "What if it belonged to someone else and you could never go back? You'd hate it, wouldn't you?"

"I guess I would," Colt conceded. "But—"

"No buts," Randy said. "Look, I've got to get out of here. I promised I'd ride over and visit a friend this morning." He grabbed his shirt from the rail where he'd left it and turned to Jenny, his face anguished. "Just don't do anything without thinking it through, all right?"

"Shouldn't you wash up first?" Jenny suggested, knowing as soon as the words were out of her mouth how much Randy would resent them.

"I'll rinse off at the sink in the barn." He practically ran down the porch steps, headed for the barn.

Jenny whirled on Colt, determined to send him away. But the words caught in her throat. She met his gaze and remembered what had happened the previous night. She had to speak quickly, or she'd lose the will to speak at all.

"When did you intend to let me in on this little plan of yours to sell the Double D?" she asked pointedly.

"It's not a bad idea."

"Forget it! If you didn't want to marry me, all you had to do was say so. I can manage on my own. I always have."

"You shouldn't have had to carry the burden by yourself for so long," he retorted. "Huck should have been here."

She looked into Colt's eyes and drew a sharp breath. "Don't you dare pity me! I don't need your sympathy. I don't need anyone. I can manage on my—"

He grabbed her shoulders and shook her. "Damn it, Jenny. Why won't you let me help?"

"I don't want you here. I don't want you touching me or kissing me or…or touching me!"

She fought him, but his arms circled around her, pulling her close so she couldn't strike out at him. He was saying something, but the sound was drowned out by the pulse pounding in her ears. She kicked his shin and heard him yelp, but he held on. One of his hands tangled in her hair, and he yanked her head back. "Look at me, Jenny. Look at me!"

She stared into eyes that were filled with compassion. And regret. And something else she was afraid to name.

"I'm glad you kissed me last night," he said.

Jenny felt her heart begin to race. "It can't happen again, Colt. Huck's only been dead—"

"We're alive. We're going to be husband and wife. It's

not as if we're strangers. We've been friends for a long time."

"*Friends.* Nothing more."

"Not yet," he said softly. His lips had a certain fullness and rigidity she recognized, and which made her heart pound all the harder.

"You're a beautiful woman, Jenny. Why are you so surprised that I find you desirable? Or that you might desire me? Why are you fighting so hard not to feel anything?"

She swallowed hard. *Because it can't last. Because it's entirely likely I'm not going to be here on this earth much longer than Huck.*

"You can grieve Huck and still go on living," Colt said in a gentle voice.

She was frightened by how persuasive he sounded. She groped for an explanation that he would accept—besides the truth. "I can't just forget Huck. He was—"

"Never here," Colt said implacably. "How often did you see him over the past ten years?"

"I saw him lots!" Jenny retorted.

"Twelve times," Colt said. "I know because I came with him every time except the last. I was here more than he was, because he spent most of his leave with his father."

"He wrote me—"

"Cards—on birthdays and holidays. I know. I made sure of it."

Jenny's stomach churned. "He loved me, Colt."

His thumb caressed her jaw, but his hold on her hair tightened, forcing her to look up at him. "I know. And you loved him. But be honest, Jenny. If you hadn't been tied to this ranch, hadn't been tied down raising four brothers, would you have kept on loving a man who was never there for you?"

Jenny's eyes misted, and her nose stung with the threat

of tears she refused to shed. "You can leave anytime, Colt. Go sniff some jet fuel. Get out!"

"I'm not going to leave you, Jenny. I'm not going to walk away, no matter how hard you push me. Between us, we're going to figure out what to do. There's got to be a solution that'll work for both of us. All we have to do is find it."

"I don't need you! I—"

He kissed her hard, cutting off speech. Then his mouth softened, and his lips moved over hers, searching for some response.

Jenny's heart skipped a beat before blood surged to her center. She clutched at Colt's bare shoulders, unsure whether she wanted to pull him close or push him away. When she hesitated, his tongue slid into her mouth for a taste, and she was undone. All thought flew out of her head, replaced by sensation.

This is what was always missing with Huck. The need to merge body and soul with another human being. The need to make two halves into one whole. The need—

The kiss ended as abruptly as it had begun. Colt looked dazed. And as distraught as she felt herself. He let her go and took a quick step back. He didn't seem to know what to do with his hands, and he finally stuck his thumbs in his back pockets. "I think maybe we'd better set some ground rules. I want—"

"Holy cow! Holy cow, Jenny! Look what I found!"

Jenny tore her troubled gaze from Colt's face and looked toward the barn. Randy was mounted on his chestnut gelding, but he was pointing at a large animal that was partially hidden from view in the corral behind the barn. "What is it?" Jenny called back to him.

"My wedding gift to you," Colt answered for Randy.

"You got me an animal for a wedding gift?" she said,

her brows lowering in confusion as she headed for the corral.

Colt kept pace with her. "Not just any animal," he said. "A Santa Gertrudis bull from the King Ranch."

Jenny halted in her tracks and turned to stare. "Are you kidding? You're *not* kidding," she said as she got a good look at Colt's face. She couldn't catch her breath.

The Santa Gertrudis breed, three-eighths Indian Brahman and five-eighths British Shorthorn, had been developed in the early twentieth century on the King Ranch, which still produced some of the finest Santa Gertrudis cattle to be found anywhere in the world. A bull like the one he described would cost a fortune—and could save the Double D.

Jenny turned and raced for the corral. Randy was off his horse and leaning over the corral, ogling the deep, cherry-red-colored bull when she reached him. "Ohmigod!" she breathed. "It's Rob Roy."

"None other," Colt confirmed with a grin as he put a booted foot up on the corral and leaned over to admire the bull. "Do you like him?"

Jenny couldn't breathe.

Rob Roy had been named grand champion Santa Gertrudis bull at the most recent stock show in Fort Worth. All by himself, this bull could put the Double D in the black.

Randy whooped and said, "Holy cow!"

"Do you like him?" Colt asked softly. "I mean, I thought about getting you something a little more romantic, like a diamond—"

Jenny clutched Colt around the neck and gave him a quick kiss on the mouth. Just as quickly, she let him go and stepped back. It was too tempting to cling to him. "It's a *perfect* gift. No woman could ever have a more perfect gift."

Then she remembered she was planning to call off the wedding.

"I guess there won't be any more talk about selling the Double D," Randy said as he mounted his gelding. "Wait'll I tell everybody about this!"

He kicked his horse into a lope, shrieking like a Comanche on a raid and kicking up a cloud of dust that Jenny waved away.

Jenny turned back to Colt and said, "How could you have teased Randy like that, saying you thought I should sell the Double D, when you'd already bought Rob Roy?"

"I wasn't teasing," he said.

"But with Rob Roy—"

"One bull isn't going to solve all your problems, Jenny. In fact, he's only going to make more work for you. I suppose with the income he'll bring in you could hire a man to help you out, but—"

"I'll still be alone, because you're not going to be around," Jenny finished for him.

"I made my choice a long time ago, Jenny."

Jenny couldn't keep the bitterness from her voice. "I know, Colt. You and Huck both. Like I said, I can take care of myself." She opened her mouth to call off the wedding, but what came out was, "Thanks for the bull. It's the nicest gift anybody's ever given me."

Jenny turned and headed toward the house. She tried to walk, but she was feeling too much, hurting too much, and she started to run. She waited for the sound of Colt's footsteps coming after her.

But she never heard them.

RANDY'S HEART LURCHED when he caught sight of Faith through the open kitchen window of her house. "Hi, Faith."

"Hi, Randy. Let me finish here at the sink, and I'll let you in."

Randy shifted from foot to foot on the back porch. Faith's dad was foreman for a neighboring ranch, and Randy noticed their single-story white clapboard house sported a fresh coat of white paint. Pink and purple petunias grew in profusion along the back porch. He had a moment to think how much Jenny would have appreciated the paint and the petunias before Faith unhooked the screen door and held it open for him.

He stared at her, stricken mute, unable to move.

Faith smiled shyly and said, "Won't you come in?"

"Uh. Okay."

The instant he stepped inside, he was assailed with a sense of order and the smell of Pine Sol. It was a far cry from his house, which suffered from too much work and too few people to do it.

"I'm glad you decided to come," Faith said.

"I said I would."

"I know but... I'm glad," she repeated, lowering her lids and hiding her eyes from him.

He recognized it for the defensive gesture it was, and couldn't help resenting it. He wasn't going to hurt her. If she'd just give him half a chance, he'd prove it.

He looked around the kitchen, not surprised to see it was pristine. The Butler girls had always come to school in starched and ironed dresses and with their hair in arrow-straight pigtails. At least, they had until Hope took the bit in her teeth and began to defy her parents. After that, it was only Faith who came to school perfectly dressed.

He took advantage of the fact Faith's eyes were averted to take a long look at her. Her left hand was hidden behind her back, so the image she presented was one of perfection. Her long-sleeved pink oxford-cloth shirt had a crisply starched collar and was belted into jeans that had a stiff crease. Her boots were so shiny he could have seen his reflection in them. Her straight black hair was tucked behind her ears.

He thought of the quick dousing he'd given himself in the barn. He'd rinsed off the worst of the sweat, but he wasn't precisely clean. His shirt wasn't ironed because Jenny had long ago given him the responsibility for doing it, and he'd decided he didn't mind the wrinkles. His boots were too scuffed to hold a shine, if he'd been inclined to give them one, which he wasn't.

Randy suddenly felt self-conscious. He should have taken a little more time to make himself presentable. He looked at the large kitchen table full of wedding paraphernalia and realized things were set up so they'd be sitting next to each other.

And me smelling like a workhorse.

"I…uh…I'm not sure how long I can stay," he said, wondering how he could make a graceful exit before she got a good whiff of him.

"Great! You're here!" Hope said, breezing into the kitchen. "I was afraid you wouldn't come, and I'd get stuck with Faith wrapping all that birdseed in net and tying it with ribbons."

Randy was relieved to see Hope wasn't dressed any better than he was. Her skintight jeans were torn at the knees, and she wore a Western shirt with the sleeves ripped out, strings still dangling, the tails tied in a knot that revealed a great deal of her midriff. Her tangled hair hung over her shoulders in disarray.

He almost smiled at the contrast between the sisters. Looking at them, you might easily get the wrong idea about which was the imperfect twin.

"You're not going to abandon us!" Faith said anxiously to her sister.

"I can help for a little while," Hope said. "But I've got other plans for later on." Hope plopped down into a chair on the opposite side of the rectangular oak table. "Let's get going. The sooner we start, the sooner this'll be done."

"You can sit here, Randy," Faith said, gesturing with her right hand to one of the two seats beside each other across from Hope.

He hesitated, then slid into the chair she'd indicated, because he wanted to sit next to her. After all, it was why he'd come. "What do you want me to do?" he asked.

"You can hold the pieces of net while I measure out the birdseed. Then I'll hold the net while you tie the bow. How does that sound?" Faith asked.

"All right, I guess," Randy replied. It dawned on him that she was going to need two hands. And that she was going to be using that hook on the end of her left arm as one of them. He felt a little jittery at the thought, and steeled himself not to shudder or do anything that would make her uncomfortable.

He glanced up and caught Hope watching him through narrowed eyes. And realized she was there not to help her sister with the wedding favors, but to protect Faith from him. He wanted to reassure Hope, but at the moment he wasn't certain how he was going to react when Faith hauled out that hook and started using it so close to his own hands.

Then he saw Faith's right hand was trembling and realized she was as scared as he was. A lump the size of Texas constricted his throat, and his chest felt like four football linemen had piled onto it.

He reached out and picked up a piece of net and placed it on the table in front of her. "Ready for—" He cleared his throat and said, "Ready for some seed."

He watched her pick up a two-pound plastic bag of bird-seed at the top with her real hand, then grasp the bottom with the hook and aim the open corner onto the net. Too much poured out.

"Oh," she said, setting the bag down abruptly. Her eyes darted nervously in his direction, then focused on the mess she'd made.

He felt his heart pounding hard in his chest. If he blew this, he was pretty sure he wasn't going to get a second chance. "It's all right," he said, reaching quickly for another piece of net. "I'll divide this in two." He suited word to deed and poured half the birdseed onto the second piece of net. "Now what?"

"Get a piece of that pink ribbon over there."

The narrow silk ribbon had already been cut into lengths. While he grabbed the ribbon, she gathered the net around the seed with one hand, and held it closed at the top with the hook.

As nonchalantly as if he tied ribbons into bows every day, he surrounded the net below her hook with the ribbon and tied a creditable bow. "How's that?" he said when he was done.

She released the hook from the net and slid it away as she surveyed his work, but he noticed she didn't retreat with it under the table. "Pretty terrible," she announced at last.

He shot her an astonished look and saw she was smiling at him. His heart did a flip-flop. He looked back at the lopsided bow and said in an unsteady voice, "I'll do better on the next one."

"Hey, there! Anybody home?"

Randy looked over his shoulder at the screen door and said, "Hi, Jake."

"Hi, Jake," Faith said.

"I'll see to Jake," Hope said. "You two just keep on with what you're doing."

"I've got that delivery of hay your father ordered," Jake said when Hope pushed open the screen door. "Ask him where he wants me to put it."

"I'll show you," Hope said. "Follow me."

Hope was glad Randy hadn't turned out to be a jerk. Otherwise she wouldn't have been able to leave Faith behind with him. She'd been waiting a long time for the chance to get Jake Whitelaw alone.

This was it.

His shirt was dirty, the sleeves rolled up to reveal strong, sinewy forearms. His Stetson was sweaty around the brim, and shaggy black hair was crushed at his nape. His cheeks were hollow, and he had a sharp nose and wide-set, ice-blue eyes. He was half a foot taller than she was, lean at the hip, but with broad, powerful shoulders. He made her body come alive just looking at him.

"How are you, Jake?" she said, walking with her shoulders back so her breasts jutted and her hips swayed.

He eyed her sideways. "Just dandy," he muttered.

"Daddy wants that hay in the barn," she said, hop-skipping to keep up with his long strides.

"Why didn't you just say so? You don't need to come with me, little girl. I know where it goes."

Little girl. Hope ground her teeth. She'd show him she was no *little girl!* "There's some stuff needs to be moved first," she hedged. "Machinery that's too heavy for me to pick up by myself."

"Why didn't your daddy move it?"

"I told him I could do it. That is, before I realized how heavy it was," she fibbed.

Jake didn't look suspicious, but it wasn't going to take long once they got inside the barn for him to realize she'd lied. The space where the hay was supposed to be stacked had been cleared out that morning. She opened the door and went inside first, then waited for him to enter before she closed the door behind him.

Sunlight streamed through the cracks between the planks of the wooden barn, leaving golden lines on the empty, straw-littered dirt floor.

He turned to confront her. "What the hell is going on, little girl?"

She was backed up against the door to keep Jake from leaving. She put her hand over the light switch when he reached for it, afraid of what she'd see in his eyes in the stark light of the naked overhead bulb. He didn't force the issue, merely stepped back and stood facing her, his legs widespread, his hands on his hips.

"What happens now?" he said. "You want sex? Take off your jeans and panties and lie down over there on that pile of straw on the floor."

Hope's eyes went wide when he started to unbuckle his belt. "Stop! Wait." She was shocked by his brutally frank speech, by the rough sound of his voice, by his plain intention of taking what she seemed to be offering without any pretense of romance. This wasn't how she'd imagined things happening between them.

He had his shirt unbuttoned and was ripping it out of his jeans when he paused and looked her right in the eye. "You chickening out, little girl?"

Maybe if he hadn't made it a dare, she would have run, which is what she realized he expected her to do. She stared right back at him and began untying the knot at her midriff.

"I'm not going anywhere."

She watched his eyes go wide, then narrow. A muscle jerked in his cheek. He no longer seemed interested in taking his clothes off. He was too busy watching her. Waiting, she suspected, to see how far she would go.

Her mouth was bone-dry, but she wanted him to know why she was doing this. "I...I love you, Jake."

He snorted. "Get to it or get out."

Her cheeks pinkened with mortification, but she refused to run. It wasn't easy undressing in front of him. She kept her eyes lowered, while she fumbled with the knot. He stood watching, waiting like a lone wolf stalking an abandoned calf, certain of the kill.

When the knot came free, her shirt fell open. She let it slide off her shoulders and onto the floor, revealing the pure white demi-cup pushup bra she'd bought with her baby-sitting money, which revealed just about everything but her nipples.

When she lifted her gaze to his face, she was frightened by what she saw. His eyes had a dangerous, feral look, his jaw was clenched tight, and his hands had balled into fists. He looked distant, unapproachable, but she forced herself to walk up to him, to slide her hands around his neck, to lift up on tiptoe to press her lips against his.

A second later she was shoved up hard against the barn door with Jake's hips grinding against her own. His tongue was in her mouth taking what he wanted, and she was so full of sharp, exciting sensations that she couldn't breathe.

Just as suddenly he backed off, leaving her with Jell-O knees that wanted to buckle, a heart that was threatening to explode and her insides tied up tight, hurting and wanting. "Jake," she said. It was a cry of emotional pain. A plea for surcease from her unrequited need.

"I'm twice your age," he said flatly. "You're too damn young for me, Hope."

"You want me," she said boldly.

It would have been hard to deny. His jeans bulged with

abundant evidence of his desire.. "I'm a grown man. Old enough to know better," he said with a disgusted sigh. He unbuttoned and unzipped his jeans, but only so he could tuck his shirt back in. He buttoned his shirt, buckled his belt and adjusted his clothes, then leaned down and picked up her shirt. "Put this on," he said.

She did as she was told. She hadn't gotten what she'd expected when she'd come in here with Jake. But she'd gotten what she wanted. Proof that he desired her. Proof that if she pushed long enough and hard enough, she might convince him that she was what he needed.

Her hands were shaking too much for her to tie a knot in the shirttails.

"I'll do it," he said, pushing her hands out of the way.

Her stomach quivered as his knuckles brushed against her flesh. She glanced up and saw the feral look was back in his eyes. He yanked the knot tight and stepped back.

"Now get the hell out of here!" he snarled.

Hope yanked open the barn door and ran.

CHAPTER EIGHT

"RISE AND SHINE, LAZYBONES," COLT said with a laugh as he pulled the covers off Jenny.

She rolled over, then sat up and stared. He'd done it again. Brought her breakfast in bed. The first time he'd arrived unannounced it had provided a few awkward moments, since all she'd been wearing was one of Randy's old T-shirts, the cotton so thin it provided a revealing display of her suddenly peaked nipples.

That incident had led to the first of a dozen silly gifts Colt had given her over the past two weeks.

"If you're really into men's clothes, I thought you'd appreciate these," he'd said when he presented her with a pair of navy blue men's cotton pajamas.

A set of flower-patterned china cups and saucers had come next. "You need to see something beautiful when you wake up each morning. I've got you," he'd said, making her blush with pleasure, "but I thought you might like these."

One morning she'd stepped outside the kitchen door and discovered the entire back porch was lined with hanging baskets of pink and white impatiens. "I owe you some flowers," he'd said. "For all the times I never brought you any."

What he meant, of course, was for all the times Huck had never brought her any.

While Colt settled the breakfast tray in her lap, Jenny fingered the solitary diamond that hung on a fragile gold chain around her neck. Colt had given her the necklace last night after Randy had gone to bed, when they were alone in the living room.

"I noticed you're still wearing Huck's ring," he'd said. "But I wanted to give you a diamond. I hope this is all right."

After he clasped the necklace around her throat, she'd reached up to touch the dimensions of the stone, to test the fragility of the chain.

An inexplicable feeling of panic had forced her off the couch and across the room to the fireplace. She'd watched the flames lick at the dry wood they'd gathered together that afternoon and fought the urge to cry.

"What's wrong?" he asked, sensing her distress. He didn't follow her. He waited for her to return on her own.

She twisted the diamond ring on her finger, adjusting it, reminding herself of its presence as she had done for ten long years. Huck's ring had been the one visible proof that they were engaged, that he intended to come back to her. Now Colt had laid his claim, slipping a chain—a delicate one to be sure—around her neck, when he had no more intention of staying with her than Huck had.

The hot tears came without warning, filling her eyes and spilling over. Colt crossed to her then, anxious and concerned. He pulled her into his arms, and she felt his lips kissing away the tears as he murmured words of comfort.

"It doesn't mean anything, Jenny. I don't expect you to love me the way you loved Huck," he said. "It's just a gift. Something from me to you. Be happy, Jenny. Please."

That made her cry all the harder, because it would have been very easy to fall in love with Colt. It was hard not to appreciate a man whose every thought was directed toward making your life easier. But, damn it, she didn't want to fall in love with another man who intended to leave her behind while he went off to fly jets. Especially not someone who was only taking care of her as a duty to his dead friend.

A certain ticking clock reminded Jenny that moments like this had to be seized and enjoyed.

She brushed at Colt's sideburns, which were already growing out, then eased her thumb across the scar on his chin where the stitches had been removed, unable to stop herself from touching him. "I'm crying because I'm happy, Colt. That's all."

He looked deep into her eyes, searching for the truth.

It was the truth. At that moment she was happy. She'd learned a long time ago, as the child of a dying mother, to relish every day for the pleasures it brought her. That lesson was standing her in good stead now.

She saw the lingering doubt in Colt's eyes and did the only thing she thought might convince him she was pleased with the gift—and with him. She kissed him gently on the mouth.

She'd had some inkling in advance of how powerful her response might be. Yet, she was surprised again. This kiss was different—more devastating—than the ones that had come before, because there was no guilt to dampen pleasure. This kiss was a celebration of joy, of delight in the man who held her in his arms. Passion rose quickly and flared hot.

Tentatively, her hands went seeking, feeling the ropey muscles in Colt's shoulders and sliding down his strong back. His hands weren't idle, and she gasped as his palm closed on her breast. The sensation was exquisite because it was so unexpected. Huck had touched her breasts many times before, but it had never felt like this. Jenny sought for the difference and found it. There was reverence in Colt's touch, along with the hunger.

He'd already eased her shirt off and was reaching for

the front clasp of her bra when she suddenly came to her senses and realized what might happen if she took this next step with him.

"Colt, no."

His mouth nuzzled the curve of her breast above her bra, and she nearly swooned before she finally grasped his hand to stop him.

"Not yet," she pleaded. "I'm not ready. Not yet."

She heard his shuddering breath, felt the tautness in his shoulders as he brought himself back from the brink. He kissed her gently on the mouth, his tongue teasing her lips until she relented and let him come inside.

To soothe, to taste, to caress.

It was the kind of kiss they might have shared as teenagers in the backseat of his Mustang, when he knew they couldn't go all the way. Deep and rich and thorough. It was lovemaking without the sex.

And she appreciated him all the more for it.

She heard a moan from deep in his throat, a grating sound of both satisfaction and the need for more, before he finally broke the kiss. When she met Colt's eyes, she saw that the fire had been banked, but it wouldn't take much to fan it back into flames. He was leaving the choice up to her. She knew she had to back away, because it was clear he wouldn't—or couldn't.

For a moment last night Jenny had thought about trusting Colt with her secret. Fear had held her back. Once he knew, he would leave for sure. She wanted to hold on to him for as long as she could.

"Good night, Colt," she said as she backed away.

He'd reached down and picked up her shirt, and she'd flushed as she realized she'd forgotten completely about it. He'd given her a lopsided smile and said, "Good night,

Jenny. I—" He'd cut himself off, swallowed hard and said, "I'll see you in the morning."

And here he was with breakfast on a tray, fresh from the shower, with eyes that crinkled at the corners with laughter...and her heart on his plate.

"You're going to spoil me, Colt," she said as she held the tray steady and scooted back against the headboard.

"You deserve a little coddling." He settled on the edge of the bed by her knees and grabbed a slice of cinnamon raisin toast slathered in butter.

Jenny picked up a flowered china cup, blew on the steaming coffee, then sipped carefully, grateful for the caffeine. She wasn't quite sure how to act after what had happened between them last night and decided to let Colt set the tone.

Colt was trying to act nonchalant, when that was the last thing he was feeling. He'd been buying Jenny little gifts ever since he'd realized how few of them she'd gotten in her life. He'd given her the diamond last night as a symbol of his love and commitment and as a first step toward asking for that same love and commitment from her.

The wary look in Jenny's eyes reminded him not to push too hard or too fast. But he couldn't shake the feeling that time was running out. His leave was more than half over, and their wedding day was rapidly approaching. Then he happened to glance at Jenny's left hand.

"Where's Huck's ring?"

"I took it off," she said, not meeting his gaze.

He watched her reach with her thumb to rub the empty spot where the ring used to be. His chest ached with hope and with fear. Maybe there was a chance for the two of them after all. He opened his mouth to speak, but she spoke first.

"Don't forget Randy's graduation ceremony is tonight," she said. "I promised him we'd go out to dinner first."

"I won't be late."

"Randy asked if he could bring a date to dinner," she said with a smile.

"Anybody I know?" Colt asked.

"Faith Butler."

Colt's jaw dropped. "*Faith* Butler? Not Hope?"

"Faith," Jenny repeated with a grin. "I couldn't believe it myself. Seems they've been seeing a lot of each other lately."

"Good for Randy. You've done a fantastic job raising him, Jenny. A great job raising all of them." He took a deep breath and plunged. "But it's time you started thinking of yourself."

"What does that mean?" Jenny asked, her eyes cautious.

"Just what I said. Why don't you sell this place and come see the world with me?"

"Colt, you promised—"

He grabbed the tray from her lap and threw it onto the dresser hard enough to make the china cup and saucer rattle, then turned to confront her. "I can't leave you here alone, Jenny. I'd worry too much about you."

"Then stay," she said simply.

He shoved both hands through his short hair, leaving it standing on end. "I'm considering that option."

Her eyes went wide. "You are? What's stopping you?"

He wanted to tell her the truth. That he didn't think he could stand waking up every morning to a wife who was in love with another man. He'd grow to hate her and himself. It was easier to go away—to stay away.

He was afraid to read too much into the fact she'd taken off Huck's ring. It might simply be that it evoked too many painful memories for her to wear it.

And that kiss last night?

Mere gratitude for the gift he'd given her. It was getting harder and harder to conceal his true feelings, but he wasn't about to let Jenny know he loved her when he had no hope of having that love returned.

"I'd like to stay Jenny," he said quietly. "But you're Huck's girl. You always have been, and you always will be."

"Huck is dead," she said, her voice cracking.

"I know," he said sadly. "I can't fight a ghost."

Jenny's brow creased. "Why would you need to?"

If she couldn't figure it out, he wasn't going to explain it to her. So he changed the subject. "I figured we'd start scraping down the barn today so we can give it a new coat of paint."

"I've got a few personal errands to run in town," she said, slipping off the bed and crossing to the dresser to run a brush through her hair. "I'll be back by six to shower and change for dinner."

"You're going to be gone all day?" he asked, startled.

She gave him a smile in the mirror as phony as a three-dollar bill. "I've put off a lot of things that can't wait any longer."

"What aren't you telling me?" he said, frowning. "Is there some complication at the bank? Some problem I don't know about?"

She laughed, a brittle sound that sent a chill up his spine. "It's nothing like that." She set down the hairbrush and turned to face him. "If I'd known you were going to get so upset, I wouldn't have told you about it."

"And then what?" he said, crossing to her, putting his hands on her shoulders from behind and looking at their two faces in the mirror. "You just disappear for the day?

You don't think that might have given me a few gray hairs?"

"You're making too much of this," she said, shaking off his hands and sliding past him toward the bathroom, where she could shut herself in—and him out.

He caught her arm and whirled her around. "You don't think I'm entitled to an explanation?"

"I don't have to explain myself to you or anyone else," she said sharply.

"I'm your husband."

"Not yet you aren't!" She jerked her arm free. "And maybe not ever, if this is the kind of inquisition I can expect when I want to go somewhere without you tagging along."

"Tagging along—" He was too furious to finish.

She poked a finger in his chest to back him off. "I've survived a very long time without you, Colt. Don't you get it? I don't need you. I don't need any man. Especially one who only wants to marry me out of a sense of guilt."

"A sense of—" he spluttered. "Where is this coming from?"

"You know very well you're only marrying me because you feel obligated as Huck's friend to make sure the widow's taken care of."

"That's not true!" He grabbed her by the arms and shook her. "I love you, damn it! I always have."

Her eyes went wide, and her jaw dropped. She was speechless, leaving a great deal of silence in which to absorb what he'd said.

Colt felt like he was going to throw up. He let her go, and she took a quick step back. "Jenny, I—"

"I don't understand. You were Huck's friend! Or you pretended to be."

"That's unfair, and you know it. Let's sit down and discuss this. Please, Jenny."

"I have an appointm—" She bit her lip. "I've got errands to run. This discussion will have to wait."

She was backing away toward the bathroom, but he wasn't going to let her escape so easily. "Wait until when?" he demanded.

"Until later."

He reached out and caught her chin with his hand, forcing her to look at him. "When, Jenny?"

"Later. Tonight," she added when his grip tightened. "Let me go, Colt."

He let her go, and an instant later she was gone.

COLT WAS STILL scraping down the barn when Randy approached him after school. Colt was hot and tired and irritable, because he knew he had to decide whether to stay in the Air Force or stay here with Jenny, and an entire day of scraping paint hadn't done much to resolve his dilemma.

It was hard to imagine his life without flying jets. It was impossible to imagine it without Jenny. He wanted both. But it was becoming very clear that he couldn't have both.

"Where's Jenny?" Randy asked.

"She's still in town running errands."

"Oh."

Colt slapped at a fly that had landed on his nose, but it buzzed away unharmed. "What does that mean, 'Oh'?"

"Nothing," Randy said quickly. "You want some help?"

Colt had three-quarters of the barn scraped free of old paint. Maybe with Randy's help he could finish today. "Sure. Why not? There's another scraper on the tool rack in the barn."

Randy slipped his book bag off his shoulder and dropped it on the ground. "I'll be right back," he said.

Colt swatted at the fly again, which was now buzzing his ear. He'd already done all the work that needed to be done on a ladder, so he and Randy worked side by side scraping the lower half of the barn.

"When did you know what you wanted to do with your life?" Randy asked.

Colt shot him a sideways look. "From the time I was a kid. Why?"

"I thought I knew what I wanted, but lately I've been less certain of what I should do."

"I see," Colt said, neither encouraging nor discouraging further discussion of the subject.

"I planned to study business because I figured that's where the money is," Randy said, keeping his eyes focused on the work he was doing. "But earning money doesn't appeal as much to me now as something else does."

"What's changed your mind?" Colt asked.

"I met someone."

Colt smiled. "A woman has a way of making you think twice about a lot of things."

Randy stopped scraping and stared at him. "How'd you know it was a girl?"

"Lucky guess."

"Anyway," Randy continued, "ever since I started seeing this girl, Faith Butler, I've been thinking maybe I'd like to study something else entirely."

Colt resisted the urge to ask what and said, "Mmm-hmm."

"Funny thing is, I don't even know what kind of courses I'd need to take to learn about it."

Colt wanted to know what "it" was, but there was an unwritten code, going all the way back to the days when people came west to escape their checkered pasts, that said a man didn't ask for information that wasn't volunteered.

Instead he said, "The university could probably tell you what you need to study."

"I suppose. I guess I'd better find out whether Texas Tech teaches anything about orthotics. Maybe I'll need to go somewhere else."

"I give up," Colt said. "What's orthotics?"

Randy grinned. "Making mechanical limbs for people who need them. Faith says there's a new silicone hand that looks a lot more real than a latex one, but nothing works as well as an old-fashioned hook. I want to invent a mechanical hand that works like a real one—you know, like in the *Terminator* movies."

Colt eyed him speculatively. "What does Faith have to say about all this?"

"We haven't discussed it." Randy began to scrape vigorously on the barn wall. Colt figured that meant he didn't want to discuss the subject with him, either, so he let it drop.

A moment later Randy's hands dropped to his sides, his chin fell to his chest and he heaved a great sigh. "How do you know when you're in love?"

Colt stopped scraping and turned to face the teenager. His first instinct was to tell Randy he was too young to fall in love, that he had a lot of living to do before he settled on one woman, and the best thing to do was ignore the feeling and it would go away. But Randy was four years older than he'd been when he'd fallen for Jenny. And that love had lasted a lifetime.

"Have you asked your sister that question?" he hedged.

Randy's face was suddenly suffused with blood, which could have been the heat, but was more likely embarrassment. "I never needed to before now. And now...I couldn't talk to her now about being in love. I mean, not with Huck dying like that, and you guys getting married in some kind of business arrangement."

"Is that what Jenny told you?" Colt said, his stomach clenching. "That our marriage is a business arrangement?"

"Well, it is, isn't it? I mean, you guys aren't in love or anything. And you're planning to leave and go back to flying jets, so what else could it be? Not that I blame Jenny for marrying you. I mean, how else can she get the money to keep the ranch?"

Colt spoke through his teeth because his jaw was clamped so tight. "Let's get one thing straight, Randy. Our marriage may have some financial benefits for your sister, but it's going to be real in every way." Colt barely kept himself from shouting that he loved Jenny. That would require an explanation that he wanted to make to Jenny first.

Randy's flush heightened. "I'm not criticizing you and Jenny. I just…I always thought people got married because they loved each other and wanted to spend their lives together. I know how hard it was for Jenny all those years with Huck gone. I hate to think of her alone when you're gone, too.

"I'd offer to come back to the ranch after I finish college," Randy said, "but I know that wouldn't really solve the problem. I think I've found the woman I'm going to marry someday, and having me and my wife living here at the Double D would just point out to Jenny how alone she is. I mean, I think I love Faith."

Which brought them back to Randy's original question. "I don't know how to tell you whether this girl is the right one for you," Colt said. "I can only tell you my own experience. When you love someone, your every thought begins and ends with her. What is she feeling? Is she happy? What can you do to make her life easier? And you want her physically. Fiercely, completely. That's part of it. Mostly, love is always considering her needs before your own. Is that how you feel?"

Colt could almost see the tension easing from Randy's shoulders. "Yeah," he said. "That's *exactly* how I feel."

Colt gave him a cuff on the shoulder. "Sounds like you're in love, pal."

"Thanks for listening, Colt."

Colt stood back and surveyed the work they'd done and realized the job was finished. "Why don't you go on in and get cleaned up? There's going to be a lot of demand for that shower if we're all going to get gussied up in time for your graduation ceremony tonight. I'll put away the tools." He reached for Randy's scraper, and the boy handed it to him, then picked up his book bag and trotted toward the house.

Colt stared after Randy, realizing that in talking to the boy he'd found his own answers. His days as a jet pilot were numbered. But to his surprise, he didn't feel resigned or sad or desperate. Because when it came to a choice between having Jenny or living life without her—there really was no choice. If he truly loved Jenny, it meant putting her needs before his own. It meant staying here to be a husband to her instead of running off to fly jets.

And it meant finding a way to handle the pain, if she could never love him back.

CHAPTER NINE

"YOU LOOK SO GROWN-UP," Jenny said as she straightened Randy's tie. She reached up to brush back the lock of golden hair that always fell onto his forehead, and he ducked away.

"Give me a break, Jenny," he said, thrusting his hand into his hair, leaving it mussed. "It's just graduation."

"Just graduation," Jenny repeated past the painful lump in her throat. The tears came without warning.

"Aw, Jenny." Randy's arms closed awkwardly around her, and she laid her head against his shoulder.

"I can't believe you're all grown-up," she said, her voice cracking. She made herself step back, quickly wiped away the tears and once against straightened his tie, while he shifted impatiently from foot to foot.

"Can I leave now? I need to pick up Faith."

"We'll meet you at Buck's Steakhouse. Drive carefully."

He rolled his eyes and said sarcastically, "Yes, Mother." He stopped abruptly, the screen door half open, and turned to face her. "Jenny, I'm sorry. It just slipped out."

"Never mind. Go. You're going to be late."

He disappeared, the screen door slamming behind him.

Jenny had been a mother to her brothers, but she'd warned them against labeling her that way. Because they knew it bothered her, they addressed her as "Mother" whenever they were angry or upset, knowing it would get a rise out of her.

Right now, she felt very much like a mother hen whose nest had just been emptied of its last chick. A huge hole gaped inside her that once had been filled up with the responsibility for her brothers. She didn't feel free. She felt empty. This didn't feel like the beginning of a new life. It felt like the end.

"Hey. Give me a break."

Jenny turned to find Colt wearing a white button-down shirt, khaki slacks and a conservative regimental-striped tie. He leaned against the doorway to the kitchen, a navy suit coat slung over his shoulder, his hip cocked.

"I suppose you witnessed that scene," she said.

"I did."

"I'm going to miss him."

"I know."

A tear slipped down her cheek, and she quickly rubbed it away. "I don't understand where all these tears are coming from," she said with a shaky laugh.

"Don't you?" Colt asked, crossing toward her. He laid his suit coat across one of the ladder-back chairs at the kitchen table and opened his arms. "Come here, Jenny."

She didn't resist his offer of comfort. She took the few steps that put her within his embrace, and his arms closed around her. "I've been waiting and wishing for this day for so long, but now that it's here, I just feel sad," she admitted.

She felt his hand smooth across her hair. Felt his lips at her temple and on her closed eyes.

"I feel like my life is over," she whispered.

"I promise you, Jenny, it's just beginning. Have you been thinking about what I said to you this morning?"

Jenny had thought of little else during the day besides Colt's confession. *I love you. I always have.* "I remember."

"I've decided to resign from the Air Force, Jenny. I want

to stay here and marry you and raise babies with you. If that's want you want, too."

Jenny felt her heart squeeze with joy and with pain. "Oh, Colt."

Tell him now, Jenny. If he really loves you, it won't matter.

She leaned back and looked up into his face, surprised at what she found. He was afraid, she realized. Of what? Suddenly Jenny knew. Afraid that she could never love him. That she would always—only—love Huck.

"I told you I've been thinking a lot today, and I have," she said. "About me and Huck. About me and you."

Colt cleared his throat, but he didn't speak. Which was a good thing, because if he'd interrupted her, she might not have been able to say what she knew had to be said.

"There was a time when I loved Huck body and soul. I wanted to make a life with him. I wanted to have his babies. I wanted to grow old with him." Jenny sighed and looked away. "I'm not sure when the loving stopped."

Colt inhaled a sharp breath of air.

She forced herself to look at him. "It wasn't until you said you loved me this morning that I made myself take a brutally honest look at my relationship with Huck. I realized that all these years I haven't been in love with Huck. I've been in love with a dream of what life could be like with him—if he ever settled down."

She lowered her gaze to Colt's throat and watched his Adam's apple bob as he swallowed hard. Her voice was barely audible as she admitted, "The last couple of times Huck came home, we didn't even make love."

"Jenny, I—"

She put her fingertips over his lips. "I'm not finished." She looked at him and said, "I never suspected how you felt. How you feel," she corrected when she felt his mouth open to protest. "I do know I've always been grateful for your friendship. You were there so many times when Huck wasn't."

She felt his lips flatten under her hand and removed it. "I'll admit I'm tempted by what you seem to be offering. But I'm afraid of making the same mistake twice. Maybe we can never be more than friends. You've caught me at a vulnerable time and—"

"Can I get a word in here?"

She gave a jerky nod.

"All I'm asking is that you give us a chance, Jenny. Can you do that?"

"Colt, there are things you don't know. Things—"

He shook his head to cut her off. "The past is the past. We start fresh from here."

Tell him, Jenny.

Jenny opened her mouth, but the words wouldn't come out. It could wait. Maybe there would be no need to tell him anything. Maybe they would mutually decide they didn't belong together any more than she and Huck had. If the buds of feeling she had for Colt began to blossom, that would be soon enough to confess her secret.

"What do you say, Jenny? Will you let me court you?"

"Court me?" she said, her lips curving. "Is that really necessary? I've already promised to marry you."

He smiled for the first time since their discussion had begun. "It's the time-honored way a cowboy wins his lady's love. How about it?"

Jenny gave him a shy look from beneath lowered lashes. "If you insist."

"I do. Are you ready to face the world as a couple?"

"As ready as I'll ever be," Jenny said with a determined smile. "Let's go."

"Do you realize this is our first date?" Colt said as he

opened the passenger door to the classic red Ford Mustang convertible he'd been storing at his parents' ranch while he was overseas.

Jenny smiled up at him as she slid into the black leather bucket seat. "This is certainly the right car for it. How about putting the top down?"

"You wouldn't mind?"

"I'd love it," Jenny said. And she did. The night was warm, and the sky was filled with a million stars. She found herself laughing as her hair whipped around her face, making it impossible to see. "I should have brought a scarf," she said.

"Look in the glove compartment," Colt said.

She opened the glove compartment and found a small turquoise silk scarf. "This is mine!"

He shot her a sheepish grin. "I found it in the car after Huck borrowed it."

"I remember when I lost this," she said as she tied back her hair at her nape. "Huck said it must have blown off. But I was sure I'd taken it off when we—" Jenny stopped herself.

"Yeah. That's what I figured, too," Colt said. He shot her a quick look. "You have no idea how much agony I suffered thinking about the two of you in the backseat of this car."

Jenny was grateful for the darkness that prevented Colt from seeing her blush. "Maybe I can make it up to you," she said.

Colt turned to stare at her. "Are you saying what I think you're saying?" His eyes looked hungry, and she felt both frightened and exhilarated at the prospect of joining Colt in the backseat of his Mustang.

A blaring horn brought them both to their senses.

"Watch out!" she cried.

Colt yanked the wheel to avoid the car coming from

the opposite direction, overcompensated and went off the road. He hit the brakes, and the Mustang skidded to a halt on the dirt and gravel shoulder.

"Are you all right?" Colt asked.

Jenny was trembling, the result of too much adrenaline. "That was close," she said with a small laugh.

"Yeah. Too close. We could've been killed. And I would've missed getting to kiss you in the backseat of this car." Colt opened his door, trotted around the front of the car, then opened her door. "Out," he ordered.

"Colt, it's the middle of nowhere. What are you doing?"

"We're taking a little trip down memory lane." Once she was out of the seat, he pushed it forward, making a space for her to slip into the backseat. "Get in."

Jenny slid into the backseat and scooted over to make room for Colt, who stepped in behind her. Before she had a chance to think, Colt slid one arm around her shoulder and pulled her close. With his eyes on hers, with their lips only an inch apart, he slowly tugged the scarf from her hair and sieved his fingers into her hair.

"I love you, Jenny. I want to hold you and kiss you and make love to you until I can't see straight."

"Oh, Colt."

Huck had never said such things, even though Jenny had always wished he would. Maybe it was because they'd become sweethearts at such a young age. Maybe it was because Huck hadn't known how much she needed to hear them said.

She couldn't honestly tell Colt she loved him, or even that she was ready yet to make love to him. But she returned the favor of asking out loud for what she wanted.

"I want to kiss you, too," she said. She put her hand at his nape and urged his mouth down to hers, feeling the desire shoot through her as his mouth captured hers.

"I want to touch you," he murmured against her lips.

She suddenly felt shy, like an innocent who'd never been touched. She reached for his hand and brought it to her breast. She moaned in her throat as his hand closed around her breast and his forefinger and thumb rolled her nipple. "Ohmigod," she gasped.

How could she feel so much? How could she need so much? There was something more she wanted. "I want to touch you," she murmured.

Colt made a guttural sound in his throat as his hand left her breast and reached for her hand, guiding it toward his mouth. He kissed her palm, then pressed it against his cheek.

His skin felt soft and smooth after his shave and smelled of piney woods. She found the scar on his chin with her fingertips first, then with her lips. Her hand slid down Colt's throat to his chest, where she felt his heart thudding under her hand.

He held his breath as her hand moved lower, past his belt until she reached the hardness and heat between his legs. He stilled as she tentatively touched, tracing the shape of him, learning the feel of him. He groaned, then grabbed her wrist to stop her exploration.

"I love the way you kiss and touch," he said. "But the first time we make love, I want enough privacy to know we're not going to be disturbed for a good long while. We're already ten minutes late for supper at Buck's Steakhouse."

Jenny managed a crooked smile. "At least I know I have a great deal to look forward to."

Colt laughed. "Come on. Let me help you out of here."

"Wait."

Colt paused halfway out of the backseat. "What's the matter?"

She grinned. "You're going to have to help me find my scarf."

Colt laughed, kissed her quickly on the mouth, then pulled the scarf from his jeans pocket and gave it back to her.

It took them only five minutes after they were on the road to reach Buck's Steakhouse. To Jenny's surprise, Colt curved his arm possessively around her waist as he led her inside. She knew he didn't give a damn what people thought. He never had. But she'd lived here for more than fifteen years as Huck's girl. She couldn't help feeling a little trepidation as they stepped inside the restaurant.

She hadn't overestimated the effect their appearance arm-in-arm would have on their friends and neighbors. Curious eyes focused on them as she and Colt followed the waitress to their table. Jenny shivered. It felt like a caterpillar was crawling on her skin.

"Ignore them," Colt whispered in her ear. "They'll get used to it."

Jenny wasn't so sure. They might get used to seeing her with Colt, but people in small Texas towns had very long memories. When she and Colt were old and gray, her name would still be linked with Huck's when it came up in conversation.

Assuming you live that long.

It had been dishonest not to tell Colt all the facts before he began his courtship. But it was entirely likely that once he knew the truth, he'd hightail it in the other direction. Jenny wanted to be wooed. She wanted to fall in love with Colt, perhaps even make love with him someday. Was that so wrong?

"You're beautiful, Jenny," Colt murmured. "I'm the envy of every man here."

She flushed with pleasure and turned to look at him.

The admiration was plain in his eyes, along with something else.

Love.

That was how she justified keeping her secret. Colt already loved her. He had nothing to lose by trying to win her love. She was the one risking everything. She was the one planning to fall in love with a man who might very well leave her in the end—as her father had left her mother—not because he didn't care, but because he cared too much.

She was glad Randy and Faith were sitting at the table, because otherwise she might have been tempted to confess everything. She was surprised to see that Hope had come along.

"Hello, girls," Jenny said. "You're both looking very pretty tonight."

"Thank you, Miss Wright," they replied in unison.

The twins did look remarkably pretty, Jenny thought, but for identical twins, they also looked remarkably different. Hope wore a sophisticated strapless black sheath that was cut low enough to reveal a great deal of cleavage. Faith was dressed in a simple, V-necked powder blue dress with capped sleeves.

Hope's hair was swept up in an elegant French twist, and she wore earrings that dangled, drawing male attention to her slender throat and bare shoulders. Faith wore her straight black hair tucked behind her ears, which held tiny diamond studs.

Faith looked like the fresh-faced teenager she was, with only a hint of pink lipstick to emphasize her natural beauty. Her dark eyes glowed from within.

Hope's face was expertly made up, but she looked like a picture in a book, not a real person, and beyond the thick mascara on her lashes, Jenny saw a hint of desperation in the girl's dark eyes.

"Hope didn't have any other plans, so Faith asked if she could come along," Randy said. "I said it'd be fine. It's okay, isn't it?"

"Sure. I'm glad you could both join us," Jenny said as Colt seated her. She knew Randy well enough to sense he was annoyed at Hope's presence, but she was proud of him for being gracious. "Looks like there's plenty of room at the table," she said.

"Jake asked if he could join us," Colt said. "So I asked Buck to make sure we had a big table."

Jenny eyed Colt speculatively, but he didn't explain why Jake had invited himself along for a celebration to which he could have only a tenuous connection.

Then Jenny looked across the table at Hope, all dressed up with no date at her side, and remembered how Hope had cornered Jake on her back porch during Huck's wake. Hope had flirted openly, but Jake hadn't seemed interested. Had Hope known Jake would be coming tonight? Was that why she'd invited herself along?

Jenny prayed the young woman hadn't developed a crush on Jake. Since his divorce five years ago, he'd been hell on women. Hope's youth might provide some protection from Jake's crude behavior, but if she pushed, Jake was likely to shove right back.

Jenny had an unsettling thought. What if Jake had arranged for Hope to be here so he could meet with her?

Once Jenny had ordered iced tea, she hid behind the menu and leaned over to ask Colt, "Did Jake say why he wanted to join us?"

Colt shrugged. "He always has a steak at Buck's on Friday night. When he realized we were coming, he asked if he could join us. Do you mind?"

"Of course not," Jenny said. "I always liked Jake." She'd liked him a lot better before he'd been married to Lucy

Palance, a girl he'd met when they were in college. Their ten-year marriage hadn't seemed to bring much happiness to either of them. She'd often seen Jake with women over the past five years, but they weren't the kind of female a hard-working rancher married.

So Jenny was amazed when Jake showed up with a schoolteacher on his arm. Miss Amanda Carter was not only a proper lady, she was also fun-loving and pretty. She was twenty-nine and still unmarried, though she'd been pursued by all the most eligible bachelors in town. She wore a tailored cream-colored silk suit that accented her female curves. Amanda was exactly the sort of woman Jenny would have chosen as a second wife for Jake. She just wasn't the sort of woman she'd expected to find at Jake's side. Was Jake turning over a new leaf?

Jenny glanced at Hope and saw from the girl's stunned expression that she might very well have known Jake was coming tonight but hadn't expected him to show up with a date. The blood leached from her face until her eyes were like two burned spots on a sheet of parchment.

Judging from Faith's equally stricken expression, she was aware of her sister's distress. Faith had seated herself so her good hand was next to Randy, so it was necessary to reach out to Hope with her prosthesis. Jenny watched in surprise as Hope tightly gripped the metal hook for comfort, as though it were a flesh-and-blood hand.

Hope's eyes never left Jake's face. She seemed to be waiting for something. *For Jake to acknowledge her,* Jenny realized.

Jake avoided speaking directly to Hope, or even looking at her, by saying to Amanda, "You know the Butler twins."

"I do," Amanda said with a smile. "You both look very pretty tonight."

"Thank you, Miss Carter," Faith replied.

Hope said nothing. Her gaze dropped to her lap, and color—an entire rose garden of color—suddenly grew on her pale cheeks. Her jaw was clamped, and she was blinking furiously.

Jenny gave Jake a surreptitious glance to see whether he was affected by Hope's despair and caught him stealing a look at Hope from the corner of his eye. It dawned on her that Jake was very much aware of Hope, that his indifference was a calculated act. He apparently cared for Hope a great deal more than he wanted her to know. And just as apparently had decided she was too young for him.

What was it about the Whitelaw men that made them fall in love with unavailable women? Jenny wondered. She only had Colt to judge by, but if Jake was crazy enough to go through such an elaborate charade to discourage Hope, he wasn't going to be happy with a substitute bride, even one as appropriate as Miss Amanda Carter.

Jake ordered a beer for himself and Amanda, then asked if she wanted to dance to the live country and western band that played at Buck's on Friday and Saturday nights. A moment later Jake pulled Amanda into his arms and began two-stepping around the wooden dance floor. Jake was a good dancer, and Jenny was forced to admit the couple looked very much like they belonged together.

A glance at Hope revealed tight lips and narrowed eyes.

Hope had obviously gotten the message Jake had sent by bringing along Miss Carter tonight. It wasn't the gentlest setdown Jenny had ever seen a man give a woman. But it was certainly effective.

She felt sorry for Hope. And angry at Jake. This was Hope's graduation night, one of the most important nights in her life. What Jake had done was cruel, even if he'd believed it was necessary.

Colt leaned over to speak in her ear. "What's got you frowning?"

"Your brother is an idiot," she whispered back.

"I've always thought so," Colt agreed with a grin. "What has Jake done this time?"

"Coming here with Amanda was—"

Before she could finish, the music stopped and Jake and Amanda headed back toward the table. Jake seated Amanda next to Hope, then sat across from her.

"Thanks, Jake," Amanda said. "That was fun."

"You're a good dancer, Amanda," Jake replied.

Jenny watched as Jake stole another glance at Hope. The teenager's chin had dropped to her chest, and she was twisting her paper napkin into a knot. It was small comfort to see the flash of pain in Jake's eyes.

As soon as Amanda was settled and had taken a sip of her beer, she turned to the twins and asked, "Have you girls decided yet where you're going to college?"

Jenny had expected Faith to answer, but to her amazement, it was Hope who spoke. She lifted her head until her chin jutted and her shoulders were squared. Her eyes gleamed with unshed tears, but her voice belied her agitation as she replied, "Faith and I have both been accepted at Baylor, Miss Carter."

"Have you decided on a major yet?" Amanda inquired.

Hope's chin lifted another notch. "Animal husbandry."

Jake choked on his beer.

"I want to learn how to put the right mare with the right stud," Hope said, staring right at Jake. "That's so important when you want to end up with good stock, don't you agree, Mr. Whitelaw?"

Jake's eyes narrowed. "Absolutely."

Jenny figured any second now things were going to

get ugly. She opened her mouth to intervene, but Jake spoke first.

"That's why I proposed to Miss Carter tonight."

Hope inhaled sharply.

"I didn't know you two had been seeing each other," Jenny said to Amanda.

"I've had my eye on Jake for a long time. He's been a hard man to pin down," Amanda said with a smile. "But he was worth the wait," she said, leaning over to kiss Jake on the mouth.

"Congratulations," Colt said, grinning and slapping Jake on the back. He stood up enough to lean over and kiss Amanda on the cheek. "I can always use another sister. I wish you both the very best."

Jenny turned to see how Hope was handling this latest announcement and discovered her chair was empty. The shredded napkin lay on the empty plate where she had been.

Jenny's gaze shot to Randy, who shrugged helplessly. To Jenny's surprise, it was Faith who saved the day.

"Hope hasn't been feeling well today," Faith said as she stood. "I think we'll wait and eat at the senior picnic later tonight. Will you excuse us, please?"

"Be careful on the—"

"I know," Randy said, cutting Jenny off as he rose to go with Faith. "I'll drive slow. See you at the ceremony, sis. Bye, Colt. Bye, Miss Carter. Congratulations, Jake."

Once the teenagers were gone, the empty seats at the table loomed large. Jenny searched for something to say, but could think of nothing. Jake's face looked pale, and Jenny noticed he had let go of Amanda's hand.

"You're not the only one with news, Jake," Colt said with a smile to his older brother. "You can wish me happy, too. I've decided to resign from the Air Force and stay at the Double D with Jenny."

Jake's lips curled in a bleak smile. "Well, little brother, looks like we're both going to settle down and live happily ever after."

Jenny shivered as a chill of foreboding ran down her spine.

CHAPTER TEN

"WHY ARE YOU so fidgety?" FAITH whispered.

Randy shot a glance at Faith, who was sitting next to him on the front seat of Old Nellie, then at Hope, who was sitting to Faith's right, and then back to the winding dirt road. "Guess I'm just excited about graduating."

After what had happened at supper, he should've known Faith wouldn't go to the senior picnic without Hope. Randy was beginning to wonder if he'd ever get Faith alone.

Everyone had brought along jeans and T-shirts to change into at the restrooms at school, because the picnic consisted of a midnight hot dog and marshmallow roast around a bonfire at the Whitelaw ranch. The Whitelaw Brats had started the tradition, and long after their youngest had graduated, Zach and Rebecca Whitelaw continued to make the site at Camp LittleHawk available for the party.

Drinking alcohol was forbidden, and couples were discouraged from wandering off into the dark. Randy figured one couple wouldn't be missed in all the excitement, and he'd made special plans for himself and Faith—if he could manage to separate her from her sister.

This year Jenny had volunteered to be one of the chaperons, along with Colt and his brother Jake. Randy supposed that meant Miss Carter would be present, too.

Too bad for Hope.

Faith had told Randy about Hope's crush on Jake. He felt sorry for her after what had happened tonight, Jake getting engaged and all, and he understood Faith didn't want to leave her twin alone at a time like this. But he was determined to have some time alone with her.

"We're here," he announced as he pulled Old Nellie in line with two dozen other vehicles. "I've got a blanket in the bed of the pickup we can sit on," he said to Faith.

"I'll get it," Hope volunteered, hopping out of the truck.

Within minutes, Randy was sitting next to Faith on a blanket beside the fire—with Hope perched on Faith's left side. He racked his brain to think of a way to distract Hope. Once he found it, he had to wait almost an hour before he found a moment when Jenny was busy enough that he and Faith could escape the party without their absence being immediately detected.

"Say, Hope," he said at last. "Why don't you see if Jake wants to roast some marshmallows? He's been standing over there all by himself with his arms crossed, just staring into the fire, ever since Miss Carter left to take care of her mother."

He watched Hope hesitate, then rise. "All right," she said. "I will."

Randy waited barely long enough to see the back of Hope before he turned to Faith and said, "Would you like to take a walk with me?"

She laid her right hand in his and said, "Sure."

He helped her to her feet and edged out of the light of the fire and into the shadows beyond. They weren't the only ones who'd decided to "take a walk." They passed several couples standing in the dark kissing. Most lingered just outside the light from the fire. For what he had in mind, Randy wanted more distance.

"Where are we going?" Faith asked as he led her farther into the moonlit darkness.

"Just a little farther," he said.

"It's awfully dark out here."

Randy stopped and looked up. "There's got to be a zillion or so stars up there, and the moon's pretty full. Trust me, Faith," he said, squeezing her hand.

She squeezed his hand back and followed without more argument. He saw the concern on her face when a glow appeared in the distance. They slid down an incline and into a gully, where he had previously set out a Coleman lantern, a blanket, and a picnic basket.

"We're here," he announced.

"What's all this?" Faith asked, turning to look at him.

Her eyes were wide and wary, and Randy knew he was about to find out whether she really did trust him. "I wanted us to have our own party," he said. "Do you mind?"

Her smile was slow in coming, but when it finally arrived, the muscles in his stomach unclenched. "I think it's a wonderful idea," she said. "Won't your sister wonder what's happened to us?"

He settled onto a ring-patterned quilt that had been made by his mother and pulled Faith down beside him. "We're no farther away than a shout, if anybody really wants to find us. I just thought…I wanted some time alone with you tonight."

"Why?"

He was gripping her right hand tightly, trying to get up the courage to say what he was feeling. "You know I like you an awful lot," he managed.

"I like you, too, Randy."

"I want you to be my girl," he blurted. He could feel the heat in his face where the blood had rushed. He was tempted to look away, but he made himself face her while he waited for her answer.

"You know we're going to different colleges in the fall," Faith said tentatively. "I'm headed for Baylor in Waco, and you'll be at Texas Tech in Lubbock. They're hours and hours apart."

"We could each drive halfway on the weekends," he said.

"We've never even kissed," Faith said with a gentle smile, "and you want me to drive halfway across Texas—"

Randy leaned over and touched her lips with his. The shock was electric. He broke the kiss and stared, stunned, into her eyes. She looked equally shaken.

Faith's right hand came up to touch her lips as she searched his face. "I've never been kissed before. Is it always like that?"

"It's never been like that for me," he said.

"It was good?"

"Better than good. Terrific," he replied. "You want to try it again?"

"Oh, yes," she whispered.

He moved slower this time, pressing his lips more firmly against hers, but feeling the same delicious, unbelievable shock to his senses. His heart catapulted in his chest, and his body turned rock-hard. His mouth slanted over hers, seeking more, and his tongue went searching.

She was breathing as hard as he was, and he felt her body quiver as the kiss grew into something greater than the thing it was. Their bodies remained separate, but their souls merged.

He wanted to hold her in his arms, to touch her. He reached out to encircle her waist and drew her close so he could feel her soft breasts against his chest. He was aware of her right arm around him, holding him, but she kept her left arm down and her body on that side angled away.

"Put your arms around me, sweetheart," he whispered.

"But—"

"Please, Faith." She had to trust him not to hurt her. He only hoped he was worthy of that trust.

Slowly, hesitantly, her arm with the prosthesis attached encircled his waist. He could feel the plastic against his back, the nudge of the metal hook at its end against his flesh. She looked up at him, searching for repugnance, for revulsion or disgust.

Randy kept his expression neutral, knowing how important it was that he accept this part of her that was no part of her. "It's okay," he said. "I can handle it."

She gave a shaky laugh. "I'm not sure I can."

"It's no big deal. Just a bunch of plastic and metal you need because you don't have a hand."

She stared at him wonderingly. "You don't mind?"

He separated their bodies, though it was the last thing he wanted to do, and slid his hands down her arms. He made himself take her hook in his left hand, while his right hand held hers. He didn't wince, though her fingernails dug into him, because he didn't want her to think he minded holding that hook.

"You've never really told me how this works," he said, staring at the hook that lay in his open palm.

"It's myoelectric."

In response to his confused look, she explained. "Impulses from the brain are received in receptors in the elbow of the device."

"So you *think* this hook open and closed?"

"That's about it," she said with a smile.

"Neat," he said. "Now, will you put your arms around me, please, and give me another kiss."

She grinned. "With pleasure."

Her enthusiasm was such, that very shortly they were lying side by side on the quilt, their bodies aligned, their mouths merged. Randy was having a hard time breathing, let alone thinking, but he knew they had to stop. Faith trusted him. He had to be worthy of that trust.

He broke the kiss and pressed his face against her neck. "We have to stop, Faith."

Her hand tangled in the hair at his nape, and he shivered at the exquisite sensations her touch provoked. She kissed his temple and whispered, "If you want, I'll be your girl."

"Oh, God, Faith." That provoked another deep kiss, to express his gratitude and his love. When her tongue traced the seam of his lips, he opened his mouth and let her in. And felt her become a part of him. Four years wasn't so long to wait. *Four years.* "I can't wait, Faith," he groaned against her neck.

"I want you, too," she confessed breathlessly.

He'd meant he couldn't wait four years to marry her, but as he looked into Faith's lambent eyes, he realized she'd mistaken his meaning. Well, he'd wanted her trust. She'd given it to him in spades. He brushed her hair back from her face with a trembling hand. "I meant—"

"There you are!" an accusing voice cried.

Randy sat bolt upright, bringing Faith with him. They found themselves staring into four disapproving faces.

HOPE WAS WEARING JEANS, a cut-off T-shirt and cowboy boots, but as she marched the twenty or so feet that separated her from Jake Whitelaw, she felt naked, as though he could see through all the trappings to the vulnerable female inside.

Jake's eyes never left hers, but his grim look warned her away. She ignored it and walked up to him, carrying the unbent hanger she was using to roast marshmallows. "How about a roasted marshmallow?" she asked.

He hesitated, then said, "Sure. Why not?"

He followed her to a table that had been set up with bags

of marshmallows and waited while she stuck a couple on the end of the wire hanger. "How do you like yours?" she asked as she crossed with him back to the fire.

"Hot on the outside, soft and sweet on the inside."

"That's me," she said softly. "Hot and soft and sweet." She looked at him and saw the glowing embers flare.

"I warned you before to stay away," he said. "I don't play games with little girls."

She held the hanger over the fire, making sure the marshmallows stayed well out of the flames. "I'm not playing, Jake. And I'm not a little girl. I know exactly what I want. I want you."

"I'm engaged to be married."

"You don't love her. You love me. You want to touch me, to kiss me, to put yourself inside me."

He stood behind her, close enough that she could feel the heat of him, but he didn't touch her. She felt his moist breath against her ear. "I thought you'd learned your lesson in the barn."

Hope felt the heat on her face and was grateful she could blame it on the fire. "It seemed to me that you liked what you saw," she said brazenly.

"Too damn much," he muttered.

She angled her head to meet his gaze, and the heat in his eyes melted her bones. She stiffened her knees to keep them from buckling. "Don't marry her, Jake. Marry me."

He swore under his breath, but he never took his eyes off hers.

"I'll make you a good wife. I can—"

"Shut up. Shut the hell up," he said in a guttural voice.

"Hey there, Hope!" Colt yelled from the other side of the fire. "Your marshmallows are on fire."

Hope jerked around and discovered the two marshmallows had been swallowed in flames. She yanked them out of the fire and blew hard to put them out, but it was too late. They were both charred beyond recognition.

"Let that be a warning," Jake murmured in her ear. "You keep playing with fire, little girl, you're going to get burned. Go away, Hope. Get as far from me as you can."

He moved away and left her standing alone. It was then Hope noticed that Faith and Randy were missing.

COLT TOLD HIMSELF he must have misconstrued the look that passed between Hope Butler and his brother Jake before her marshmallows caught fire. He considered whether he ought to confront Jake but decided it wasn't necessary. His brother knew better than to get involved with a girl half his age, especially when he was engaged to another woman.

But he had to admit that an evening campfire in the middle of the prairie had a way of encouraging romance. Colt had fond memories of a night he and Huck and Jenny had roasted marshmallows with friends and family around a similar campfire. Mac Macready, who'd later married his eldest sister, Jewel, had sat around the campfire vying for Jewel's attentions with Gavin Talbot, who'd ended up marrying his sister Rolleen.

"What's put that smile on your face?" Jenny asked.

"I was remembering a time when we were fourteen and we did this."

"The night Mac Macready warned off Gavin Talbot from Jewel?" Jenny inquired.

"You remember that, too?"

She laughed. "The way sparks were flying between Mac and Jewel, we didn't need a fire to roast marshmallows."

"They're an old married couple now with three kids. Gavin and Rolleen have four between them. Where has the time gone? I can't wait till we've got a brood of our own."

Jenny's face blanched.

"Jenny? What's wrong?" Colt asked.

"I never realized you wanted a big family."

"I guess I never thought about it before, because I never wanted to marry anyone but you. I assumed you'd still want kids. Are you saying you don't?"

"I've already raised one family, Colt. I'd like a little time for myself. I'll understand if that changes your mind about marrying me."

Colt felt like he'd been kicked in the stomach. But Jenny and kids went together like peanut butter and jelly. She'd always loved kids. Apparently, raising four boys by herself had taken its toll. "I suppose I can live without having kids," he said slowly.

"Don't do me any favors," Jenny snapped.

He caught her arm before she could escape. "Hold it right there! I've told you it's okay."

"You don't mean it," she said. "I saw the look in your eyes, Colt. You're shocked and disappointed."

"So what if I am? It's not the end of the world. I'll get over it."

"Will you?"

"When it comes to a choice between you and kids," he said, "there's no question which I'd choose. I've waited too long for you, Jenny. I love you too much to give you up for any reason."

"You say that now," she said. "What about later? What about a year from now or five years from now? What if you change your mind?"

"All I can do is tell you how I feel right now," Colt said. "Nothing could make me leave you, Jenny."

She looked stricken. She opened her mouth to speak, but they were interrupted by Hope Butler.

"Miss Wright, my sister is missing and so is your brother Randy."

"They've probably gone for a walk," Colt said.

"I've looked around, but I can't find them," Hope said. "I'm worried."

Colt exchanged a glance with Jenny. They both knew why the couple had probably disappeared. If it was up to him, Colt would have waited for them to return. He was in a position to know Randy's feelings about Faith, and knowing Jenny, he was sure she'd raised her brother to respect a woman's feelings. Randy wouldn't be doing anything Faith didn't want.

But the fear in Hope's eyes was real and couldn't be ignored.

"What's up?" Jake asked as he joined them.

Colt watched as Jake exchanged an inquiring look with Hope.

"Faith and Randy are missing," Hope said.

"I'll go take a look for them," Jake said.

"I'm coming with you," Hope said.

Jake halted in his tracks.

It was plain Jake didn't want her along, and equally clear Hope wasn't going to be left behind. Colt remembered the look he'd seen pass between the two of them at the campfire. "Why don't we all go?" he said. "It shouldn't take us long to find them."

Jake shot him a look of appreciation, then headed into the shadows with Hope a step behind him.

"She's in love with him," Jenny murmured as they followed after them.

Colt frowned. "I hope you're wrong."

"I don't believe I am."

"She's only eighteen."

"I fell in love with Huck when I was fourteen," she reminded him.

"Poor Hope," Colt said, shaking his head.

"Poor Jake," Jenny countered.

"What do you mean?"

"Have you seen the way he looks at her?"

Colt remembered the look he'd seen Jake and Hope exchange. "He can't be thinking of doing anything about it," he said half to himself.

"Oh, he won't do anything about it," Jenny said. "The idiot."

"What are you saying? That he should go after her? He just got engaged!"

"He's a fool to ignore his feelings. He should admit he loves her, and let her love him back."

"I suppose you think I should have told you I loved you, even when it was hopeless."

Jenny stopped and turned to face him. "Maybe if you'd said something fifteen years ago we would've been together when there was still a chance—" She cut herself off and hurried to catch up to Jake and Hope.

Colt's mind was reeling. Jenny had always—only—loved Huck. Hadn't she? As soon as he caught up to her he demanded, "Are you saying you had feelings for *me* fifteen years ago?"

"It doesn't matter now," she said. "We can't look back, Colt. We can't focus on what might have been. We have to live in the here and now. I shouldn't have said anything."

Colt should have felt ebullient at Jenny's revelation. It took him a moment to figure out what was bothering him.

Maybe if you'd said something fifteen years ago we would have been together when there was still a chance— A chance for what? Colt wondered. For true love? For a family? What was it she'd been about to confess when Hope Butler had interrupted them.

In the far-off glow of a lantern, Colt spied Randy and Faith lying on a quilt. Jake and Hope reached them first.

"There you are!" Hope said in an accusing voice. "What are you doing to my sister?"

"I'm fine, Hope," Faith said, quickly rising to her feet and self-consciously rearranging her blouse.

Hope turned on Randy. "What's the big idea sneaking off into the dark with my sister?"

"Hope, that's enough," Faith said. "I came with Randy willingly. We were just talking."

Hope snorted. "Talking. Right. That's why your lips are all puffy and—"

"That's enough," Jake said.

"Can't you see—"

"Leave them alone," Jake said. "Your sister's entitled to make her own choices."

"But—"

"Randy, why don't you take Faith back to the fire," Jenny said. "Colt and I will gather up these things for you."

"Thanks, sis," Randy said. "Come on, Faith."

"I'll walk you back," Hope said, reaching a hand toward her sister.

"I'm going with Randy," Faith said, meeting her sister's gaze, but not moving toward her.

Colt saw the shock and pain on Hope's face as Faith took the hand Randy held out to her and began walking back to the fire, leaving Hope behind.

Colt would have stepped into the breach, but Jake beat him to it.

"I'll walk you back," he said to Hope.

"I don't need an escort," she retorted, turning and marching back toward the fire.

"I'll make sure she gets back okay," Jake said as he left Colt and Jenny alone.

Instead of picking up the blanket, Jenny sat down on it. "Join me?"

"We're supposed to be chaperoning kids."

"They'll manage without us for a few minutes," she said, patting the blanket beside her. "Join me."

Colt wasn't going to turn down the chance to be alone with Jenny under a moonlit sky. He sat down cross-legged on the blanket. "Now what?" he said.

"If I have to ask, you aren't the man I think you are," she said teasingly.

Colt leaned over and kissed her on the mouth. The sound of satisfaction in her throat made him ache. He reached out to palm her breast and heard a moan of pleasure that sent his blood thrumming through his veins. He lowered Jenny onto the blanket until they were fitted together from breast to belly. "We missed doing this as kids, didn't we?" he said.

"Uh-huh."

"I'll make it all up to you, Jenny," he promised.

"I only wish you could," she murmured against his neck.

"What does that mean?"

"Only that some moments are lost forever, Colt. That's all."

The sadness in her voice made him want to weep. "Just promise you'll let me try, Jenny."

She leaned over and gave him the softest of kisses. "All right, Colt," she said as she met his gaze in the moonlight. "I promise to let you try."

CHAPTER ELEVEN

"You look good enough to eat," Colt said.

Jenny blushed as she stepped farther into the living room. "Thank you, Colt."

He held out his arms, and she walked into his embrace, letting her body settle against his. "This feels good," she said.

"No argument from me," he said. "I can hardly wait till you're my wife. How's that wedding gown coming along?"

"It's not finished yet."

Their wedding was one week away, but Jenny hadn't finished making her wedding dress. There was a good reason for the delay. She still wasn't sure there was going to be a wedding, for the simple reason she hadn't yet told Colt her secret.

He'd become so dear to her that she couldn't bear the thought of losing him. The temptation was overwhelming not to tell him at all. But how could she take vows "to love and honor and cherish" in the midst of such a deception?

Trust him, Jenny. He loves you. It won't matter.

Colt's arms tightened around her. "Is it my imagination, or are you losing weight?"

Jenny stiffened. "It's this dress," she said.

He held her out at arm's length and critically surveyed the short black satin sheath held up by narrow rhinestone straps. It was cut low enough in front to reveal her modest cleavage and short enough to reveal her long, slender legs.

He whistled, long and low. "You're one gorgeous lady, Miss Wright. But once you're mine, I think we're going to put a few pounds back on those beautiful bones."

She didn't dare meet his gaze, afraid he would find something in her eyes that would give her away. Worry had caused her to lose her appetite. But explaining even that much would require her to reveal the source of her anxiety—the secret she was keeping from him. "We'd better get going. Your mother and father will be wondering where we are."

"I'm not sure I want to share you with anybody else just yet."

"Randy will—"

"Randy left fifteen minutes ago to pick up Faith."

"Your parents—"

"My parents won't mind if we're a little late to our own engagement party."

"Colt, I don't think—"

"Don't think," he murmured as he pulled her back into his arms. "Just let me hold you. I can't believe this is real. For so many years I dreamed of moments like this, and now I want to enjoy every one of them."

She hid her face against his neck and clutched at his shoulders. "I love you, Colt."

She heard his sharp intake of air before he separated them so he could look into her eyes. "I've been waiting a long time to hear you say that."

"There's just one thing—"

His mouth captured hers in a kiss of claiming, preventing the words that might have torn them apart.

A frisson of pleasure shot through her. How could Colt make her feel so much, so fast? It had never been like this with Huck. Never. Her nipples peaked with the brush of his hand across the satin. He kissed her throat, then suckled, causing her insides to draw up tight. She moaned, a sound of desire and despair.

Her heart beat against her ribs like a butterfly caught in a jar, as he reached for the zipper at the back of her dress. It slid down easily, and the straps fell off her shoulders along with the top of the sheath. Beneath it she wore a black merry widow. The avid look in his eyes made her body quiver with anticipation. He reached behind her to unhook the bra, and she panicked.

"Colt, no!"

His hands paused, but his eyes quickly sought hers for an explanation. "What's wrong?"

"I…" Her hands gripped his arms, as though to shove him away. *Tell him. Tell him. Tell him.*

"This isn't the right time," she said breathlessly. She saw the disappointment in his eyes, but, thank God, no suspicion. "We're supposed to be at your parents' home in twenty minutes."

His lips curled in a lopsided grin. "I'm sure I'd enjoy making love to you however little time we took." He held up a hand to stay her protest. "But I'm willing to wait, if that's what you what."

"It's what I want."

He lifted the straps back onto her shoulders and reached around her to zip up the dress. All the while, his hips were pressed against hers, so she could feel his arousal. She ached for him, yearned for him. And feared his discovery of the truth.

"It's all right, Jenny," he murmured in her ear. "I understand why you're afraid."

"You do?" she said, her voice catching in her throat.

He nodded solemnly as he brushed her hair back behind her shoulders. "You're afraid it won't be the same with me—" He swallowed hard and corrected himself. "As *good* with me, as it was with Huck. Just remember that I love you. If you want me to do something differently, all you have to do is ask."

She wanted to tell him he was wrong, that he made her feel so much more than Huck ever had. But she bit back the words. It wasn't Huck's fault he hadn't made her feel more. It wasn't Huck's fault she hadn't been in love with him. She hadn't known what a difference love would make. Until Colt had come along and shown her.

Jenny leaned forward and kissed Colt gently on the lips, feeling the need that arose whenever she touched him. "I love the way you touch me, Colt. I love the way you kiss me. I want to make love to you. But I need a little more time."

"We're getting married in a week," he reminded her. "Do you want to wait until our wedding night? Is that what you're telling me?"

She couldn't wait that long. Colt had to know the truth before they stood in front of a preacher and said vows that bound them for a lifetime. *A lifetime. Who are you kidding, Jenny?* She couldn't mislead Colt any longer. It seemed time had run out.

Jenny swallowed past the lump in her throat. "Tonight," she said. "After the party."

"I'm going to hold you to that promise," Colt said, leaning down to kiss her tenderly on the mouth.

As she stepped out onto the back porch, Jenny stopped abruptly. Parked at the door was a brand-new forest-green Jeep with a gigantic yellow bow on the hood. She turned to Colt, who was grinning.

"Do you like it?"

"Oh, Colt. It's too much." *Especially when you may not want anything to do with me after tonight.*

"I'd hand the world to you on a platter, if I could."

"I don't know what to say."

"Say you like it."

Jenny smiled. "I like it." She stepped off the back porch and walked completely around the Jeep, peering inside.

Colt pulled the ribbon away from the vehicle, then reached into his trouser pocket to retrieve the key. "You want to drive?"

"Oh, yes, please."

Jenny didn't say much on the trip to Hawk's Pride because her heart was lodged in her throat. This was all a dream, and she was afraid to wake up. Colt was everything Huck had never been—generous, thoughtful, helpful—and he made her body hum whenever he touched her.

But he wasn't perfect. He had one fatal flaw. He couldn't bear to be around sick people. She'd gotten the measles when she was sixteen, and Colt hadn't come to visit her once until she was well again.

When she'd questioned him later, he'd admitted, "Something happens inside me when I see somebody I know who's sick in bed." He had put a hand to his belly. "My insides sort of squeeze up tight, and I can't breathe."

She'd laughed at him and asked, "What do you do when you get a cold?"

"Oh, I don't have any problems when *I'm* sick. Only when somebody else gets ill."

"What do you do when one of your brothers or sisters gets sick?" she asked.

"I stay away until they're well."

"You can't mean that," she said.

"I most certainly do."

"You don't even bring them magazines or something to drink?"

Colt shook his head.

"That's awful!"

"I didn't say I was proud of the way I act," he said. "And believe me, I've tried to get over it. I visited Avery's bedroom when he got the mumps, but it was a disaster. I was with him maybe a minute when my hands started trembling, and I broke out in a sweat. I barely got out of there before I lost my lunch!"

"Why do you suppose that happens?" she asked.

"I think I'm afraid," he confessed in a low voice.

"That you'll get sick, too?"

"That someone I care about will die."

"People don't die of a cold, Colt, and not very often anymore from measles or mumps," she chided.

He grimaced. "I know that! I didn't say what I feel makes sense. It's just what I feel. I can't help it. So don't give me a hard time about it. Okay?"

In all the years she'd known Colt, she hadn't once seen him visit anyone in the hospital. When her mother was sick, he only came by when he was sure he wasn't going to catch a glimpse of her in bed. Another time, when he discovered Tyler and James had chicken pox, though he'd already had the disease himself, instead of coming inside, he offered to help with the chores in the barn.

Jenny wished she had told Colt the truth from the beginning. It was going to be much harder to give him up now than it would have been before he'd come to mean so much to her.

"For a lady on her way to a party, you don't look very happy," Colt observed.

Jenny made herself smile. She was determined to enjoy their engagement party, especially since it might be their last night together. "I was thinking how strange life is. If Huck hadn't been killed...I would have missed so much."

"I feel the same way. I miss him a lot, but if he were here, I wouldn't have you."

Jenny reached a hand across the seat to Colt, and he gripped it tightly. "I'm glad we found each other," she said.

"Me, too."

Jenny brought the Jeep to a stop at the back door to the Whitelaws' ranch house. The whitewashed adobe house, with its barrel-tile roof, had been built in a square around a gigantic moss-laden live oak, and the party had spilled into the grassy central courtyard.

Jenny felt Colt's arm slide possessively around her waist as he escorted her into the fray.

"Hey, there, Slim," he said, shaking hands with an old high school friend. "Buck, Frank," he said, shaking more hands.

"Congratulations, Colt," Buck said. He dipped his head, touched the brim of his Stetson and said to Jenny, "We all wish you the best, Miss Wright."

"Thanks, Buck," she said.

There was something lovely about being surrounded by friends who'd known you since the days when you'd all played ring-around-the-rosie together. At the same time, it was unsettling to see the speculation in their eyes as they tried to gauge whether she and Colt might have been lovers when she was still Huck's girl.

A huge beef was being barbecued on a spit, and there was a keg of beer, along with iced tea and soft drinks. A group of women, Amanda Carter among them, were setting up a buffet table with side dishes everyone had brought. Jenny's brother Tyler was pounding on one leg of the sawhorse table with a hammer, while Colt's brother Rabb held it up.

She looked for Jake and found him standing in a circle of ranchers and their foremen, including Zach Whitelaw, her brother Sam, Wiley Butler—and his daughter, Hope.

She located Randy and Faith talking with a bunch of teen-agers beneath an arbor of bougainvillea.

She looked at Colt and realized he was making a similar survey to locate his siblings and his myriad aunts, uncles and cousins. "You've sure got a big family," Jenny murmured.

"Yeah," Colt said. "And a close one. It was great growing up as one of the Whitelaw Brats."

Jenny turned her eyes away. If Colt married her, he wasn't going to be adding any branches to this awesome family tree. He'd said he didn't mind, that she was enough for him. But seeing all these Whitelaws with their children and grandchildren made her realize how much Colt would be giving up if he married her.

It would be easier to push him away now than to endure the regret in his eyes for however much time they had together.

Stop it, Jenny. Stop looking for reasons to break up with Colt. Oh, you can come up with a few. He'd be happier flying jets than living with you. He'd be happier marrying someone who could give him kids. He'd be happier if he didn't have to hang around and maybe watch you die. But isn't the choice really up to him? Are you going to give him a chance to choose you?

That was the crux of the matter. Jenny wasn't sure she had the strength to survive Colt's rejection. It was easier to avoid that possibility by rejecting him first. She could drive him away. He wouldn't stay where he wasn't wanted.

But one of the lessons the past two precarious years had taught her was to reach out for happiness. Loving Colt made her happy. Making love with Colt would bring her joy. After that... Life was uncertain. No one got any guarantees.

Jenny turned to Colt and let him see the need she felt,

the yearning to be held and loved. "How soon do you think we can leave without our absence being noticed?"

Colt's eyes lit with a fire that warmed her insides. "My father wants to say a few words and make a toast. After that, I think we could slip away."

"Why don't you see if he wants to do that now?" Jenny said.

"Come with me," he said. "We'll ask."

Colt's parents were surprised that he wanted them to make their speeches so early in the evening, but they were more than willing to accommodate their youngest child.

"May I have your attention, please," Zach said, arranging Jenny and Colt between himself and Colt's mother Rebecca. "Before we carve up that beef, I'd like to say a few words to my son and future daughter-in-law."

The noise died down, but it didn't get completely quiet. Babies still cried and children still played. But the adults gathered around them, drinks in hand, ready to offer toasts to their future happiness.

"First I want to thank Jenny for loving my son. And my son for being smart enough to settle down and marry her."

There was general laughter, shouts of "Here! Here!" and clinking beer glasses.

"I want to tell my son how proud I am of him. How much we feel blessed for having been given the chance to make him a part of our family. I only hope he and Jenny find as much joy in raising their Whitelaw Brats, as we did in raising ours."

There was more laughter, more clinking glasses.

Jenny felt her face turn to stone. She was afraid to look at Colt, afraid to look at anyone. She prayed that Colt would let the statement pass, that he wouldn't feel the need to tell his parents, "My future wife doesn't want children."

From the corner of her eye, Jenny saw that Colt's face

was frozen in a smile. A muscle in his jaw jerked, and she realized his teeth must be clenched.

Then it was Rebecca's turn to speak. Colt's mother put her arm around Jenny and said, "We know you and Colt could live on love alone, but we've decided a little bread wouldn't hurt. We hope you'll let us pay off the mortgage on the Double D as a wedding present."

There was a gasp and then applause.

Jenny's heart was stuck in her throat. There was no way she could speak. She could barely breathe, she was so overwhelmed with joy and with pain. This good family had raised a wonderful son, and all she had offered him— all of them—was deceit.

"I'm sorry," she blurted. "I can't accept your gift. Because I can't marry your son."

COLT DIDN'T KNOW when he'd been so angry with anyone in his life. "Don't you dare run away from me," he snarled, grabbing Jenny's arm as she reached for the door to the Jeep. "What the hell's going on, Jenny?"

She was panting, and her eyes look frightened. "You heard me. I can't marry you."

"What is it you're so scared of?" he demanded.

She looked like a deer caught in a set of headlights. "This—the two of us—would never work."

Colt realized they'd acquired an audience. Not surprising, considering the bombshell Jenny had dropped. He was still reeling himself. "Get in," he said. "We're going home."

"You are home, Colt."

"Get in the damned car, Jenny." When she didn't move, he swept her up in his arms, carried her around the hood of the Jeep and deposited her in the passenger's seat. "Don't get any smart ideas," he warned.

He half expected her to leap out of the Jeep and run.

She was good at running from trouble, his Jenny. But the running was going to stop. Here. Tonight.

Colt started the engine and spun the wheels, kicking up dirt and stones as he backed out of the driveway. "Buckle up," he said. "It's liable to be a bumpy ride."

He didn't say another word until he cut the Jeep's engine at Jenny's back door. "Come inside. We're going to talk."

"I have nothing more to say," Jenny said as she shoved open her door and hurried up the back steps. "Go home, Colt. Leave me alone. I don't want to see you again."

"That isn't going to cut it, Jenny. I told you I wasn't going to leave you. And I meant it."

Jenny reached the porch first and whirled on him. "What if I don't love you?"

Colt froze with his boot on the bottom step. "What?"

Jenny turned her back on him and thrust both hands through her hair. "I lied when I said I loved you."

"I don't believe you," Colt said, his voice soft but furious. "Turn around and look at me. Say it to my face, goddamn you!"

Jenny dropped her hands to her sides. She turned slowly until she was facing him. Her eyes brimmed with tears, and her mouth was curled down at the corners. "I thought I could go through with this. To save the ranch. But I can't."

Colt hissed in a breath. It sounded like the truth. "Oh, God, Jenny."

"Go home, Colt."

"I can't," he said, the words torn from his throat. "You're home for me, Jenny. I still want you. I still need you."

"I won't marry you, Colt. That would be a living hell for both of us."

"You made a promise to me earlier this evening. I expect you to keep it," he said implacably.

He saw her confusion, the moment when she realized

what he meant. Her nostrils flared, and her lips thinned. "It wouldn't be lovemaking, Colt. It would be sex."

"Sex is fine with me," he said, moving up the steps toward her.

Jenny took a step back. "Don't come any closer."

"I intend to get a hell of a lot closer before the night is over," he said, backing her up against the frame of the house. He shoved his knee between her legs and pinned her body against the wall with his hips. His hands thrust into her hair, angling her head back at a painful angle. "You're mine, Jenny. You've always been mine. You just didn't know it."

"Colt, I—"

His mouth covered hers, angry and afraid, searching for answers that always seemed a step beyond his reach. A spark of electricity leaped between them, shocking his senses. His body hungered as much as his soul, and he felt a sense of desperation that was impossible to deny. There was nothing gentle about his kisses. He forced her lips open for his intrusion, biting them, sucking on them, demanding a response.

Her body betrayed her. And he knew he had her soul.

He lifted his head and stared down into her panicked eyes. "You lied, Jenny. I don't know why. But before we're through, I'm going to find out the truth."

"You can't handle the truth," she cried. "Why do you think I've been lying!"

"We can discuss this later," he said as he thrust his hips against hers. "After we've made love."

"Colt, you can't—"

"Watch me." He picked her up and carried her into the house.

Colt snapped on the tiny lamp that sat on Jenny's chest of drawers, then threw her onto the four-poster. He began stripping himself while she watched in stunned disbelief. He took off his shirt, then yanked off his boots and socks. He pulled down jeans and Jockey shorts together and stood before her completely naked.

He heard her gasp, saw her eyes go wide.

"That's something else Huck and I *didn't* have in common," he said. "Move over, Jenny. Make some room for me."

She scuttled across the bed and landed on the floor in the shadows on the opposite side. He stalked around the foot of the bed and dragged her to her feet. "Need a little help getting undressed?"

Before she could protest, he had her zipper down and the black sheath stripped off her shoulders. His arms imprisoned her as he unsnapped the black merry widow. He felt her tense as he pulled it free and threw it onto the floor. Her eyes slid closed as he looked at her naked breasts for the first time. He leaned over and kissed the tips, one at a time, and heard her harsh, indrawn breath.

Then he slipped one nipple into his mouth and suckled.

She cried out and her hands reached for him, grabbing handfuls of his hair to hold him where he was. "Oh, Colt. It feels...it feels..."

She didn't finish the sentence. But she didn't have to. He could see the ecstacy on her face.

He shoved the sheath the rest of the way down, only to discover she was wearing a garter belt and black nylons. "This is the kind of gift a woman plans for her lover, Jenny."

She didn't deny it.

"I thank you," he said as he looked his fill.

He took off her black silk panties but left the nylons and garter belt, since they weren't in his way. He pulled her close, reveling in the feel of the soft fabric and her even softer flesh against his own. He kissed her eyes, her nose, her cheeks, her lips. He caressed her arms, her back, her stomach. Any part of her he could find. But he came back often to her breasts, because she seemed to have so much sensation there.

To his surprise and pleasure, she touched him in return. Her hands marveling, seeking, scratching, squeezing, making his body pulse and tighten and yearn.

It had been too long since he'd had a woman. He was afraid if she kept touching him, he would spill himself too soon. So he laid her on the bed and caught her hands and pinned them against the pillows and made himself go slow.

"Colt, I can't wait," she begged.

"Another kiss here," he said, his lips against her belly. "And here," he said, moving his mouth lower.

Her body writhed beneath his caresses and then became taut. "Please," she gasped.

He took his time. And he brought her joy.

She was like no other woman he had ever known. Softer. Sleeker. More responsive.

He kept his weight on his arms as he spread her legs with his knees and positioned himself between her thighs. "I'll be as gentle as I can, Jenny. Let me know if I hurt you."

He was so big. And she was so small. Suddenly he was afraid. He looked into her eyes and saw that she was not.

Then she reached for him, pulling him toward her, and he pushed slowly into the warmth and wetness of her. She angled her hips, gasping as he sank to the hilt.

"You fit," she said, surprise evident in her voice.

He couldn't help smiling. "Did you think I wouldn't?"

"I wondered," she said, her hands brushing the hair from his forehead. "But I'm glad you do."

"Me, too," he said with a smile.

He took his time, moving slowly, kissing her face and her throat, his hands moving over her, feeling, touching her perfect body—except for one spot on her breast. He felt her stiffen as his fingers traced the blemish. A dimple in her flesh. And some kind of scar.

His body didn't allow him time to consider what he'd found. It demanded culmination. He lifted her legs and wrapped them around his waist and drove them both toward satisfaction. He waited for her. And it wasn't easy. But he was many times rewarded, because her climax came so close in time with his own, that both of them were lifted higher. He threw his head back and gritted his teeth against the almost unbearable pleasure, as he spilled his seed in her womb.

Afterward, he pulled her close, kissing her again.

"I love you, Jenny. I love you," he said between panting breaths.

"And I love you, Colt," she admitted in a quiet voice.

He didn't have the strength to ask all the questions that were tumbling around in his head. So long as she loved him, they could work everything out. He still had no idea what had made her so frightened. But he felt certain that whatever it was, they could handle it together.

As he held her close, his fingertips grazed the blemish on the side of her breast, almost beneath her arm. He lifted his head to look, but he could barely make out the dimpled flaw in the shadowy light. "What is that?" he asked.

"A scar," she said.

"I didn't know you were hurt. How did it happen?"

"I wasn't hurt. I have cancer. Had cancer. May still have cancer," she said breathlessly.

Colt sat up and stared down at her. He swallowed hard.

Sweat beaded on his brow. His body began to tremble. He bolted from the bed and ran for the bathroom, his hand over his mouth. He barely made it in time.

CHAPTER TWELVE

IT TOOK COLT a moment to realize where he was when he woke up. Not in Sam's bedroom at the Double D, but in his own at Hawk's Pride. He felt the sweat break out on his forehead at the mere thought of *Jenny* and *cancer* together in the same sentence.

Oh, God: What had he done?

Memory returned like a hideous nightmare, and he saw himself, eyes wide with horror, stomach churning, and then his ungainly race for the bathroom. He recalled the foul taste of vomit, and the hot wash of shame.

Colt groaned in agony and pressed the heels of his hands against his grainy eyelids.

He'd failed her. She'd shared her trouble with him, trusted him, given him a chance to prove his love. And he'd failed her...and himself.

Oh, God. Why cancer? Of all the maladies in the world, why give my Jenny cancer?

Then he remembered more. Jenny had come into the bathroom, dampened a cloth and gently wiped the sweat from his brow and the spittle from his mouth. He'd kept his eyes closed, afraid of what he'd see in her eyes if he looked at her. Then her touch was gone.

"Go home, Colt," she'd said in a flat voice. "Go home."

When he'd come out of the bathroom, he'd found his clothes laid out on the bed and Jenny nowhere in sight.

He'd had an urgent need to see her. To make excuses for himself. To explain what had happened.

But he didn't need to explain. Jenny understood his irrational fear of illness better than anyone.

Sick people sometimes die.

No. Not my Jenny. Not so young. Not when she's barely had a chance to live!

Colt struggled to remember her exact words. *I have cancer. I had cancer. May still have cancer.*

The terror of what she'd said had kept him from asking for more information. He speculated with what little knowledge he had.

The dimpled scar meant she'd had some sort of surgery. A lump removed? And then what? Radiation? Chemotherapy? How had that been possible without anyone noticing the effects of such treatment? The vomiting. The hair loss.

Of course. It had been easy to conceal her illness when she was so very much alone. She'd only have to hide it from him and from Huck for a few days at most while they were home on leave. For the past two years she'd been alone on the Double D except for Randy, who was probably in on the secret. It was likely Randy knew everything and had been sworn to silence. He had to talk with Randy. Randy would be able to tell him the details he hadn't gotten from Jenny.

Colt leaped out of bed and dragged on some clothes. He shoved his feet into a pair of boots, grabbed his battered Stetson and left the house as quietly as he'd returned late the previous evening.

As he approached the Double D ranch house, Colt felt the bile rise in his throat. He swallowed it down. His skin felt clammy as he quietly shut the door of his Mustang and moved up onto the back porch. The back door was unlocked. Even in these dangerous days, Westerners left their doors open as a gesture of range hospitality. Strangers were welcome.

A man who betrayed his woman's faith and her trust likely was not. So he entered as silently as he could and made his way down the hall to Randy's bedroom. Colt knocked once, then opened the door and stepped inside, closing it behind him.

Randy was still sound asleep, the covers thrown off, so Colt could see the boy wore only a pair of cotton pajama bottoms. Colt sat on the edge of the bed, gave Randy's shoulder a shove and whispered, "Wake up."

Randy rolled over, scraping at the sand in his eyes and yawning. "Oh. Hi, Colt." He shoved himself upright and scratched at his belly. "Sorry I was so late getting in last night. I saw Jenny's door was closed and your bed was empty and I figured… Well, I didn't want to bother the two of you, so I just—"

"This visit isn't about how late you came in last night," Colt interrupted. "It's about—" His throat constricted, making speech difficult, but he forced the words out. "About Jenny's cancer."

Colt saw the flicker of pain on Randy's face before it was replaced by guilt. "She finally told you, huh?"

"Yeah," Colt said, releasing a gust of air.

Randy looked anxiously over Colt's shoulder toward the door. "Is she coming here to tell me about it?"

Colt was confused. "You mean she hasn't said anything to you before now?"

Randy swallowed hard and shook his head. "I—" His voice broke, and he cleared his throat. "I figured it out for myself. There were days she'd be sick. And she lost weight. And once I heard her crying. Then I found a bill from the doctor, and I knew."

"You never confronted her and asked for the truth?" Colt asked, incredulous.

Randy shook his head. "If she'd wanted me to know, she'd have told me."

"Did you at least share what you knew with your brothers?"

Randy's chin dropped to his chest, and he shook his head.

"It never occurred to you to write to Huck. Or to me? To tell someone who could give her some help?" Colt said, his rage as palpable as his voice was quiet.

Colt saw a tear drop onto the sheet.

"I was scared," Randy said in a voice hoarse with tears he was trying not to shed. "I kept hoping it would go away. Jenny's always been so strong. I figured if she really needed help, she'd ask for it. But she never did."

Colt pulled the tearful boy into his arms, and felt Randy's arms close tightly around him. How awful it must have been for him to know. How terrified he must have been of losing his sister. Colt offered comfort and received it in return. In a little while he asked, "When did you first notice Jenny was ill?"

"Two years ago," Randy answered.

Two years, Colt thought. And she hadn't yet succumbed to the disease. But she looked so frail. And she'd lost weight even since he'd come home. Didn't she have to see the doctor sometime?

Then he remembered the day she'd spent in town, the day she hadn't invited him along. *She must have seen a doctor then.* Maybe he could find out who it was and ask— No. A doctor wouldn't tell him Jenny's secrets. And he shouldn't be asking. If he wanted to know anything, he should get it from her.

He patted Randy's back and said, "Don't worry, boy. I know now, and I'm going to take care of her."

Randy sat back and scrubbed at his eyes with his hands. "You don't know what a relief it is to hear you say that."

Colt tousled Randy's hair. "Go back to sleep." He rose and headed down the hall toward Jenny's room, stiffening his buckling knees and determinedly swallowing down the nausea that rose as he approached her door. He felt the sweat bead on his forehead and fought back a wave of dizziness as he reached out to knock on her door.

"Jenny, it's Colt. Let me in."

There was no response. He wouldn't have blamed her if she never wanted to see him again. But he wasn't going to leave this time—or ever again. Even if he spent the rest of his life hanging over the toilet bowl every morning, he was here to stay.

He knocked again. "At least say something," he said. "Let me know you're all right."

Silence.

"I'm coming in," Colt said. "We need to talk." He turned the doorknob, but it was locked.

He laid his cheek against the smooth wood. She'd locked him out, and herself inside. "Please, Jenny. Give me another chance."

He waited, his ear pressed against the door, for any sign that she might relent. And then he heard her reply.

"Good-bye, Colt."

HE'S GONE.

Jenny stared, dry-eyed, at a water mark in the ceiling where the rain had leaked before Colt fixed the roof. There was no repairing such a stain. It could be painted over, but in her experience, it had a way of seeping back through. It was better just to tear down the ruined part and get rid of it.

Better to send Colt away, than to let him try to make amends. She would never—could never—forget his reaction last night. Or forgive it. It was hard enough facing her illness, without seeing her own terror reflected back in his eyes.

What did you expect? a voice asked. *That he would be miraculously cured? That his abhorrence of illness would magically disappear because you were the one who was sick? Did you think he'd pull you into his arms and tell you everything would be all right, that he was there for you, always and forever, "in sickness and in health"?*

Foolish woman. Did your father stay to help your mother? Whom have you ever been able to rely on besides yourself?

Jenny felt cold and empty inside, as though a block of ice had frozen around her, insulating her from the world, from its pain and its joys. She wanted to spend the day in bed with the covers pulled up over her head. But there were animals to be fed, chores to be done and a life—however brief—to be lived.

She left the bed and walked across the room to stare at her naked body in the mirror. The slight defect in her breast didn't even show from the front. She had to turn sideways and lift her arm to see it. There was only a slight indentation in her skin and a thin scar where the cancerous tissue had been removed.

She turned away and headed for the shower. She made the spray as hot as she could stand it and stood there as long as she dared, wishing the warmth would seep into her bones and melt the ice that held her feelings frozen inside. If only she could cry, she might feel better. But all she could muster was an awful sense of desolation.

She dressed in the most comfortable jeans she owned and her favorite shirt. She made herself smile into the mirror as she dried her hair, hoping that would make her feel better. Her grin had the look of a corpse in rictus.

That did make her smile. The curl of her lips was fleeting, a single instant of relief from the oppressive sorrow she felt. But it gave her hope that she could survive this second, even more devastating loss of a loved one.

She smelled coffee as she headed toward the kitchen. She was grateful there would be something hot and strong to drink, but she wasn't looking forward to seeing Randy. The two of them were going to have some hard times together—considering it was no longer possible to save the Double D.

She stopped dead on the threshold to the kitchen. Colt stood with his back to the sink, his hips resting against the counter, his hands gripping it on either side.

"What are you doing here?" she said cuttingly.

"I thought you might need some coffee," Colt replied.

She watched him swallowing furiously. Any second, he was going to have to bolt for the bathroom.

"Oh, for heaven's sake! Eat a cracker," she snapped.

"Will that help?" he said, his face tinged with green.

"It works for pregnant women with nausea. It ought to work for you." She crossed to the cabinet and pulled out a box of soda crackers, ripped open the bag and stuck a cracker in front of his mouth. "Open up." He opened his mouth, and she stuck it inside.

He bit off a bite, chewed carefully and swallowed. He took another small bite, and another, until the cracker was gone. "Thank you," he said at last.

His color still wasn't too good, and sweat dotted his forehead, but at least he didn't look in imminent danger of puking. "Sit down," she ordered. "Have you tried drinking any of that coffee you made?"

"Not yet," he admitted.

"Something carbonated might be better for your stomach." She crossed to the ancient refrigerator, pulled out a can of ginger ale and popped the top. "Drink this."

He looked wary. "My stomach—"

"Drink it," she ordered, shoving the can into his hand.

He took a sip, then looked down at her. "Satisfied?"

"I'll be satisfied when you're gone from this house."

"I'm not leaving," he said.

"I make you sick, Colt. Physically ill. You look worse than a calf with the slobbers."

He grimaced. "That bad? Then you shouldn't be shoving me out the door. Sick as you make me out to be, I'm likely to ruin the upholstery in my Mustang. Now *that* would make me truly ill."

Jenny felt a rising hope shoving its way upward from inside, trying to get out. But there was no way it could get past the ice that was frozen around her heart.

"Why are you here, Colt?"

"I need some answers, Jenny. I want to know about your cancer."

She was shocked to hear him say the word aloud. She watched to see if he was going to be sick, saw him swallow hard and reach for another saltine.

He's trying, Jenny. Give him a chance.

She'd given him a chance. And he'd broken her heart. It had taken all night to put the pieces back together. Why should she let herself be hurt again?

"All I want to do is talk," he said, anticipating her refusal. "Have a cup of coffee and talk with me, Jenny. You owe me that much."

She stiffened. "I don't owe you anything. Not after last night."

She watched all the blood leave his face. She pulled a kitchen chair out from the table, grabbed him by the arm and shoved him into it. "Put your head down before you faint," she said, shoving his head between his knees.

Too late, she realized she should never have touched him. His hair felt soft beneath her fingertips, and the warmth of the skin at his nape heated her skin. Melting the ice. Thawing her heart.

She jerked her hand away and backed up. She turned and crossed to the percolator and poured herself a cup of coffee. He started to lift his head, and she snapped, "Keep your head down!"

She placed a handful of saltines and the can of ginger ale on the table in front of him, then retrieved her cup of coffee—a mug, not one of the delicate china cups he'd given her—and sat down on the opposite side of the table from him. "All right. Take your time and come up slow."

He looked pale, but at least he was no longer white as a ghost.

"Ask your questions. Then get out."

"Why didn't you tell Huck? Or me? Why did you keep it a secret?"

"I was afraid if I told Huck it would be the excuse he needed never to come back," she said. "And we both know how you feel about sick people."

"You didn't give us a chance."

"You were both thousands of miles away. In Germany, I think. Or was it somewhere in Southeast Asia? Huck had a dozen chances to quit flying and come home and marry me. He never took one. Why should I think my being sick would make a difference?"

She saw the pain and regret on Colt's face, but he didn't contradict her.

"How far along was the cancer before you discovered it?" he asked.

"Because of my family history, my gynecologist suggested I get a baseline mammogram when I turned thirty, a healthy mammogram for comparison purposes, to make it easier to identify anything abnormal if it showed up in the future. Since my mother got breast cancer when she was thirty-four, I figured it might be a good idea.

"Except, that first mammogram revealed a tiny spot, not much bigger than a pencil tip, but there, just the same." She shivered and took a sip of hot coffee to warm the cold inside.

"It was a shattering moment," she admitted, meeting Colt's gaze with difficulty. "There was something hard and foreign inside me, attacking me, trying to kill me."

She watched Colt swallow hard and reach for a saltine.

"I couldn't even feel a lump," she continued inexorably, mercilessly detailing the facts he'd demanded. "But it was there. Without the mammogram, I might not have known until it was too late."

"So you had surgery to remove the cancer?" Colt asked.

"My doctor performed a lumpectomy."

She saw Colt cringe and remembered how she'd felt the first time she imagined a knife slicing through the soft flesh of her breast. "My doctor told me she thought she'd gotten all the cancerous tissue. But there was no way to know whether the disease would come back. I had radiation."

"How?" he asked, his brow furrowing. "I mean, without anyone but Randy finding out."

"Randy knows?" she said, her eyes darting toward the doorway that led to his room. She started to rise, to go to her brother, to assuage his fear.

Colt grasped her wrist from across the table and held her in place. "Randy's fine. I want to hear the rest of it."

She sank back into her chair, staring at his hand until he released her. Her eyes locked with his. "The rest of it.

You mean the fury and resentment I felt? The fear of losing a part of me to the surgeon's knife? And of all things, a breast—the part of a woman that most symbolizes her femininity, the one truly sensual gift she can give to her husband and lover, the means of nursing her children.

"I ranted at fate. I was quite melodramatic. I frightened the horses in the barn. Better them than Randy or any of my brothers."

"You should have told them."

"Don't tell me what I should have done! Do you think I don't know they would have dropped everything to come running? Do you know I don't know how much they care? But I love them just as much as they love me. What could they do, really, to change anything? The cancer is either going to kill me, or it's not. Nothing they do or say is going to change that.

"In the meantime, their lives would have been turned upside down. They would have been miserable worrying about me. It was better my way."

"How do you think they're going to feel when they find out the truth?" Colt asked.

"If the lumpectomy had worked, they would never have needed to know."

She saw Colt go still. Saw the growing awareness in his eyes of what she'd just revealed.

"It's back?" he asked, his voice grating like a rusty gate.

She threaded her hands together in front of her, gripping them so hard her knuckles turned white. "I had a follow-up mammogram the day I went into town by myself. The doctor called last week. She wants me to come in for a needle biopsy. She's afraid she made a mistake not doing more radical surgery the first time."

Jenny saw Colt was swallowing furiously. He closed his eyes and gritted his teeth so hard she saw a muscle jerk in his cheek as he fought off the nausea. When he opened his eyes, the terror was barely hidden behind a facade of composure. "Is that why you never finished the wedding dress?" he asked.

She nodded.

"When is the biopsy scheduled?" he asked.

"I was going to spend the day in town tomorrow 'running errands,' for the wedding," she confessed. "I have to be at the doctor's office at eight-thirty. I planned to have the surgery, recuperate at her office, and be home in the afternoon."

"I'll go with you," he said.

"You don't need—"

"How the hell do you know what I need?" he said in a voice filled with barely controlled rage. "I need to live my life with you. I need to go to sleep with you in my arms and wake up with you in the morning. If all we're going to have is a few months or years together, I want every minute I can get."

"I have *cancer*," she said, emphasizing the word.

"And it makes me sick—literally—to know that," he retorted. "I'm as angry and frightened as you are, Jenny. Maybe more so, because I've wanted you all my life, and now, when I thought we'd have a lifetime together, you tell me you may already be dying. I don't know how to cope with the anger I feel. Or the fear."

They stared at each other for a long moment, both aware of the crossroad they had reached. Jenny could go on alone, or she could ask Colt to join her.

"You could hold on to me," Jenny said at last, reaching a hand across the table.

Colt grasped her hand like a lifeline. Their fingers entwined, but soon that wasn't enough for either of them. As though led by some unseen hand, they both rose and moved around the table toward each other. Colt's arms closed around Jenny, and she knew she was where she belonged.

"Give me another chance, Jenny," Colt whispered.

The ice cracked around her heart, leaving the pulsing organ exposed and vulnerable, capable of feeling…everything. "Oh, Colt."

"Don't deny me, sweetheart. Let me love you. Let me be a part of your life for however long we have left together on this earth."

What woman could refuse an offer like that? "All right, Colt. For as long as we have together, I'm yours."

CHAPTER THIRTEEN

THE HARDEST THING Colt had ever done was sit in the doctor's office, surrounded by sick people, and wait for Jenny while she underwent a needle biopsy on her breast. Jenny had explained Colt's problem to her doctor, who had prescribed something to control his nausea.

But no pill could relieve his dread that Jenny might die from cancer. The disease was arbitrary; it killed with equal disregard for age or gender, race or creed. And Jenny was right; there was nothing he could do about it.

Except live life with her to the fullest every day.

The instant they left the doctor's office after the outpatient surgery was completed he said, "Marry me, Jenny. On Saturday, as we planned."

"We won't have the results from the biopsy by then," she countered as he helped her into his Mustang.

"I don't care."

"There's no time to finish my wedding gown."

"I dropped it off with my mother this morning. She's taking care of it," he said as he settled into the driver's seat. "Any more excuses?"

She eyed him solemnly. "I don't think it's fair to you. I may not have very long to live."

"I'll take whatever time I can get."

"You seem determined to do this."

"I am."

"What will people say?"

He shot her a triumphant grin. "I know I've won when that's the only argument you can come up with. You know I don't give a damn what other people say. If it feels right to you and me, that's all that matters. Will you marry me on Saturday?"

She chewed on her lip for a moment, then seemed to make up her mind. He held his breath until she said, "All right. Okay. You win. I'll marry you on Saturday."

He hit the brakes and swerved the convertible to the side of the road, skidding to a stop on the shoulder.

"What's wrong?" Jenny cried.

"Nothing's wrong," he said. "I simply felt an irresistible urge to kiss you silly, that's all."

Impossibly, unpredictably, she laughed. "You're crazy, Colt!"

"Crazy in love with you," he said, leaning over to touch his lips to hers.

She moaned, and he deepened the kiss, slipping his tongue inside her mouth and tasting her. His heart beat wildly in his chest, with joy and with fear. She was so very precious. How would he bear it— Colt forced himself to focus on the delicious sensations caused by her tongue sliding between his lips, touching the roof of his mouth, then withdrawing to be followed by his tongue, tasting her.

He would find a way to make her understand that, even if more radical surgery became necessary, it wouldn't matter to him. The only thing that mattered was keeping her alive. He broke the kiss at last, but pressed his cheek against hers. "I love you, Jenny."

"And I love you," she whispered.

"We'd better get going," he said, forcing himself back to his own side of the car. "We've got lots of company waiting at home."

"Oh, Colt. What have you done?"

"What you should have done two years ago. I called your brothers, had them meet me at Hawk's Pride, and told them about the cancer."

"You had no right!" Jenny said, her hands clenching into fists.

"I have every right," he retorted. "I love you. That means I'll do everything within my power to make your life easier and happier. Even if it means making your brothers' lives a little unhappier."

"What did they say?" she asked anxiously. "How are they taking the news?"

"How do you think they took it? They were angry and hurt." He rubbed his jaw and said, "Sam took a swing at me. He thought I'd known all along and had kept it from them."

"I'm sorry. Sam always was a little hotheaded."

"Once I explained, he apologized. But now that they know, they want to be there for you, Jenny. It was all I could do to keep them from coming to the doctor's office this morning. They compromised by agreeing to see you after the surgery at the Double D."

"How can I face them?" she said.

"Just remember they love you."

When they arrived at the house, they found all four of her brothers putting a coat of fresh, white paint on the house. But they weren't the only ones at work. All of Colt's brothers and sisters had joined in to make various improvements on the property.

The shutters on all of the windows, as well as the front door, had been painted a deep green that matched Jenny's new Jeep. Flowers and shrubs had been planted around the front porch, and an entire lawn had been laid in thick patches of green.

"Ohmigod, Colt! Look what they're doing," Jenny said.

"It's a wedding gift, Jenny. From my family and from yours. They're helping to make our house a home."

Colt saw the sheen of tears in Jenny's eyes and felt his own throat swell with emotion. "You don't mind, do you? James and Tyler suggested it, and I said it sounded like a good idea. When Mom and Dad and Jake heard what your brothers planned to do, they wanted to be a part of it. And when my brothers and sisters—"

She cut him off with a kiss. "I love them for it," she said simply. "All of them." She let herself out of the car before he could get the door for her and headed around to the front of the house to survey their work.

Colt had to walk fast to keep up with her. "Jenny, are you sure you're up to this?"

She smiled at him over her shoulder. "I want to thank them, Colt. I want to tell them all how wonderful I think everything looks."

And she did, even going so far as to drop onto her knees and tuck a little extra earth around the red geraniums his mother was planting beside the front steps.

Jenny had guts, all right. And stamina. He kept a wary eye on her, wanting to make sure she didn't do too much. The surgery had been done with a local anesthetic, and Jenny swore she was okay. But Colt had seen enough of Jenny to know that if someone she loved asked her to pick up a house, she would give it try.

When the painting was finished, Jenny watched over the cleanup, and more than one brother said, "Yes, Mother," as she issued instructions on how it should be done. As the afternoon wore on, her too-bright eyes and her too-fast speech told him she had reached the limits of her endurance.

He announced it was quitting time, and everyone should gather on the back porch for a glass of iced tea and fresh-baked, hot-from-the-oven chocolate chip cookies his sister Cherry had made. Jenny sat in one of the two wooden rockers on the back porch—a gift from his parents—while his mother occupied the other. His father stood behind his mother, in much the same protective way Colt stood behind Jenny. Some of his siblings sat in chairs that had been brought outside from the kitchen.

Sam and Tyler leaned on the porch rail, while Randy sat cross-legged at Jenny's feet, with Faith by his side. His brother Jake leaned against the house, his eyes focused on Faith's sister Hope, who was sitting with Colt's sister Frannie on the wooden swing Jake had hung by ropes from the porch rafters that afternoon.

There was a lot of laughter and joking, everyone careful to keep the mood light. No one had spoken the "C" word all afternoon. No one had mentioned the desperate disease that had brought them together.

"I can't thank you all enough," Jenny said for the umpteenth time. "This was a wonderful surprise."

"You should have told us sooner," Sam said curtly.

Jenny stopped rocking. It got so quiet Colt could hear the single fly buzzing around the last chocolate chip cookie on the plate. He put a hand on Jenny's shoulder and squeezed.

I'm here, love. You're not alone.

She smiled gratefully at him over her shoulder, then met Sam's embittered gaze. "I thought I could spare you this pain," she said. "I was wrong. Please forgive me."

"We can't get back the two years you stole from us," Sam said.

Jenny arched a brow. "I've been right here, Sam."

"But I didn't know— I would have come—" Sam lifted his hat, forked his fingers through his hair, then resettled the Stetson low on his brow. "What are we supposed to do now?"

"What you've always done," Jenny said. "Be there when I need you."

Once the subject had been opened, it seemed there were others who needed to speak.

"When will you get the results of the biopsy?" Tyler asked.

"On Monday."

"What about the wedding? Is that on or off?" James asked.

Jenny reached up and laid her hand over Colt's, which still rested on her shoulder. She smiled and said, "The wedding is on."

"On Saturday? Before you know the results?" Sam asked, staring hard at Colt.

"On Saturday," Colt confirmed.

"Which reminds me, I have a wedding dress to finish," Colt's mother said, rising from her rocker.

"I've got some errands to run," Jake said. "Can I give anybody a lift anywhere?"

"I need a ride into town," Hope said, jumping up from the swing.

"If you're driving Hope into town, can you take me and Faith, too?" Randy said, rising and then helping Faith to stand.

"Why not?" Jake said. "Anybody else? I've got one of the vans."

Everyone else had their own transportation. In a matter of minutes, the porch was empty except for Colt and Jenny. "Come sit with me on the swing," he said, taking her hand and helping her out of the rocker.

As Colt sat down on the hanging swing and lifted Jenny into his lap, she slid her arms around his neck and laid her head in the crook of his shoulder. He could feel her warm breath against his throat.

He set the swing in motion with the toe of his boot, and they sat without speaking and watched the sunset. The sky was streaked with bright yellows and rosy pinks, and the sun looked like an orange ball as it began its descent beyond the horizon.

"All we need to make this picture-perfect is a dog at your feet," Jenny murmured.

"That can be arranged," Colt said as his lips curved in a smile.

A jet broke the sound barrier, and Colt looked up, knowing he wouldn't be able to see it, but searching the sky anyway.

"Will you miss it very much?" Jenny said quietly.

"Flying? Sure. I'd be lying if I said I wouldn't. But life is about choices, Jenny. Being with you is the right choice for me."

"What if—"

"You want to play that game? All right. What if I get bucked off my horse tomorrow and break my neck? What if we get abducted by aliens? What if—"

Jenny giggled. "Abducted by aliens?"

"What if the cancer does come back?" he said seriously. "It won't change anything. I plan to treasure every moment I have with you—however many there are."

He felt her kiss his throat, then his chin, then the side of his mouth. He turned his head and blindly found her mouth with his. He felt her moist breath against his flesh as she whispered, "I have the irresistible urge to kiss you silly. Will you please take me to bed?"

Living life to the fullest, Colt mused as he lifted Jenny and carried her into the house, definitely had its compensations.

As Randy helped Faith into the backseat of the van, Hope jumped into the front with Jake. Randy shot a glance at Faith to see whether she thought he ought to try to do something to get Hope to sit in back with them. She gave a slight shake of her head, and he slid into the backseat with her.

As they headed toward town, the silence in the front seat was palpable.

"How about some music?" Hope said finally, turning on the radio.

Jake glanced at her, then aimed his eyes back at the road without speaking.

Randy was grateful for the noise, because it meant he could talk to Faith in the backseat without being overheard. "Does Hope really have something to do in town? Or is she just trying to get Jake alone?"

"Do you really have an errand?" Faith countered. "Or do you just want to get me alone?"

Randy grinned and slid his hand along her jeans from her knee upward along her inner thigh until she reached over to clamp a hand over his to stop him. "I definitely want to get you alone," he said. "But I actually have an errand in town. I promised I'd pick up some white ribbon for Jenny. Now, answer my question."

Faith removed his hand and set it on his own thigh, then laid her hand on the inside of his thigh close enough to his zipper to cause serious repercussions. She shot him a mischievous sideways look from beneath lowered lashes. "My suggestion is that you mind your own business. I plan to keep you so well occupied that you won't have time to worry about what's going on between Hope and Jake."

Randy made a strangled sound in his throat as Faith's hand brushed tantalizingly across his erection and disappeared back onto her own side of the seat. "That sounds fair," he said.

For the rest of the ride into town, Randy wasn't aware of anything except Faith's teasing touches, her impish glances, the intimate promises she was making that he hoped she planned to keep. He responded with caresses of his own and heated glances and a whispered question. "When?"

He saw her cheeks pinken, and knew she'd heard him. "We can slip away during your sister's wedding reception. My parents won't miss me for a few hours during all the celebration."

"Will you let me see your other hand? I mean, without the prosthesis?"

Her mouth flattened into an unhappy line. "You may not like what you see. Is it really necessary?"

He took her hand in his, caressing the normal fingers. His mind had conjured up an image of deformity beneath her prosthesis that he was sure couldn't be worse than the real thing. "You take it off at night, when you go to bed, don't you?" he asked.

She nodded.

"If we're going to spend our lives together, I figure I better get used to how you look without it."

"Maybe you won't want to be with me anymore after you see me without it."

He was surprised that Faith was able to state her fear so clearly and succinctly. If he could accept the hook and the plastic arm, he didn't think real flesh and bone—no matter how malformed—could make him reject her. But he knew words alone weren't likely to assuage her fear. "You'll just have to take that chance," he said at last. "Unless you want to break up right now."

He watched myriad emotions—doubt, fear, hope—

flicker across her face as she evaluated the risk, and balanced the possible reward. *Like Colt did with Jenny,* he realized. *Balancing the risk of losing her against the joy of loving her.* As Faith must balance the risk of trusting him against the joy of being fully loved.

"All right," she said at last. "I'll let you see my hand. But only if you promise—"

He squeezed her trembling hand to cut her off and said, "It'll be all right, Faith. Believe me. It won't make a difference."

He only hoped he was right.

JAKE WAS ANGRY. Hope recognized the signs. The vertical lines on either side of his mouth became more pronounced because his jaw was clamped, and his eyes narrowed to slits. There was an overall look of tautness to his body— shoulders, hands, hips—that suggested a tiger ready to leap.

She knew she shouldn't have invited herself along. She knew Jake didn't want her around. She also knew he didn't want her around because he was tempted by her presence, like a beast in rut responding to the relentless call of nature.

Hope let her gaze roam over Jake and saw his nostrils flare as her eyes touched what her hands could not. She wondered whether she ought to push him into something irrevocable. Like taking her virginity.

He would marry her then. She was sure of it. But would he love her? She didn't want him without his love. She knew that much. But she was running out of time. Why, oh, why, had he gotten engaged to Miss Carter? She wouldn't feel this desperation if he hadn't forced her hand. She knew in her bones that they belonged together, and she didn't intend to lose him to another woman.

When they arrived in town, Hope was surprised that Jake volunteered to drop off Randy and Faith first after setting a time to pick them up again. She offered a reassuring smile in response to Faith's anxious look as she and Jake drove away.

"You haven't asked where I want to be let off," she said when Jake had driven half the length of the main street in town without stopping.

He shot her a look filled with scorn. "Don't insult my intelligence. You haven't got any errands to run. But I do. So sit there like a good little girl and be still."

It was the *little girl* that did it. It was a flash point with her and always would be, because it diminished who she was, which was more than the sum of her age. She began to unbutton her blouse right there, driving down Main Street.

Jake glanced in her direction and nearly had an accident. "What do you think you're doing?"

"Taking my clothes off?"

"Do you want to get me arrested?"

"I'm not a minor, Jake. We're two consenting adults."

"I'm engaged. I'm promised to another woman."

"Not once word of this gets around," she said, glancing at the passersby who gawked in through the window as she pulled her shirt off her shoulders, leaving her wearing only a peach-colored bra.

Jake swore under his breath and gunned the engine, heading for the old, abandoned railroad depot on the outskirts of town. He braked to a halt in front of the depot and turned to glare at her. She saw the flicker of heat as he glimpsed the fullness of her breasts above her bra.

"What the hell do you think you're doing?"

"I'm not a little girl, Jake. I don't know what I have to do to prove it to you."

"I'm not going to marry you, Hope. You're not what I

want. I want someone who can share my memories of the world, someone who's lived a little."

"I can catch up," she said desperately.

He shook his head. "No, little girl. You can't."

Hope felt her chin quivering and gritted her teeth to try to keep it still. "So you're going to marry Miss Carter?"

"Yes, I'm going to marry her. Put your blouse back on, Hope."

She grabbed her shirt and tried to get it on, but the long sleeves were inside out, and her hands were shaking too badly to straighten it.

She heard Jake swear before he scooted across the bench seat, pulled the shirt from her hands and began to pull the sleeves right-side out. He held the shirt for her while she slipped her arms into it. Her cheek brushed against his as she was straightening. She turned her head and discovered his mouth only a breath from her own. Their eyes caught and held.

She wasn't sure who moved first, but an instant later their mouths were meshed, and his tongue was inside searching, teasing, tasting. He was rough and reckless, his hands cupping her breasts as a guttural groan was wrenched from his very marrow. His mouth ravaged hers as his hands demanded a response.

She couldn't catch up. He was moving too fast.

And then he was gone. Out the opposite door. She scrambled after him, pausing in the driver's seat when she spied him leaning against the van, his palms flat against the metal, his head down, his chest heaving.

He stood and faced her. "That was my fault," he said. "I…" His eyes were full of pain and regret. "You're formidable, Hope. I'll grant you that. Somewhere out there is a very lucky young man."

"I want *you*," she cried.

"I belong to someone else."

"You're only marrying Miss Carter because you don't think you can have me. But you can," Hope insisted. "There's nothing stopping us from being together except your own stubborn bias against my age."

"Your youth," he corrected.

She snorted. "Eighteen years isn't that much. Lots of men marry younger women."

"You need to go to college. You need to find out what you want to do with your life. Maybe you'll decide you want more out of life than simply being some rancher's wife. If I were to marry you now, the day might come when you decided marriage to me wasn't fulfilling enough, that you needed to go find yourself."

"Is that what happened with your first wife?" Hope asked, her eyes wide.

"I've seen it happen," Jake said without answering her question directly. "You're too young to know what you'd be giving up, Hope. Go to school. Get an education. Find out what you want to do with your life."

"If I do that, if I go to college, will you wait for me?"

She saw the struggle before he answered, "In four years I'll be forty. I—"

"Wait for me," she said, stepping out of the van. "Don't marry Miss Carter. Promise you'll wait for me."

"I can't promise anything, Hope. There's another person in this equation you're not considering. I've proposed to another woman, and she's said yes. Unless Amanda breaks the engagement, I'm honor-bound to marry her."

"Even if you don't love her?"

"Who says I don't?"

The shock of his words held Hope speechless. "How could you love her and want me like you do?"

He shoved a frustrated hand through his hair. "I respect and admire her. And she loves me. We can have a good life together."

"You *don't* love her," Hope said accusingly.

"I don't know what I feel anymore," he retorted. "You've got me so damned confused—"

"Wait for me," Hope said. "There are such things as long engagements."

"That wouldn't be fair to Amanda," Jake said stubbornly.

"It is if you don't love her. Don't you think she'll notice? Don't you think she'll miss being loved?"

Jake stared at the ground, then back at her. "I'll go this far," he said. "I won't press her to get married. But I'm not going to walk away if she sets a date."

"Thank you, Jake. At least that gives me a chance."

Jake shook his head. "I'll say this much. Life with you would never be boring."

Hope laughed. "I hope I get a chance to prove that to you someday."

CHAPTER FOURTEEN

"STAND STILL, JENNY, or I'll never get all these buttons done up," Rebecca said.

Jenny looked at herself in the oval standing mirror in the corner of her bedroom, hardly able to believe that she was the beautiful woman reflected there. She looked like Cinderella, ready for the ball, except her dress was white, instead of pink. She'd pieced the dress together herself, but Colt's mother had finished it, adding lace and ribbons and seed pearls like one of Cinderella's mice.

The satin gown had a wide boat neck, open almost to her shoulders, with long sleeves that tapered to the wrist. The bodice was fitted to the waist with a wide skirt belling out below. A narrow train decorated with tiny seed pearls began where the last cloth buttons ended in back and trailed several feet behind her.

Jenny reached up to adjust the net veil, held in place by a circlet of fresh white daisies, and brushed at a stray wisp of hair at her temple that had escaped the knot of golden curls at her crown. "Are you done yet?" she asked.

"Not yet," Rebecca said.

"Whatever made you decide to put thirty-two buttons down the back instead of using a zipper?"

Rebecca smiled. "I was thinking of my son."

Jenny's brows lowered in confusion. "I don't understand. A zipper would make it easier for him to get me out of this dress in a hurry."

Rebecca's smile became a grin. "I know. But think how much his anticipation will have built by the time he gets the last button undone."

"If his patience lasts that long," Jenny said with a laugh.

Rebecca joined her laughter. "There. All done." She put her hands on Jenny's shoulders and looked at their side-by-side faces reflected in the mirror. "My son loves you, Jenny. I'm only beginning to understand how much. I wish you both all the joy that love can bring. I'm sorry your mother isn't here to see you today. I know she'd be very proud of all you've accomplished."

Jenny felt the sting in her nose and the tickle at the back of her throat. "Thank you, Mrs. Whitelaw."

"I wish you'd call me Rebecca. Or Mom, if you wouldn't mind."

Jenny turned and hugged Colt's mother. "I've missed having a mom. It'll be good to have one again."

Rebecca levered Jenny to arm's length and looked her over. "You're beautiful, Jenny, inside and out. I wish you much happiness with my son."

Jenny looked at Colt's mother through misted eyes. "Thank you, Mom."

Rebecca grabbed a Kleenex from the box on the dresser and dabbed at the edges of her eyes. "We'd better get moving if you don't want to be late to your own wedding." She reached down to pick up the dragging train, brought it around and layered it carefully over Jenny's arm. "There. Are you all set?"

"Ready as I'll ever be," Jenny said.

"Are you sure there's nothing else you need?" Rebecca asked.

"Let's see. Something old—my mother's pearl necklace. Something new—this beautiful gown. Something borrowed—the Whitelaw family Bible you gave me to carry.

Something blue—my wedding bouquet of bachelor's buttons. I have everything I need."

"Except a groom," Rebecca said with a laugh. "I'll see you at the church."

Once Rebecca was gone, Jenny didn't linger long in her bedroom. She knew her four brothers were waiting in the living room to escort her to church. As she came down the hall she heard Randy say, "Holy cow!"

The moment she stepped into the living room, her brothers, who'd been lounging on the furniture, all stood up. Sam spoke first.

"I'll be damned. You're gorgeous, Jenny."

Jenny smiled. "Thank you, Sam."

"Stunning," Tyler said.

"The prettiest bride I've ever seen," James added.

"Holy cow!" Randy repeated.

Jenny laughed. "I'd love to stand here and listen to more of your compliments, but I think it's time we left for church."

The four brothers exchanged looks before Randy stepped forward. "We got together and decided to give you something special as a wedding gift."

Randy looked into the inside pocket of the navy blue suit jacket he was wearing but didn't find what he was looking for. He looked in the other side of the coat and pulled out some papers. He stepped forward and handed them to Jenny. "For you."

"What's this?" she asked.

"A honeymoon," Sam said.

"At the Grand Canyon," James added.

"We figured you deserved a *monumentally* good time," Randy said with a grin.

"We'll take care of the ranch while you're gone," Tyler said, cutting off the objection on the tip of her tongue.

Jenny was astonished. "I don't know what to say."

"'Thank you' might be nice," Sam said.

Tears filled Jenny's eyes, and she tried to sniff them back.

"Don't you like it?" Randy asked, confused by her tears.

"I'm overwhelmed," Jenny said. "Thank you all." She held her arms wide, and her brothers moved to hug her all at once. She gave them each a kiss wherever she could reach.

Randy wiped the kiss from his cheek and said, "We don't have time for any more of this mushy stuff right now. We're gonna be late if we don't get outta here."

"Right, brat," Sam said, tousling Randy's hair. "So get moving."

Jenny laughed, banishing her tears, and followed her brothers out of the house.

Her wedding day had dawned sunny, but the ceremony was scheduled for eleven-thirty to avoid the heat of the day. The reception was being held in the courtyard at Hawk's Pride, beneath the cool shade of the moss-draped live oak.

Jenny's stomach was full of butterflies, which she suspected was normal for a bride on her wedding day, but she had put her fears on hold. Today was about joy and love.

Once they arrived at church, she waited by herself in a small room off the vestibule, while her brothers helped to seat guests. In a departure from the norm, Jenny had neither bridesmaids nor a maid of honor. She didn't have any close girlfriends, and she didn't know any of Colt's sisters well enough yet to feel comfortable asking them to stand in such a role. She had asked her four brothers to stand up with her instead.

"If you're going to be unconventional, I don't see why I can't do the same thing," Colt had said.

"Meaning what?" Jenny asked.

"How about a Best Lady instead of a Best Man?"

"Who did you have in mind?"

"My sister Jewel," Colt said. "She was like a second mother to me, and we've always been close. If you don't mind, I think she could hang on to the rings as well as one of my brothers. And Frannie will kill me if Jewel gets to dress up and she doesn't. So I guess I'd better include her.

"Actually, it might balance things better if I use all my sisters for 'groomsmen,'" Colt mused. "That way, with Rolleen and Cherry, we'll have an even number of girls and guys coming down the aisle. What do you think?"

"It sounds like a wonderful idea!" Jenny said.

"Who's going to give away the bride?" Colt asked.

"I don't know. I forgot all about that."

"It's usually a parent or an older relative," Colt said.

"I don't have any of those. Any suggestions?"

"As long as we're being unorthodox, how about my parents? They've adopted eight of us kids. I don't see why you can't adopt them."

Jenny smiled. "Done."

"Then it's all settled," Colt said.

"What will people think?" Jenny wondered.

"This is our wedding," Colt said. "We can do as we damn well please."

COLT WAS WISHING they'd eloped. He was standing in his father's bedroom, dressed in a black dinner jacket, studded white dress shirt, cummerbund and black trousers, fidgeting nervously as his father tried for the third time to tie his bow tie. His brothers watched the comedy of errors from vantage points around the room.

"Hold still," Zach said as he adjusted the black silk, "and give me a fighting chance to get this straight."

"It's too tight," Colt said, slipping his finger between the bow tie and his throat.

"That's the marital noose you feel tightening around your neck," Jake said.

"Just because your marriage didn't work out—" Rabb began.

"The bride's got cancer," Jake said.

"*Had* cancer," Avery corrected.

"May still have cancer," Colt said quietly. "And if she does, we'll deal with it. I love her. Be happy for me, Jake." He met his brother's remote, ice-blue eyes and felt as though they were miles apart.

Jake shrugged. "It's your funeral."

Avery hissed in a breath.

"Bad choice of words," Jake said repentently. "I don't know what's wrong with me today. I hope you and Jenny have a long and happy life together, Colt. I really do. I'll see you after the ceremony," he said, backing his way out of the room.

It was clear, at least to Colt, that Jake considered marriage on a par with walking through a minefield barefoot. Which made Colt wonder why his brother had gotten himself engaged to Amanda Carter. And whether Jake would follow through and take a second trip down the aisle. Only time would tell.

"I'd better get going," Rabb said. "I promised Mom I'd help greet people at the church."

"Me, too," Avery said as he followed Rabb out the door.

Colt's father stepped back to admire his handiwork. "That ought to do it," he said.

"Any last words of advice?" Colt said.

"Be happy," Zach said.

Colt saw the tears in his father's eyes and felt his throat swell with emotion. "Thanks, Dad."

He took the step that put him within his father's reach and felt his father's arms surround him. As a child, he'd found support and succor, even surcease from pain, within these strong arms. Zach Whitelaw had taken a child that was not his own flesh and blood and made of him a devoted son.

"I love you, Dad," he said.

His father gave him a quick hug, then pushed him away. "We'd better get going. Your mother will kill me if I don't get you to the church on time."

"Sure. Then she'll kiss you all over till you're well again."

"Maybe being late isn't such a bad idea," Zach said with a laugh.

They made the trip to the church in Colt's Mustang convertible with the top down. The wind ruffled Colt's hair and left his bow tie once more askew.

"Let me fix that tie," Zach said.

Colt waved at friends and neighbors as his father arranged his bow tie, then watched his father head for the front of the church. He headed for a door at the rear, where the choir usually assembled, and which was used during weddings for the groom and his "groomsmen."

The room was filled with his sisters, arranging their hair and putting on makeup and getting dressed. Colt grinned as he observed the cacophony and confusion. It felt like old times. Cherry was walking around in a bra and half slip; Jewel's hair was still in hot curlers; Frannie was buttoning up Rolleen's dress, while Rolleen talked on a cell phone.

"Hi," Colt said.

"Finish buttoning Rolleen for me," Frannie said. "While I pin some flowers in my hair."

Colt crossed to Rolleen and began buttoning up her dress. "Who's that on the phone?" he asked.

"Gavin's grandmother," she whispered back. "The baby's teething and has a little fever."

"When you finish with Rolleen, can you do me?" Cherry said, pulling her dress on over her head.

Colt crossed to the sister who'd been most like him in temperament, the other rebel in the family. Cherry had come to the Whitelaw family as a mutinous fourteen-year-old juvenile delinquent and ended up—in Colt's humble opinion—as a damned good wife and mother. "How're the twins—both sets—and what's-his-name?" he asked.

"The girls are in the high school pep squad, and the boys are into G.I. Joe. What's-his-name hit a home run in his Little League game this morning. Why do you think I'm running so late?"

"Tell Brett I said congratulations," Colt said.

"You can tell him yourself at the reception. He'll be there, along with forty-three dozen other screaming Whitelaw brats."

Colt groaned. "Surely you jest!"

"I'm not off by much," Cherry warned.

"Colt, will you come hold this mirror so I can see the back of my hair?" Jewel said.

"Duty calls," Colt said as he buttoned the last button on Cherry's dress. "Hey there, Jewel," he said as he took the mirror from his eldest sister and held it up for her. "How's it going?"

"There's a lump in my hair," she said. "Right..." She reached up, trying to locate it backward in the mirror.

"There?" he said, poking at a cowlick at the back of her head.

"That's it. Stubborn little cuss." She took the mirror from his hand and threw it onto the table in front of her. "Why do I bother? Plain brown eyes, plain brown hair, plain old face. You'd think I'd get used to it."

Colt tipped her chin up and surveyed her face, which still bore remnants of the faint, crisscrossing scars she'd acquired in the car accident that had originally left her orphaned. "You look pretty good to me," he announced.

She brushed his hand away and wrinkled her nose. "You have to say that. You're my brother."

The organ began to play and Jewel looked at her wristwatch. "Oh, Lord. Five minutes. Is everybody ready?"

Colt looked around. The chaos had ceased. Before him stood his four sisters looking remarkably lovely in pale rose full-length gowns. Every dress was cut in a different style that had been especially designed by Rolleen to make the most of each sister's assets.

"You all look...wonderful," Colt said, his voice catching in his throat.

"You look pretty wonderful yourself," Jewel said, crossing to link her arm with his. "Come on, Colt. It's time we made our appearance in church."

They walked out to stand in front of the altar and wait for Jenny to appear. Her brothers had already taken their places on the opposite side of the altar. Colt found his parents sitting in the front pew, waiting for the appropriate moment to give away the bride, and smiled at them. His mother dabbed at her eyes with his father's hanky and smiled back.

Their choice of attendants might have been unusual, but Jenny had selected Lohengrin's "Wedding March" as the processional. At the sound of the familiar opening chords, the congregation stood, and Colt searched the back of the church, waiting for his first look at the bride.

Jenny walked down the aisle alone, as she had lived most of her life. Colt felt his throat constrict as he caught sight of her. She looked ethereal. He could see her face through her veil, and her joyous smile made his heart swell with love.

His parents met her and said the words that gave her into his care. He reached out and took her hand, then turned with her to face the preacher.

"Dearly Beloved," the minister began. "We are gathered here…"

The vows were familiar, but they seemed to have a great deal more meaning, Colt discovered, when you were the one taking them.

"Do you, Jennifer Elizabeth Wright, take this man to be your lawful wedded husband, to have and to hold…to love and to cherish…all the days of your life?"

"I do," Jenny said.

Then it was his turn.

"Do you, Colt David Whitelaw, take this woman to be your lawful wedded wife, to love and to honor…in sickness and in health…as long as you both shall live?"

Colt's throat was so swollen with emotion, he couldn't speak. He nodded, but the minister was waiting for the words. He felt Jenny squeeze his hand. "I do," he rasped.

Putting the simple gold band on Jenny's third finger somehow linked them together. When she placed a gold band on his finger in return, it felt as though the two of them had been made into one.

Then the minister was saying, "By the power vested in me, I now pronounce you husband and wife. You may kiss the bride."

Colt's hands were trembling as he lifted the veil and looked into his wife's shining eyes. He lowered his head slowly, touched her lips gently, then gathered Jenny in his arms and gave her a kiss that expressed all the tumultuous emotions he felt inside.

The congregation began to applaud.

Colt lifted his head, grinned sheepishly, then slipped Jenny's arm through his and, to the swell of organ music, marched with his bride back down the aisle.

THE NEWLYWEDS WERE SPENDING one night at the Double D before they left for their honeymoon at the Grand Canyon the following morning, so Randy was supposed to spend the night in Colt's room at Hawk's Pride to give his sister and her new husband some privacy.

It had been difficult for Randy to keep his mind on the wedding ceremony, when he knew he had a test of moral courage coming up in a matter of hours. Once the wedding reception was in full swing, he planned to sneak into Colt's bedroom with Faith—and see what she'd been hiding beneath her prosthesis.

He hadn't seen Faith before the ceremony began, and in all the excitement afterward, they'd ended up going to Hawk's Pride in separate cars. He searched for her in the courtyard and spied her near the punch bowl. He hurried in her direction, but stopped ten feet away and gawked.

She wasn't wearing the prosthetic device.

She had on a pair of white cotton gloves that ended at the wrist, exposing her arms. The left glove had something inside it to fill out the fingers, but apparently the gloved hand wasn't functional, because Faith didn't use it when she helped herself to a cup of punch. Her left arm, including the wrist, which was usually covered by the prosthetic device, looked perfectly normal.

It was the rest of her hand—or rather lack of it—he needed to see.

But suddenly he was in no hurry to see it. He stayed by Faith's side all afternoon. He laughed with her as Jenny cut the wedding cake and stuffed a big piece into Colt's laughing mouth. He shared a shy glance with her as Colt retrieved the garter from Jenny's leg, and he cheered with her as Colt's brother Rabb caught it. He stood by her side as Hope leaped high and grabbed Jenny's bridal bouquet.

He even took her with him when he helped decorate Colt's Mustang convertible. The guys ended up spraying as much shaving cream on each other as on the car, and made water balloons and threw them, too, before finally tying a bunch of old cowboy boots to the back bumper and declaring they were done.

Shadows were growing on the lawn before Randy finally acknowledged that putting off this reckoning wasn't going to make it any easier. He took Faith's right hand in his and said, "Will you come with me?"

"Where are we going?"

"Colt's room."

He saw the flash of fear in her dark eyes before she gripped his hand and said, "All right."

The house was built in a square, and it should've been easy to find Colt's room, since he'd been there once before, but he went down the wrong hallway, and they ended up going down three more hallways, full of wandering wedding guests, before he found the one he wanted.

He knocked on the door, in case anyone was in the room, then looked both ways to make sure no one was watching, and stepped inside. Once he and Faith were both inside, he closed the door and locked it. When he turned back around, Faith was sitting at the foot of the bed staring back at him. He crossed and sat down beside her...on her left side.

"I've never seen you wear gloves before," Randy said, unsure how to begin.

"I've had this special glove for quite some time. My doctor designed it especially for me. I just never had a reason to wear it." She held out her hands for him to see. "I look pretty normal," she conceded. "But it's more aesthetically pleasing than functional. In an emergency I can use the heel of my hand." She waggled her left hand to show the flexibility allowed by the bit of palm she had. "But I miss the versatility I get with a hook."

She was chattering, Randy realized, because she was frightened. And he was listening, because he was afraid to speak. They made a fine pair, he thought wryly.

"Take off the glove," he said. "Or would you rather I do it?"

"I'll do it," she said quickly.

He had situated himself on her left side purposely, to make sure there'd be no hiding anything—neither her hand, nor his reaction. He steeled himself for what he would see, tensing his muscles, gritting his teeth to hold back any sound of disgust or dismay that might come out.

She kept her eyes lowered. The glove was attached around her wrist with a Velcro strap, and there was a tearing sound as she pulled it free. She laid the glove on the bed beside her and dropped her left hand into her lap.

Randy kept his own eyes lowered as he examined what she'd revealed. The skin was pale, because it never saw the sun. There was a bit of a wrist and five tiny nubbins that had never grown into fingers. He reached over and slid his hand under hers, feeling her tremble as he did so.

"It's okay, Faith. Your hand just stopped growing. That's all."

She laid her head on his shoulder and closed her eyes. A tear dropped off her lash and onto his palm where he cradled her hand. He leaned over and licked up the tear. And kissed her hand.

He felt her right hand on his head, and then her kiss on his hair.

"I love you, Randy," she said.

He sat up, then lifted her left hand and drew it toward his cheek. "I love you, too, Faith."

He knew the courage it had taken for her to trust him. He willed her to believe in him and felt his heart thump hard in his chest when she lifted her left hand and caressed his cheek. He covered her hand with his own, then leaned over to kiss her lips.

A hard knock on the door broke them apart.

"Who is it?" Randy called, jumping to his feet.

"Who do you think?" Hope said. "Have you got my sister in there?"

"I'm here," Faith answered, crossing to open the door for her sister. "What's wrong?" she asked.

Randy watched as Hope looked down at her sister's uncovered hand, then up at his face. A smile curved her lips. "Why, nothing's wrong," she said with a grin. "Nothing at all."

At that moment Sam came walking past the door, noticed Randy and Faith and said, "Jenny and Colt are getting ready to leave the reception. You might want to come and see them off."

"Just let me get my glove," Faith said, turning back to the bed. "And I'll be ready to go."

"I'll see you two out back," Hope said, heading for the courtyard.

Randy and Faith weren't far behind her.

Randy had stuck at least a dozen pieces of net filled with birdseed into his coat pockets, so he'd have plenty of birdseed to shower on Jenny and Colt.

"Untie those ribbons," Faith instructed. "And pour the birdseed into your hand, so it'll be ready to throw."

"Oh."

"Will you untie mine, too?"

"Sure," Randy said, realizing that she was essentially

one-handed without her hook. "I'm gonna invent something, Faith."

"What?"

"A hand—like in the *Terminator* movies—that you can really use."

"Oh, Randy. I hope you do."

Randy heard cries of "Here they come! Get ready!"

He turned to find his sister, Colt's arm wrapped tightly around her waist, her eyes bright, her smile wide, making her way through the crowd.

THE RECEPTION WAS half over before Jenny realized the significance of the wedding gift her brothers had given her. She searched frantically for Colt and found him drinking champagne and laughing with his brothers. She dragged him away to the arbor, chasing away at least a dozen shrieking children to have even a modicum of privacy.

"My brothers gave me a wedding gift," she said. "A honeymoon trip to the Grand Canyon."

"I know all about it," he said, alternately tickling his sister's, Cherry's five-year-old twin boys, Chip and Charlie. "We leave tomorrow morning, 7:00 a.m. flight out of Amarillo."

"The doctor's office doesn't open till eight."

"So what?" Colt said, hefting Rolleen's ten-year-old son Kenny up over his shoulder and letting him drop until he was dangling by his heels. Kenny howled with glee.

"Don't you see? We won't have the test results before we leave," Jenny said.

"We're going to have a honeymoon whether you have cancer or not," Colt replied. "The news will wait till we get back." He leaned over and kissed her on the nose, struggling to stay upright with Chip and Charlie each entwined around one of his legs like vines around an oak. "Anything else bothering you?" he asked.

She lifted a brow and said, "Well, if we're going to get up so early in the morning, isn't about time we took our leave?"

Colt's eyes went wide, and then he smiled. "Mrs. Whitelaw, that's the best suggestion I've heard all day," he said, prying the twins off his legs.

"Thank you. I love getting compliments from my husband."

Colt's gaze locked hers. "Husband. That has a nice sound." He slipped his arm around her waist and headed for the car. "Let's go, wife."

Jenny went with Colt to tell his parents they were leaving, and the word spread quickly.

"Hurry up if you want to get a last look at the bride and groom before they take off!"

"Does everybody have some birdseed?"

Jenny ducked and laughed as birdseed caught in her hair and her eyelashes and slid down the front of her dress.

Colt laughed and ducked right along with her. "Hurry up, wife, or we're going to turn into two bird feeders!"

Colt didn't even open the door to the convertible, just dropped her in over the top, then came running around and jumped in behind the wheel.

As they drove away, Jenny reached across the seat and took Colt's hand. He smiled at her, and she smiled back. This was the beginning of a new life. A new love. And happily ever after.

EPILOGUE

BENIGN. JENNY HAD never heard A sweeter word. She still had three more years before she'd feel satisfied that the cancer was truly gone. But she'd been given a respite, a time in which to live life to the fullest. And a husband who was determined to help her do it.

Jenny snuggled closer to Colt, spooning her body against his. She heard him make a sound of pleasure in his throat and whispered, "Are you awake?"

"I am now."

She pulled his arms tighter around her, and he cupped her breasts and held her close. It was always like this after they made love, holding each other, reaffirming their joy with each other.

"I visited my doctor today," Jenny said.

She felt Colt stiffen. "Oh?" he murmured cautiously.

"I wanted to ask her what she thought about me getting pregnant."

"I see," Colt said. "And what did she say?"

Jenny turned over in Colt's arms, so she could see his face. "She said it was up to me."

"There's no risk to you?" Colt asked.

"I didn't say that. But I think what we have to gain is worth what risk there is. I want us to have children, Colt. Is that too much to ask?"

"I already feel like I've dodged a bullet," Colt confessed. "I want kids, but not at the risk of losing you."

Jenny pressed her face against Colt's throat and felt his arms close around her. "If we have a boy, we can name him Huck."

She heard him chuckle. "Huckleberry Whitelaw. Now there's a name to give a kid nightmares."

Jenny smiled. "Growing up in a houseful of boys, I always wanted a little girl."

"We could name her Becky," Colt said.

Jenny laughed. "And the next boy Tom."

"Three kids," Colt said. "That's a houseful."

"Not like the eight your parents raised," she pointed out.

"Three's plenty for me," he said, lifting his head and finding her mouth with his.

They kissed slowly, letting the passion rise, feeling the hope and ignoring the fear. They would find a way to be happy, living each day and loving each night. For all the rest of their lives.

* * * * *

POWERFUL HEROES... SCANDALOUS SECRETS... BURNING DESIRES!

TEMPTED BY A COWBOY
by Sarah M. Anderson

Available October 2014

**The 2nd novel of the *Beaumont Heirs* featuring
one Colorado family with limitless scandal!**

*How can she resist the cowboy's smile when it
promises so much pleasure?*

Phillip Beaumont likes his drinks strong and his women easy.
So why is he flirting with his new horse trainer, Jo Spears,
who challenges him at every turn? Phillip wants nothing but
the chase...until the look in Jo's haunted green eyes makes him
yearn for more....

Sure, Jo's boss is as jaded and stubborn as Sun, the
multimillion-dollar stallion she was hired to train. But it isn't
long before she starts spending days *and* nights with the sexy
cowboy. Maybe Sun isn't the only male on the Beaumont
ranch worth saving!

———————————————

Be sure to read the 1st novel of the *Beaumont Heirs*
by Sarah M. Anderson
NOT THE BOSS'S BABY

Available wherever books and ebooks are sold.